The Abyss line of cutting-edge psychological horror is committed to publishing the best, most innovative works of dark fiction available. ABYSS is horror unlike anything you've ever read before. It's not about haunted houses or evil children or ancient Indian burial grounds. We've all read those books, and we all know their plots by heart.

ABYSS is for the seeker of truth, no matter how disturbing or twisted it may be. It's about people, and the darkness we all carry within us. ABYSS is the new horror from the dark frontier. And in that place, where we come face-to-face with terror, what we find is ourselves.

"Thank you for introducing me to the remarkable line of novels currently being issued under Dell's Abyss imprint. I have given a great many blurbs over the last twelve years or so, but this one marks two firsts: first *unsolicited* blurb (*I* called *you*) and the first time I have blurbed a whole *line* of books. In terms of quality, production, and plain old storytelling reliability (that's the bottom line, isn't it?), Dell's new line is amazingly satisfying . . . a rare and wonderful bargain for readers. I hope to be looking into the Abyss for a long time to come."
—Stephen King

Please turn the page for more extraordinary acclaim . . .

PRAISE FOR ABYSS

"What *The Twilight Zone* was to TV in 1959, what *Night of the Living Dead* was to horror films in 1968, what Stephen King was to dark fiction in the mid-70s—Abyss books will be to horror in the 1990s."
—Mark Hurst, editor of *The Golden Man*

"Gorgeously macabre eye-catching packages . . . I don't think Abyss could have picked a weirder, more accomplished novel [than *The Cipher*] to demonstrate by example what the tone and level of ambition of the new line might be." —*Locus*

"A splendid debut." —*Rave Reviews*

"Dell is leading the way." —*Writer's Digest*

"They are exploring new themes and dimensions in the horror field. My hat's off to Koja, Hodge, Dee and Dillard, as the others forthcoming! And hats off to Dell Abyss!"
—Gary S. Potter, *The Point Beyond*

"Consistently excellent, the most likely place to find innovative horror fiction." —*Science Fiction Chronicle*

"Horror fiction's equivalent of Vintage Contemporaries."
—*Arkansas Democrat-Gazette*

"A MARVELOUS DEBUT . . . COMPULSIVELY READABLE."
—*Locus*

HIGH PRAISE FOR

Daniel H. Gower's previous novel

THE ORPHEUS PROCESS

"At times it's so good, it's scary, and other times, it's so scary, it's good. . . . A strong first novel for Daniel Gower, and, as many times as you hear this cliché, I look forward to his next book." —*The Cthulhu Mythos*

"Gower has a fine grasp of characterization, and his reanimation process, as well as the pseudo-science which underlies it, creates sufficient verisimilitude for the reader to suspend his disbelief for the duration. And that is the toughest job for any novelist, but especially a first-timer, to pull off." —*Midnight Graffiti*

"Ambitious . . . this first novel shows a lot of promise."
—Tyson Blue, *Cemetery Dance*

Also by Daniel H. Gower

THE ORPHEUS PROCESS

DANIEL H. GOWER

A DELL BOOK

Published by
Dell Publishing
a division of
Bantam Doubleday Dell Publishing Group, Inc.
1540 Broadway
New York, New York 10036

If you purchased this book without a cover you should be aware that this book is stolen property. It was reported as "unsold and destroyed" to the publisher and neither the author nor the publisher has received any payment for this "stripped book."

Copyright © 1993 by Daniel H. Gower

All rights reserved. No part of this book may be reproduced or transmitted in any form or by any means, electronic or mechanical, including photocopying, recording, or by any information storage and retrieval system, without the written permission of the Publisher, except where permitted by law.

The trademarks Dell® and Abyss® are registered in the U.S. Patent and Trademark Office.

ISBN: 0-440-21456-4

Printed in the United States of America

Published simultaneously in Canada

December 1993

10 9 8 7 6 5 4 3 2 1
OPM

To Joan,
for whom words don't corrupt

. . . when I start falling
in that inhuman pit
of dizzy death
I'll know (if
smart enough t'remember)
that all the black
tunnels of hate
or love I'm falling
through, are
  really radiant
right eternities
    for me
      —Jack Kerouac
        Mexico City Blues, Chorus 184

PART ONE

*Portrait
of an Artist*

1

The Naked Business Lunch

As always the subway car smelled like the bottom of a trash can, and that mixed with the arrhythmic rocking of the speeding vehicle gave Julian Stormer some nausea to add to his low mood. He hated traveling through the bowels of the city almost as much as he hated going downtown, his destination. But if he didn't want to starve or end up working some tedious, menial job, he had to find out what was up with his agent. Seven months was too long not to hear from the man, and Julian's funds were getting close to nonexistent. So it was time to swallow some pride and sacrifice some peace of mind and venture into the towers of steel erected on plains of concrete that formed the hub of the big midwestern city of Groveland.

There was no place to sit, so he stood gripping a noose-shaped hand-hold of steel, trying to identify the stains on the floor and reading the graffiti on the walls. With a little care he could discern some of the words. They formed trailing sentences: *I just don't care anymore —A concerned citizen. I feel number than the Beast, Sick,*

Sick, Sick. I don't know who I am—Anonymous. The beginning is nigh, so repent. These were sentiments with which Julian could heartily identify. He was an artist and his paintings were off-center dissections of the world, the phenomena of existence stripped down to their bare essences, rather like these off-the-wall bits of wall wisdom. Anger, despair, and biting wit screamed out from these scratchings and scribblings, as they did from his canvases. Nobody seemed to be listening lately, however.

He studied his nearest fellow passengers, a withered old woman in a babushka, a fat man straining the seams of his business suit, and a tragically homely teenage girl. They looked miserably bored and self-absorbed, like everyone else on the train. In spite of himself Julian sometimes thought that the bulk of humanity was a grotesque menagerie, the inhabitants of a Bosch painting. He didn't hate them, though he certainly didn't love them, but he did feel somehow apart from them. And when he was among them in large numbers, as in the city center toward which he was headed, they frightened him. All those nameless faces, all those lives with their own problems and desires, a shuffling horde of clothed bodies with hundreds of pairs of eyes staring at him. It was sometimes too much for him to take. That, partly, was why he lived on the periphery of the city, out in a rundown section where few were brave enough to dwell, where much of the property was condemned. It was also the only place he could afford to live.

The train screeched to a halt, the doors clanked open, and the passengers started shoving their way out onto the platform. Julian rushed through the surging herd to the stairs and up to the street level above, hyperventilating a little. He took out a cigarette and lit it, and then he felt somewhat steadier, less nauseated. The harsh, stark lines of the massive skyscrapers filled his eyes with their gray geometry as they blotted out the sun and the clouds. They seemed to similarly eclipse his sense of himself. Among such huge constructions, in the midst of thousands of anonymous citizens, how could anyone possibly hope to retain an identity? He took a breath of exhaust-fouled air and moved with the procession of pedestrians, keeping his head down.

His destination was a restaurant called Elle's Kitchen, a currently trendy lunch spot where his agent, Nolan Voight, had agreed to meet him. It was located just around the block from the Charteris Street Station, Nolan had told him, so even he would have a hard time getting lost on the way there. The cracks of the sidewalk passed beneath his feet and he finally turned the corner. He looked into the storefront windows as he passed a printing shop, a bookstore, and some office buildings; then he spotted the restaurant sign with its delicate blue lettering. He suddenly found himself face to face with some guy shouting in his face.

"Are you saved?"

Julian took a step back from the man, who stood blocking the restaurant entrance. He was young, wearing a white shirt and a dark tie, and was waving a black book.

"From what?" Julian asked.

The street preacher ignored his response. "Beware the Scarlet Woman, harlot of Babylon, mistress of the pit! She drinketh from the cup of iniquity and copulates with the Beast."

"Yeah, right." When he tried to go around him, the man continued to block his way.

"Her agents are beautiful female demons who look like unto angels, but whose bitter souls are infested with serpents. They will deceive you and drag you down to deepest hell. With fleshly lust they enslave you, with pleasing visions they blind you, with soft, sweet words they deafen you, until you can no longer obey Scripture or see heaven or hear God."

"Hey, do you mind?" Julian tried again to bypass the stranger, but he still wouldn't move clear of the door.

"Beware of she who bears the forbidden fruit, she who bleeds for her sins, she who paints herself, adorns herself with gold, and makes men unclean. She visits men in the dark of night, haunting them with erotic nightmares and causing them to pollute themselves. Her tongue speaks vileness and drinks dry the springs of their virility. May God hide us from her face with its scarlet lips and eyes of painted purple. May He keep our souls safe from the black pit of her heart. May he save us from falling into the dark hole of foul vapors in which she seeks to devour the world!"

Julian snorted out an incredulous laugh. He'd always thought a lot of religion was caused by sexual hysteria, but he'd never heard it expressed in such blatantly Freudian terms before. It was impossible not to wonder what this poor fellow's past trauma with the female gender had been. The preacher scowled at him, however, not amused by his lack of reverence.

"Have you been born again?"

"Uh, no." He couldn't resist the temptation for a comeback. "I think I got it right the first time."

Now the preacher leaned toward him with an upthrust forefinger. "Do not mock the Almighty, brother, lest His devils be loosed upon you to torment your body and spirit for all eternity, for Christ is lord of death and the demonic."

Great, he thought. Not only did he have to put up with the dangers the streets presented to his physical person, but now this guy was threatening to brutalize him metaphysically. He had nothing against believers, but he personally couldn't take anything that seriously. And he had no patience just now for this particular proponent of the faith.

"Right. Excuse me." He managed to slip behind the man and reach the door.

"Remember that Jesus loves you!" the preacher called after him.

Going inside, Julian wondered if he looked like a conspicuously lost soul, for he seemed to attract the attention of creed hawkers of all types. Moonies, Hare Krishnas, Jehovah's Witnesses—you name it, he'd been a target of their proselytizing.

"Is that guy still out there?" asked the hostess, looking over Julian's shoulder as he stepped up to her. "I'm sorry about that. He's been pestering our customers all morning."

He crushed out his cigarette in the white sand of a cylindrical ashtray nearby. "Oh, I guess he's just adding a little local color. I'm here to meet someone. The reservation would be under the name of Voight."

Nolan had assured him that the place had no dress code, but now that he saw how posh it was, he feared he might not get in, dressed as he was in blue jeans, a sleeveless sweatshirt, and his black leather jacket. The hostess seemed to take no notice, however.

She was a moderate beauty, he noticed as she consulted her record book. Nice eyes, wonderful cheekbones, but a somewhat unintelligent expression.

"Mr. Voight isn't here yet," she told him.

Nolan had never failed to be late. "Okay. I'll wait for him at the table. Smoking."

"Fine. This way."

She led him to a dark corner in the cool depths of the glittering-crystal and polished-oak ambience, sat him down at a small square of thick wood, and left him with a silver menu written entirely in French. He thanked her and scanned his surroundings. The place was crowded, filled with the young and upwardly mobile engaged in animated conversations, absorbed in the arcana of business deals and high finance. Or maybe just gossiping about office politics and adulterous affairs of friends and enemies alike. He didn't know. He'd never been part of that world and he never would be. They held a certain fascination for him, however, with their complete unabashed immersion in the material. From their Italian suits to their ludicrously expensive cars and their stratospheric house-sized apartments, he couldn't help but contemplate what it would be like to live that way. Was it as spiritually deadening as he thought it must be? Certainly he wouldn't be averse to a little more monetary wealth for himself, but for him the driving force of life was creation, the making of images moving and profound that no one had ever seen before. That was what he lived for, not power over others or the accumulation of physical objects. Sensation and imagination were his gods.

A waitress appeared, a pretty one, and he smiled at her in what he hoped was a charming way. Being around such attractive females was agitating his already long-starved lust, but he didn't for a moment believe he had a chance of scoring with these women. They would no doubt prove to be too normal and demanding. No point in even trying.

"What can I do get for you today?" she asked brightly.

He ordered a martini and nothing else, wondering how much it would cost and how much he had in his wallet, warning himself that he shouldn't be drinking on an empty stomach. He could always try to stick Nolan with the bill, but there was no guarantee that the man was even going to show up. The drink was delivered and he resisted the urge to gulp it, sipped at it in a civilized manner instead. He lit a Camel cigarette, predicting it would be the first of many he smoked in that spot. There was a painting on the wall nearby, he noticed, like an abstract sketch from an old musical. Four stripe-shirted French sailors danced in a chorus line as they ogled a streetwalker wearing a short slitted skirt and a beret, with the spidery gantry of the Eiffel Tower erected in the background. Julian was very unimpressed.

He stood up, took off his jacket, and hung it on the back of his chair. Seated again, he munched his olive and tapped on the tabletop with the toothpick. A glance at his watch informed him that he'd been waiting for twenty minutes. When the waitress came by again he ordered another martini, and when this one arrived he gulped it down.

You are the people who live high in the light, he thought at the crowd, all smartly dressed and flawlessly coiffed. *You dwell aboveground in the land of plenty, while my kind and I inhabit the sparse subterranean regions.* He was getting melodramatic, feeling really out of place. The other people were staring at him, he felt, though he couldn't catch them in the act. They must be wondering what this long-haired bum was doing in their posh establishment, a scraggly intruder on their impeccable feeding grounds.

After his third martini Nolan finally joined him, sounding slightly out of breath. Nolan had a pudgy face that made him look more jolly than he was, but Julian had long ago ceased to be fooled by it. "Hello, Julian. How are we today?"

"I don't know about you, but I'm fine. Is that holy roller still hanging around outside the door?"

"Is the what?" Nolan pulled out his chair, then settled his corpulent mass in it. His suit was black and his tie was an orange diamond pattern.

"Skip it." The urban prophet must have moved on.

"Well, you're looking good. Have you been working out?"

Julian shook his head. "Neither my musculature nor my life."

His agent laughed, the pudgy face crinkling up. The waitress put in another appearance and Nolan ordered a tossed green salad with a glass of mineral water. He just asked for another martini. It was okay, he told himself. He'd eaten three olives, so his stomach wasn't exactly empty anymore.

"I'm sorry I'm late, but I was on the phone with Anna Kurtz. That lonely old spinster will talk your ear off, you know."

Yeah, he knew, though it had been so long since he'd talked to someone of importance in the art community that he might have forgotten by now. And Anna Kurtz wasn't that old, though her biological clock was certainly ticking away, if such a thing mattered to her. She was known to be a fag hag, but hanging out with gay males was not a good way to land a man. Nolan had just given him a pertinent piece of information, however, for Anna was co-owner of the Pickman Gallery. "One of your clients is having a show at the Pickman?"

"Uh, yes, as a matter of fact. Neil Marco has an exhibition there now. Very bright boy, very striking work. Are you familiar with his stuff?"

"Vaguely." His martini arrived and he poured half of it into his stewing innards, well on his way to being drunk. He fired up his tenth or so cigarette. "What are you doing for *me,* Nolan? It's been over two years since my last show and the wolf is going to be at the door soon."

Nolan studied him for a moment, looking worried. "Yes, well, interest in your work has dwindled somewhat. You must understand that this business is subject to the principles of supply and demand just like any other, Julian. And if you will recall, your last show was something of a disaster."

Indeed it had been. He'd sold only two paintings, both of them smaller works. The critics had savaged him. His first show had been a near sellout, however. "Yeah, I remember. But this isn't a business, Nolan. It's a professional field of culture."

The waitress came over with the salad and set it before Nolan, who began picking at it with the correct fork. "Well, you came here to ask me why your contributions to this professional field of culture aren't making you any money, so obviously there is a business aspect to it, isn't there? Look, Julian. You're good. I like your work, even though I don't always understand it. When you do things like landscapes of living flesh and embryos inside of eyeballs you sort of lose me a little. And you've lost the public a little, you see. The shock value of your stuff has worn off, lost its impact. Now it just leaves people bewildered."

Julian narrowed his eyes on the man, on his piggy Captain Bligh face and his feathery brown hair. Nolan kept shoveling pieces of lettuce into his mouth. How could he get so obese grazing on rabbit food? He had to be sneaking pastries in the middle of the night, maybe whole lasagnas.

"Are you suggesting that I should start doing more commercial sorts of paintings?"

"Nothing of the sort," he said, waving this idea away. "I'm just telling you that you're a victim of the fickle winds of taste. I would have talked to you about this sooner, but you got rid of your phone. You've got to be patient. The people who raved about you and made you a hit the first time around were, shall we say, a bit ahead of their time."

"I seem to recall you describing them as rich, drugged-out young decadents."

Nolan conceded the point with a shrug. "It takes all kinds, and when it comes to appreciating your pictures it takes even weirder kinds. You'll be discovered again. Just give it time."

He'd been inclined to blame Nolan for his decline in popularity, but now he realized he'd been jumping to conclusions. If his work was just too strange for most people, then that's just the way things were. "Okay. I've been really productive, you know. I've got about twenty-four new paintings done."

"Good. Then I'll come around and see them sometime soon. Oh, I almost forgot. Someone did a sort of retrospective review on you." Nolan reached into his coat pocket and pulled out a folded-up photocopy. "It was in an article about modern surrealists by some critic named Duburry, in a magazine called *Enigma*. Not very complimentary, I'm afraid."

Julian was suddenly suspicious as he took the sheet of paper and started reading it. The pertinent paragraphs began two thirds of the way down the page:

> Then there's Julian Stormer, a flash in the palette who caused a minor sensation some years ago. His paintings are sexual, viscerally mystical, angry eruptions from the subconscious. There is, to be sure, an honored tradition of surrealist art, but true surrealist art has something to say. Stormer's paintings don't say anything. He tries to make darkness beautiful, savagery romantic, death desirable, but he only succeeds in making art nauseating.
>
> Now, a creator of such obscene and blighted images will probably say that he doesn't care what people think of his work, but he cares a lot. That's why he dreams up such outrageous affronts to human eyesight, to attract notice and become the center of attention. But he doesn't paint art. He portrays madness. There are no numinous elements to Stormer's sick visions, only sensory distortion. The only thing he has to say to the world is that he perceives it through a diseased mind.

He was shaken, wondering just why Nolan had sprung this critical assault on him. There had been times when he sensed that the man didn't really like him very much. He'd even formulated a theory that Nolan was a frustrated, failed artist who was envious of his own clients.

Or was this just Nolan's way of trying to goad him into doing paintings that were a little more accessible to the public mind? If so, it was a very crude and cruel tactic.

"Uh, that's pretty cold," he said, shaking the photocopy, then dropping it on the table. "Of course, I think that guy is full of shit."

"Of course he is," said Nolan, not sounding terribly sincere. It would have given Julian great pleasure to knock the table over on him and watch him fall on his flabby ass, but the artist was not prone to violence.

"Yeah, well, listen. I've got to be going. Come by anytime and have a look at my output, huh?" He couldn't believe Nolan had done this to him. He stood, grabbed his jacket, and staggered out of the dining area, smiling that he had after all stuck Nolan with the check.

On his way past the restaurant bar he was accosted by a short brunette, who asked him if he had the time. He looked over her head at the clock on the wall behind her and pointed at it uncertainly.

"Oh, yeah," she said, briefly turning but never laying eyes on the timepiece. "Uh, have you got a light?"

She was holding an already lit cigarette, he noticed. What was going on here? "Look, lady. I've got to get out of here. I've had enough of this town for one day."

"Wait. Listen. How would you like to go to a party?"

His alcohol-hazed brain started to work finally. No. Could it really be? First John the Baptist and now Mary Magdalene. "And just how big would this party be?"

With practiced affection she touched his left arm. "Just the two of us. You see, my lunch date has stood me up, so I've got some time on my hands. And you look like you're nice. Would you like some company?"

She did appeal to him, he had to admit, with her

round face, full lips, boyish haircut, and big breasts (though he had to wonder if they were original equipment). The blue dress she was wearing revealed more than enough of her legs for him to give them his seal of approval. And he had not known carnal love with a woman since Mercy had broken up with him ten months ago. *But this is a call girl,* he reminded himself. *You can't afford her, and besides that there is a sexual plague abroad in the land. She's not safe.* The alcohol made him silly.

"Are you the Scarlet Woman?" he asked her, slurring his words a little.

Her expression was predictably puzzled. "Huh?"

"If you lie down with beasts you get up with fiends. Sorry, but I've gotta run."

He left Elle's Kitchen, thought about it a few seconds, then hailed a taxi. Once he was inside he told the driver, "Take me to the Pickman Gallery, on Hilliard."

It was time he had a look at the output of the new boy who had replaced him in Nolan Voight's good graces, his rival who was now all the rage. And if it weren't for his pleasant martini high, rage would be all he was feeling, rage at the Neanderthal critic slandering him in the article, rage at that bastard Nolan for having made him read it. His ego was fragile enough these days without having his flesh torn by the culture vultures. Alone with himself, he spent countless hours applying color to canvas, feeling that he was creating marvels but never entirely sure. He needed feedback, reinforcement, nurturing. He required the sustenance of being appreciated.

If I killed myself, thought Julian, *the value of my works would skyrocket.* Fame regained and lasting, if posthumous. But no, it wasn't a good idea. Suicides became trees in hell according to Dante, losing in death the freedom of movement they failed to appreciate in life. That was no way to spend eternity.

The Pickman wasn't a large gallery, but it was a classy place. He thought of it as ultramodern Roman in design, built in what the architectural style might be like now if the empire had never fallen. Sleek columns, slanted arches, triangular lintels. When the cab pulled up in front he paid the driver, tipped him generously, and strolled inside for a bit of gratuitous self-torment.

It was a depressingly large crowd for this time of day. He wondered how long the show had been running. Even more depressing was the number of paintings with glossy golden stickers beside them, meaning they'd been purchased. Almost half had been sold already. That made it a totally no-win situation for Julian: if the show had just started recently, then the exhibits had gone awfully fast; on the other hand, if the show had been running for some time and it was still drawing a lot of attention, then it must be causing quite a stir. There was nothing for him to gloat over. He berated himself for thinking like that, being petty. There was nothing worse than pettiness, except maybe self-pity.

He tried to be objective as he examined the paintings: glittering spheres of metal and light, silver people with featureless faces, cityscapes of chrome frameworks and mirrored monoliths. They made him think of the sterile, dehumanized future. It was a future that would probably never be, he mused. Science had not prevailed over the ancient dogmas, energy and resources had turned out to be all too finite, and utopia was totally out of vogue. Humanity had already been defeated by entropy, it seemed, buried in its own wastes and choking on its own pollution. He decided he didn't like Marco's paintings.

They said something, all right, but they lied. Hollow illusion was all they had to offer, pretty, superficial visions and nothing more. He hated them.

"Well, well. The creature walks among us," said a voice behind Julian. He turned to see the speaker, who was a short-haired young man in a blue sweater and casual brown slacks. It was Corey Rucker, a fellow plier of the paint trade.

"Hey, Corey. What are you doing hanging out in this mausoleum?"

Corey came over and shook his hand. "Just committing chronocide. Jerome insisted that we come and see Marco's show. Wretched, isn't it? A regular atrocity exhibition. What brings you out of your lair?"

He shrugged, pleased that someone shared his opinion. "Oh, I'm just slumming. I was downtown on business so I thought I might as well see the sights."

"Well, you've come to the wrong place. These sights aren't fit for man nor beast. Jerome's formed a knot of people around himself in the central concourse. Of course. He was being obnoxious, so I took a walk. But now that I've run into you, you should come and say hello."

Facing a whole group was the last thing he was in the mood for, but there was no way he could gracefully refuse. "Sure. Lead the way."

Because of all the vodka in his bloodstream, and because Corey had echoed his reaction to Marco's creations, Julian felt very warmly toward the man. It was good to see a friendly, familiar face again. He always meant to keep in touch with the people he knew and liked, but they either clustered around the Village like it was a cultural colony or dwelled in lofty high-rises in the high-rent districts, while he was living his lone existence out in the boondocks. Someone would drop in once in a while, but not often. Only his best friend, Vern Doyle, was a regular visitor.

Everyone seemed inexplicably happy to see him, as if he'd just stumbled in on his own surprise birthday party. He figured he'd been out of circulation longer than he'd thought. Besides Jerome there was Pauly, Wes, Charlene, Andrea, and a skinny bald-headed guy he didn't recognize. And Anna Kurtz, looking vaguely bohemian in a long black velvet dress.

"Julian!" Jerome called to him. "Come and join us. Some kind of karma seems to have drawn all the geniuses here today."

"It sure seems that way," he said, waving at everyone. He didn't really think of anyone else here as a genius, but it would have been impolitic to say so. Corey's paintings were mildly inspired, Jerome was a competent sculptor, Pauly's music was incoherent to him, Wes and Charlene wrote poetry he found insipid, and Andrea was just a sophisticated groupie. The bald guy, who introduced himself as Ron, he couldn't comment on. As for Anna, he felt that she was not only untalented but didn't know talent when she saw it. He had to make nice with her, however, for people like her held his life in their hands.

"Hello, Anna. Long time no see."

She sauntered over to him, clasped his hand, and kissed him on the cheek. "Where have you been keeping yourself, stranger?"

"Uh, I've sort of gone into involuntary semiretirement."

Anna was not an unpleasant-looking woman, but her

nose was too large and her lips were too thin for his taste. He was mesmerized, however, by the diamond necklace hanging above her modest breasts. It looked like a cluster of stars in a midnight sky against the fabric of her dress. "Well, come sit down and tell me what you've been up to."

Julian let himself be guided to a chair, which he made use of, with Anna sitting on the left arm. Her casual invasion of his personal space made him a bit uncomfortable, but he tolerated it.

"So what do you think of the show?"

He'd been afraid she was going to ask. "Um, Marco has some very nice strokes in some of his pieces. He seems to be very into light."

Corey, standing nearby, chortled when he overheard this.

Anna grinned at Julian. "I know. Your work is much more shadowy and organic, and that's what you like. But Marco's work really calls to something deep in the human spirit. It moves people."

It moves their jaws to yawn, he thought. "I'm sure it does. Say, I don't suppose you'd have an opening for an opening anytime in the near future? I've got a whole series of real eye-popping stuff just waiting to adorn these hallowed walls." God, was that what he'd really come here for, to beg for a show? He couldn't take his eyes off the sparkling stones around Anna's neck, and he feared she would think he was staring at her tits. It made him want to do a painting of her, something like the towering queen of night with the silvery, shimmering backbone of the Milky Way shining out through her black torso.

"Doesn't Nolan handle you anymore?" she asked, frowning slightly.

His celestial vision of her faded. "Uh, yeah, sure, but I'm never quite sure if he's doing as much for me as he can. It doesn't hurt to ask, anyway."

"Oh. Well, Nolan *is* a bit of an ass. I don't know about arranging you some space. We're all booked up for some time to come. Still, I could see what I can do for you."

Both her tone and the look she gave him were a bit patronizing, but he didn't care. He found it amusing. *You're a real patron of the arts, Anna.* He wondered if she was interested in him. Probably not; he was always misreading signals from women. Did she think he was gay? Not that it mattered, except that he disliked giving out mixed signals himself. It only made life more complicated.

"Yeah, I'd really appreciate that." His nausea was threatening to return, caused by the martinis now, so he thought he'd better get out of there. "Well, I hate to schmooze and run, but I've got to be going. It was good seeing you again." He stood and said his good-byes to the rest of the gang.

Just as he was leaving Anna called to him, "Keep in touch, Julian."

In his present state of mind he thought that sounded like really excellent advice.

2

Sweet Young Things

It was starting to get dark as he walked from the subway station back to his apartment. He regretted not taking an earlier train now, for it was a long walk through perilous territory. A teenage gang called the Crucifixers claimed it as their turf, though he'd never heard of any other gang challenging them for it. Who would want it? It was a whole lot of nothing as far as he could tell. So far in his five years of living in the area he'd managed to avoid any confrontation with the young hoodlums. He'd seen them around, though, with their black headbands and golden jackets. Their colors sported an interesting symbol, that of a snake nailed to a cross. More than that he did not care to know about them.

Julian felt lethargic and he had a headache, a symptom he always suffered when he drank in the middle of the day. If anyone decided to harass him he wouldn't even be able to give them a good run for their money. Or his money, more likely. He would just stumble over his own feet and then get robbed or beaten or both. God, he had to move out of this neighborhood sometime soon. Every day it seemed to fall even farther into decay. There were more broken windows, more fire-gutted buildings, more abandoned cars, more furniture and appliances put out on the sidewalks. A majority of the streetlights had been shot out and never replaced. Even the smell of the place was beginning to get to him, the stale and sour odor of human beings living too closely and too long in one spot, of old housing begrimed and deteriorating. It wasn't quite yet a slum, but it would soon qualify as such.

He came to an alleyway not far from his building, looked in, and saw a pile of ragged clothing lying near a wall. It appeared a bit too motionless for his comfort, so he approached it.

"Fred? Are you okay, Fred?"

The lump of rags stirred and sat up, revealing a grubby man with ancient features. Julian didn't know if Fred was genuinely old or just prematurely aged by years of living on the street. Whichever it was, he lived in fear of one day finding his destitute friend dying or dead in this or some other nearby alley.

"Julian," Fred mumbled. "Hey, how ya doin', young man?"

"I'm just fine. How about you?" Even through Fred's animal odor the fumes of alcohol wafted out. Where the hell had the derelict gotten hold of a bottle?

"I'm doing great." The man spoke with a trace of an accent that Julian thought might be Italian. "Found a prize in the trash. Incredible what people will throw away. So I'm feeling pretty good."

That explained that. "Yeah, I had a few too many myself this afternoon."

Fred belched, rubbed his crusty eyes, then picked his nose with the little finger of his left hand. "So how's the rat race in the city?"

"Still going full tilt. You know, I don't understand why you don't sleep in one of the abandoned buildings around here. It would be safer and warmer for you."

"Nope. No, thank you. I'm the outdoor type. I like to sleep under the stars. Got a butt you can spare?"

Julian shook a cigarette out of the pack and handed it over, lit it for him. He had to get close to do this, so he got a noseful of the homeless man's gaminess. Fred tried to keep it clean, but pavement dwelling was not very conducive to hygiene. He had taken a mild interest in this man who had shown up in his neighborhood a few weeks ago, for Fred was the most unpretentious human being Julian had ever met. The old man didn't want to work or put up with the complexities of society, so he very simply refused to do it.

"Well, stay out of trouble, Fred."

"Yeah," he said, choking on smoke and phlegm. "And you go ahead and get into a little."

"Right. See you around." Julian continued on to his building, one of the least dilapidated structures in the neighborhood. As he approached the front entrance he looked up and smiled at his favorite feature of its architecture, a gargoyle leering out from above the doorway. It wasn't a gargoyle like the bored-looking horned-and-winged apes of Notre Dame Cathedral; it was just a grimacing face almost sticking out its tongue, but he liked it. It was whimsical, mysterious, and completely frivolous.

He went inside, passed the door of the elusive Mr. Bonewitz, and mounted the stairs to his loft on the second floor. They were the only two people inhabiting the building, as far as he knew. When he came to his door he found a note tacked to it. It read:

> Tried to catch you at home. When are you going to get your phone reconnected? I got us a date tonight with a couple of sweet young things. Be ready by seven and we'll paint the town blood-red.
>
> Vern

Julian stifled a groan as he tore the note free and unlocked his door. The women Vern found for him were never his type. They were, in fact, usually hand-me-downs from Vern. Besides that, the whole dating scene was beginning to get him down. It had been so much easier meeting girls when he was in high school. He saw so many every day that at any given time one or more of them was bound to like him. Life in those days had been less demanding in a lot of ways, back in the small town where he grew up. His friends and he would get drunk or high or both and drive around for hours at night without a care in the world, oblivious that they were endangering their lives and others'. They cruised for chicks and often found them; back then females would do a lot for a joint, a few beers, a little excitement in their dreary lives.

All that had changed drastically over the years, he thought as he went in and flopped down on the unmade bed. Now to get and keep a woman he had to impress her with money, with style, with novel experiences, with skillful lovemaking and ever-increasing pleasures. With coke-headed Mercy he'd had to compete with a chemical to keep her sufficiently stimulated. It had obviously been a losing battle. They had met in the Village when he was at the height of his notoriety, a somebody, a hot artist worthy of her notice. She had been a little repulsed by his paintings, but she'd at least had the humility to admit that she didn't know a whole lot about art. Yeah, she'd sure got that right.

He got up and trod over to his collection of antique objects and curios spread out on a couple of wooden shelves. There was a Viking helmet, a Celtic torque, an Aztec stone skull, a Merovingian crystal ball, and the adder stone Mercy had given him shortly before their breakup. She had gone to England with some friends, where they'd ended up pub-hopping up the east coast of the island in a van. In the town of Whitby she'd seen the abbey and heard the story of St. Hilda expelling the serpents from the edifice and over the cliffs into the sea. For some reason this had plucked a string in her imagination, so when she came across the adder stones for sale around the town she'd bought one as a gift for him. It was really just a fossilized ammonite, an extinct snail-like creature with a spiraled shell, with a snake's head carved at the end. Locals said such charms were the petrified bodies of the unfortunate snakes St. Hilda had vented her wrath upon. They were supposed to protect the owner from evil.

Julian had hated the thing as soon as he saw it, and he'd told her so. It was a scientific specimen, not a work of art, and he despised the confusion, the superstition. He supposed in retrospect he could have been more tactful, for Mercy had thought she was giving him something very special to add to his collection. In reality, he believed he'd been angry at her for having left him alone, for having gone off and had fun with other people. He was afraid to travel because he felt lost and empty when he was away from home for any length of time. Also, her beauty made him constantly jealous. She was always too flirtatious with other men, too friendly. Mercy called herself a free spirit, but she was really a restless spirit, afraid to be alone, unable to sit still for more than a few minutes, loath to engage in serious conversations. He had never succeeded in getting her to calm down and focus her energies.

After his rejection of her present, things had gone downhill very fast between them. She accused him of being too withdrawn, too caught up in himself, complained that she wanted a man who was going to make a difference in the world. She was tired of being tied down, and she thought Vern was creepy. Julian decried her drug dependency and said her friends were shallow. So they parted, and he kept the adder stone, just to remember her by. And he missed her.

He decided he needed a shower to wash away the soot of the city and refresh his dulled senses. On the way to the bathroom, he stopped at his easel to take another look at the painting he'd finished last night. It was a naked young woman turning the corner in a passage of some dark, bonelike material, trailing a thread from her left hand. This strand was unraveling from the fiber of her own flesh, for she was already weaving it through skeletal fingers, though the rest of her body was still sound. He called it "Ariadne in the Labyrinth," but he wasn't entirely happy with it, felt its meaning might be too obscure. The idea was that the deeper she progressed into the labyrinth, the less would be left of her. And was she weaving a web within the maze?

He hoped he wasn't losing his touch. The next work, he'd already resolved, would be a big one, something he could really let himself get drawn into. A magnum opus. Stripping, he stepped into the shower stall and let the torrent of steaming water wash over him. Sensation flooded back into his skin, relieving him of the wounds inflicted on his mind by a harsh world determined to chew him up and spit him out. And the day wasn't over yet. He wondered just how much of a disaster tonight would be. If he had his way he'd skip it altogether, but Vern hadn't given him the opportunity to do that. Besides, there was always the chance that he might actually like the girl, or at least have a little good, clean, impersonal sex with her.

As soon as he'd shut off the water, there was a knock at the door. Maybe whoever it was had been knocking while the shower was running and he just hadn't heard it. It had to be Vern, of course. Julian slipped on his jeans, soaking them in the process, and dripped water across the floor to let him in.

"Hey, Julian," said Vern Doyle, striding in like he owned the place. "You look like a drowned rat."

"Hello, Vern." His friend was a tall, dark drink of hyperactivity with a fondness for tattoos, black attire, and situations in which he could act menacing. Bad acne had left him with a scarred complexion, but he had beautiful light brown hair, the kind that women really did like to run their hands through. Julian had witnessed this phenomenon himself on a number of occasions.

"Aren't you ready yet, man? The Monique and Margie Show is on the road and raring to go. Why ain't you?" Vern stood in front of the painting of Ariadne, bouncing up and down on his heels as he studied it.

Julian grabbed a towel from the bathroom and started

drying himself. "I don't know if I'm up for this, man. I've had a rough day."

"Yeah, yeah. Come on, let's have none of that. If you've had a rough day, then you're in dire need of a smooth night. These girls are wild and crazy, best friends with each other from way back. They're waiting downstairs right now in Monique's car. It's a sure thing, I'm telling you. You can't miss. All you have to do is show up."

A likely story, he thought. Vern was an expert thrill salesman, but the thrill was always harder to obtain than he made it out to be. He sat down on the edge of the bed. "Well, tell me something about them."

Vern fell back on the bed beside him, leaning on his elbows and crossing his legs at the ankles. "Margie works at a cosmetics counter. She's mine for the evening. Monique works in a record store. She's a dazzling redhead and she's yours for the taking. She's very into music. And she's female and she's alive. What more do you need to know?"

So far it didn't sound very promising. Julian didn't know much about music. All he knew was what inspired him, what stimulated him as he worked or conceived a work. He didn't care if it was pop, classical, underground, or heavy metal. If it emotionally moved him, he liked it, and that was all that mattered. However, if Monique was knowledgeable about any art form at all, then she might be interesting to be with.

"Okay. I'll go. Give me a few minutes to make myself human."

"Attaboy. I'll be waiting down below with the babes." Vern thrust himself onto his feet and headed for the door. "I like the painting, by the way. Looks to me like that poor girl is spreading herself a little thin, though."

Julian grinned at the door as Vern closed it behind him. The man was no intellectual, had barely graduated from high school, but he had an uncanny knack for grasping the gist of Julian's paintings. It reinforced the idea in Julian that art was created and understood on a level beyond known mental functions, interpreted by a sense not restricted to the physical world. He hesitated to call it spiritual or psychic, preferred rather to think of it simply as altered consciousness. It made sense, for Vern definitely had a different way of looking at things.

As he got dressed, he remembered how they'd met. It had been at Julian's first opening, at the Milton Blake Gallery. The place had been broken into and robbed just prior to his show and Vern, who ran a security systems consultant firm, was personally handling the installation of the new alarms. Julian was understandably nervous about the safety of his paintings, so he approached the man and spoke to him, hoping to gain some reassurance. At first Vern had been arrogant, standoffish, and condescending; artistic types were all wimps to him. Then he took a look at Julian's work and was genuinely fascinated by it. Such savage and sensual images struck a chord in the hard, wild man. A deep friendship quickly formed between them and had lasted ever since, as incompatible as they often seemed to be.

Julian combed his hair and put on his leather jacket, suddenly feeling very hungry. He wished he'd eaten something earlier in the day. Lately he'd been forgetting to have meals, which was something new for him. It was beginning to show, too, in the bones pressing against the inside of his skin. He hadn't been this emaciated since his addiction to amphetamines as a teenager. Oh, well, it was nothing to worry about. Maybe it made him look lean and mean. He shut off the light and left the loft, anxious about meeting someone new.

Monique's car was a cherry-red Mercury Cougar with a license plate that read REDHDGVR. He found that funny, tacky, and a little exciting all at once. Someone swung the passenger-side door open from the inside and he got in, sitting in the front seat. Marijuana smoke hung heavy in the car's interior and Bon Jovi was playing on the stereo. The driver was a petite woman, presumably Monique, wearing a jacket and skirt of blue denim and a lacy white shirt. She had gorgeous red hair, long and thick and not at all wiry, and she was very cute, but he thought she had too many freckles. And she was wearing too much eye makeup.

"Julian," said Vern from the backseat, "this is Monique. And back here with me is the lovely Margie."

He shook hands with Monique, who was busy choking on some smoke. Then he turned around to greet Vern's date. She had long, dark hair, a voluptuous figure, and a meticulously made-up face of considerable beauty. Her clothes looked expensive, a gold silk blouse, a black leather miniskirt, and black velvet boots. Her eyes looked a little blank, but that could have been from the effects of the weed.

"How are you doing?" he said, addressing both women at the same time.

Margie giggled. "Real good and getting better. Here." She held out a lit joint over the back of the front seat. He took it and toked on it without inhaling, just to be polite, then handed it to Monique.

"Thanks," said Monique, sounding hoarse. She had

not yet looked directly at him. "So what are we doing tonight, guys? We gotta decide where we're going."

"Let's go to the Boiler Room," suggested Margie. "Dr. Strain is playing there tonight."

"What do you say, Julian?" Vern asked him. "It's a blues band. Is that okay with you?"

He hated blues, but he didn't want to be a dissenting voice. "Yeah, sure. Fine."

"Then we're off," said Monique as she crushed out the joint in the dashboard ashtray. She twisted the key in the ignition, revved the engine, and accelerated down the street. Julian strapped himself in, trying not to wonder if she was in any condition to drive.

"So what do you do for a living?" she asked him.

"I'm a painter."

"Oh, yeah? Well, my apartment could sure use repainting. Think you could give me a good deal?"

He cringed, felt like getting out of the car right then and there. Without waiting for it to slow down. "No, I'm an artist. I paint pictures."

"Oh." Monique seemed to think about this for a few moments. "Hey, wanna do my portrait?"

The pleasant idea of her posing nude for him diluted his despair a bit. "I'm not that kind of an artist. My models are nightmares, when I can coax them out of my head to pose for me. I take snapshots of hallucinations."

"Huh?"

"He does weird, freaked-out paintings, Monique," Vern explained. "Monsters and demons and stuff like that."

"Oh," she said uncertainly. "That's really something."

Now she probably thought he was a lunatic. His

chances of making it with her might have just been reduced to nil.

"Maybe he can paint you anyway, Monique," said Margie. "After all, you are pretty weird."

Monique shrugged, unoffended by this remark. "Yeah, maybe. I've always seen myself as an Irish witch, maybe a reincarnation of one of my ancestors."

"What was that?" jeered Vern. "You see yourself as an Irish bitch?"

"Shut up, Vern. What were those people called, Julian? You must know. They worshiped trees and carried out ceremonies at Stonehenge."

"Druids." She was genuinely beginning to spark his interest.

"Yeah. You could paint me as one of those."

It had possibilities, but he didn't know much about Druids. No one did, really. They pulled into the parking lot of a bar that looked like it had stood for half a century. Monique parked the car deep in the shadows behind the building, and it turned out there was a reason for this. She produced a small mirror and a vial full of white powder from her purse, and began cutting lines with a razor blade. Vern and Margie leaned forward in anticipation.

"You're all going to love this," said Monique as she worked. "This is high-grade Peruvian flake. The old Indian peoples would get so stoked on this shit that they could cut off their own heads with swords and not even feel it."

Vern seemed to think this was a hilarious thing to say. Julian wondered how anyone could take it as a recommendation for something. Dollar bills were rolled up and the snorting commenced. When Julian's turn came he reluctantly indulged, having long ago seen and felt everything he wanted to see and feel on mind-altering substances. The visions came to him now unassisted, and in fact he needed alcohol to block them out on those occasions when they too furiously deluged his weary brain. Drugs tended to imbue his nightmares with the power to overwhelm him.

With everyone's nerves buzzing ecstatically, they got out and walked toward the bar. Julian realized that if he didn't get a drink and some food soon he would collapse or suffer something worse. They paid the cover charge at the door, Julian paying Monique's way, then they went in and found, at Monique's insistence, a table near the stage. The place was crowded, which didn't make him feel any more at ease, the audience consisting of a slightly larger proportion of black people than whites. Smoke formed a fluid layer in the darkness near the ceiling, undulating with the air currents. The stage was the only well-lit area and it was vacant at the moment. True to the name of the bar a huge iron boiler stood in one corner, old and unused.

An unattractive waitress appeared and Vern ordered a pitcher of beer. Julian mumbled out a request for some corn chips with cheese sauce, wishing his head would stop spinning. He fumblingly got a cigarette out of the pack and lit it with a trembling hand. None of the others seemed to notice his shaky state. Monique and Margie were lost in girlish small talk and Vern, understandably, couldn't seem to keep his hands off Margie's body. Her cowlike expression had not changed in the least, so Julian suspected it was her natural aspect.

The beer and his chips arrived. They tasted like cardboard and the cheese was like melted plastic, but he devoured them as if he were a starving man. He had to get some solid nutrition into his system or it would fail somehow. It was underfed and overloaded. Passing out didn't seem possible—he'd never done it before, so his body didn't really know how it was done—but he might throw up or start acting like an idiot.

Monique turned to him finally. "So, Julian, are you a big blues fan?"

Now she asks me, he thought. "Um, I like some of it, mostly when it's done by a band that does harder rock, like Led Zeppelin or AC/DC. They kind of give it more of an edge, more coherence."

She nodded slowly, her eyes wandering. "Yeah, I can see that. I'm a big fan of Stevie Ray Vaughan. I was really broken up when he got killed."

Julian didn't know who she was talking about. He wanted to steer the conversation toward something more relevant to him. "You said you think of yourself as a witch. Are you into the occult?"

"The what?"

"You know, ghosts, witchcraft, contacting the dead, that sort of thing."

"Oh." Her head tilted and her eyes grew distant. "I'm into astrology and tarot cards. And I believe in reincarnation. I really feel that I've lived before."

He sighed, deciding that he'd asked for that. For him, occult matters were merely amusing and interesting, sometimes serving as source material for his art. They provided forms for his murky musings, offered him symbols through which he could express what might otherwise be inexpressible. They seemed to be real to her. "Well, that's cool."

"What sign are you?"

This was getting worse by the minute. "I'm a Scorpio."

"Really? That's the sexiest of the signs. I'm a Libra. We have a hard time making up our minds."

"I thought you were Fellatio, the sign of the phallus," said Vern, laughing at her.

Monique threw a corn chip at him. "You can't be serious about anything, you prick. You just don't believe in anything."

"I believe in my own abilities. I know them and I trust them."

"Me too," said Margie, giggling again. "I believe in his abilities. He's going to demonstrate them to me again tonight."

"You don't have the ability to save your own soul," Monique said to Vern. "Only God can do that."

"I have noticed that most people profess a passing belief in God," said Julian, pleased that the discussion had finally taken on some substance. He was also feeling better. "That belief, however, in no way influences their behavior."

Monique stared at him, for the first time all night. "What, you mean that they still go on taking drugs and fucking like bunnies and swearing like sailors? Like me? Well, I think the original Holy Scripture was lost, covered up by people who want life to be miserable. God wants us to have fun and be happy. He doesn't want us to be down on our knees all the time."

He smiled at the naive simplicity of the concept. "If divine revelation is so hard to perceive accurately, then maybe there's no such thing."

That seemed to stun her into silence.

"I think the end of the world is coming," said Margie, serious now.

Vern sneered. "You do, do you?"

"Yeah. I mean, think about it. How much longer can the world go on the way it is? How much further can things degenerate? Everybody's sex crazy, there's violence and killing everywhere, and it just keeps getting worse. Pretty soon we're all just going to be totally out of control and it'll all fall apart. We'll have hell on earth and that'll be the end."

Julian decided she was smarter than she looked, and a lot more paranoid.

"I suppose the devil is behind all this?" Vern said to Margie, mockingly.

"Well, yeah. Of course."

"Then can I ask you, if the planet is headed toward hell on roller skates, why are you contributing so enthusiastically to the general decadence and wholesale sin?"

Margie shrugged. "Well, I figure I might as well have a good time while it lasts."

Vern shook his head at this. "Devil, what is man that thou art mindful of him? It's as big a conceit as a supreme being watching over humanity."

"It's not the devil," said Monique in quiet earnest. "That's not where evil comes from. It came here from somewhere else, out in space maybe. It lives inside of us all and feeds on our souls. It invaded our minds a long time ago."

"Yeah?" Vern said with weary annoyance. "Well, I personally wouldn't know what to do without my pet evil spirit. It gives me the strength to get up in the morning."

The band had come onstage while they were talking and now started playing, making it impossible to be heard over the music. It didn't matter, for the conversation seemed to have ground to a halt anyway. Monique was obviously into some hard-core mysticism and Vern had a way of making anybody sound ridiculous. Julian concentrated on downing several beers and keeping the chaotic din of wailing sax, twanging guitars, and frantic drums from grating on his nerves. Vern and Margie lost themselves in each other while Monique lost herself in the music.

They finished off four pitchers and the women made two trips to the rest room to "powder their noses," so by the end of the evening everyone was pretty wasted. Vern seemed the least debilitated, however, so when the time came to leave, Monique handed him her car keys. This gave Julian cause to wonder if the man even had a driver's license. He didn't own a car and Julian had never seen him drive one before. It would be a blessing if the night didn't get too much more interesting than it already had.

Monique leaned against Julian as the four of them stumbled out to the parking lot. He liked the feel of her, small and soft and warm, and he ventured to put his arm around her shoulders. Her hair smelled of some fruity shampoo, with the slightly medicinal scent of her perfume beneath it. They settled into the backseat of the Cougar. Vern situated himself in the driver's seat like he was strapping himself into a cockpit, and Margie flopped into the passenger side in the front, her eyes only half open.

"Is everybody ready?" Vern asked, starting the car and spinning gravel as he pulled out before anyone had a chance to answer. "Let's take the freeway back to Julian's place. I don't feel like waiting for traffic lights."

Julian interpreted this to mean that Vern was in the mood for some speed. Vern had bragged a number of times about his high-velocity exploits in other people's cars, such as outrunning a police cruiser in a stolen vehicle as a kid. These stories hadn't seemed worth paying attention to at the time. Now Julian worried about what he'd gotten himself into.

Vern located an on ramp and turned onto the four-lane thoroughfare, rapidly accelerating. He found a radio station playing heavy metal and let it blast from the speakers, which were just behind Julian's and Monique's heads.

"God, I hate that stuff," she muttered. "You should see all the sleazy no-brainers who come into the store to buy it, like bodies with no one really inside of them. They look at me like they could fuck me for a few minutes then kill me and never think twice about it."

He didn't tell her that he liked the music, though he would prefer that it weren't threatening to make his ears bleed. She slid her hand between his legs, surprising him, but he thought he was too drunk to get an erection. He remembered what her license plate said and wondered how serious she was about it, discovered that even this failed to arouse him. It was an old dilemma with him: he couldn't perform in social situations unless he stayed in control of himself, but he couldn't even face social situations unless he let himself get out of control. Maybe his physical apparatus would start responding in a few minutes. If not, this blind date was going to end on a rather embarrassing note.

Vern slammed on the brakes and spat out a stream of loud, vicious profanity. Jerking his head up, Julian saw the cause of it: a silver Mercedes coming down an on ramp had cut them off as it sped onto the freeway. He had a pretty good idea of what was going to happen next.

"Now, that wasn't nice at all," said Vern, snarling. "I'm gonna have to teach that dickhead a lesson." He pressed hard on the gas pedal and the chase was on.

"Get him!" Margie urged. "Get the fucker! Go get him, man."

Monique sat forward. "No! Cut it out, Vern. I'm warning you. If you scratch the paint on this thing or get a dent in it I swear I'll cut your balls off."

Vern said nothing, just zeroed in on his prey and kept on coming. The Cougar roared up alongside the Mercedes, both doing about seventy-five miles per hour, Julian noticed, and he saw that there was a young couple in the other car. The guy was driving. Margie flipped him the bird, and he took this as his cue to get away. He pulled ahead and Vern pursued, moving over behind him.

"Let's bang heads, motherfucker." Vern punched the accelerator and the front bumper briefly kissed the back bumper of the Mercedes.

"Goddammit, Vern!" screamed Monique.

"Chill out, babe." He switched back to the other lane and raced up to the left side of the Mercedes. The driver's face looked shocked and angry at this harassment.

"Uh, Vern," said Julian, "why don't you just let this go, huh? Let it slide."

"No way, man. Me and this dude are gonna dance." Vern turned the wheel to the right and the Mercedes swerved out of the way. They were doing ninety now. It would be very easy to get killed at this speed.

Julian sat back in his seat, feeling petrified. He'd been in a car accident, a long time ago, and he didn't like being reminded of it. His aunt Dora had been driving and she didn't survive. And Julian had almost died. Of fright.

Vern steered the Cougar at the other car again. "Come on, little doggie. Heel."

The Mercedes yielded and this time Vern forced it off the road, onto the shoulder. Vern skidded the Cougar to a stop a thousand yards down the way and backed up very fast at the Mercedes, slamming on the brakes at the very last second so that he avoided a collision by less than a foot. Julian sighed with relief as he unclenched his white-knuckled hands.

"Now I'm going to kick some ass," announced Vern, getting out of the car. Margie got out to do some cheerleading and Monique went around to inspect her front bumper, so Julian thought he'd better follow them.

The driver of the other car, dressed in a dark business suit, emerged and started to stalk toward Vern. Julian knew this was a mistake; it was not wise to cross Vern Doyle. "Are you some kind of a psycho? What the hell is your problem?"

"I've got a very bad attitude," replied Vern, slowly approaching him. "Always have."

When the man got a good look at what was stomping his way, a thin but muscular guy, tall and extremely ready for action, he backed up and withdrew into his car. Vern rushed forward with startling speed, yanked open the door before the man had a chance to lock it, and reached in to grab the keys from the ignition. Then he stood back and let the man and woman lock the doors.

"I'm not going to drag you out, you weasel," said Vern, pocketing the keys. "I'm going to wait until you come out of your own free will and fight me like a man."

Julian felt this had gone far enough. Vern never knew when to quit. "Come on, Vern. Leave them alone."

"Nope." He didn't look at Julian, just stared at his human game. "This guy is going to step out and let me beat the crap out of him. Then he's going to apologize for cutting me off and making me beat the crap out of him. Then I'll leave them alone."

"This is getting boring!" Monique informed him.

That seemed to spur Vern on to action. He jumped up on the hood of the Mercedes, no doubt scuffing and denting it. For a moment he knelt down on all fours, making faces at the couple through the windshield, then he leapt back to his feet, still on the hood.

"You know, your windshield looks kind of dirty to me," he said. "It's not safe. Don't fret about it, though. I'll fix it."

He promptly unzipped his black jeans, took his penis in hand, and proceeded to piss on the tinted glass. His urine steamed in the cold night air. A number of cars drove by, but Vern was oblivious to them as they caught him in their headlights. Margie laughed hysterically, and even Monique joined in after a moment. Julian had to admit that it was an inspired bit of revenge, exactly the sort of thing Vern was so good at.

His bladder emptied, Vern zipped himself up and bounded to the ground, grinning. He swaggered around to the driver's-side door and dangled the keys near the window. "Now maybe you'll remember to drive in a more sportsmanlike fashion. Speed kills, folks."

Then he threw the keys deep into the weeds by the side of the road. This seemed unnecessarily cruel to Julian, but it would be futile to point this out to Vern. One of these days he'd have to find some saner friends.

Everyone was mostly quiet the rest of the way to his apartment. Vern was basking in the afterglow of his street theatrics, Margie had passed out, and Monique claimed she wasn't feeling well. He was tired and emotionally exhausted from the day's events, so aside from some soothing words to Monique he said nothing. If she felt ill, then probably nothing would happen between them tonight. There didn't seem to be any chemistry there anyway.

They arrived at his building, and Vern parked the car in front. Monique suddenly sat forward. "Oh, God. You stopped too fast. Let me out."

Vern opened his door and she tumbled out, staggering around the front of the car to the sidewalk, where she started vomiting. Julian got out and, careful not to get any on him, held her as she heaved violently. No, he wasn't going to have any company in his bed on this night. He looked up and saw Vern smirking at him from inside the car, shaking his head.

All in all it seemed an appropriate end to the evening.

3

A Walk on the Dark Side

The juices were not flowing, the fires were not burning, the Muses were not amusing him tonight. It was nine o'clock on a Wednesday night and Julian was standing before a large, nearly blank canvas. He hadn't sold a painting or been laid in a very long time—he hadn't heard from Monique since the double blind date last week—and now his inspiration seemed to have dried up on him. Something was trying to suggest itself on the white surface, medieval towers, Gothic cathedrals, underground caverns, or a modern city in ruins, but the image refused to be revealed. He had to trick it into exposing its bones and flesh to him, leave and catch it by surprise by coming back too soon or too late, or by going out on a quest for a new set of eyes from which it could not conceal its nature. Thinking this, he squinted at his embryonic creation and smoked his last cigarette. *He was out of cigarettes;* that clinched it. Everything pointed to getting out of the loft and seeing some of the outer world for a while. Out there somewhere he would find an as yet unused door back into his inner world. He hoped.

So he grabbed his jacket and strode out the real-world door, wondering where he should go in search of creative input. He thought about calling Vern, asking his friend to meet him somewhere. A brief walk to the end of the block informed him that the pay phone standing there was out of order. What the hell. He would go solo tonight, stop relying so much on Vern for protection and amusement. Nor did the idea of going down to the Village appeal to him. It was so full of writers, poets, musicians, sculptors, and painters trying to soak in the soul-stirring atmosphere that it had become drained, a spiritual void, a pretension of depth and transcendent perception. There were just the same old faces and places there, and he'd end up getting drunk, staggering home, with nothing to show for it but a hangover. No, he wanted someplace shadowy and dangerous, someplace where the shadows and the dangers were real, not painted and postured. *Painted shadows;* that was something to think about. He'd made the right decision, was getting inspired already.

There was a short stretch of the city not far from his abode called the Crescent, so named because it was a curving block of bars, pool halls, and flophouses, located on the edge of slumland and a vast plain of vacant lots left by building demolition. Urban renewal. It seemed like just the sort of place he was looking for, raw and real, so he started walking down that way, to the east. The neighborhood didn't look so bad at night because you couldn't see just how far gone it was. The rats and stray dogs got bolder after the sun went down, but they pretty much stuck to rummaging through the garbage cans. Competing with Fred.

"Hey, Julian," a scratchy voice called to him from within an alley.

Speak of the devil and he appears. "Hi, Fred." Fred had made a fire and he was cooking what looked like a small carcass on the end of a stick. Julian hoped it wasn't what it looked like. He couldn't bring himself to ask.

"Where are you off to?"

He shoved his hands into his pockets and shuffled his feet. "Oh, I don't know. I'm just getting some air. Maybe stroll over to the Crescent for a drink or two."

Fred nodded, cleaning out a nostril with a pinky again. "Try a bar there called the Quarry. It's the only one for miles around that'll serve me. It's not like you to be wandering around alone in the dark, though. Not safe."

"Yeah, like you've got a lot of room to talk. You'll be lucky if you don't wake up some morning with your throat cut."

"I can take care of myself," said the shabby man, laughing. "Can you keep me company for a while?"

This was not really what Julian had in mind, chewing the fat with a skid-rower. "Uh, I really can't. I need to stretch my legs, recharge my mental batteries."

Fred held out whatever was on the end of the stick. "I'll share my dinner with you."

He blanched a little. "No, thanks. I'm on a rodent-free diet."

"It ain't rat. It's flying rat. Pigeon. European royalty used to eat this as squab and consider it a delicacy."

"I'll pass anyway," he said, laughing.

"Then can you spare a few bucks?"

"No way. I refuse to contribute to the deterioration of your liver."

Fred turned away and went back to his cooking. "Go away, then."

"I'll see you later." He tramped on toward the Crescent.

Textures smooth and rough blazed at him, the chiaroscuro of streetlight, moonlight, and neon light brushed against his retinas, shapes geometric and chaotic tugged at his churning subconscious. Something was breeding in there, but it might yet come out stillborn. Like any child, a painting had to be lovingly gestated, nurtured with adversity's sweet milk, and he was quite happy when his brainchildren turned out to be freaks of nature. Hungry for experience to feed his imagination, he shambled along the Crescent and into the tavern called the Quarry.

It was a very long room, almost a hallway with nowhere to go. The lighting was low, the air was smoky, the wallpaper was peeling, the floor was stained, and the barstools had burst their seams, but Julian liked the place. Gritty human essence permeated the fabric and furniture of the establishment, the sweat, breath, spit, and drowned dreams of desperate spirits who came in to lose their misery in spirits of another sort. Two old men sat at a small, rickety-looking table crammed against the wall to his right. One of them had had his right arm amputated from the elbow down, which made Julian's skin crawl a little. A group of young male toughs played pool on the splotched and torn green-velvet-covered table at the far end of the room, and there was a potentially fine-looking blond girl talking on the pay phone at the end of the bar to his left. She was wearing dress bluejeans, a white shirt, black high heels, and a brown corduroy jacket. Her body looked excellent, but he couldn't yet see her face because of the way she was half turned. A fine mane of light gold hung down a little past her shoulder blades. *This could be a most productive expedition indeed,* he thought as he took a seat at the bar.

The bartender emerged from the back room, a large man who was obese but also amply muscled, an ex-biker type, his long, wavy hair tied in a ponytail. Julian guessed that in spite of its danger-zone location there weren't many brawls in this dive, or that at least they didn't last long. There had to be some heavy artillery under the counter, a sawed-off twelve-gauge or maybe a blunderbuss.

"What's your poison?" the man said in a remarkably friendly voice.

"I'll take a draft." As the barkeep drew the beer and Julian fished out his billfold, he tried to listen to the young woman's telephone conversation. He couldn't make it out; she was speaking very softly. Maybe she was making a drug deal. Or talking to her pimp? No, she didn't look like a hooker, wasn't putting it on display. The beer arrived, he paid, then he occupied his time wishing she would turn around so he could get a good look at her face.

The face was important. He was a face fetishist, got a hard-on for beauty. Couldn't help it. He had to be gazing into a visage of aesthetic ethereality when in the throes of orgasm between a woman's thighs. His desire for a smoke hit him at the same moment he noticed the cigarette machine in the rear corner, giving him the idea that he could inconspicuously check her out while doing one of the things he had come in here for. So he nonchalantly stood and made his way toward the back of the room, passing close by her to hear what she was saying.

He caught a whiff of her scent and it smelled like incense, spicy and musky and musty, like an ancient temple or an opium den. It was wonderful. And he heard her clear, full voice say into the mouthpiece she was holding:

"Okay, so like, if it's not Bogomil then I'm thinking Benandanti. You know, the good walkers, born of the caul. Christ, you're supposed to be the expert. I don't know about this shit."

She was staring at a small, crumpled sheet of paper clutched in her left hand, obviously half reading from the dense scrawl covering it. As he walked by, she lifted her eyes long enough to briefly meet his, and they were the bluest he'd ever seen. They were alert, lively, and smiling, and part of a very pretty face. But they didn't really seem to see him, so intent was she on her phone call.

As he shuffled on to the cigarette machine, he couldn't keep the thought out of his head: What was a girl like that doing in a dump like this? And what was that weird fucking conversation she was having? No matter; she was a looker and for once he seemed to be in the right place at the right time. Julian resolved to definitely hit on her and he didn't care if she shot him down in flames. Being a slave to his art, he could derive inspiration even from failure and rejection. No gain without pain, no light without darkness.

He dropped the coins into the slot, then pulled out the glass knob that delivered him a pack of filterless Camels. How should he proceed with this somewhat intimidating fox? He had to think up something clever, slick, cool, and unusual. Opening lines started going through his head, none of them sounding promising. As he turned to look back at her he accidentally nudged one of the pool players just as the guy was about to make a shot. The balls clicked but nothing rolled into a pocket, though Julian didn't really think that was his fault. He hadn't disturbed the shooter all that much. It didn't make any difference, however. Five sets of eyes suddenly fixed on him, glaring.

"Hey, *pendejo*," said the shooter. He was a muscular, baby-faced youth. "You fucked up my shot, man."

"Hey, I'm sorry, man." That sounded lame; Julian sincerely hoped he wouldn't soon be in a similar condition. He'd forgotten that this was a section of the city where logic didn't apply, where the effect was sometimes way out of proportion to the cause. Innocent action could result in a far vaster and negative reaction.

"Yeah?" said the other manchild with a cue stick in his hands. "You look pretty sorry. Just how sorry are you?"

Shit, he thought. Now he'd gotten himself in a tense situation and the girl on the phone was watching him, would gather her first impression from how he handled himself in a crisis. And he seldom handled himself well under pressure.

"Uh, look guys. I really didn't mean it. It was an accident. But here." He took out a quarter and placed it on the edge of the pool table. "Have a game on me."

All five of them laughed, then the shooter spoke. He also seemed to be the leader. "Yeah, we might have a game on you." Picking up the coin, he rubbed it between thumb and forefinger. "But it might not be the kind of game you like."

They slowly surged toward him. This was nothing personal, Julian knew. They were just bored and full of hostility born of frustration, of barren uncultivated lives, and he had just walked in, drawn attention to himself by doing something careless, and thus become their quarry in the Quarry, their victim for tonight. He looked for the bartender, but the big man seemed to be in the back room again. Great. This could easily result in more pain than he could learn anything from, except maybe never to leave his loft ever again. At least, not without Vern along to keep him out of trouble, though Vern was almost as dangerous as the trouble he needed to avoid.

"Hey," the girl called to Julian, now done with her phone call. "You in the leather jacket. Can I borrow one of those smokes you just bought?"

It looked as if she'd taken more notice of him than he'd first thought, or else she was just taking pity on a poor chump about to get his ass kicked. "Sure," he said, and started to walk over to her, but the shooter detained him with a heavy hand on his shoulder.

"Wait a minute, geek. We're not through rapping here. You made me miss my shot and there's a lot of money riding on this game. So maybe you owe us for more than just one."

The girl walked over very casually, hands at her sides, hips swinging confidently. She looked the shooter straight in the eyes.

"Look, tough guy. This hard-ass routine is really tiresome. Five on one, messing up someone who hasn't really done anything to you, is a very childish way to get your rocks off."

The shooter grinned, looking her up and down once. "Maybe so, bitch. How about if we get our rocks off by throwing you down on the table and pulling a train on you? You like that? A good old-fashioned gang bang. How about that?"

She returned the grin. Then the light in the room seemed to shift, getting somehow darker and somehow brighter at the same time. All the shadows became the most real and solid things that Julian could see. Her eyes deepened into pools of blackness for the merest split second, eclipsing all the whites. No, not black, just a very dark violet. Julian blinked to clear his vision and when he reopened his eyes things appeared normal again. The shooter had jumped back a few feet away from her, looking pale. Had she kneed him in the groin or something? He looked more scared than injured.

"Get away from me, *bruja*," he angrily gasped at her.

"How about that ciggy?" she said to Julian as she strolled back to the bar. Nobody stopped him as he followed her, and the two of them assumed stools near his warming mug of beer.

"So tell me," he said as he tore open the pack, tapping it until several tobacco cylinders projected from it. "What's a nice guy like me doing in a place like this?"

Taking one of the Camels, she smiled. "Do you live around here often?"

She was quick to pick up on the game. He liked that. "Lots of weather we've been having lately, isn't it?"

Led by the shooter, the pool players filed past them toward the door, donning their golden jackets. A snake nailed to a cross adorned the backs of them. *Jesus Christ!* thought Julian. He'd narrowly escaped getting sliced and diced by the Crucifixers, the local teenage mafia. Suddenly, he was very grateful to this strange female stranger.

"You really freaked them out, I guess," he said, pointing with his thumb at the last of the Crucifixers exiting. "How did you do that?"

Her smile turned wry as she looked down at the counter. "Oh, I guess I reminded them of my sister and they remembered that she kicked the shit out of one of them a few years ago."

It wasn't hard to tell that she wasn't completely serious, but he decided not to press the matter. "Oh. Well, thanks. You saved my skin."

"Yeah, I did. Maybe you'll let me borrow it sometime. When you're not using it, I mean." Her gaze returned to his face.

He laughed, marveling at her. This lovely young woman could easily be the most bizarre person he'd ever met. Her intriguing and unidentifiable fragrance, the way she talked, an air of untamed unknown passions about her. It turned him on something fierce. "Yes, of course. Anytime. Uh, my name's Julian Stormer."

"Hey, cool name." She seemed to think about something for a moment, then extended her right hand. "Ashley Herrin. Pleased to make your acquaintance. Care to buy your skin-savior a drink?"

"Sure." The bartender was back, leaving Julian to wonder if the man hadn't been conveniently absent when an unpleasant scene was developing. He'd evidently misjudged the hulking brute.

"White wine," she said to the big man. "And something halfway drinkable if you please, huh?"

The drink was brought and he paid for it. "So, are you a student or something?"

"Huh? What do you mean?" She didn't seem to blink much, and she kept looking away from him, as if she was self-conscious about her face. Or maybe just her eyes.

He pointed at the phone. "Well, I eavesdropped a little on your phone call. Sounded pretty esoteric."

HARROWGATE 53

Her eyebrows twitched and there was a momentary twinge in the corner of her mouth. "Oh, no. I'm not a student, not formally. I've just got this friend who's into some really weird, wild shit and I'm a little worried about her. That's all. So I'm doing some investigating."

He nodded. "Very thoughtful of you."

"So tell me, Julian. Are you a poet or something?"

"A painter." He recalled Monique's reaction to this reply and waited to see if she would do better.

Ashley sipped her wine. "Close enough. One paints with words, the other rhymes with images. Are you any good?"

"On the canvas? I manage to go a few rounds, even get a knockout now and then. How about you? What do you do?"

She averted her eyes again. "Anything I want. Actually, I'm a curatrix."

Julian rolled the word around in his head for a moment. "Does that mean you cure people, or that you're the caretaker of a museum?"

"I could probably cure you," she said, giggling. "I'm a caretaker of a private legacy. Boring work, you don't want to hear about it."

He leaned closer to her, putting his hand on the bar. "Actually, it sounds fascinating. I used to practically live at the museums and libraries in this burg. Antiquities and ancient artifacts enthrall me. I've got a few in my loft, nothing valuable or spectacular. But you're the keeper of a personal collection, huh? Does the owner ever show it off? I'd like to see it sometime."

She crushed out her cigarette in the glass ashtray on the counter between them. "I don't think so. It's priceless, truly one-of-a-kind stuff. Actually, I'd much rather see your collection. What do you say?" The ruby swell of her lips formed a come-hither smile. "Let's go to your place."

A thrill shot through his viscera to his groin, kindling a euphoric fire in his brain. So he had come away from his walk with not just a little ambrosia for his soul, but a bit of nectar for his flesh as well. She made him even more nervous than most beautiful women, however. The trick with the lighting still bothered him, what he had glimpsed in her eyes. He could probably convince himself without too much trouble that he'd imagined it. Such a minor enigma only intensified her aura of mystery, arousing him all the more. Besides, this was an opportunity he couldn't possibly pass up. The opportunity of a lifetime.

"Yeah. It's not far. Let's go."

He left an undeserved tip on the bar and led the way out of the Quarry, with Ashley Herrin close behind.

4

Rapid Heartbeats

"The moon reminds me of a skull," she said, gazing up at the white orb in the sky as they walked down the sidewalk.

"Yeah? You know, I've never been able to see the man in the moon." He had to keep up the clever chatter. Couldn't afford to lose her interest now. "It just looks like a battered sphere to me."

Ashley smiled at him. "That's strange. I would expect a painter to see patterns and faces everywhere, beneath the superficial solid world. It should be all cracks and fragile facades to you."

Julian didn't quite get that. "Well, yeah. I guess my art is more philosophical than perceptual." That sounded pompous. He had to get a rein on his tongue before he said something really stupid.

"You mean you try to get people to think when they look at your work."

"Exactly." God, she was sharp. She couldn't be much older than twenty, but she was smart beyond her years. *Who was this woman?*

She looked at him, then studied the crumbling tenement they were passing by. "I like that idea. People don't spend enough time thinking. Or feeling. They're so much like dumb animals, just going blindly through their lives. They need something to shake them out of their stupor. Is that what your paintings do?"

Stop it or you'll make me fall in love with you. "Yeah, I guess it is. I've never thought about it that way before. You've got gifted insight."

"Oh, not really." Ashley shrugged off the compliment. "You'll find I have a different take on things, that's all."

They came to his building and she paused, looking up. "Love your gargoyle."

This chick is too good to be true, he thought.

As soon as he'd let her into his loft she started exploring the place like a cat. Julian just stood back and bemusedly watched her, a warm, breathing, sensual work of art moving gracefully through the sanctum where he created his art. She paused to finger through his extensive compact-disk collection, browse through his sparse library populating two bookshelves, glance at his stack of videocassettes, and drink in every poster, print, and painting on the walls with her eyes. As she came to each metal sculpture and stone statue she caressed it with affection, giving special attention to his ancient objects. When she came to the adder stone she traced the spiral of the ammonite inward with her slender forefinger.

"The authenticity of a lot of that stuff is doubtful," he said when she'd finished examining his curios.

She seemed to ignore this. "It's here," she said, wistfully distracted. "In the walls, at the walls, beyond the walls."

Reflexively, he looked at the walls. "What is?"

With a dimpled smile she swept over to him and stared into his eyes. "The powers of creation. If I were blind I would know this is an artist's digs. I can feel it in the air."

"That's just ninety percent perspiration and ten percent inspiration." Quieting his nerves with some effort, he ventured to put his hands on her hips. She did not resist or withdraw in the least. Neither did she respond.

"It's not quite accurate, is it? Art isn't creating. It's searching."

She's too intellectual to be a street chick, thought Julian. If she was so damned cultured, what was she doing in this center of urban decay? Well, what was *he* doing there? "I guess so. Searching for truth, for unveiled reality, for the hidden aspects of ourselves."

Her head shook slightly. "I want to see your work."

His paranoias began to stir. What if she was an art critic trying to get an advance look at Julian Stormer's latest output? Ready to pounce on him and eat him alive like that bloodsucker in *Enigma*? No, he wasn't thinking clearly. Their meeting had been accidental, and besides that he'd been out of the scene for so long, he'd fallen beneath the notice of the culture vultures. Aside from minor derisive mention in an obscure article, that is. So he decided that her interest was sincere, but there was a catch.

"Uh, I never show it to strangers, unless they're potential buyers brought over by trusted friends. Never."

Biting her lip, Ashley raised her hands and dug her red nails into his upper arms. "I think you can make an exception in my case."

The pain surprised and excited him. Apparently she liked to play rough, so he let go of her hips and grabbed her slight shoulders. "No, I'm sorry. I just can't do it."

A laugh gushed out of her as she hooked her left foot around his right leg, trying to trip him. "Oh, you can. You will, sooner or later."

She was a lot stronger than she looked, for it was all he could do to maintain his balance. "You've got a lot of nerve, you know. Coming in here and making demands. My work is very personal to me."

"Oh, so you don't want to get personal with me, huh? This here sort of tells me different." With her right hand she reached for his crotch and squeezed hard. He yelled and went down on the floor, with her on top of him. She didn't let go.

"Okay. So, now do I get to see the paintings?"

"If you expect me to use that thing later you'd better let go of it."

Ashley squeezed harder, making him howl. "Don't worry. I know exactly how much punishment it can take and still function. Do I get to see them?"

"All right, all right. Just don't turn me into a soprano."

Grinning triumphantly, she released his sore genitals and stood up. As painful as it had been, he hated to break their first physical contact. It made him feel like he hadn't felt anything in a very long time. For a fleeting moment, however, he wondered just how far she would have taken it. Would she have done him actual bodily harm? The fact that he wasn't certain of the answer both scared and delighted him. He'd sure caught himself a live one here.

"You really know how to get your own way," he said, rising to his feet.

She held her hands behind her back and bounced on her heels. "I always have."

HARROWGATE

"Well, you won, though not exactly fair and square. Right this way, milady, to my etchings."

Julian led her to the dark end of the loft, flicking on the lights to reveal the two dozen cloth-covered squares and rectangles leaning against the wall. He still felt uneasy about doing this, for he'd received so many bad reactions to his art that it didn't seem worthwhile anymore to show it. When it was hanging in a gallery he didn't have to hear their insults, snide remarks, or leering innuendos, so that was safe. It was rare when someone was not offended, rarer still for someone to truly understand what he was trying to do. Now he had to risk Ashley's displeasure, but he couldn't deny her, refuse her. Fool for love, idiot for a fetching face. Or was it more than that? He felt she had eyes that couldn't fail to appreciate what he would reveal to them. Silly idea. *Well,* he thought, *just look at it this way: You owe her for getting you out of that jam with the Crucifixers.*

"Voilà," he said, removing the covers one by one and tossing them into a corner.

Ashley pressed her forefingers together and touched them to her lips, her gaze intent. At first she walked back and forth in front of the disorganized exhibition, seemingly trying to absorb the general flavor of the surrealistic images. Then she squatted down before the painting he called "Nightmare Lands," a dark desert inhabited by fungus and slugs, reached out to touch it, and pulled it closer. She did the same with the worm-infested, brainlike hive of "Teratogenia," the fleshy female gargantuan of "Primal Madonna," and "Ariadne in the Labyrinth," lingering long over this last picture. Julian watched silently with his arms crossed, smoking a cigarette and another after that.

"I see the influence of Bosch and Dalí," she said, finally standing back next to him and folding her own arms, gently gnawing a knuckle. "There's also some Giger and Dean in it. But you've blended it all together around the heart of something completely new. I'm very impressed, Julian."

Catching him totally off guard, she turned and closed her arms around his body. He clumsily reciprocated the gesture.

"You're looking very deep," she said, her high-cheeked face very serious. "Do you know what you're looking for?"

He shrugged involuntarily. "What hasn't been seen yet? I mean, just whatever it leads to, what I can expose."

She nodded so quickly and slightly that it was more like a twitch. "And just how far do you want to go?"

Ashley was clutching him hard, though without stabbing him with her nails this time. His heart had accelerated to a furious beat, he realized, and it wasn't entirely from arousal. She'd startled him as much as stimulated him, and now she was scaring him. Her eyes bored into his and he prayed that they wouldn't change, as they had in the bar. What was she getting at? What did she want? Him, obviously, but what part of him? Well, he knew what he wanted from her.

"All the way, of course," he replied.

To his relief she grinned at the double entendre. "I believe you, Julian. It's obvious from your work. You've glimpsed something, something only the gifted and the damned get to see. But it's not true that what you can't see can't hurt you."

Some sense of normality was returning to him and he

was getting a little pissed off at her. She was talking so weird, he began to wonder if she was flighty, like Monique and her ilk. "Ashley, what the fuck are you talking about? It's all just imagination. You know, diffracting the world through the prism of the subconscious mind."

Holding him even tighter, she began rubbing her leg between his legs. "Yeah, I know. Now let's fuck, lover."

That was a little more like it. They kissed in a very long, hungry embrace of lips and tongues and mouths, then he took her horizontally into his arms and carried her to the corner he'd curtained off as a bedroom. Though she waited for him to undress her, there was nothing really passive about her; she did little, but he felt she was in control the whole time. He stripped off his own clothes, gently pushed her down on the bed, and suddenly remembered there wasn't a single condom in the place.

"Uh, I hope this doesn't spoil the mood," he said, "but I don't have any protection."

Ashley giggled. "Um, I can see you have a real active social life."

His erection was stiff and throbbing, totally out of patience, and she was laughing at him. "Well, I could run out and get some. There's a drugstore just a few blocks away."

She looked down at his cock. "No, I don't think you could. Listen, Julian. I can't get pregnant and I don't have anything contagious, and I'm not worried about you. So go ahead. Get on with it or I'll beat you up again."

There was a slight viciousness in her tone that startled him, almost as if she was urging him to rape her. If he wasn't careful, she could make him really crazy. "Okay. Tonight's my night for living dangerously."

He kissed her from head to toe, sucked at the nipples stiffening on her breasts, licked her lightly furred mound to slick wetness, then carefully penetrated her. Initially she seemed to be barely reacting, but he soon sensed that her passion was building slowly, in intense, sinuous movements. It was a bit strange, as if she wasn't responding to his actions but was drinking in every nuance of the experience, or as if something long dormant in her was gradually being coaxed back to life by his sexual attentions. At no point did she lose control; she did not thrash or spasm or jolt. She just writhed and undulated with the tension of a skilled dancer. Julian couldn't take offense at this, as it in no way seemed to be a performance. It was simply the way this enigmatic woman experienced pleasure, seeming almost to spread her orgasm out over half an hour instead of climaxing all at once. He just went along with it, luxuriating in the sleek, silky feel of her skin, breathing in the exotic spiciness of her fragrance, which seemed to exude from her very pores.

She finally seemed to reach some sort of peak, stretching as taut as an Inquisition victim on the rack, with her heart beating almost impossibly fast against his, and she clawed deep into his back with her nails at that moment. Stinging pain blazed into his flesh and he was sure she'd drawn blood, but he didn't stop. This sort of thing had happened to him a few times before, discovering a sadistic streak in a partner during sex, though it had never been this extreme before.

Since she was already there, he let himself go. She laughed very mildly as he ejaculated, held him close as he spurted inside of her. As the waves of rapture flowed through him he saw something appear behind his closed eyelids, in the fabric of his thoughts. It was a strange image, partly geometric and partly organic, like a bright Maltese cross flung across a dark diamond-shape. Wriggling lines of purple vibrated within it, toward four tiny eyes staring outward, and mushroom shapes pulsated around the outside. It was a very puzzling and ungainly vision, not erotic in any way. What the hell had made him conceive of it at that particular instant? Was this what happened when you went so long without making love to a woman? Your id short-circuited?

It faded after a few seconds, to the point that he couldn't even visualize it in his memory. That was okay with him. It was better forgotten anyway.

"What's the matter?" she said. "You've got a funny look on your face. Wasn't I good, the best you ever had?"

"It's nothing. And you were fantastic." She relaxed as he withdrew from her, but he didn't want it to be over so soon, so he began nibbling on her neck below her ear. In spite of the injury she'd inflicted on him he felt very affectionate toward her, she who had not existed to him but hours before.

He found himself licking at a nearly invisible scar that ran clear across her throat. Must have missed it before in the heat of lust. His skin prickled when he realized what his tongue was touching, but he was careful not to show his shock. Apparently she'd lived very violently, at some point in her life.

"You've found my permanent necklace," she said cheerfully, a bit wearily. "Yes, I had my throat cut open once. It was a long time ago. I was in on a drug deal that went down real twisted."

Very tentatively, Julian traced the faint line of discolored flesh with his right forefinger. "It healed really well. How deep was it?"

Ashley sat up, unrudely pushing him away. "Just about fatal. The funny part was trying to cry for help. The sound wouldn't get any farther than the hole in my windpipe. It was like I'd swallowed a waterlogged piccolo and was playing it very off-key."

He was very close to astonishment. Never had he met someone who'd gone through such severe trauma, let alone one who could discuss it so casually. It reminded him of his own brush with death, as a child, in which he sometimes believed he'd actually been dead for a few seconds. That was the worst of it, the not knowing. And what he'd thought he'd seen . . . He wanted to tell her about it, the worst experience of his life, in the wreckage of that car, but he couldn't bring himself to share it. Not even with this kindred ravaged soul.

"Did they get the guy who did it?"

"Not for that, but he got his in the end. And I might see him again someday, though I won't recognize him when I do."

Was she always going to talk in riddles? "Well, you're over it now, right?"

She laughed at that, a touch grimly. "It's something I'll never get over, Stormy. It'll be with me until my . . . it'll be with me forever."

Julian nodded. Sighing, he finally risked exploring the wounds on his back. Sure enough, his fingers came away dripping with vivid red blood. Ashley looked a little stricken when she saw this.

"Gee, I'm sorry about that. I get kind of carried away sometimes. Are you all right?"

"Yeah, but I think I'd better put something on it. I've heard there are few things filthier than what's under human fingernails. I don't want it to get infected." He got up and headed for the bathroom.

"I'll help you." She padded after him. "I mean, I assure you that you can't catch anything from me, but it's better to be safe than sorry, I reckon."

"I've got alcohol and peroxide. Which do you think will hurt less?"

"Uh, alcohol." In the full glare of the bathroom lights her physical perfection stunned him all over again. He wondered how the world treated such an exquisite creature, if she was constantly tongue-tying men and inflaming jealousy in women. Maybe that had something to do with her violent tendencies. It was a good bet that she was terrifying to behold when she was genuinely angry.

"Then I guess I'll use peroxide. You'd probably like it to sting even worse."

"Don't be such a baby. Here. I'll do it." She grabbed the bottle of peroxide and poured it on the scratches. He practically screamed as he whirled around to face her.

"Not like that! Soak some cotton with it, then dab the wounds."

Ashley was laughing so hard, she could scarcely breathe. He liked the way her breasts jiggled when she did so, like globes of milky white Jell-O, but he was in true agony. And she was having herself a good old time. *"The wounds.* You make it sound like I tore the skin half off your back or something. Be a man, Stormy."

"I *am* a man. I'm just not a masochist."

She snatched a cotton ball from the edge of the sink. "All right. Turn around so I can finish."

He did so. "Be careful."

The pain was less as she gently wiped the markings she'd carved in his flesh, but he still grunted from the discomfort.

"Want me to kiss it and make it feel better?"

"No. You're probably poisonous."

There was a giggle in his ear, then she stopped applying peroxide. Next thing he knew he felt her hands on his buttocks, spreading them. What he thought was her tongue then touched him in a place no tongue had ever before touched him. He pulled away and turned around again.

"Ashley, that's not very sanitary."

"My, you sure are fastidious, aren't you?" She remained kneeling, with her face close to his penis. "How about if I kiss this?"

The prospect made him breathless, but he still wasn't going to let her off the hook so easily. "You're not going to bite it off, are you?"

Ashley shook her head. "Not my style." She placed his hands on her head and he let his fingers get tangled in her hair. Then she pleasured him with her lips and her tongue, more expertly than any other woman ever had, and when he came she swallowed his semen without the slightest reluctance. Julian believed he could easily get used to this.

They returned to the bed and he lit two cigarettes for them.

"I'll bet you forgot all about your back, didn't you?" she said, puffing away on hers.

"Don't let it go to your head. You were never a sorority girl, I see."

"Huh?" Then she looked at the digital clock on the

nightstand and jumped up. "Shit. It's almost midnight. I've got to be going, I'm afraid."

I'm afraid too, he thought, but of what he wasn't sure. "Why don't you spend the night here? I make a terrific breakfast. It's the only meal I know how to cook."

"No, sorry." She started to get dressed. "Don't worry. I like you. A lot. We'll see each other again. Soon. I promise."

That made him feel better, but he was still a little disappointed. And that surprised him; his emotions usually moved a lot slower. "I don't usually fall in lust so quickly, but I think I dig you too." Having made that admission, he began to feel awkward. It was hard letting someone get so close so fast, as it caused him to lose his severe detachment from the world. Well, Anna Kurtz had told him to keep in touch. Ashley made him *want* to keep in touch, with his feelings, with the world, with the human race. Especially with this one specific female human.

"I might as well ask, Cinderella. What do you turn into at midnight?"

Ashley looked at him sharply, then smiled. She slunk over to him and kissed him voraciously on the lips, making him taste traces of himself. "A real bitch. You got a phone and a number to go with it?"

"Uh, no. Since my agent stopped calling me I didn't see any point in keeping one around. You?"

She stood and put on her coat. "Would I be using the one at the Quarry if I did? Well, I know where you live. I'll be around."

Pretty sure of herself, wasn't she? He resented that a bit. "What if I have company?"

Her grin turned mysterious, like the Mona Lisa on

acid. "I'll know if you do or not. Good night, Stormy. Bittersweet dreams."

There wasn't much he could say to that. "Good night, Bittersweet."

Then she was gone, out of his apartment but hopefully not out of his life. He fell asleep shortly after that and had some very vivid dreams, of which he remembered not a one.

5

Early Worm

The sun had not been up for long when Julian joined it, wondering if the previous night had really happened. The still-drying wet spot in the middle of the bed told him that it had. Ashley Herrin, lovely riddle wrapped in an enigma, had actually come home with him and shared his bed, letting him know that he was still among the living, that his life wasn't over yet. It was not a good day to die, venerable Native American philosophy notwithstanding.

He rolled over to the edge of the mattress in a prelude to rising and spotted a wrinkled piece of paper on the floor, recognizing it as the one Ashley had been holding during her phone call. It must have fallen out of her coat pocket when she was getting dressed, he reasoned as he picked it up. A lot of her writing was illegible, but he could make out a few words: *Labartu, daughter of Anu; Ne-Gaib; Marbabeta Salomon.* Most of it was like that, foreign words and incomprehensible phrases, sounding like bits of very obscure occult lore. One line—*sister of the gods of the streets*—seemed to describe Ashley perfectly.

Suddenly, the Muse stirred in him, compelling him to go to his canvas. A shape had formed in his mind's eye and he wanted to make it real. This was doubly fortuitous because the early-morning daylight was at that magic moment when it beamed through the loft's skylights at just the right angle, so that it looked like the very first light to shine down on the earth, a naked primal light fresh from the sun, the kind of light that energized and purified. He did his best work in the dead of night, when the rest of the world was so silent that he could hear the voices in his head, but he had found this enchanted interval by chance and took advantage of it whenever he could. He leapt out of bed and strode to the big white rectangle he was trying to turn into a masterpiece. Moving the screen he used to conceal it, he stood naked before it and regarded it the way a matador looked at a hoof-scraping bull.

There was a large empty space near the center of the painting. He transferred the image his mind held to this blankness and tried to figure out what it would look like, something like a controlled symmetrical explosion. It certainly had nothing to do with what was already contained in the painting, but he decided that was a lost cause by now. This new invading shape might offer him more to work with. Sparkling solar radiation eight minutes old streamed upon the spot at which he was staring, crystallizing the image. Julian squeezed out white paint onto a palette, barely taking his eyes off the point of impact. He picked up a brush and attacked the canvas with vigorous strokes, producing what looked like a bright Maltese cross left open and unconnected at the center. There the vision faltered. His subconscious must have seen the completed shape while he walked in a dream state, a place from which he often came back with viable ideas, but returning reason and the aging rays of the sun had dissipated it. The perfect light was gone, taking the magic moment with it. He hadn't gotten up early enough to capture it. The early bird catches the worm. And what happens to the early worm? It gets eaten by the bird. This morning he felt more like the worm, devoured by the mental block obstructing his creativity.

Giving up, he cleaned and tossed down his brush, then took another look at the four flaring streaks of white he'd just painted. Whatever design they were supposed to be part of had completely fled his brain. Or had it? He had seen it before, he believed. Where? When? Wait. Of course. Last night, while making love with Ashley. It had come and gone then too. It was still in his head, but far too deeply buried for his conscious self to get at it. Sex and dreaming seemed to dredge it up. But where had it come from in the first place? No matter. If it had any significance at all, it would come back to him.

He concealed the painting, then put on his jeans and a white T-shirt. He shuffled over to the kitchen alcove to make coffee. It was time to start taking his daily dose of caffeine and nicotine. For a long time he sat at the table, drinking coffee and smoking, trying to sort out what last night had been all about. The memory of the bloodletting shook him up some, all the more because it thrilled him. He liked the idea of living on the edge, flirting with danger, but he didn't really have the guts or the drive to do it. That was why he hung around with Vern, who was an amphibian of the underground, an expert swimmer in the criminal element as well as a denizen of the dry land of society. He could report to Julian from that darker, rawer realm of dirty dealings and shady characters that Julian was afraid to enter himself. Julian could vicariously live the fast, wild life through Vern.

Ah, but now that he'd met kinky, weird Ashley he could have a bit of that for himself. He could experience it instead of just fantasizing about it. He wondered whether he was sick for wanting to, whether his reason was slipping. No, he didn't think so. He was an explorer of the depths of human nature, and where had Freud looked to learn about the basic formations of the mind? To the primitive and the abnormal. In the tribesman and the madman the skeleton of the psyche was laid bare. So it was high time for him to get to know a little savagery and mania firsthand. That was probably why his inspiration had abandoned him, because he'd relied too long on form instead of substance.

And Ashley Herrin was a woman of substance, far more so than Monique or Mercy. He often doubted that he'd really loved Mercy. How could he have? She'd mostly been just a shallow ornament, a socially skilled companion, someone to help guide him through the demands of everyday existence. Someone to put him down when he was already feeling low, never showing him the very quality after which she was named. Ashley challenged him, agitated his senses, forced him to live up to his conception of himself. This woman seemed to be his muse incarnate, an inhabitant of one of his paintings come to life, and he wasn't about to let her go. She was as much worth hanging on to as his sanity, so long as she didn't cause him to lose it.

On the other hand, he couldn't be a complete fool

about this. He had to go into it with open eyes. Besides her fierce sexuality, there was the hint of her entanglement with pagan worship of some kind. He pulled her notes out of his pocket and studied them. Whether or not her story about being a curatrix was true, he didn't know, but there was obviously far more to it than she'd told him. Right now he knew nearly nothing about her, except that she'd once come close to being a severed head. And that pain and pleasure blurred together to a degree in her mind.

There was a familiar knock at the door, an assertive pounding that made the wood tremble. He crossed the broad space of the loft and opened it. "Hello, Vern."

Vern loped in, looking bigger than his wiry frame really was, ever the space invader. That described him exactly, thought Julian. An invader of people's space, pushy and taunting, the kind of guy who liked to unsettle people by getting right up into their faces. He was a predator and a prankster, a wolf in clown's clothing.

"Julian, my man. How goes the creative process?" Julian sat back down and Vern pulled out one of the kitchen chairs. As small as it was he still managed to sprawl across it.

"It comes in spurts."

Vern snorted. "Sounds more like your love life. Got any beer?" He leapt up and stalked to the refrigerator.

"One, I think. Christ, Vern. It's not even nine o'clock in the morning."

"I haven't been to bed yet," said the man as he once more flung his lanky body across the chair and popped the top of the beer can. He leaned forward. "Not to sleep, anyway. Been doing speeders all night. When you sleep, you miss out on all those hours. It's all just dead time. I can't bear the idea of that."

Julian shook his head in wonder. "How you manage to run a successful business is beyond me. You're never there, and when you are there you're fucked up or coming off of being fucked up."

This got a shrug from Vern. "Hey, I hire good people, good people who know that if they screw up I will ream their asses. Besides, I'm stronger than any drug known to Man."

Vern had spent some time as a not-very-successful private investigator before going into the security-systems business, Julian knew. Detective work had turned out to be boring and anything but glamorous. So now the man helped people protect their homes and businesses, but he could also be called upon to perform a number of shadier services. Though Julian wasn't sure just how far such services went, he believed that professional hit-men were never involved. There had been a few cases not long ago in which Vern had aided parents in the abduction and deprogramming of their children from so-called brainwashing cults. Vern was good at the strong-arm tactics and he liked doing them. He'd also become somewhat knowledgeable about the crazy things such mystical sects believed in, so Julian decided it would be worthwhile soliciting Vern's opinion.

"Tell me what you think of this," he said, sliding the sheet of paper across the tabletop to his guest.

Vern picked it up as he took a long gulp from his beer and belched loudly. He muttered as he read, wide eyed with alertness at first, then frowning, setting it down when he was through. "As my ancestor Conan would say, it looks like a lot of bloody nonsense. Actually, I think some of that is from Assyrian mythology, but I can't be sure."

"Assyria. That's like Babylon, right?"

"Babylon, yeah. Uh, this here looks like a Scripture reference. Romans six: seven. You got a Bible around this dump somewhere?"

Julian leaned forward to see. "Is that what that is?"

"Yeah, that's what it is. What did you think it was? An ancient baseball score?"

He sat back. "I couldn't read it. You're a lot better at deciphering handwriting."

"Oh. Well, I've had a lot of practice on the job. Do you have a Bible?"

"No. I loaned it to old Bonewitz a few months ago and he never returned it. He had some theory about it being written in code and he wanted to prove it."

Vern guzzled more of his beer. "What is this? Where'd it come from?"

The memory of it made him smile. "I met this really strange girl at a bar called the Quarry last night. She's blond, very smart, very quick wit, and a feast for the eyes. You see, I went out for some cigarettes and a little motivation and almost got myself into a scrap with some Crucifixers. Ashley—that's her name—sort of talked my way out of that hassle. Then we came back here, she asked to see my paintings, we got into sort of a wrestling match, I showed them to her, then we made love. She clawed the hell out of my back at the moment of truth. She left just before midnight and accidentally dropped that on the way out."

Scratching his right cheek, Vern eyed Julian pensively. "I'm very happy for you, man. She faced down a bunch of 'Fixers?"

It sounded a lot more improbable when someone else said it. "Yeah. Ashley's kind of a tough girl. Used to be a member of a local gang, I think. She has a scar clear across her throat where it was cut once."

"She what?" He guffawed incredulously. "Julian, what the devil are you getting yourself into? Or what she-devil are you getting into? This hellcat intensifies her orgasm by inflicting pain on her partner and walks around with a shopping list of musty mumbo-jumbo. Is that the picture?"

"Uh, yeah, that's about it." Somehow the way Vern put it made it seem a lot sleazier than it felt to him.

"Well, what was she doing in the Quarry? I know the place. It's a real low-rent watering hole."

Now came the questions. Vern could never let him have something for his own, had to come on like a know-it-all all the time. "She was talking to someone on the pay phone about that stuff." He pointed at the scrawl-covered page.

A smile that was half snarl came to Vern's lips; he looked like a dog that was preparing to pounce. Julian had seen that expression before, whenever his friend smelled blood or sensed fear, when he thought he might have a trail to follow with some righteous ass-kicking at the end of it. "Christ, Julian. This chick could be a Satanist or worse. Maybe you're being set up as a sacrifice or something. An innocent Adonis like you just might attract such trash."

"Don't talk shit, Vern." A wave of anger swept over the fear in Julian's guts, but the fear was not entirely washed away. "How the fuck can you call me innocent?"

More teeth showed in his snarl-smile. "Because though you may create images that embarrass and disgust people, your soul has never been violated. You've never met real corruption. Until now, maybe."

Why was he doing this? Why was he trying to cast last night's fling in such a sinister light? They were friends, but Vern always had to have the upper hand in their relationship. Vern attacked reality, while he could only remotely probe it. Never without female companionship, never at a loss for something clever to say, never at loose ends in his life, Vern was always sure of himself. Julian hung around him partly in the hopes that some of Vern's confidence would rub off on him. Vern was an only child, born and bred in the city, someone who'd had to make things happen for himself all his life or they wouldn't have happened at all. There was more to it than that, however. Vern had no calm, secure place within himself. He had to be the center of some action or he didn't know where he stood, didn't feel alive enough.

"You're just upset because you didn't find her for me. I found her myself."

Vern spread his arms, pleading innocence of this charge. "Hey, I'm just worried about you, man. It's a mighty mean city out there."

There could be some truth to that, he thought. He might be in over his head. "Come on, Vern. She was very sweet in her own way, certainly not the kind of girl who could fuck a guy then hand him over to a bunch of maniacs to have his heart carved out."

"How would you know? You ever meet that kind? Well, I have, and you know what? You just can't tell. They are expert liars, consummate actors. What's inside of them is not the same as what's inside of you."

What about what's inside of you, Vern? "Yeah, maybe, but this mystical shit isn't about her. She said it was for a friend of hers, someone who was getting into something weird."

Vern laughed harshly through his snarl. "Oh, man, you poor naive schmuck. Her friend, huh? Oldest lie in the book and you fell for it. Ashley must have real nice titties and buns—oh, and knowing you she's gotta have a face that can make a man come just looking at it—because you're not usually this dumb."

Julian had to concede that point. Then he remembered what Ashley had said about her sister having kicked the shit out of some Crucifixers a few years back. People always substituted friends and relatives when they didn't want to implicate themselves. Suddenly a lot of her very odd behavior made more sense. Talk of another reality underlying this one, claims about the gifts of the damned, and a midnight curfew. It all added up to her will and her mentality not being entirely her own.

"Yeah, she's beautiful. Achingly gorgeous." Did that explain her presence in this collapsing area of the city? Some group was using her as a lure for potential victims? "Shit, Vern. I really like this babe. Last night was one of my best ever. There was something—I don't know—ethereal about her. Like she was my own personal muse come to me in the flesh." He pushed away his coffee cup and sat back hard in his chair. "Ain't that just my luck? I meet the girl of my dreams and she's Dracula's daughter."

"Wait a minute, wait a minute. Just hang on, Slick." Vern got that spark in his eye signaling that he was about to take control. "I could still be wrong. I'm just looking out for you. You gotta be careful these days. After Jonestown and Matamoros you've just gotta wonder about people, and I don't want the world making a meal out of my friends. You make my days more interesting, Julian, and I don't want to lose that. So listen. When are you seeing her again?"

Julian shrugged glumly. "I don't know. We didn't exchange phone numbers or make a date. She's kind of, uh, elusive."

"Ethereal and elusive. Sounds like Tinkerbell in black leather. What else did you learn about her?"

"Not too much. She said she was the caretaker of some fat cat's priceless private collection. That's about all."

Digging his elbows into the tabletop, Vern nodded. "No wonder you fell for her, a guy who's queer for old junk the way you are. Did she mention her boss's name? A personal hoard like that would need mucho security and I would remember hearing about a deal like that."

"Uh, not that I recall."

"Uh-huh." Vern searched his face until he was looking at Julian eye to eye. "What about her last name, Julian?"

He thought about what he was doing. With a name, even an alias, Vern Doyle could learn just about anything about anybody. Those kinds of connections were among the man's contacts. As much as he loathed the idea of anyone's privacy being invaded, he had to know about the girl, whether she was a threat to him, whether she was lying to him.

"Ashley Herrin. Her name is Ashley Herrin."

Vern didn't even bother to write it down. "Okay. I'm going to check her out. And you know what? I sincerely hope she turns out to be clean. I really do. No one deserves the love of a good woman more than you do. I mean, you're an artist. You feel more deeply than most people. Besides, you're my friend and loneliness is a killer. And I guess it would take kind of a bizarre woman to put up with you."

Julian smiled as Vern stood and patted him on the shoulder. "Thanks, Vern. Let me know what you find out."

"Will do." He finished his beer, vertically crushed the can, and strutted to the door. "Well, the early bird gets worms. I'm going home to sleep the day away. Chin up, Picasso."

"Take it easy, Vern."

When his friend was gone, Julian wondered if he would soon learn things about Ashley that he would really rather not know.

6

Some Enchanted Oddness

Julian finally surrendered to the fact that he wasn't going to get anything constructive accomplished that day, so he decided to take care of some domestic chores. He straightened up the place a bit, then gathered together his wash, including the passion-soaked sheets, and headed out to the Laundromat.

The street was sunny but cool as he walked along, the laundry bag slung over his shoulder like he was a sailor on leave. Fred was sitting on a stoop a few addresses down, so he stopped to chat.

"Hey, Julian. Did you find what you were looking for last night?"

He rested one foot on a step, noticing that Fred looked more cleaned up than usual. The swarthiness of his skin wasn't entirely the result of grime, apparently, for it remained dark despite having been scrubbed. Fred even looked slightly noble, with his long hooked nose and his projecting chin. "I think I might have. I met a real pretty lady, one after my own heart." After Julian said this he realized it could be taken two ways, one of them ghastly.

Fred nodded knowingly. "She go home with you?"

"Uh, yes, she did. We had a great time." Why was he telling Fred this?

"Yeah. It's been a very long time since I made love to a woman. Even the whores won't let me touch them anymore. I guess I've just let myself get too far gone."

There was a nostalgic look on Fred's face, an expression of loss. Julian felt sorry for him, though he knew pity was the last thing the man needed. This was one of the few times he'd seen Fred during the day, and the derelict wore many layers of baggy, ragged clothing, but Julian could swear that Fred actually had a big belly. Not exactly the trait of a near-starving man. Did he find that much to eat in the local garbage cans, or was he simply bloated from malnutrition? Julian certainly knew little of such matters, never having gone hungry except when he forgot to feed himself. That could change, of course, if he didn't start selling some paintings. Poverty did not look like fun.

"Well, what are your plans for today, Fred?" He tried to sound cheerful in the hopes of keeping Fred from getting depressed.

"Me? I guess I'll just sit here and watch the world creep closer to its end."

Not him too. It was like an epidemic, this mass doomsaying. "Yeah, well, try to keep your spirits up, man. I'll see you around."

"Good day, Julian."

Why the devil was everyone's outlook so gloomy? he asked himself as he trudged down the sidewalk, avoiding the gazes of the people he passed. The evil empire had fallen, so the war of splitting atoms seemed like an extremely distant possibility. Maybe people felt guilty about feeling good. Optimism was a sin in a nation founded by strict believers who asserted that everyone was born corrupt and deserving of the fiery pit. On the other hand, why didn't he paint pictures of flowers and kittens and green valleys with blue skies? All those bright joyful things? Why did his brush conjure up exhibits that would not look out of place if they were hung in a gallery in hell? Well, darkness had its beauty, or rather there was beauty in that which had been condemned as darkness. He was simply trying to reveal that it was there if you opened your eyes to it.

None of this was what he really wanted to think about. Ashley weighed heavily on his mind. His dilemma with her seemed to boil down to this: If he could come up with a convincing explanation why she might be attracted to him, then maybe he could persuade himself that their encounter had been more than a one-night fling or a menacing interlude. He was a good-looking guy; even Vern had referred to him as an Adonis. His face appeared younger than its thirty-one years. But he was shy and awkward, whereas Ashley was as cool and agile as a feline. He was talented and original in his outlook. His eloquence was limited to the canvas, however. Ashley seemed to speak with her very flesh, from the marrow outward. Her words were charged with a profound and intimate awareness of what made people tick. There was a certain vulgarity beneath her style and flare, though, as if she had come up from very crude origins. She lapsed into it when her concentration flagged. So maybe he represented culture to her, a chance to rise above her lowly lot in life.

He entered the Laundromat and picked out a machine. No, this wasn't getting him anywhere. They hadn't been together enough yet for him to make educated guesses about her. He'd found a straw to grasp on to, however. Just maybe Ashley saw him as Pygmalion to her Galatea.

"That one's out of order," said a black woman standing next to him.

Julian looked down and saw a handwritten OUT OF ORDER sign taped to the washer. "Uh, thanks."

"You best pay attention to what you're doing, young man," she said with a smile. "You'll end up walking into the middle of traffic and not even know it."

More sound advice. He switched to another machine and stuffed his clothes into it. There was no point in sorting them anymore. Everything was too old and faded to run into anything else. A vending machine on the wall dispensed a tiny box of detergent to him; he poured it in, slid four quarters into the washer, then sat down to wait.

She just might show up tonight, he thought. He had to make contingency plans. This time he would sweep *her* off *her* feet. But how? What would a freaky feral creature like her be into? There were probably few sights he could show her that she hadn't already seen. Still, he had to make the attempt. He twirled a lock of his hair in his fingers, realizing it was greasy and in need of washing, as he considered the matter.

Aside from the black woman and her two kids—a boy and a girl—who were remarkably quiet for children, there was a skinny woman of no real beauty with curlers in her hair sharing the Laundromat with him. She was doing a load too large for one person, so he guessed that she was married but still childless. She didn't look very happy. Julian mourned the emptiness of her existence, wished he could fill it with something. His own life was spasmodic, a stormy sea of ups and downs, but he always had the sublime act of creation to fall back on, to give him purpose. What did this poor young woman have? Ah, for all he knew she was enormously contented. You couldn't tell from the look on someone's face while she was performing a mundane task. But he suspected that she really was as silently desperate as she appeared to be.

His eyes turned to the cheap literature scattered about the place. Religious tracts, some newspapers, a few public service pamphlets. *How to Avoid Sexually Transmitted Diseases.* Near the door there was a stack of *Street Signals,* a free magazine dealing with the local music scene. Julian went over and picked one up. Leafing through it he saw that Red Ripper, a punk rock band whose disks he liked a lot, was playing at the Grotto that night. There was the answer to his prayers. He would show Ashley that he could walk that line on the edge of the infernal, stride boldly through the ambience of apocalypse. That should adequately impress her.

He took the *Street Signals* with him when he left with his laundry. The Grotto was one of many clubs he'd never been to, and he had to know how to get there. His mood was much lighter as he walked home, for in the light of day Vern's talk of cultic conspiracies seemed absurd. And he felt brave, certain that the long sheltered phase of his life was over. He was about to break out of it with a vengeance, storm the gates of his own inhibitions.

Back in his loft he felt brought down just a bit, for the thought of his stalled painting filled him with inertia.

That was a whole other nut he had to crack. For now, some sleep seemed like the best thing. If Ashley *did* come over, he had to have the strength to keep up with her.

So he flung himself onto his bed and napped, drifting into dream.

Just about the time Julian was falling into slumber, Vern Doyle was coming out of it in his brownstone flat four miles across town. His lair, as he called it. *Wolfschanze*. He got up, paced into the black-and-gray living room, rewound his answering machine, and fixed himself a rum with Coke as he listened to the messages. The first drink of the evening, perhaps the first of many.

Margie had phoned three times, asking him to call her. Vern sighed. He was tiring of the woman. She was getting too serious, demanding commitment, sinking her claws into him. It always happened that way. Women couldn't settle for just running with him. They wanted to tame him. Someone else had already captured his interest anyway, a meter maid named Roslyn. He'd been driving one of his employees' cars—he saw no sense in owning one of your own in the city—and left it parked too long without feeding the meter. She'd been writing up a ticket just as he walked up, so he proceeded to talk her out of it. Not that it mattered to him, as poor Greeley would have had to pay the fine, but he liked the challenge of getting around the law. And Roslyn was damned cute.

The next message on the machine was Roslyn, informing him that she had her meter running for him.

Well, that would have to wait, thought Vern. He had some business to attend to, a favor for a friend. The case of Ashley Somebody was on his agenda for tonight. Was her last name spelled Heron, like the bird? It was probably phony, as her first name might well turn out to be as well. A woman who ran with gangs and had gotten her throat cut at one point would most likely possess a criminal record, so he decided to start there. If the cops had already done the work, that would save him a lot of effort.

He took a quick shower, then dressed in black chinos and a dark-gray madras shirt. Looking in the bathroom mirror, he bared his teeth at his reflection, admiring their whiteness, recalling the meat-eating ancestry they betrayed. What he saw pleased him, even his rugged skin. The horns and eyes of the goat-head tattoo on the left side of his neck peeked just over his collar, a souvenir from his younger, somewhat more ritualistic days. With a drop of styling gel rubbed together in his hands he slicked back his fine hair. Then he was done.

When he'd donned his brown leather coat he was off, into whatever the night had to offer him. He walked a ways down the road and hailed a cab when one came into view. In this city there was a bar where mostly cops hung out, and there was a bar where mostly reporters hung out. There was a third bar, however, where both cops and reporters hung out. Vern told the driver to head for that one.

It was dusk as he arrived at Petrovich's Pub. The crowd wasn't real thick, but he did see several people right off the bat who might prove informative. He got a seven and seven from the bar—Vern had no qualms about mixing his drinks—and selected his first target. There was a crime reporter from the *Tribune* sitting at the end of the big bar of mahogany and black marble, a man who had been on the beat for a long time. His name was Clu Malington, but Vern (and others) thought of him as Clueless because of his stubbornly square disposition. Vern sidled up to him.

"Say, Clu. You drinking alone?"

Clueless didn't seem all that happy to see him. "Hello, Vern. At least I'm drinking. I had a long day. It's good to see you're still out and about. I guess the powers that be still haven't caught you at whatever it is you do."

He laughed icily at that. "My reputation precedes me. But I'm really a good citizen. I look out for the public interest."

"Yeah? Last I heard you'd declared war on some kind of commune located upstate. What the hell was that all about?"

Vern narrowed his gaze on Clueless's pasty aged face. "Is this off the record?"

A mercenary smile beamed at him. "Sure."

"Yeah, right." Vern sat on the stool next to him. "Look, I'll admit it's a gray area of the law."

"There's nothing gray about kidnapping, Vern."

"Well, anyway, that was a few years ago and I don't do that anymore. You should try interviewing the parents of the kids who get sucked into those zombie cults, though. You might see it differently."

"I'd find that they paid you a lot of money, I'm sure."

So the evening was starting off with a bit of aggravation. He could put up with it. "Look, Clu. I'm tracking something else down at the moment. I'm running a security check on some prospective tenants for a couple of friends of mine who own some rental property. One of them is a single woman named Ashley Heron. The name kind of rang a bell with me, maybe an a.k.a. for a member of a female gang, but I can't quite place it."

Clu sighed and started thinking about it. "Yeah, I have to admit that it sounds familiar. About thirteen years ago there was a big buzz in the downtown vice squad about a charming chronic offender named Ashley something, among other names. Now, what was she? Coke dealer, I think."

A teenage coke dealer didn't sound very threatening, Vern thought. "Why all the commotion if she was just some punk selling blow?"

"No, wait! I remember now." Blood seemed to rush into the reporter's sallow cheeks too fast. It might soon be time to put this newshound out to pasture before he had a heart attack on the job. "There was this beautiful young hooker that they busted a couple of times. Blond hair and blue eyes. She was real expensive, had real high-class customers. One of her aliases was Ashley Herrin. *Herrin,* the German word for mistress, because she specialized in domination. You know, whips, spikes, leather, humiliation, that whole scene. They said she would also let herself be tortured. Very sick case."

Vern laughed, more at the irony than at Julian's expense. His friend had hooked up with a hooker, and a very kinky one at that. Amazing. Poor Julian would be heartbroken. "So what was her real name?"

Clu was still thinking hard, furrowing his shaggy brows. "Uh, Prender or Preeter or something like that. But there's no way this could be the same woman."

Uh-oh. Barked up the wrong tree on the first try. "Why is that?"

"Well, this little Nazi pro left the life and went into dealing coke. She crossed another dealer and got rubbed out in the basement of a bar somewhere. So it couldn't be her."

Back to the drawing board. He started to get up. "Oh. Well, thanks, Clu. You've been a big help."

Clu tapped him on the shoulder, an unpleasant sensation. "Hey, you know, there was something weird about that murder. Besides the fact that the lovely victim had her throat cut from ear to ear, I mean."

Vern's spinal cord wriggled within its column of bone. Also an unpleasant sensation. "And what was that?"

The reporter laughed heartily. "Those klutzes with the coroner's team lost the corpse. No one has any idea what happened to the damned body!"

He settled back onto his seat. "Yeah, that sure is funny, Clu. Maybe you ought to tell me everything you can remember about the case. From the beginning."

The next round was on Vern.

It was cold, dark, and he was lost in the labyrinth, which seemed to be the interior of the vast carcass of some monstrous thing long dead. There were countless tunnels and endless turns, leading nowhere, taking him ever closer to the heart of the maze, where something unfaceable dwelled. Not completely human, not completely living, it waited for him with supreme patience. It knew him and it needed him, but it thought of him as less than animal, barely worthy of its attention.

It was the thing he'd met long ago, the thing he'd seen on the other side of death.

There was more than one, he remembered now. They were the Slug People, glowing sickly in their lair, telling him of the terrors they had to offer him. He had fled from them then, and he fled from them now, screaming through the labyrinth.

Julian awoke with a lurch, the afterimage of that strange haunting shape burned onto his brain but fading. Slanted eyes, bulbous forms, sharp edges. What did it mean? He recalled something of the dream, a bad one, but the shape had not been anywhere in it. Of that he was certain. His REM sleep seemed to stir it up rather than creating it. As for the dream itself, well, he thought of nightmares as rehearsals for hell. Previews from below and beyond, run-throughs for those last few seconds while you're dying.

He realized he wasn't alone. A slender figure stood by his bedside in the shadows and he knew her by her scent alone. Ashley was there, redolent of tangy sea, earthen dust, and sweet smoke. When he switched on the lamp she blazed red at him, for a shiny crimson jumpsuit was stretched over every curve of her body, with lace gloves and spike-heeled boots to match. Her eyes were occulted by mirrored sunglasses and a red velvet choker hid her scar. He thought she looked magnificent, but he was startled to find her hovering over him.

"Ashley. How did you get in here?"

Her voice was almost a whisper. "Your door wasn't locked."

Julian rather doubted that. He knew what kind of area he lived in and he wasn't about to become a crime statistic while he slept. The door was always locked when he had his back to the world. If she'd picked the lock, however, he couldn't be too upset. It seemed in keeping with the on-the-edge game they were playing with each other. "I'm glad you came."

Ashley's lips, redder than her outfit, twisted into an

ironic smile. "Yeah. Let's think of this as my second coming. I'm in the mood for some action. How about you?"

She was standing awfully still, like a brightly painted idol. He wished she would move. "Uh, yeah. In fact, I was thinking along exactly the same lines." He sat up, swinging his legs over the side of the bed. "There's a band called Red Ripper playing at the Grotto tonight. They're really good. We could go and see them. I mean, you're certainly dressed for the occasion."

His joke didn't seem to amuse her at all. Her smile turned to a grimace and she recoiled slightly, as if from an unseen blow. "No, Julian. Not the Grotto. I don't like that place. Somewhere else, maybe."

There was actually someplace this fallen angel feared to tread? He found that fact intriguing, and a little reassuring. If she wasn't completely fearless, then she might harbor some understanding for his own myriad dreads. "Okay. There's a copy of *Street Signals* over on the kitchen table. It tells who's playing where and when. Why don't you pick out where you want to go while I change my clothes?"

With a nod she ambled over to the table and sat down, started reading in the dark with her sunglasses still on.

"You'll ruin your eyes doing that," he said as he turned on the overhead lights.

She smiled at him again. "Don't worry. The fire of my feverish desire burns with a light all its own. I can read anything by it."

"Uh, right. Sure. Is it okay if I take a quick shower before we go?" He headed for the bathroom.

"No, it's not."

Julian didn't stop, thinking she was joking. "You can join me if you like."

"I mean it, Julian." Now he stopped. "I like the natural smell of you. Don't wash it off. Come as you are."

Shrugging, he sniffed his armpits. They weren't seriously offensive yet, so he relented. "Have it your way. One gamy bohemian at loose in the night, coming up."

This seemed to please her. He joined her at the table. "Made up your mind yet?"

"I think so. There's a three-band show playing at Pandemorgue: Hellhead, the Exhumes, and Out of Body. Let's go see that one."

"Whatever you say. You're the boss."

Her big silvery lenses flashed at him. "Yes, I am. And remember that."

There was peril in the air tonight, and he hoped he was up to facing it. Certainly he had as good a guide for it as Dante had, in virtuosity if not in virtue. She was not Virgil, or virgin, but she *was* a brilliant pagan. "Then let's be off. I'm ready for anything."

"That is yet to be seen." She giggled, slung her small red purse over her shoulder, and stood.

"I don't suppose you drove here," he said as they trampled down the stairs.

"Huh-uh. I haven't owned a car in years. I think I've forgotten how to drive even."

That was a curious bit of information, he thought. He couldn't afford a car, and he'd never liked them much, but he did know how to drive and took pains to keep his license renewed. It just seemed like a basic requirement of living in the modern age.

They hit the street and started walking. "Well, the club

is pretty far, so let's start walking and keep our eyes peeled for a cab."

"Fine with me." Judging by her easy tone one would think she didn't have a care in the world. He wished he made her half as nervous as she made him. Did he dare hope that he was the cause of her buoyant mood, that she was just plain happy to be with him?

He wondered how they looked together, strolling side by side along the cracked and pitted sidewalk, she with her swaying, fluid stride, he in his shambling gait. Ashley was the more glamorous of the two, of course, in her sleek and striking semiuniform. Compared to her he must look unkempt, in his wornout jeans, off-white T-shirt, and black jacket of battered leather. His simple black shoes were badly scuffed and the right one was splitting its seam in the back. Perhaps she'd planned it this way, kept him from grooming and changing so that she would stand out against him. It seemed pointedly unnecessary to him, for no matter how he decked himself out she would always outshine him, in fashion, poise, and allure. He was sure to be the envy of every heterosexual male at this subcultural nightclub.

The night sky was overcast, obscuring the stars and the moon. Anna's diamonds and Ashley's skull. City light and foundry fire reflected dully off the lower-lying clouds. The flames of heaven, he mused.

"It looks like a rolling sea of embers and ashes," she said, following his gaze. The ruddiness from above glinted off her shades.

"Red sky at night, sailor's delight. I never understood that saying. You suppose it has to do with how much fun sailors have in red-light districts?"

Her smile briefly lit on him. "Any port in a storm, I guess."

The thrill was still there, he was pleased to find. It wasn't just flawless first impressions. There was something real between them. He reached over to hold her hand but she pulled it away.

"Don't, Julian. It's too high-school."

So he didn't, a little stung with hurt. It seemed there were some rules to this game he had yet to learn. She might not want from him what he wanted from her, might not have the same idea of what love was, and he had to be ready for that. Should he even be thinking about love? Just how serious would he be willing to get with such a quirky, daring creature?

"Have you always lived in the city?" Changing the subject seemed wise to him.

The question garnered a long look from her and put a strain on her smile. "Must we exchange a lot of personal information?"

His shoulders shrugged defensively, almost wincing. "It's a harmless enough thing to ask someone. Is there a lot about yourself that you're ashamed of?"

Ashley didn't answer.

"Okay. I'll tell you about me, then. I'm a small-town boy from a typical middle-class family. Two brothers, two sisters, all of them good little socialized citizens. I'm the youngest, the black sheep of the family. I couldn't wait to get away from there, although this city hasn't been so easy to take either. I don't make friends easily."

"I love the city," she said, seeming to relax a bit. "Especially at night. This is my time. I come alive in the night. When I was a teenager I used to sneak out after everyone else was asleep and go out running around with my friends. Sometimes with my girlfriends, sometimes with a boy. God, the crazy things we would do. A little breaking and entering, into the houses of people we knew were on vacation. That was our idea of a slumber party, raiding their liquor cabinets and sleeping in their big opulent beds. Or we'd smoke pot and fuck in the local graveyard. It was like having the whole planet to ourselves, in which we could do whatever we wanted."

He wondered if she'd ever held hands with any of those boys. "I know what you mean. Most people seem content to lose the intensity of youth, but not me. I've tried to hang on to it as long as possible."

She nodded emphatically. "It takes a lot of will not to let yourself get beaten down by the demands of normal reality. There's a taxi."

"Is it on duty?"

The cab was waiting for a phoned-in fare that was taking too long to show up, so the swarthy, curly-haired driver told them to get in. Julian tried to identify the man's accent, guessed it was either Hungarian or Lebanese, more probably neither. He was no good with languages. The guy's name on his license clipped to the sunvisor, Faludin Varasi, offered no clue either.

"You very nice young couple," said the driver after Julian gave him their destination. "Your girl very pretty. Why you want to go to hangout of skinheads? Skinheads spit on me, call me terrible names."

Julian leaned forward. "Uh, I'm real sorry about that, uh, Faludin." He hoped he'd pronounced the man's name correctly. "You see, there's always that two percent, but not all skinheads and punkers are like that. You'll find boneheaded jerks in every part of society, full of hate and anxious to spread it. We're just going to Pandemorgue for the music."

That last statement wasn't quite true, he realized. They were going there looking for trouble to avoid.

"Well, I know that place. Is violent. You be careful you don't get you skulls smashed in, huh?"

"Thanks for your concern. We'll be all right." He sat back and leaned against Ashley. "That's right neighborly of him, don't you think?"

"Yeah, but it's misguided," she said with a smirk. "He should be asking us politely not to severely damage anyone when we get there."

Such wickedness lurking behind her sweet face never ceased to amaze him. Or excite him. He watched the city fly by his window in a stream of neon signs, flashing lights, pedestrians, and brief street vignettes. An escalating conflict between a black man and a white man, two cops questioning a hooker, lovers embracing against a plate-glass window full of activated TVs, a woman in a fur coat walking her poodle. Ordinary people on a typical night. Julian wasn't one of them. He was a seeker of dark secrets on a magic-carpet ride with a ravishing temptress of utter abandon. Exactly where he wanted to be.

The driver pulled the cab onto the edge of the parking lot of a big flat building and stopped. Big bonelike letters spelled out PANDEMORGUE on the black front wall of the club. "I go no further," he said. "No want get stones thrown at my cab."

This seemed paranoid to Julian, but then he'd never been a target of ethnic hostility. He paid the fare with a tip and Ashley and he got out. The parking lot was moderately crowded with rowdy young people of both sexes, laughing, yelling, and getting playfully rough with each other.

"No parental guidance here," he said as they entered the fray. Mohawks, orange and purple hair, torn clothing, and a general burlesque aura characterized the raucous mob they were passing through. And there were indeed some skinheads here and there.

Ashley nodded. "So far from death and yet so close."

He considered this. "You mean because they haven't yet lived much of their lives but they're so willing to risk them?"

"Exactly."

They came to the door, he paid the cover charge for both of them, and the backs of their hands were stamped with fluorescent winged skulls by a girl with black eye makeup and long scraggly hair. A narrow corridor lined with ultraviolet lights led the way to the main room. He experienced some apprehension as they entered, never having been in a place like this before.

"I don't get it," said Julian, studying the glowing stamp on his hand as they entered the dark, smoky depths of the place, which smelled like a warehouse. Music was already vibrating the walls, though it wasn't live.

She stood on her toes to check out the people in attendance. "It's kind of a joke. Your skull flies so it's high. You know, you can drink anything you want. People under drinking age get a wingless skull, you see."

"Oh. You've been here before, I guess."

"Sure. I can just relax and be myself here."

To the degree the interior had any decor at all it seemed to be that of a crypt. The curtains around the stage were like ragged burial shrouds, the bar was sculpted to look like a sacrificial altar, and candles burned in glass skulls on the tables. The effect seemed a bit forced to Julian. They sat down at one of the tables on the edge of the dance floor, which he knew in a place like this was more properly called the "mosh pit."

"That fact they know you here explains why you didn't get carded," he said to her. "I mean, if I was working the door I'd take one look at you and think you might be underage. How old are you, anyway?"

She leaned over close, reflecting his face back at him in her sunglasses. "Oh, Julian, I'm old. Older than you can imagine."

He studied her grinning face, wishing she'd stop hiding behind the opaque lenses. "Why are you wearing those things over your eyes?"

"Don't you like them? They're the perfect way to remain both conspicuous and anonymous at the same time."

"It's just that I know women who would envy you the color of your irises. They would die to have what you see the world through."

Ashley seemed to think this was hilariously funny. "You know, someday you may discover just what a genius you really are. Now go get me a drink. Some peppermint schnapps would be nice."

There was obviously no way to get past her masterful evasiveness. "I hear and I obey."

The place was filling up with tender-aged libertines of mutant culture, the hordes of the seventh seal, but he didn't have to wait long at the bar. He ordered a beer for himself and Ashley's schnapps, considering that he might be spending too much time lately drinking in public establishments.

"That was Hitler's favorite drink," said the hippieish bartender.

"What?"

"Peppermint schnapps. Der Führer loved the stuff."

"Oh. Well, thanks for that bit of information." The evening's strangeness wasn't wasting any time getting the jump on him. And making him jumpy.

Hellhead had taken the stage by the time he got back to the table. They were four shirtless emaciated young men, all with black suspenders, all with the sides of their heads shaved. Their trademark, it seemed. There was one lead guitar-vocalist, one bassist, one keyboardist, one drummer. Without any ado they went right into their first song, which was about the French Revolution. It seemed to have more to do with a certain sexual technique, however, than the eighteenth-century political uprising in France. "Off with his head," the refrain of the jarringly disjointed tune, took on a whole new meaning.

Soon the slam-dancing began in earnest. Julian was intrigued and appalled all at once. People on the dance floor in front of the stage intentionally collided with one another, whipped each other around, threw people at each other, and just seemed to be having one hell of a good time. It was extremely violent, but there didn't seem to be any real aggression involved, at least not toward each other. To Julian it seemed like a way of making physical contact without risking intimacy, without dropping one's barriers. They were together with others but still safely alone, getting the affection they craved while still looking tough.

"Lamia!" someone shouted nearby.

Ashley turned with a wary look on her face, then smiled at the person walking toward them. He was a small bearded man wearing a seedy black tuxedo, and he hugged Ashley in a way that made Julian jealous. Old boyfriend?

"You're looking far out, Phil. Phil Gory, this is Julian Stormer."

Julian shook hands with him. "How's it going?" He had to yell to be heard over the band.

"Hey, all right. Lamia, where have you been lately? I haven't seen you in many moons."

She shrugged as if it wasn't relevant. "Oh, I've been tied up for the past few weeks."

"Yeah, I'll bet you have." Phil leaned on the table near her and they talked animatedly for several minutes about subjects he couldn't overhear. They seemed to be just close friends, fellow subculturals. So Julian let his mind and his eyes wander, smoking a cigarette. Someone appeared to be staring at them from across the room, a man with thinning hair and a stubble of beard who looked to be one of the oldest individuals there. He wore an army jacket and motorcycle boots. Perhaps he was staring specifically at Ashley, which was understandable.

Julian turned back to the show. When he saw one of the teenage dancers jump onto the stage and leap off into the crowd, his heart clutched itself in shock. When twelve arms gently caught the young man he was unaccountably moved. This scene repeated itself dozens of times throughout the performance, egged on by the members of Hellhead: young men and women climbing onto the edge of the stage, launching themselves gleefully into the air, and people they might not even know casually breaking their fall and setting them on their feet again.

"Nice meeting you, man," Phil said to Julian, tapping

him on the shoulder. "Keep this lady entertained, you hear? She'll be less trouble to others that way."

"I'll do that." When Phil had gone, Julian leaned toward Ashley. "That's quite a nickname you've got. It refers to an ancient Greek she-demon, doesn't it?"

"That's right," she said, nodding. "She was a real maneater. Can I have another drink?"

So he made another trip to the bar. When he came back, Ashley was talking to another guy, the one who had been staring at her, in fact. They seemed almost to be arguing. Julian fervently hoped he wasn't going to have to come to blows with the man.

"What's the problem here?"

The man looked at him. "No problem. This is Sophie Darrell, isn't it? I know her. It's Sophie and she hasn't aged a day in a whole decade."

Ashley appeared flustered. "I don't know what you're talking about. I don't know you and that's not my name. Now, go away, will you?"

"Her name's not Sophie, friend," said Julian, staying calm. "So leave her alone, okay?"

"Now, wait a minute," countered the man, making no move to leave. His leathery, lined face appeared elated but puzzled. "This chick knows me. You know me, Sophie. Jack Sanders? Don't you remember me?"

"For the last time, I don't know you!" She stood up angrily. "Come on, Julian. Let's get out of here. There's too many fucking psychos in this place."

So Julian set the drinks down on the table and started to follow her out. Her harasser dogged their heels.

"Why won't you admit knowing me?" he pleaded. "Hey, we fucked a couple of times and I never forget a woman I've fucked."

Julian's cheeks grew hot and his heart throttled up. Was he expected to turn around and punch this guy out? Would Ashley resent him if he didn't? She'd stood up for him against five gang members, but he wasn't able to defend her honor from one lone maniac. He felt a bit sheepish.

"How the hell did you stay so young?" were the last words they heard from the man before they cleared the exit. He didn't pursue them past that point.

"What the hell was that all about?" Julian asked her as they crossed the parking lot.

"Nothing. A case of mistaken identity. Don't worry about it." She was irritated and shaken. "Christ. This city's full of nut cases."

The episode disturbed him, but he judged it would be unwise to question her about it. He wasn't entirely certain that she hadn't recognized the man, but if the guy was part of some unhappy time in her past, then she was entitled to her privacy. "Would you like to go somewhere else?"

She nodded apathetically. "Yeah. Anywhere."

They walked a few blocks until they came to a yuppie bar called New Orleans and went inside. The place was very clean and lavishly appointed, but the music and the clientele left much to be desired. An inane DJ was playing remixed dance songs of the most vapid sort. Julian motioned toward an out-of-the-way booth and they occupied it, sitting across from each other.

"One thing's for sure," she said, sounding more relaxed. "No one in here will recognize me."

He lit a cigarette. "I know what you mean. This is a sexual stalking ground for all the beautiful empty-headed people. AIDS fodder."

Ashley giggled. "What kind of fodder?"

"AIDS. The plague of the twentieth century, the Blue Death."

Her face remained blank and his skin went cold. Was she putting him on? "It's a venereal disease?"

"It's a lot worse than that. You mean you've never heard of it before?"

Now Ashley looked worried, as if she'd just committed a major social blunder. "Oh, of course I have. I didn't quite hear what you said, that's all."

She didn't sound very convincing. How could she not know about it? And if she didn't, he'd had unprotected sex with a potential carrier. He reminded himself to definitely obtain some condoms before they went back to his place. But he couldn't get over her ignorance in this matter. Had she been living in a cave for the past ten years?

A waitress came up and they ordered, the same as they'd been drinking at Pandemorgue. He felt an urge to get rip-roaring drunk, but if he did he wouldn't be able to perform in the sack later. Ashley could probably get a performance out of him no matter what condition he was in, however.

"You ever hear of a thing called primal scream?" she asked him.

"Sure. It's supposed to be a way of getting all your inner tensions out." This was certainly an abrupt change of subject.

"Inner tensions, right." Her finger pointed at him. "I've got a lot of those right now. I feel like standing up and screaming right here, in the middle of all these fine, upstanding citizens. If we'd stayed at the club I would have done some slamming with the kiddies." She looked deceptively calm.

"Troubles with your employer?"

A harsh laugh tore from her throat. "Something like that."

The drinks came and as he paid for them a whole new possibility occurred to Julian. Could she be married, maybe to some rich guy who owned a big cold mansion in Groveland Heights? Her husband was old and boring, maybe, so she ventured into the hazardous quarters of the city looking for excitement. Was she a battered wife? Were her eyes blackened beneath those mirror shades? He hoped she was single, but if she wasn't it wouldn't bother his conscience at all.

"You know, Ashley," he said, moving around the table to sit next to her, "I've heard there's a better cure for stress than screaming in public. I mean, sex always worked for me."

Her full lips smiled at him. "It works for me too. Come on. Let's go to my place."

"Shouldn't we finish our drinks first?"

She stood, carrying her schnapps. "Take them with us."

He followed her through the crowd with his beer in hand, waiting for someone to try to stop them. They came to the emergency door and left through it.

"We never seem to stay in one place very long," he said.

"I have a way of using a place up pretty quick. Story of my life."

He wanted to hold her hand again, but he didn't try. Would she mind if he put his arm around her? "Where do you live?"

"It's a small apartment, back toward your neighborhood." She sipped her drink. "It's a bit of a dump, but it's only temporary lodgings."

What the hell? he thought. *Go for broke.* He slipped his arm across her shoulders and she ducked away. "What's with all this touchy-feely stuff, Stormy? Keep your paws to yourself."

Now he was getting pissed off. "What's with me? What the fuck is with you? You'll suck my dick but you won't let me show you a little affection. Are you queer or something?"

Ashley quit walking and stared at the ground, seeming to compose herself. "Look. I'm sorry. I just have a problem with it, okay? You'll just have to bear with me." She gulped the rest of her drink, then threw the glass at the base of a wall, where it shattered.

"It's just hard for me to understand, Ashley." He regretted having yelled at her, but he was beginning to fear that she was too weird even for him.

Looking up, she poked him in the ribs. "I'll make it up to you when we get to my bedroom. You'll see."

Some of the night's charm had been chafed away by their first argument, so they said little as he waved down a cab and they rode in it to her place. It looked more like a fleabag hotel than an apartment building, perhaps a year or two away from being condemned, but he was not one to judge someone's abode. In fact, there were times when he found inspiration in squalor.

"I live on the second floor," she said, leading the way up the creaking stairs. There was a TV turned up loud somewhere, and someone was coughing his lungs out. Three kinds of mildew seemed to have infested the bare wooden walls of the hallway, as if nature was painting a mural with fungus. Ashley unlocked her door, flicked on the light switch, and they entered her dismal dwelling.

"Bet you never saw a crash pad that looked like it actually crashed before." She sounded a bit embarrassed about the accommodations.

"It's no worse than some of the places I lived in before I got my loft." What struck him most about the two small rooms was that they didn't feel lived in. She evidently didn't spend much time here at all. There were no kitchen appliances, no dirty dishes in the sink, no knick-knacks of any kind, nothing to make it feel homey or comfortable. Not even a television set. Black curtains separated the bedroom from the combination kitchen and living room, and the area surrounding her big brass bed was the most furnished. There were candles, posters, a stereo, and lots of cushions. The fact that she had this little love-nest didn't defeat his theory that she might be married, for this was probably not where she really lived.

"Would you like a drink?" she asked as she set about lighting candles and sticks of incense.

He studied a cockroach racing brazenly across the counter. "Not right now."

"Well, take off your coat and stay awhile."

This he did, laying it on the badly stained top of the shaky kitchen table. His beer bottle was drained, so he set that down and lit a cigarette. A baby was crying in a distant corner of the building.

"Turn off the light, then come in here and lie down," her voice beckoned, and he complied. She remained standing as he crawled onto the bed, finding it soft and clean. He loved the atmosphere in here, darkly dreamy and lurid, a pleasure chamber cut off from everything else. Day-Glo lovers embraced on the wall next to Elvira in dominatrix wear, wielding a whip and promising to be Yours Cruelly. Streams of scented smoke curled through the candlelit air, making him reminisce about pot parties, teenage gropings, a simpler age.

"Prepare for ecstasy, lover." She unzipped her jumpsuit, revealing a leather teddy and matching nylons beneath. He'd never seen a woman look so exquisite, vulnerable, and threatening at the same time. Finally she removed her sunglasses—her eyes were unbruised—and joined him on the bed. She started pulling his shoes off.

"I want to do a painting of you sometime. Maybe as Lilith, the first mother of humanity."

"I've heard that story," she said, pushing up his shirt. "Adam rejected her because she wanted to be on top when they screwed, right?"

"Uh-huh. So she went off and mated with demons, spawning a race of vampires." He watched her lick his nipples.

"Now you're seeing the real me, Stormy."

When he was naked, she took his penis in her mouth and with a few rhythmic strokes inflamed him into a frantic erection. Then she unsnapped the crotch of her teddy and straddled him. Her body smoothly received him, slippery and snug, and he just lay back and let her do most of the work. There was an ease to her lovemaking that had been absent the night before, as if she was now reconnected with the part of herself that enjoyed the act. And she seemed more aware of his presence, more focused on him.

"Now, wasn't Adam a moron for not liking this?" she said with a languorous giggle.

His answer was a groan of delight.

They climaxed at almost exactly the same moment, she

with faint gasping cries, he with gratified grunts. Two things struck him instantly: Once again he'd forgotten to wear something on his organ, and his unbidden vision had returned. A hideous flower sprouting from a scabrous jewel, it was there again in his head, complete and even expanded. A web of dully glowing lines radiated outward from it into infinity, like a vast net cast out across the world. What the hell was it? Why was it plaguing him? And the coincidence, the timing of its intrusion . . . how could sex with a woman bring it on? It was anything but erotic, and it made him feel rattled, a bit tainted, like finding an ugly growth on his skin. Maybe Ashley was hypnotizing him somehow. Implanting subliminal suggestions in his brain. Should he confront her about it? No, it was just his feverish imagination getting the best of him. A deeply buried cluster of his overworked neurons had fixated on this bizarre image, and the chaotic energy of orgasm thrust it to the surface. That was all it was. Once he'd externalized the thing in pigment and cloth it would cease to haunt him. The slate of his mind would be cleared.

As before, the image faded from his thoughts, and he was unable to recall its specific details. This time, however, he knew it would be back. It wasn't an event he was looking forward to.

Ashley nimbly dismounted and stretched out next to him, reaching into a box on the floor to pluck out a joint. She crossed her stockinged legs at the shins as she put a lighter to it. "You're a good fuck, Stormy."

"Yeah? Well, you're the tenderest, most tactful lover I've ever had."

Laughing out a lungful of marijuana smoke, she nudged him hard. "Come on. You know that all those sweet nothings people say to each other really are nothing. Pillow talk is for fools. I'm just refreshingly blunt."

He accepted the joint she handed to him and inhaled from it. A conversation with Ashley required some reinforcement. He passed it back. "Haven't you ever been close to anyone? Didn't you ever want to hear soft words spoken from the heart by one who cares for you?"

"Don't be a drag, now." She concentrated for a moment on smoking the reefer. "I've been through a lot. I know how heartless people can be. Hell, I've looked death square in the face, so I know what life has to offer. The only way to survive is to be stronger than death or life."

This set him to thinking, wondering how he could reach her on a personal level. Pierce her shell of toughness. If he wanted her to open herself to him, he had to open up to her. Taking a deep breath, he let his mind drift down through the years. It was a memory far entombed in his consciousness, but when it exhumed itself it was always vivid. More caged than interred, really. The circumstances weren't completely clear, obscured by time, trauma, and the unreliability of a five-year-old's mind.

"Ashley, I want to tell you something. I think you of all people should be able to understand it."

Like a striking snake her gaze darted to his face. "You're not going to get sappy on me, are you?"

He raised himself on an elbow and turned to her. "No, no. It's like a story I want to tell you."

"Oh, good. I like stories." She relaxed. "Fire away."

"Okay. This happened when I was five. I was a nervous kid, as you can imagine. Afraid of everything. Dogs, fireflies, my own shadow. I was always ill disposed toward the idea of death. I experienced terrifying black oceanic thoughts of what death must be like. I don't recall who first explained death to me, but I became aware of my mortality at a very tender age. I also had a terrible fear of being mutilated, of suffering terrible physical afflictions. No one told me that minor things tend to go wrong with the human body and they're nothing to worry about. So when I'd get a pimple or something on my arm it would send me into a panic. I'd hide it for as long as I could, but bath time would inevitably roll around, my mother would see it, and adding to my shock she would yell at me, then violently pop it."

Judging by Ashley's expression, she was finding this less than interesting. "Is this going somewhere?"

"I'm getting to the point." First he had to light up a cigarette. "My mother and father both worked in the city here. One day, when I was five, my mother was hit by a car while crossing the street. So she was in the hospital, my father was with her, and I don't know where all my brothers and sisters were. One was at college, the others stayed with friends, I think. But my parents had Aunt Dora pick me up at kindergarten to drive me into the city to be with them. At least, that's how I remember it. I couldn't stay with Aunt Dora because she was a boarder somewhere and she didn't have room. I guess.

"Anyway, Aunt Dora wasn't truly a relation, just a close friend of the family. On the day I was riding in the car with her it was winter, and it was snowing. There was ice on the road. Someone veered out of their lane or something, Dora swerved to avoid a collision, and we went flying off the highway, down the embankment, and into a tree. It all happened so fast, I didn't have a chance to be scared, but then the really bad things started happening."

Recalling the incident was closer to reliving it than he was comfortable with, but he had to tell it. It was his most potent weapon in this love war with Ashley. "Both of us were wearing our seat belts, but Aunt Dora's seems to have failed because her head had smashed into the windshield. The car was on an angle, with me at the lowest point and Dora suspended above me in her loosened strap. She was all busted up, but still making noises like she was alive. There seemed to be a point of bone projecting from her left nostril. And then I noticed that I was covered with blood.

"There are no words for what I felt then. The blood was warm and dark, and it soaked into my clothes. Dora was making grotesque gurgling sounds, groaning as her broken bones and crushed organs squeezed the life out of her. Seeing the stark wretchedness of her dying state only further convinced me how horrible it must be to die. I assumed that the blood all over me was my own, even though I wasn't in any great pain. I don't know if I thought my nerves might be severed or not, but I thought I was seriously hurt and would soon die. The fear of that grew in me, so rapidly and vastly that my mind and body couldn't contain it. The terror of dying scared me to death.

"I blacked out, lost all touch with my flesh. I believe that for a moment I was dead. I was in the blackest place you can be in, and something was there to meet me. Several somethings, actually. They were like upright slugs and they glowed a putrid yellow. They seemed to speak to me, but I didn't have enough mind with me to understand them. All I knew was that I didn't like them at all. They were the foulest, nastiest things I had ever seen. After a moment they rapidly receded from view, and I seemed to fly across a blank expanse to my place in the car. I was so happy when they went away and I came back to myself that Dora's gory corpse was a welcome sight. I then realized that it was her blood I was drenched in. She was dead, I was alive, and it was over. Except for the nightmares and bad memories."

He waited for Ashley to respond. She was quiet for a very long time. When she did speak there was a hint of wonder in her tone, along with . . . was it reverence?

"Your paintings. It's through them that you deal with that experience. That weird trauma is what drives your art."

With his right hand he cupped her left breast. "To a very great degree, yes. It's like having an itch in your soul that you can't scratch."

"Do you really believe you were dead?"

"Yes, I do."

She grasped his hand and interlaced her delicate fingers with it. "Then what was it you saw on the other side?"

The sight of their hands together was a marvel to him. Hers was applying a lot of pressure to his, however, almost as if they were arm-wrestling. "I don't know. Ghosts, demons, the dead. Maybe hell is run by a committee."

Ashley laughed long, hard, and viscerally at that remark. "I'm really glad I met you, Stormy. You make me look at things in a way I haven't looked at them in a very long time."

"I'm glad I met you. You make me feel fifteen again."

"Really?" She disposed of the roach and rolled over

on top of him. "I'll bet you don't have half the stamina you did when you were that age."

His stiffening member disagreed. "Want me to prove you wrong?"

"By all means, lover. Do your worst."

He did his best instead.

PART TWO

Below and Beyond

7

On Harrowed Ground

"We seen her, man," said Angelo Gusano, sweating. "We watched the place last night, me and Jesus did, and this woman came right out of there. Up from the sewer, through a manhole, but there must be a way in through the basement."

Guillermo Esposito, known mostly as Guilly, leader of the Crucifixers, looked at Angelo the Loco and his lamebrained friend, Jesus Langosta, and felt bored, a bit annoyed. He sat in the back of the storefront office that the gang rented as its headquarters, like a king in his throne room. His lieutenants, Arturo, Miguel, and Esteban, stood around him waiting on his pleasure.

"What do I care about some squatters in the Wasteland?" said Guilly, brushing at his blue gabardine pants. Neatness counted when you were a ruler of men. "Besides, you guys aren't nothing to me anymore. You're too stupid to be in the gang. You bought from a narc, got yourselves busted, then you got sprung a little bit quicker than you should have. You keep coming around here and we might just do a ritual on you."

He could smell their fear and was surprised that they stood their ground. These two losers had obviously got some crazy idea in their heads that they weren't going to let go of easily. He hated wasting time on them. Angelo always wore way too much of some cheap cologne and Jesus always had his shirttail hanging out, his fly unzipped, or a booger hanging out of his nose. Sometimes all three. Both of them invariably wore white socks and black shoes. Guilly wondered why he'd ever let them into the gang in the first place.

"Yo, man, we wanna do you a favor," Jesus explained, trying to sound cool and friendly. "For old times' sake, like. Angelo and me will take care of these trespassers for you, see. We'll drive out these freaks and ask nothing in return."

Guilly smiled. Did they think for a minute that they were fooling him? "Except to be back in tight with us."

Angelo and Jesus shifted nervously.

"Hey, man, we weren't really thinking of that," Angelo said. "But if, like, you did see that we could still be useful to you—"

Silencing him with a wave of his hand, Guilly rubbed his knuckles against the fine skin of his boyish face, thinking. What did he have to lose? Even if these two idiots made a total mess of it and brought the cops down on the gang, he could take the heat. Knowing how to deal with trouble was how he'd gotten where he was.

"Okay," he said, nodding ever so slightly. "We'll see how it goes down. But you're totally on your own. We're not backing your play. When you goin' in?"

"Tonight." Angelo grinned and nudged Jesus, who didn't seem all that happy that they'd gotten what they'd come for.

Guilly turned his hands out. "Then go do it."

The two of them turned to leave.

"And remember to bring back some proof of what you've done," Guilly called after them. "I don't take the word of cowards."

On that note of encouragement they departed.

When Julian woke up he was alone in the dingy apartment. Ashley wasn't in bed with him and the silence in the place was deafening. From where he was lying, he could see through the open doorway to the empty bathroom, so she wasn't in there. She was gone. It amused him to find that he was actually sore from their nocturnal acrobatics; he couldn't remember how many times they'd done it. At some point she'd bitten into his shoulder until he'd bled, but at least she'd spared his back this time. Sex with her was definitely not safe. Sometime around dawn they'd stirred against each other and embraced in an exhaustive sixty-nine, then he'd fallen back asleep, utterly spent. She never seemed to tire in the least, so it came as no surprise that she'd risen early and left.

He got up, dressed, explored his surroundings. Looked for a note and didn't find one. In the daylight, filtering in through filmy windows that faced out on a brick wall, the rooms looked even more seedy and less inhabited. This was where she escaped to from somewhere else, he felt sure of it. Elusive, evasive, a woman of many names and many games, she held all the cards in their relationship. Even that was okay with him.

For now.

Since there wasn't much to see he'd soon seen enough, so he decided to get out of there. He didn't have to worry about her few possessions' getting stolen, because the door locked when he closed it behind him. One less thing on his mind. When he reached the street he realized he wasn't quite sure where he was. East of his neighborhood, he believed. Somewhat south maybe. Every road led somewhere, so he started walking and looked for familiar landmarks.

There was no way to put their second date in perspective. Actually, it had been more like round two than a second date. It was too anarchic, too tumultuous. Being with her bombarded him with more sensation than he could process in his head. One fact seemed definite: He had penetrated her street-hard facade, struck sensitive layers beneath. True, she had lanced far deeper into his soft spots than he had into hers, but there was no emotional victory without risk. They were both hooked into each other's flesh and feelings. There was no backing out now.

A main avenue suddenly opened up in front of him and he recognized it. Cologne, which led into Hudson, which would take him home. His growling stomach reminded him that he was starving himself, and the aroma wafting into his nostrils from his own body informed him that he was approaching the grubby state of the homeless people scattered about. A hot meal and a hot shower might make him feel human again.

The sun was high and bright, but the air was cool and clouds were moving in. It was probably going to rain. He smoked as he walked, wishing his head would clear. His brain cells were no doubt screaming for nutrition. Man does not live by head alone. He laughed out loud at that and several passersby glared at him like he was a lunatic.

Maybe he was. If madness felt this good, he wanted more of it.

By the time he was back in his loft he was dismayed to find that the walk had nearly drained what strength he had. He couldn't rest, however. Not without doing something first, facing his accusing failure-in-progress. Whipping away the screen, he looked at the painting with wincing eyes. The curving symmetry of the white splashes triggered the image in his mind and he saw more of it on the canvas. It hungered to be let out, so he shuffled over to the painting and tried, feeling almost as if he were in a trance.

Hours passed without his noticing. The work went slowly, absorbing all his faculties. It had to be just right. Line and form must match unseen contours perfectly. Long did he labor at it, but he accomplished little, having no idea what the image was, where it had come from, why it clung so viciously to his imagination. What he'd started as a Maltese cross ended in spiked mushroom formations at the corners of a diamond shape. More than that he really couldn't see for now. The strangeness and insistence of the design consumed his thoughts, so he did more staring than brush-stroking, striving to divine what the damned thing meant.

When he was finally forced to admit that he'd arrived at another impasse he staggered to the kitchen table and fell into a chair. He'd never been eaten alive by a painting before. Obsessed, yes. Certain previous works had wounded the functions of his life, but never out and out slain them. Somehow he had to get on top of this compulsion. Surrendering to it seemed to be the only way.

Eat or be eaten, he told himself. There were some stale crackers in a cupboard and he munched on those for a while. Not much else there. Nothing to drink, so if Ashley came over he'd have nothing to offer her. And he badly wanted to stay in tonight. He didn't think he could take another one of her nights out so soon.

After he'd finished the crackers he took a walk to the local liquor store and bought a bottle of cherry brandy. The expression of the old man behind the cash register told him he looked like shit, which fazed him not in the least. Only when he noticed the setting sun on his way back did it occur to him how late it was. A whole day gone in a flash. *Time sure flies when you're having fun with paints and paranoia.*

A woman was waiting by his door. Dark haired, not Ashley. Anna Kurtz. Well, well. His popularity hadn't entirely waned.

"Jesus, Julian. You really live here?" The shift she wore was silver, but her feather boa and gloves were black. She was actually smoking through a cigarette holder.

"Hi, Anna. Yeah, I really do. If you want to hear the despair and passion of the common folk you've got to get down amongst them. What brings you out this way?" It occurred to him that she might be here to take a look at his work, perhaps with a mind toward showing it at her gallery. Then he remembered that he'd forgotten to cover the painting. There was no way he could let her in until he did. It was the first thing his hands had created that he was even close to being ashamed of, a departure so radical and ill-considered that he had to shield it from other eyes until he understood it himself.

"Oh, I just got to thinking about you. You've made yourself rather scarce lately. Aren't you going to ask me in?"

Think, Julian. Or lie. "Listen, Anna. I have a date tonight. She'll be here soon."

Anna's stark features remained neutral. She blinked at him. "Fascinating. I'd love to meet the lucky girl."

This was another no-win situation. He couldn't afford to offend her, so he decided to shrug off the new work as a crazy experiment. That should do it. "Uh, okay. Just let me find my key."

He opened the door and she followed him in. "It suits you," she said of the place.

His gaze shot to the painting. Something about it looked wrong, a dark patch at the center. Just a trick of the shadows, no doubt, for it quickly vanished. But it had sure looked odd for a moment there.

"This is interesting." Anna approached his unfinished symphony of oils, almost dancing as she walked. An aristocratic waltz. "I can't say I see what you're trying to do here."

"It's just something I'm fooling around with. Nothing serious. Would you like some brandy?"

"Love some."

Maybe she'd leave after they shared a drink, he thought as he poured some of the sweet red fluid into two snifter glasses. He wasn't in the mood for company. He was in the mood for Ashley.

"How have you been, Julian?" she asked when he handed her a glass.

So she wanted to make small talk, something he didn't feel like doing. He wanted to eat a big dinner, take a shower, finish the painting. The shadowy spot on the canvas was back, he saw. "I've been just fine, Anna."

"You don't look well. You aren't so broke that you can't buy food, are you? If it's that bad I can help you out." Her face showed concern, with perhaps an opportunistic edge to it.

"I've just been living in the fast lane lately. That's all. I'll be all right."

"Oh. Okay. Can I use your bathroom for a moment? I need to fix my makeup."

"Sure." He pointed the way and was glad when she left the room. There was a hole in the center of his painting and he hadn't put it there! It was square, like a window cut through the canvas, and filled with a violet darkness. A familiar violet darkness, similar to that which he'd glimpsed in Ashley's eyes that first night. The sheer impossibility of it shook him, made him feel dizzy and nauseated. As he watched, it seemed to adjust to the light and disappear, so he flicked off the light switch. The glowing void was there again, even though it seemed darker than the room's shadows, and he felt he could almost fall into it. It quickly adjusted to the darkness and vanished again.

A knock sounded at his door and he jolted as if he'd just been shot. He turned the lights back on, hid the painting behind the screen, and took a moment and a half to compose himself. Hallucinations now. Then he opened the door.

"Hiya, babe," said Ashley, casually striding in. She was into leather tonight: halter top, short skirt, and thigh-high boots all in black. A black felt choker concealed her throat scar, a large bag of brushed brown leather was slung over her right shoulder, and she had her sunglasses on. He would have found the outfit very arousing if he hadn't just suffered a good scare.

"Good evening, Ashley." He shut the door, then leaned against it, just watching her move. There was such a strange profound grace to her, very catlike, so much looser than that of other people, as if she were cut free from something to which everyone else was chained. Another crazy thought; she seemed to spawn them in his mind when she was around. Once more his nostrils were brushed by the subtle but entrancing scent of her—cinnamon, sandalwood, and lavender long aged in an alchemist's retort. He still couldn't get over the fact that this smashing creature was interested in him, but here she was again.

She stopped in the middle of the floor, slid off her shades, and looked at him with her body in profile. "Got any work done, Stormy?"

Anna emerged from the bathroom then, and the eyes of the two women locked solidly for a moment. Ashley's face transformed into grinning fury.

"You're not alone, huh?"

Advancing smoothly with an extended hand, Anna said, "I'm Anna Kurtz, an old friend of Julian's."

"*Old* is the word for it," said Ashley in the moment before she grabbed Anna's wrist and kissed her on the lips. Julian was pretty sure she slipped her the tongue as well. Anna was so severely shocked that she dropped her glass on the floor. It miraculously didn't break, just released a flood of brandy on the wooden boards.

There was a distinct smacking sound as Ashley released her victim. "Any friend of Julian's is a friend of mine."

Anna wiped her mouth with the back of her hand, glaring in horror at her attacker. It took a lot to blow Anna's cool, but it was blown. "Your lady here is a bit of a sick bitch," she said, smoldering. "You should keep her on a leash, Julian."

Sheer disbelief still had him in its grips. Had he really just seen that? "Ashley, are you nuts? What do you think you're doing?"

She stared right back at Anna. "There's only room here for one bitch."

With a flourish of her boa Anna stomped to the exit. "I guess I'll go before I get raped. I'll see you around, Julian. If you manage to stay alive." She left, slamming the door behind her.

Now that the reality of what had happened had sunk in, Julian felt himself getting furious. He confronted Ashley. "What did you do that for?"

Her head was tilted, eyes not looking at him, as if his anger puzzled her. "I was just eliminating some competition."

Jealousy was the one thing he'd never expected from her. "She wasn't competition! She runs a fucking museum. Are you always such a cunt to complete strangers?"

"Don't talk to me like that!" She swung her eyes on him, blue and blazing daggers. "If she's nothing to you, then what are you so upset about? She'll get over it."

Did she really not understand? "That's not the point. You can't treat people that way. Anna never did you any harm."

This seemed to get through to her, turning her rage to a frown. Walking backward, she retreated to the bed and sat on it. "You're right. I'm sorry. I've just been feeling insecure lately."

Strained silence hung heavy between them for several long moments. "I bought some cherry brandy. Would you like some?"

"Sure."

Picking up Anna's glass, he took it into the kitchen alcove and rinsed it off. Then he partially filled it and carried it along with his own to the bed. He sat down next to her, admiring the lengths of her thighs exposed between her skirt and her boots. Even through his annoyance he began to anticipate exploring the mysteries between those thighs before the night was over.

"Did you miss me?" she said, trying to sound cheerful.

"I couldn't help but miss you." He handed over her glass, from which she sipped. "I've been meaning to ask you. How's your friend doing?"

Her face looked perplexed again. "Friend?"

"Yeah, the one who's tangled up with the weird cult."

"Oh. Her." She twirled her sunglasses in her right hand, then started to put them back on and checked herself. "She's still okay, as far as I know. I myself am thinking about making a big change, putting my old life behind me. But it won't be easy."

A moment of truth was coming, he sensed, so he said nothing.

"After that story you told me last night, about dying or at least coming close to death in that car crash, I feel I can ask you something. You fear death, you said, more so even than most people."

He shrugged uneasily. "It would be fair to say that, yes."

Ashley nodded ever so slightly. "So you would do almost anything to stay alive, wouldn't you? Maybe even get into some bad shit?"

Now she had him worried. Exactly what was she involved with? "Uh, that's a pretty heavy question. I guess I've never really thought about it, but I don't think I could live with myself if I ever seriously hurt anybody. I'm a creator, not a destroyer."

Her nod was more emphatic this time, a little resigned. "You're an innocent, Stormy. You know that?"

"You're the second person to call me that this week," he complained. "How can I be? I drink, I smoke, I paint dirty pictures and I think lewd thoughts. I live in the gutter, where my mind is, and I'll screw with any woman who gives me half a chance. So how am I an innocent?"

"Because you've never harmed anybody. You experience pain, visualize pain, but you never cause pain." Standing, she sashayed to the screen hiding his latest work. "Can I see what you're working on now?"

Julian braced himself for a fight. "No, you can't. You see, I believe a painting is like a baby: neither one is improved by looking at it before it's finished. You're not going to beat me up, are you?"

A laugh, a bit forced, escaped her lips. Tonight was not going well. "No, of course not. This one I'll wait for."

Since she'd all but broached the subject already he thought he might as well press it. "Ashley, are you a married woman?"

The question seemed to startle and amuse her. "Uh, no. Not at all. And I never have been. Most likely never will be."

"Well, concerning the question you asked me earlier. You're not in some kind of trouble, are you?"

"Of course not," she said, coming back to the bed and climbing on it. "Come on, this is supposed to be a party. Let's just have fun. Here. I've got a present for you."

Reaching into her oversized purse, she removed a long curved object wrapped in soft white cloth and handed it to him. "This is for you, for inspiration."

He accepted it, surprised by its weight, and felt sharp, clean edges under the fabric. There was nothing unusual in her act of generosity, he reflected. People were always giving him peculiar gewgaws with the notion that they would fuel his fever-dream fires, which sometimes they did. Seldom, though. Witness Mercy's adder stone. Carefully he unfolded the cloth from around the hard, heavy object and found himself holding a crescent moon of translucent purple crystal about ten inches long, three inches thick at its widest point. It was simply gorgeous, rendered with geometric precision and infused with bigger-than-life color.

"It's incredible," he said. "Amazing. Look, I know it's really gauche to ask where a present came from, but if there's an artist around who does this kind of work I've got to meet him."

Ashley smiled devilishly. "That's not possible. You see, the person who fashioned that is long dead. It's very old."

Then he got it. This was one of the artworks in her keeping! She had stolen for him, for his sake. It was flattering, true, but he wanted no part of art theft in any form. Talk about ruining your reputation; if it ever got out even as a rumor, he wouldn't be able to get a job as a house painter. He handed it back to her like it was the proverbial hot potato.

"I can't let you give this to me, Ashley. Not if you took it from your employers."

The accusation did not upset her. "I didn't steal it. It was given to me. I happened to mention how beautiful I thought it was and my superiors told me I could have it. It's a Shadow Prism. Let me show you."

She swung her legs over to the other side of the bed,

set her glass down on the floor, and jumped up, moving to the corner where the light from his shaded bedside lamp did not reach. A pile of dirty clothes occupied a wicker chair there. He'd missed them on laundry day. Watching his expression, she held the crystalline crescent in the shadows, tilted it so that it faced the wall at about a forty-five-degree angle, and gazed at it in grinning anticipation. Julian riveted his own gaze on the object, feeling giddy because he didn't have the slightest idea what was going to happen next. After a few moments the purple moon-shape seemed to rapidly absorb darkness out of the air around it without diminishing the shadows. To him it looked like a reverse explosion, filling the crystal with a blackness so deep that Ashley appeared to be holding a crescent-shaped void in her hand. The sight frightened and fascinated him, for it was as if a rip had been torn in the reality of his room and a darkness beyond mere absence of light was filtering through the crystal into the everyday world. In this way his mind scrambled to define what his eyes saw, as something began shooting out of the concave side of the crystal toward the wall, something like a narrow stream of sooty liquid smoke, curling, coiling, and writhing into tendrils where it struck the plaster without damaging it. Ashley turned her head to see his expression, smiling with euphoric mischief, her eyes bright and curious, and for just an instant more violet than blue.

"Ashley, what is that thing? How is it doing that?" It was just a parlor trick, he told himself, a very clever illusion. But it sure looked real. No, it looked more real than real, like it involved forces that would outlast mere physical things.

She paused theatrically before answering. "I told you.

It's a Shadow Prism, a lens that can focus the voidlight of the Abyss, of which shadows are but the faintest rudiments."

Once again she was speaking utter parapsychobabble, but her words put him in mind of what he'd seen in the center of his painting just before she arrived. There had been a great deal of synchronicity in his life of late, he'd noticed. "What the fuck are you talking about?"

Ashley pulled the Prism out of the gloom into the dim yellow lamplight and it assumed its ordinary but exquisite aspect once more. She sat down on the opposite side of the bed, cupping the crystal in both hands. "I'm talking about what will remain when most everything has fallen away, Julian, that place you were at when you thought you were dead. I want to help you figure out what it is."

He sighed wearily. Having had a so-called supernatural experience of his own at a very young age, he was as much game for this mystical stuff as anybody, had had his palm read, his tarot dealt, had put in his time with Ouija boards and seances. One time he'd even undergone hypnotic past-life regression and was not surprised to find himself having Goya's memories. But enough was enough. Ashley's trippy witchy shtick was wearing thin.

"All right. A good magician doesn't willingly reveal the secret to a really good trick like that one. My guess is you've got some sort of tiny smoke-machine with you, but it doesn't matter. Even if it is just smoke and mirrors, it's a very entertaining act."

Her smile didn't disappear, just became a lot more intimidating. "It's not a cheap trick, Julian. Not an optical illusion. This is simply how reality works on another level, on the most fundamental plane, near the very core."

"At the heart of darkness?" he sneered. "Okay, Ashley, have it your way. Go ahead and come clean with me. Is it you who's into some kind of cult or coven? What is it? Golden Dawn? Ordo Templi Orientis? Order of the Silver Flame? And just how seriously do you take all this nonsense?" As an afterthought he reached into a pocket of his jeans, pulled out the oft-crumpled page of notes she'd left behind, and tossed it on the Paisley print quilt.

"You don't understand." Her fine features contorted in utter bafflement. "I'm trying to help you. I'll make you the greatest artist who ever lived. Through me you'll capture visions that people won't be able to take their eyes off of. You'll snag their imaginations for years at a time. They'll talk about what they've experienced in your paintings to the exclusion of all else. Civilization itself will be changed by the images blazing out from your pictures."

So she was having delusions of grandeur now, he grimly mused. All he'd wanted was a simple if unusual girl whom he could love and cherish, along with enough money from his paintings so he could spend his time on his art. Instead, he now found himself with some sort of cryptic crusader, a messiah of the macabre who wanted to use him to get her message out. *Used again, Stormer. Way to go.*

"Is that all I am to you? A hand and an eye and a brush through which you can spread the weirdness with pretty pictures?"

"No! Oh, no!" She quickly scooted across the bed and took his hands in hers, dropping the Shadow Prism onto the quilt. "I just thought you would want this. You gave me something last night that means a lot to me, and I wanted to repay you. This is the only way I know how. It's the only thing I have to offer."

Freeing his right hand, he used it to touch her cheek. "That's not true. You've got yourself to offer. I wasn't asking for anything more from you."

She lowered her head and shook it violently. "No. You don't know what I am. I thought I could give you what you most desired, but I judged you wrong. God, I got everything wrong. I don't know human nature anymore. I've forgotten how people think and feel."

With his hand to her chin he raised her head up to look into her face. The soft swelling of her lower lip quivered and she had turned pale, as if pure dread was possessing her. "I've been out of it too long," she said. "Human feeling must die after a while."

These struck him as the words of a recovering junkie, but there were no chicken tracks on the creamy skin of her arms that he could see. "Hey, relax, babe. You're being way too hard on yourself. People misread each other all the time. I mean, we've only known each other for three days, right?"

Ashley looked away, then remet his eyes with tears in her own. "But I used to read people so well, except at the end maybe. It was my profession. I was a—" She choked back the words so hard that she actually gagged. "Now the company I keep isn't the kind anyone should be around. I'm no good for you, Julian. I'll just destroy you. I shouldn't be here. I'm sorry. I've got to go."

Now he really felt as if he'd been kicked in the gut. "Ashley, what is it? You can talk about anything with me. You know that."

For a moment she considered it, then wildly shook her

head. "No. Not this. I can't." Their contact was broken and she slipped off the bed, fled toward the door.

"Wait!"

"No, don't," she sobbed, her last words before leaving.

Julian sat there for quite some time, stunned and drained, a hollow wretch of a man. *Lord, you sure can pick them, Stormer. What a huge black secret that chick must have haunting her life, a veritable closetful of skeletons.* And he'd gravitated right to her. What did that say about him?

Had he totally lost her? He could hang around the dump she occasionally occupied, wait for her to show up there, but he had a feeling she'd never go near the place again. Tonight she'd been about to run away from something, to him, but things had gone wrong and she'd changed her mind. Now she'd gone back, maybe for good.

Idly, he picked up and fingered the Shadow Prism, admiring its clean beauty in spite of his misery. It seemed to tingle lightly in his hands, almost as if it were singing to him. The tune summoned the image that had been taunting his brain for the past few days. There seemed in his mind to be some kind of spongy formations projecting from the edges of the diamond shape, for no good reason. Well, it wouldn't hurt to add them onto his canvas. Perhaps he could at least solve one riddle in his life, complete the painting and escape his frustration and depression in creation. And drink.

Rising and retrieving the brandy bottle, he obeyed the call of his tyrannical work of art.

In an area of the city that was a now-abandoned industrial zone, christened the Wasteland by the Crucifixers and claimed by them as their turf, Angelo Gusano and Jesus Langosta skulked in the dark of night. They had nearly reached their destination, and they had not yet lost their nerve. Camouflaged in black attire, on foot, and bearing six knives, two swords, and one handgun, the two teenagers felt prepared.

"We'll be a two-man hit squad," Angelo was saying, just to keep their morale boosted. "Whoever's living in that old place won't know what hit them after we get through. We're about to make history, man."

Jesus was in agreement with all this, but he was still a bit concerned about his personal safety. "I think you should let me carry the gun, man."

"No way." Angelo was adamant. "This was my idea, so I keep the gun. Besides, I'm a better shot."

"Well, what if *they* have guns?"

"They won't have any guns. It's just a bunch of hippies or punks, living like animals. Just stick with the plan. If we meet too much resistance we retreat. Simple as that."

"Yeah," said Jesus, marveling at the simplicity of it. "Stick to the plan. What could go wrong?" What he was really thinking was *Why am I here?* The answer, of course, was because Angelo had talked him into it. It hadn't been real hard, of course. He wanted to get back into the gang, and he had a lifelong habit of getting persuaded by his friend to do things. In fact, he had a burning need to be a Crucifixer because his friend had him believing it was the only thing worth being. He was stupid and Angelo was smart. He was afraid, except when he was too stupid to be afraid, and Angelo was brave. But he also sometimes suspected that his friend wasn't quite right in the head. It was a suspicion, but he wasn't smart enough to be sure.

Angelo kept up his propagandistic patter. "Remember this is Crucifixer territory. Territory is everything. These people are invaders. They gotta be driven out, you know? We don't have to kill anybody. We don't even have to hurt them. We just have to scare them, let them know that the wrath of the cross cannot be evaded."

It all sounded good to him, but he had a strong feeling that someone was going to get hurt. They were raiding someone's home, and people defended their homes to the death. Even he knew that. But he had to go along with his friend. Angelo took care of him. Without Angelo he'd be a complete nobody. Which didn't alter the fact that he didn't want to harm anyone, especially that beautiful blond girl they'd seen come out of that place last night. She'd shone like a star in his eyes. When Angelo had told him that a girl like that would never let him touch her, Jesus had felt that he could hurt her. Hurt her bad. He knew he was fat, stupid, and ugly, but he had brute strength. That was his one saving grace.

"There's the manhole she came out of," said Angelo, pointing. "We go down there and head that way, toward the building."

The building he was referring to was dark and round, with ten oblong additions radiating from it. Its central roof was wide and high, a pretty big place. He knew from past expeditions that it was very solid and all the doors were locked tight. In spite of its location Angelo doubted it had ever been used for any kind of manufacturing. Storage, maybe. But he rather thought it was some kind of temple or cathedral. They would soon know for sure.

There was no cover on the manhole, so Angelo just shone his flashlight down to see what was there. It looked to be more an access tunnel than a sewer. No smell of shit was wafting up from below. Of course, no one lived around these parts anymore.

"I'll go first," said Angelo. "You stay close behind."

"Right, man."

Angelo climbed down the rusty ladder, glad he'd worn thick gloves. Cut yourself on rusty metal and you risked lockjaw. Then they had to knock out your two front teeth and feed you through a tube. Or so he'd heard. It wasn't very far down, and at the bottom it was remarkably sanitary for an underground passage. Maybe the rains had washed it clean.

"This ain't so bad," he said as Jesus joined him in the tunnel. "It's even big enough to walk through. Let's go."

There were some rats, but not many. They looked scrawny and weak. Must be real slim pickings in the Wasteland. The two of them followed the passage thirty yards or so before they came to a brick wall that had apparently collapsed due to age and neglect.

Angelo smiled at the sight. "This is too easy. It's like they're just beggin' us to break in. Come on. Let's pay them a surprise visit."

Beyond the wall the tunnel changed, widening into what looked like a maze of catacombs with sides made of stone blocks. They had no clue how to proceed.

"We could get lost in there real easy," said Jesus.

"Shh." Angelo was frowning. "Keep your voice down. We'll go this way."

His guess was good, for after they made a few twists and turned a few corners they came to a curving passage that seemed to lead out of the maze. They started to follow it but suddenly found two shadows in front of them, which they quickly realized were their own cast by a light from behind them. Turning, they saw a man and a woman with no eyes and discovered they were paralyzed. Angelo never completed his move for the gun in his belt.

"Your fear prevents you from moving," said the woman. Tall, thin, she had long dark hair and a bony but beautiful face with a harsh mouth slashed across it. She wore a full-length dress of moldy, moth-eaten brown velvet. "Knowing that won't help you, however. You're a slave of your fear."

Her companion, holding a flaming torch, looked no friendlier. He was a small black man with a shaved head and hardened features, wearing denim coveralls. If he'd ever smiled at all, it had been many years ago, thought Angelo.

"What are your names?" demanded the woman. There were eyes in her sockets, he realized, but they were so dark, they looked as if they weren't there. They had no whites. Same with the black guy.

"Jesus Langosta," Jesus blurted out.

Angelo heard himself say, "Angelo Gusano."

The woman grinned, and it wasn't a pleasant sight. "The messiah himself and a heavenly messenger. How utterly enchanting. Well, I have some ill tidings for you, I'm afraid. You're on harrowed ground and we eat angels and saviors here."

Jesus got the black man and the woman chose Angelo. The two creepy people stepped up real close to them, face to face, boring into their eyes with eyes that weren't eyes. Angelo suddenly saw nothing but the purplish depths of two eye-shaped holes. Cold shadow seeped into his brain as a strange smell hit his nostrils, like rotting flowers and decaying leaves. Her smell. His head seemed to fill with freezing darkness, driving out all sense of his body, all memory. She was emptying him!

HARROWGATE

He was becoming hollow, filling up with something from below, a nothingness that was like fluid flowing into his flesh. Void devoured him. Void devoured.

Until there was only void.

8

A Spy in the House of God

This is crazy, this is crazy, this is crazy, thought Vern Doyle as he stamped out one cigarette and lit another. *This is so goddamned fucking crazy, I don't even know how to describe it.* He stood in the recesses of a doorway across the street from his friend Julian's building, out of the light rain that was sprinkling from the night sky, manning a stakeout. But it was the craziest damned stakeout he'd ever done.

He hadn't had too much trouble finding out who Ashley Praetor, alias Ashley Herrin, was. After all, a rough-trade hooker who successfully bugged out of the life (with her life) from that maniac pimp Cadge's stable was the stuff of legend. It would have been hard enough informing Julian about that, but there was more. *Jesus wept, was there ever more!* This gutsy little ex-pro went into business for herself, only it involved a very different kind of blowjob, this being the kind that was white, powdered, and taken in nasally. That was before the heavy bad vibe world of crack came down, but that age had its risks too. By all accounts she'd been a very cool dealer, honest, professional, and keeping kiddie sales taboo. Just the kind of dealer street-slime pushers love to hate. Inevitably her impeccable business habits had allowed her to encroach on another dealer's territory, some rodent punk named Stitch because of the sloppy surgical embroidery done on his face. Stitch then conspired with a heavy-duty coke supplier named (or aliased) Ernesto Frost (who did *not* like to be called Frosty the Snowman), to snare Ashley in a raw deal.

A cutthroat deal.

Frost intercepted a substantial shipment headed for Ashley's regular supplier, leaving her high and dry with many orders to fill. Enter Stitch to generously offer her a deal she couldn't pass up, at least not without losing a large portion of her clientele, buyer and dealer loyalty by necessity swaying with the winds of market demands. So she agreed to do business with the Snowman. The time and place for the meeting were set, just after hours in the basement of a punk club called the Grotto, the owner of which Ashley knew personally. What she didn't know was that the premises were being used without his knowledge, the door being opened by a bouncer deeply in debt to Stitch. All parties showed up, Ashley with her bodyguards Ruby and Jules, Frost and Stitch and four goons. What exactly happened after that was not clear, but Ruby, Jules, and two of the henchmen ended up with multiple stab wounds and various broken bones, Ruby with a half-garrotted throat. Rumor had it that Frost sought private medical attention for the knife-inflicted injury to his groin area, which cost him his right testicle. The next time Stitch showed up in public he was shy his right eye.

Apparently Ashley had fought like a hellcat with a

switchblade in each hand, once she'd realized the deal was a setup. Amazingly no shots were fired, in anger or otherwise, the ban on handguns perhaps having been insisted upon by the bouncer. But Ashley's bodyguards were put out of commission and she was disarmed with great difficulty. Then Frost, bleeding profusely from his crotch, picked up one of her blades as the two of his goons left standing held her firmly.

He might have raped her, if he hadn't been gay, if he hadn't been cut in the genitals.

Instead he sliced her throat, deep and wide, then left her to die as they left their own casualties behind and made good their escape. Fate seemed to have some sense of justice, however, for Frost met a messy end a few months later at the hands of some ruthlessly ambitious Colombians. It was the bouncer who found the five grievously bleeding bodies, returning to the closed club perhaps out of guilt, and called the police and the ambulance. By the time they arrived, Ashley Praetor was dead.

That's right, Vern old boy. You have a dead woman under your surveillance. What do you know about that?

The death certificate with the coroner's signature and the murder investigation report were on file, plain as day. So was the photograph of her inert form lying inside the chalk lines on the basement floor of the Grotto. Vern had a photocopy of it in a pocket of his coat. Ashley Sonya Praetor, alias Ashley Herrin, alias Sonya Gray, alias Sophie Darrell, twenty-four years of age, known prostitute, suspected drug dealer, died from massive loss of blood and asphyxiation due to a gaping wound to the throat, on April 2, 1979. *Over ten fucking years ago!* Officially the corpse just got lost in the shuffle, the transportation of the other victims to emergency rooms and her to the city morgue, but Vern had the real poop on that. The forensics team had looked away for just a moment, discussing some evidentiary detail or maybe a fine point of procedure, and when they looked back the body was gone. Vanished. Vamoosed. Only the chalk lines and the poor pretty girl's blood were left behind.

Vern wasn't sure what he thought about all this. It was just possible that Julian's sweetheart was only going by the name of the deceased. But with a scar across her neck right where Ashley had been cut? What a weird trip that chick must be on if she took emulation that far. And if it wasn't that, then what? Someone come back from the dead? *Ain't no such animal*, he told himself.

He didn't know the answer. This caper really was beyond him. The young woman he'd seen go into Julian's loft half an hour ago had looked like the deceased, but he hadn't gotten a good look at her face because of his wandering attention. By the time he'd noticed her and realized her destination, she'd had her back to him. All he knew was that if she came out wearing the face of the stiff in the police photo, he'd be liable to piss himself, maybe dump a load in his shorts. Leave it to Julian to snag himself a sexy spook for a lover. It was a blackly scary idea, but it also ensnared him on a gut level. Here was a real challenge, the damnedest mystery he'd ever confronted. This was something more than sadistic hoods, greedy mobsters, conniving killers, and power-mad cult leaders. There was a thrill of sinister wonder here, a wild dark side that promised to go right over the edge. It was an edge over which Vern deeply wanted to peer, into whatever lay beyond.

As stoked as he was, he was having a hard time figuring his options. What if he followed her and she led him straight to a graveyard, hovered above a particular plot, and sank through the ground to her resting place six feet under? Would he just hike back to Julian's place and nonchalantly tell his friend he'd never have pegged him for a necrophiliac? Or what if she shambled home to some run-down house with her coffin set up in the parlor, packed with wormy dirt from her burial in the old country, where she stayed during the daylight hours? Would he get a stake and a mallet and pierce her heart so that she turned to rot and then dust? That's the way it was done, wasn't it? He'd seen it a hundred times in the movies. Now, he was going to be awfully disappointed if all this turned out to be some kind of absurd scam, but he still wasn't too hot on the idea of facing off with a corpse that refused to admit it was dead. That would be *falling* over the edge, not just looking to see what was there.

The door he was watching opened. *That sure was fast.* Either a quickie or a lover's spat, he guessed. She emerged, and, *oh, God it sure does look like her, not aged a single day.* Still, he was pretty far away yet and there were other possibilities. A twin, a sister, even a cousin maybe, or even plastic surgery. Or how about a really expert makeup job? No, that wouldn't hold up unnoticeably during a bout of hot and heavy fucking. Was he grasping at straws? Why the hell would anyone go to so much trouble to impersonate a dead woman? *A dead woman:* even Vern's supersteady nerves were jarringly strummed by that phrase repeating in his head. But he kept himself still.

She proceeded down the street the way she had come, walking like someone who was very much alive, with a swishy, sensual gait that was the farthest thing from a zombie's rigid shuffling he could think of. Even from this distance he could tell she was an exceptional piece of ass, and he loved the black leather fuck-me getup she was wearing. Normally he would have been instantly in lust with her, but somehow the hint that she might once have been a candidate for a cadaver's slab dampened his libido a bit. He left his hiding place and tailed her with supreme stealth and skill, so unless her senses were also supernatural she would never suspect she had an extra shadow.

Ashley, if that was her name, had looked very sad coming out of the building, actually teary eyed. *Do ghosts cry?* he asked himself. Well, this one did. She walks, she talks, she fucks, she cries, she crawls on her belly like a reptile. (Sure hope not, that last.) Maybe Julian had blown her cover, ripped the skin off the skull, so to speak, in a burst of brilliant insight. Vern doubted it. If anything, this fetching phantom was feeling guilty about haunting such a nice guy and had rushed out in a fit of remorse. *Hey, that's pretty good, Vern: you can diagnose the behavior of the dead as well as the quick.*

The rain didn't seem to bother her at all. She had two chances to hail a cab and passed them both up. The air was a bit nippier, too, than she was dressed for, though she didn't shiver or rub her bare arms. She was also trekking quite a distance, six blocks already. Should he accost her directly and ask her what her game was? He suspected that was a bad idea, for in legends the living dead had a reputation for ruthlessness, even bloodthirst, which he had no desire to mess with. Not that he believed for a moment that she was a walking corpse or an apparition. Ashley cast a shadow, the chill of night turned her breath to mist the same as his own, and her skin color looked healthily human. But if he could flash a mirror in front of her or expose her to sunlight . . . *Shut up, Vern.*

They were entering a decaying industrial district now, rows and rows of abandoned factories and unused warehouses, just a whole lot of nothing. Miles of it. He had to be careful at this point: she could slip into any one of a hundred doorways or other ingresses and he wouldn't have a clue where she'd gone. Past a crumbling steel plant, she turned left down a street and crossed to the other side, making him nervous. It was hard to see her with no streetlights on. Fortunately the clouds above were parting to let the moon shine through. Her blond hair all but glowed in the silvery light, like spun platinum.

He relaxed a little as they reached the end of the avenue, for he believed he saw her destination, a building so out of place in its Gothic architecture that it had to be where she lived. Oh, it was just too weirdly perfect. Filling the corner of an intersection, it looked like a cathedral of some kind. The building was big and circular, like a railroad roundhouse, with a conical roof and several rectangular annexes projecting from it like the spokes of a wheel. Large blocks of brownstone formed its high walls, in which not a single window was visible. No steeple, no belltower, no cross pointing at the heavens, but it did have the feel of a house of worship, denomination totally unknown. Vern hung back now that he knew where she was going. Sure enough, she strode up to a door at the end of one of the oblong wings, rooted in her big purse for a key, unlocked the door, and went inside.

He found himself another doorway and sat down on the steps, thinking. How far did he want to take this tonight? He had an address in his possession, so he could do more checking before he entered the breach. Well, there was no harm in scouting out the building from the outside. He could at least do that much, couldn't he?

So he got his legs moving and ventured onto the sacred grounds. They weren't extensive and they seemed overgrown by weeds. It must not be a very successful church if it couldn't afford to pay a groundskeeper. The lack of windows worked to his advantage now: he couldn't see in, but whoever was inside couldn't see out to notice a spy on their lawn. There was no detail on the radiating sections, of which there were ten, so he went right up to the central rotunda. Something was carved into a panel of gray stone set into the curving wall high above his head. The lettering was weathered, but he thought he could make it out.

COLD STORAGE, it said.

No, wait. That wasn't what it said at all. *Settle down, Vern.* He laughed out loud and it sounded hysterical enough to startle him. The sign actually read GOLD STORAGE, as in someone named Gold having used this place as a warehouse long ago. Had the bizarre revelations of the day affected him more than he'd thought? To the point at which he could seriously entertain the idea that a lovely perambulating corpse would return to cold storage to keep from spoiling? *Get a grip on yourself, man. Keep a level head.* How could he, when none of this added up? Any way he looked at the facts, they led to unacceptable conclusions. Ashley was some woman posing as a murder victim, for reasons unknown. She liked to hide out in the middle of nowhere, for reasons unknown. In recent days she had been observed doing research on obscure Middle Eastern mythology and had become sexually involved with his friend Julian, an artist with a bent toward the strange. Where was the thread that linked all this together? No logical explanation presented itself.

It was time to consider the improbable, maybe even the impossible. She could be a member of an underground cult of some kind, one in which the initiation required getting yourself killed and coming back to life. Good trick, one that only a really devoted follower would succeed at. That was worse than impossible. It was ridiculous. The trail dead-ended here, however. Literally. He had nowhere else to look for clues. Talking to Julian and looking up the owners of the property would offer minor details at best and red herrings at worst. The answer was inside the ugly mound of masonry standing in front of him, so he couldn't walk away from it just yet. Riddles troubled him, drove him nuts until he solved them, and this one was threatening to put him in a straitjacket and a rubber room. He wouldn't be able to sleep, eat, or live a normal life until he got to the bottom of this. And when he finally did, a rush of near-orgasmic joy at solving it would surge through him.

Right, so it was definitely decided: he was going in. Now the problem was how to gain entry. He retreated and made a wide circuit of the outlying area, finding an open manhole. It could lead into the cellar of the place, but entering from below didn't seem like a wise notion. He'd rather come in from above, take the high ground and observe from elevated vantage points. So he turned his attention to the roof of the roundhouse. There were no skylights or belfries, but he believed he saw vents up there, closed now but maybe large enough to squeeze through. The walls were too even to scale and there were no rooftops close enough from which he could jump. That was a damned dangerous way to do things anyway. There was, however, a big diseased-looking tree nearby with one long thick branch that just might project to within sufficient distance of the cathedral. He walked around to the side where it was growing, a truly impressively sized trunk of dying timber, fatally wounded perhaps by all the pollution it had breathed in when the surrounding factories were still in operation. It was hard to muster a great deal of confidence in its solidity, but he began climbing it, shinning first, then using the lower branches like the rungs of a ladder. A wave of nostalgia flowed through him, for he hadn't climbed a tree since he was a teenager.

When he reached the intended limb, he started rethinking this proposition. First, the wood of the branch looked rotten and worm-eaten. Second, he would have to leap quite a distance to land on the roof, and he would probably make a hell of a racket besides. He could easily drop onto the top of one of the wings, but that wouldn't help him reach the vents. There was just too much vertical distance between the two roofs. Taking one step out on the limb, he considered the odds.

Granting this idea of yours works, Vern, what are you getting yourself into? He was unarmed save for the jackknife hidden in his right boot and the small Mace canister in an inside pocket of his coat. *Yeah, you're out on a limb all right, man.* If these were kill-crazy cultists and they caught him breaking into their headquarters, he was liable to have one fucking big fight on his hands. His judgment was clouded—by his concern for his friend, his vaulting curiosity, his need to pump himself full of adrenaline by testing his limits. It wouldn't do to examine his motives too closely at this point; it might unsteady his nerves, distract him with too much thinking. *Leap before you look, Vern.*

And a leap was exactly what it would take. He could use the branch as a springboard, run to its end and then jump, and come down on the slanted wood of the roof with his feet still moving to space out his impact. It sounded like a plan, so he put it into action. Braced against the trunk, he shoved off and rushed along the length of the limb, leapt from its tip into the air, felt his stomach sink as it cracked under his feet, and knew he was in trouble. He didn't have anywhere near enough momentum to land where he wanted, so he came down awkwardly on the edge of the roof and instantly lost his footing. Falling on his belly, he began sliding to his death. Forty feet or more of sheer drop-off gaped between him and the hard ground before he found himself holding on to something for dear life with his legs dangling below him. It was a metal gutter he was hanging from, and he was eternally grateful it was there. At some time, probably fairly recently, someone had fortunately attached rainspouts to the rim of the roof of this dusty old hall. *Well,* thought Vern, *thank whatever dark little god is worshiped within for that small favor.*

There were two more bits of luck worth mentioning: The tree branch hadn't completely broken off and gone crashing to the earth, and he didn't think his clumsy landing had made very much noise at all. So far, so good, so nothing. The most perilous part was yet to be faced. He swung his leg up and hoisted the rest of his body after it, thankful for all that weightlifting and working out, without which his muscles would have been too weakened by his heavy intake of drugs and drink to effect his own rescue. Once erect on the conical roof, he crept up the slope to the nearest vent.

He knelt down and tried to lift it. Good; it wasn't locked from the inside. It looked as if it opened on an attic crawl-space, bitterly stale with rat droppings and tapestried with spiderwebs. Not at all inviting and dark as hell. With uncharacteristic lack of foresight he had worn his good leather coat. Well, if it got stained or torn he had no one to blame but himself. Before he went in there, he tried to spot a trapdoor in the floor of the attic by the glow of the moon, failed to, and entered anyway. There was no percentage in turning back now.

Just inside the vent, half buried in the dust on the floor, he found a rusty iron rod that had presumably been used to prop open the shutter, and he used it for this purpose. In this way he afforded himself at least some illumination. If he went around and did the same with all the vents, he would have a lot more light to see by, but he would have to cross expanses of filth and breach curtains of cobwebs. The prospect didn't appeal to him, so he didn't do it. If cleanliness really was next to godliness, then this place was definitely ungodly.

His good fortune was still holding up, however. About fifteen feet away, near the wall, he found a door in the floor, round and hinged and fitted with a corrosion-covered ring for a handle. Beyond it could lie the point of no return, he reminded himself. He was about to trespass into the lair of a woman who might be something other than living or dead, whatever the fuck that meant. *If you've truly got balls, Vern, now is the time for you to prove it. I fear nothing, not ghost stories or maniacs with knives. I am the meanest son of a bitch in the valley of the shadow. Nobody fucks with Vernon C. Doyle and lives to tell the tale. I'll spit in the devil's ugly face and rule hell if I die.* He reached down, pulled open the horizontal door, and dim gray light flooded upward through the hole.

Leaning over, he poked his head into the opening. He saw statues, fancy columns, white tiled flooring, and crudely carved shapes in the gray stone of the walls and ceiling. The medieval-looking interior was lit by white globes held aloft in the arms of small demonic sculptures. This area seemed to be an outer gallery ringing the cavernous chapel at the heart of the building, sufficiently vacant and out-of-the-way for him to make his entrance. One problem remained: Once he eased himself through the hole to the floor below, he wouldn't be able to reach it again, would be forced to find a ladder or another way out. Well, he'd cross that bridge when he came to it. He slipped his body through the opening, clinging to the rim with his hands and letting the lid rest heavily on his fingers, then let go. It closed with a soft thud above him as he dropped to the tiles. He crouched down to avoid being seen through the stone railing to his left. Entry gained. Now what?

Out of habit, his eye assessed the art objects lining the gallery, and he instantly decided that Ashley's job was unnecessary if these were what she took care of. The statues were quaint and unusual, but not the products of any great talent. He doubted they were worth much. They might fetch a price with some eccentric whacked out on grotesque figures in marble and bronze, but it would be too much trouble tracking down a rich nutter like that to make them worth stealing. Nonetheless, Vern decided that if he was caught, it would be better to play the thief than the spy he was. In wartime spies were shot. So he kept his weapons, such as they were, concealed.

Using every bit of cover at his disposal, he moved beyond the columns, still hunkering low, to the balcony looking down on the central chamber. He peeked through the balusters. It definitely looked like the altar room of a temple, though not Christian, Jewish, Muslim, or any other faith he recognized. A truly impressive quantity of white marble had gone into its construction. Vern thought it was probably the brightest, purest, cleanest room he'd ever seen. The center of the floor was covered with a painted black circle containing a tight dizzying spiral, about sixteen feet in diameter. At ten points around the circle round flaming eyes had been painted in dark purple. One section of the wall was dominated by what looked to him to be a shrine carved in golden-brown stone. The object in the shrine was like a diamond in shape, with mushroomlike forms sprouting out of it at the corners and edges. It had a square hole at its center and a slanted eye stared out of each corner of this opening. Was this the idol of the cult? God of geometry and nuclear explosions? Wavy lines snaked around the eyes and the big corner-mushrooms had spines on top like cacti. The whole thing was a little like a cross between a Hindu mandala and a Native American God's Eye. He'd once had a girlfriend who decorated her apartment with such things. For quite some time Vern studied it, remembering every detail for future reference. Then he noticed movement below and made sure his position was sufficiently concealed.

A line of people filed into the room, ten individuals cloaked in hooded robes of satiny gray. He looked around instinctively for the cameras. Was he on the set of a bad movie or what? As far as he could tell, five of the performers were women and most of them looked fairly young, mid-thirties at the oldest except for one elderly man. One of the females, he was reasonably sure, was Ashley. These were the cult members, or maybe just the priesthood, and he was apparently about to witness a ritual. Perhaps a black mass. No young virgins were present, so a sacrifice seemed unlikely. Somehow, he didn't find that particularly reassuring.

The robed figures took their places on the fiery eyes surrounding the spiraled circle, standing very erect and serious. Looking absurd. Vern suddenly felt as if he'd been zapped into a time warp, for he was looking upon supposedly civilized modern people in the grip of pure and ancient superstition, performing a rite as old and irrational as the rolling of bones and the reading of goat guts. But he'd encountered this before. As a student of human nature he liked to know lots of different kinds of people, which was one reason he valued Julian's friendship. So he had Satanist acquaintances who geeked cats and chickens, Catholic relatives who paled at the sight of communion-wafer crumbs spilling onto the maculate ground, and New Age friends who clutched and entreated their crystals. Same thing with these Stone Age characters he was spying on. He personally didn't buy into any of it. Wit and will were what he believed in, and they had not failed him yet.

One of the worshipers pulled back their hoods, and sure enough there was pretty Ashley, standing at about ten o'clock around the circle from where Vern was crouching. Three of the other females were also lookers, and the last one he would have boinked after three or four drinks. One of the males was a small but tough-looking black man, standing right at midnight. Vern's legs were cramping up but he dared not move, for if the man raised his eyes even a fraction he might well spot the intruder. A dreadful and peculiar thought squirmed into Vern's mind at that moment: *Are all these people dead?*

With one very clear voice they began chanting, but he couldn't make out what they were saying. Foreign-sounding words, maybe names of some kind. After he listened awhile he concluded they were repeating the same thing over again, the exact words or phrases a dozen or so times. Then the room changed.

The black circle seemed to sink down into the floor, spiraling into infinity below. Vern grabbed the railing as vertigo seized him, nearly robbing him of his already precarious footing. For the first time in his life he understood what people meant when they spoke of a bottomless pit. When he felt himself being drawn into the endless emptiness, he tore his gaze away with considerable effort, only managing to shake off the sensation of falling by rapidly blinking his eyes, then staring up toward the ceiling. The sight he saw there wasn't much better: ten glowing shapes hovered near the top of the room above the pit, their precise details obscured by their vivid golden auras. He received the distinct impression, however, that they were human bodies wrapped in crystalline shell and translucent flesh, ornately contoured but in-your-guts disturbing, reminding him more of Egyptian sarcophagi than anything else.

Looking down again, he watched as the flaming eyes in the floor blazed to life, engulfing their occupants in columns of purple light. More wonders met Vern's eyes.

He didn't believe what he saw.

9

White Velvet

Someone was banging on the wall of his slumber, a wall that was made of the bone of his skull.

Julian clawed his way back to semiconsciousness, slowly becoming aware that he was lying on his stomach on the floor in front of his painting, with the empty brandy bottle nestled against his chin. There was someone at the door, pounding the hell out of it and calling his name. It sounded like Vern. He struggled to his feet, staggered over to the door, and yanked it open, solely motivated by the desire to have the noise stop tormenting his hung-over brain. Through bleary, squinted eyes he verified the identity of his unwelcome visitor, then turned and got a good look at the big canvas on which he'd been agonizing a picture into completion. It made him do a double take. Apparently he'd done quite a bit of work on it before drinking himself into oblivion last night. Or rather the image had invaded more of the white surface. However you wanted to look at it. The mushroomlike projections looked inflamed and swollen.

He covered it before his friend had a chance to see the extent of his folly.

Vern said nothing until he'd looked in the fridge to assure himself there was no beer in there and resigned himself to a glass of water. He guzzled some from a not-so-clean snifter glass and exhaled loudly. His eyes hesitantly met Julian's blurry gaze as he spoke, and for the first time since the artist had known him those eyes shone with a glint of fear. "My friend, you've got a problem. A big weird one."

"I know." Julian's lips felt numb, were not completely responding to his will. "I've got the mother of all hangovers. Unless you're referring to yourself. You certainly qualify as one of my bigger, weirder problems."

He shook his head. "Come here and sit down. I'll fix you something for your bottled blues. Then I'll make some coffee. And then I've got something to tell you that'll blow your mind and turn your soul black."

Julian shrugged without enthusiasm, gave in to the absurdity of what Vern had just said, and seated himself at the kitchen table. "Couldn't I at least have some cream with my soul?"

Vern winked at him. "Good man. Keep your sense of humor. You're going to need it." On the counter Vern mixed tomato juice, pickle juice, one raw egg, two shots of Worcestershire sauce, and three shots of grenadine together in a glass. Then he placed it in front of Julian. This done, he set about making coffee.

"Vern, do you really expect me to drink this?" he said, grimacing at the concoction.

"Sure. It'll pep you right up. Then we'll pump some caffeine into you and you'll be able to bear the weight of the underworld one more day."

Julian sighed. "You're being even weirder than usual, man. What's with you today?"

Vern sat down at the table and lit a cigarette. "Sorry to be so mysterious. I've been up all night, but I feel wired to the max. I'm having a hard time collecting my thoughts. You see, I've got to say something to you that has never been said before. You've got to be ready for it. I mean, I don't even know what I think about it, even after what I've just been through." He stared at the dark fluid dripping into the glass coffeepot.

The man was making no sense at all, thought Julian. He sipped at Vern's remedy, then quickly put it down. Bad memories of last night with Ashley were starting to come back to him, knotting his stomach. It seemed he might actually have to vomit, though booze never affected him that way. "You look like you didn't have a very good time staying out all night."

"That's about right. Who's that guy you're always talking about who took a tour of hell?"

"Dante?"

"Right." Vern pointed at Julian. "I feel like him. God, there's some strange shit going down in this city. You'd never suspect it's there, but it is, uglier than sin." He got up, poured two cups of coffee, brought them back to the table, and reseated himself. "Where was I?"

"Something is uglier than sin."

"Yeah. Look. I'm not a very tactful guy, but I'll take a crack at it. I know you're not superstitious. You don't believe those things you paint exist, or so I've heard you say. But do you think that maybe, in some way, it's possible they could?"

Julian let out a groan, rubbing his aching head. "Man, it's too early in the morning for mind games."

"Hey, you're telling me it's early. You're lucky I waited for the sun to come up to wake you. I've been walking around the block for hours, waiting for dawn and watching to see if she comes back. You don't know what you've gotten yourself into. But this isn't a joke or a trick. Just answer the question. Please."

He tapped his fingers on the tabletop, frowning. "Watching to see if who comes back?"

"Just answer the question!" Vern demanded. He seemed unusually short-tempered this morning.

"All right! But you've got to be more specific."

"Okay." Holding out his hands and calming himself. "Okay. How do you feel about ghosts, the living dead, that sort of thing?"

Here was a question right out of the blue if he'd ever heard one. "Uh, well, I guess I'm intrigued by the idea of it, but I feel it can't happen. It's all fairy tale and folklore."

Nodding as he let out a stream of smoke, Vern said, "Yeah, but what if it's not? Can you get behind that idea at all?"

This was getting infuriating. "Vern, what the fuck are you driving at?"

"Okay, okay. Um, I looked into your ladyfriend's past a bit. What I've come up with is mucho bizarre, to say the least. Now, I don't know how or why, or what it means, but someone who looks a lot like your lover was murdered over ten years ago. Her name was Ashley Praetor, but she sometimes used the alias Ashley Herrin. *Herrin* is the German word for mistress, which this girl probably chose because she specialized in sexual domination."

"Looks like Ashley?" Humoring Vern would be easier

than arguing with him, Julian decided. Vern liked to argue and he didn't.

"That's right. She had her throat cut. The authorities showed up at the scene of the crime and were ready to ship the body to the morgue, but it vanished right out from under their noses. It was gone and it was never found."

He couldn't muster a laugh at his friend's words, but not because he didn't find them outlandish. It was just disappointing to find that Vern's wit was sicker than he'd thought it was. And crueler. Julian's mind was cloudy, his mood was low, and he didn't have the strength to deal with this nonsense.

"So she wasn't really dead."

Vern reached into an inner pocket of his jacket and pulled out an orange envelope, his expression very stern. He began spreading photocopies out on the table like he was dealing cards. A death certificate, a mug shot of a woman, and a photograph of a prostrate body.

"I couldn't get a copy of the police investigation report. I had to call in a lot of favors on this one and my department contacts were losing patience with me. This case is still an embarrassment for everyone involved."

Julian leaned forward and studied the mug shot first. Facing front and in profile, it was either Ashley or her dead ringer. Her expression was haughty and impish, as if she deserved to be able to do whatever she wanted and the world could go to hell. The name on the identification plate in front of her read PRAETOR, ASHLEY SONYA. The charge was prostitution. Her birth date was listed as 3-17-55, age 21. Date of arrest was 7-29-76.

Ashley had barely aged at all since the picture was taken.

"Now, I know women lie about their age," said Vern in an even tone, "but let's get real. Is the woman you've been seeing in her middle thirties?"

Next he read the death certificate. It said just what Vern had told him it did. Someone named Ashley Praetor had had her throat cut in 1979 and died from the wound. His hands were shaking, but he attributed it to all the brandy he'd drunk.

Finally he looked at the crime scene photo. If Vern had selected it, he'd picked the right one, for it showed the victim's face as plain as day. It was clearly Ashley in all her dimpled, angelic beauty, head turned to the right, eyes staring lifelessly into space. Her throat gaped like a huge and ragged open mouth. The slender fingers of her right hand seemed to be reaching out to touch something. Blood, her own blood, was spread so thickly beneath her that she seemed to be lying on a red carpet.

It was Ashley, but of course it couldn't be.

He looked up at Vern, his arms resting on the table. "Vern, if anything, you are more rational than me. Maybe not in your behavior, but in the way you analyze things. This woman is dead, unless she got up and walked away with no blood in her body. Ashley is alive. Or do you think I made her up?"

Vern shook his head in emphatic denial. "Oh, no, man. I know she's real. I followed her last night."

Julian had a feeling he didn't want to hear this. His stomach was flopping around inside of him, partly from the residue of the brandy and partly from the goriness of the photo on the table. And partly because the murdered woman looked so much like Ashley and had her name. He wished he would throw up, but he knew he wouldn't. He hated doing it too much.

"Okay, so you know she's real," Julian said. "She's not a ghost. So the woman in these pictures is not her."

"I didn't say that, but we can assume it for the moment if you like." Vern sipped his coffee.

"Let's." Julian ran his hand through his limp hair, scratching his grimy scalp for a few moments. It had been three days since he'd taken a shower, hadn't it? Have to do something about that. A question came to him and he hated to ask it, but he had to. "Did the woman in these pictures have any other aliases?"

"Yes, as a matter of fact." Vern sat back and furrowed his brows, recollecting. "Uh, Sonya Gray and Sophie Darrell."

A gasp burst from Julian's lips, as if he'd been punched in the guts. The guy at Pandemorgue had mistaken Ashley for someone named Sophie Darrell, was certain it was she. What else had he said? *That she hadn't aged in ten years.*

"What are you thinking?" he heard Vern ask from a distance.

"Huh?" He realized he was leaning onto the table, so he sat up and composed himself. "I'm thinking that you're obsessed with this delusion and you've gone off the deep end."

No offense registered on his friend's coarse face, just rallied patience. Julian knew what he was waiting for.

"All right. You say you followed her last night. What did you see?"

Vern slurped down the last of his coffee, crushed out his cigarette, and lit another. "I waited across the street for her to leave here. It looked like she was crying when she came out. Anyway, she led me into that run-down industrial zone west of here. There's some kind of big cathedrallike building located pretty far into it, a real odd-looking place. It's got a dome in the center and ten wings extending from it. No windows. Well, that's where she went. She went in through one of the side doors, just took out a key and opened it. I climbed a nearby tree and got in through a vent on the roof. Inside there's a central chapel with a design painted on the floor, a big black spiral surrounded by ten purple eyes with, like, tongues of flame flaring from them. I saw a ritual carried out there."

Though he was listening intently, Julian had no idea how to deal with this information. Did it mean she was living with squatters in the midst of the dead factories falling to ruin out that way? It was a worse neighborhood than his own.

"Ten gray-robed people came into this room as I watched," Vern continued, increasing excitement saturating his voice. "There were five men and five women. Ashley was one of them. They took their places on the purple eyes and began chanting real weird shit, foreign names or phrases. Then the special effects started. First the black spiral fell through the floor clear to China and beyond. I didn't like looking at that much, so I looked up. There were things hanging in the air, glowing shapes, like half-melted wax figures or something. They weren't all that pleasant to look at, either, so I looked down again."

At this point he paused and briefly laid his face in his hands, drew his fingers down his cheeks. Then he took a deep breath and resumed with some effort. "What I saw scared the shit out of me. These people, they changed right before my eyes. Purple light rose from the eyes under their feet and changed them. Each one became something different, mostly monstrous things. Ashley, your Ashley, had lost all her hair and it looked like her whole face and head were covered with white velvet. Like a white rabbit but without the ears. Another was red and scaly, one had a blue shell, and one had what looked like a naked skull of brown bone with a bunch of orange horns sticking out of it. I mean, words can't describe them. At least I can't. These freaks were standing where people used to be. Oh, and they all had one thing in common, at least the ones I could see. Their eyes had turned dark purple, with no whites at all."

The last few lines were all that kept Julian from laughing this whole story off, but that's all it took. He remembered that first night in the Quarry, Ashley confronting the leader of the Crucifixers, a fleeting instant when her eyes had looked stained with a purple so dark, they seemed almost black. Just the way Vern described. He wanted to plead with Vern to take it back, to deny it. This was the one thing Julian couldn't do, however, for that would be admitting there could be the slightest shred of truth to the tale.

"It really got to me, I don't mind telling you," Vern was saying, a little boastful now. "I mean, it looked so real, but it only took me a few seconds to figure out that it was all clever illusion. Projections, holograms, masks, that sort of thing. Probably meant to enhance the beliefs of the cultists. It looked goddamn convincing, though. The scaled skin, the shell—it seemed to breathe. It was incredible. Even after I knew what it was, it still freaked me out, so I didn't look at it long. When I'd had enough I left. They were so intent on their trippy mass that they didn't hear me sneak out a side door."

His account complete now, Vern leaned back in his

chair with his hands behind his head, staring fiercely at Julian. Words were like alien things to Julian in that moment, but a few finally came to him.

"Okay. So it's like you say." There was a strain in his voice he'd never heard there before. Something like the uprooting of deep denial. "It was all a hoax. Just fakery."

He pressed a finger down on the photo of the dead woman. "So that's what this is too. A hoax, a trick. Someone playing with people's heads. With your head."

"Fine. Let's say that." Vern waved his hands impatiently. "That's most likely all that's going on. But are you afraid to explore the other possibility? Like, I've been watching your face and I can tell that you know more than you're saying. There are things about Ashley that are making you wonder. I've scored points off you that you aren't giving me credit for. Let's talk about those."

Julian tasted his coffee, found it tepid, and got up to pour it into the sink. "This isn't some kind of game, Vern. We're talking about a very disturbed woman here. Besides, I don't want to discuss it anymore. I feel nauseous."

"You mean nauseated. *Nauseous* means you cause disgust. *Nauseated* means you feel disgusted."

"I don't feel disgusted!" The rage came out of nowhere as he whirled around. "I'm just hung over from drinking a whole bottle of brandy all by myself."

Vern's tone switched to one of sympathy, conciliation. Deception. "If you don't want to talk about it I don't mind. Just sit down and let me tell you what else I've learned."

There was more? Julian sat down, pulled a Camel out of the pack in his shirt pocket, stuck it in his mouth, and ignited a match from the box on the table. He put flame to cigarette with an unsteady hand. "Go ahead."

"You see, you really should be sure, because if it's the same Ashley, then she comes with quite a history." Vern pointed at the mug shot. "This one was a kinked-out hooker when she was alive, specializing in the leather, whips, and chains scene. Sometimes she'd be torturer, other times victim. She got free of it and turned coke dealer, but she got rubbed out for her troubles. Let's say that somehow she survived the attempt on her life and she's the same person you've been seeing. Has she told you any of this? Don't you think you have a right to know this about her? And what if she's still turning tricks? Any idea about the infection rates among hookers?"

His brain had absorbed enough already. Too much. It couldn't take any more. "Please go away, Vern."

No chance. The man had shifted into relentless mode, leaning forward, glaring wide eyed at him, pointing with his finger, and puffing furiously on his cigarette. "Can you love someone like that? To say the least, she's no good for you, Julian. You've had a brush with insanity and you should leave it at that. Forget about her."

"That's easy for you to say." He was remembering the smell of her, the feel of her, the sound of her voice as she echoed his innermost longings. Moments came back to him when he'd sensed the wise, wounded, confused soul inside of her and been drawn to it. "You haven't looked into her eyes."

"I've told you what's in those eyes, man. Blackness. She's weird and fucked up. Inhuman." Vern's snarling smile had emerged once again.

He vaguely shook his head. "I don't know what human

is anymore, but I know her. She can't be what you say she is. Whatever she's into, she wants to get away from it. I'm sure of that."

"Hey, I'm just looking out for you." He sat back, adopted a mellow smile, and spoke in a calm voice. Now Vern was coming on like a big brother, instead of a sadistic psychiatrist. A long ash projected precariously from his cigarette, which he studied intently. "I mean, who knows what's really going on here? We live in truly strange times. But you know me: I'm a bloodhound when it comes to danger, and this reeks to high heaven with bad vibes. Deadly ones. I'm only telling you this as your friend."

"I know that." *And you're probably digging it to no end, hoping it will turn out to be just what it looks like.* Vern Doyle, danger junkie, would then have found the ultimate peril, tangling with a cult of the living dead. "I'll think over what you've said, but I've got to have that address, Vern. I probably won't do anything with it, but having it will make me feel better. You can understand that, can't you?"

Vern's gaze darted over his face in a patronizing search pattern. "Nope, sorry. I'm afraid I can't do that. It's for your own good. I've seen a lot more dark, heavy shit in this world than you have, and this is like the very darkest. I can't explain it, but I feel a responsibility to keep you as far away from it as I can. Stay out of it, Julian."

Interesting choice of words, that last line. Evidently the man wanted this mystery all to himself. Alone would he take on these urban demons, sharing the thrill and glory with none. If he'd had the emotional strength, Julian would have been furious at Vern for making these decisions about his life for him, but right now he was just tired. "All right. Have it your way. Maybe you're right after all. Now, if you'll excuse me, I think I'll sleep a few hours. Or days."

"Right. Good idea." He put out the cigarette he was smoking and stood up. "I guess I'll go down to the shop and see how things are going there. Have to make a living, you know."

At the door Vern hesitated. "Oh, yeah. There's one more thing. You know that Bible reference in the notes? I looked it up. It goes: 'For he that is dead is freed from sin.' "

It figured. Death and sin seemed to be Ashley's specialties. "Uh, thanks, man. See you later."

When he was gone, Julian lay facedown on the bed and dropped rapidly out of consciousness. His sleep was haunted by the image taking shape on his canvas, struggling to form itself from shadow and light, urging its contours and texture out of deepest darkness and purest essence. For the first time he received the impression that there were things hovering about on the far side of the configuration, hazy and hideous blights of being.

They seemed to be waiting to come through.

10

Late-Night Thriller

Of course, Vern couldn't leave it alone.

He had a contact in the Hall of Records by the name of Tess Gorman, whom he'd met during his short-lived days as a private investigator. Her husband had hired him to find out if she was remaining a faithful little wife or messing around on the side in a sleazy affair, and together she and Vern ended up making the man's unfounded fears come true. She was still married, and they still indulged in the occasional dalliance. Vern liked to keep in touch with old friends.

One phone call to Tess informed him that the aging structure at 2160 Avernus Avenue had been purchased in 1926 by someone named Sylvio Desiderio in the name of a religious sect called the Paracletes of Earthly Transfiguration. It had originally been constructed as a Masonic temple in 1841, then it was sold to the Mormons in 1892. When all the heavy industry moved into the neighborhood after the century turned, the Latter-day Saints sold the place to one Herschel Gold, who used the premises as a storage facility until the present owners took possession of it.

Factory noise, air pollution, and urban decay didn't seem to bother them at all.

Vern had used the pay phone in the Quarry, going there on the off chance that another clue might present itself. This was where it had all begun, after all. He'd been to the office to work and he'd been home to sleep, but he was anxious to pick up the trail again. When he hung up and turned to the bar, he saw that matters were already getting interesting. She wore a leather fedora, big sunglasses, white sneakers, and a black raincoat, but he was pretty sure that the brunette seated there was one of the comely female cultists. Somewhere along the line he'd picked up a tail, probably coming out of Julian's building, and she was damned good at it. He hadn't suspected anything at all, until now. Unless, of course, this watering hole just naturally attracted the thirsty dead. One glance out the plate-glass window assured him that the sun was still up; apparently they didn't come out only at night.

That he would approach her was not in doubt, for the prospect of this confrontation was irresistible. To talk to one of these spellbound loonies, mess with her head, show her what bad really meant, would be too much fun to pass up. But he had to consider what might be going on. No one had spotted him leaving the cathedral, he was certain, for all those deep purple eyes had stayed fixed on the dazzling shapes floating above them, their idols or whatever. Someone may have heard something, however, and afterward searched the place from top to bottom, in which case they would have found the open vent and his footprints all over the dusty attic. They would know their holy hideout had been invaded. Not much thought would be needed to link that event with Ashley's wanderings in the outer world, so spies would be dispatched to see what she had stirred up, whose unwanted attention she had drawn. And they had found *him*.

There was another angle to look at, though, the one Julian refused to. It made him wonder how someone with so much imagination could have so little imagination. Vern had seen people on the streets who looked worse than dead but were still walking around. Was it so much more farfetched to think that maybe a few remarkable individuals wrestled with their deaths and won? Out of stubbornness, out of meanness, out of sheer will—who could say? Maybe it happened. So, was his stalker dead or undead? Living psychotic or enslaved zombie? Was she live or was she memento mori?

He slid onto the stool next to her, lighting a cigarette. She pretended to take no notice as she sipped her clear lime-slice-accessoried drink.

"It sure is dead in here," he said.

No response.

"You know, you're about the prettiest little tail I've ever had. Or would it be more accurate to call you a shadow?"

Finally she looked at him, utterly expressionless. "Are you talking to me?" Her face was round, girlish, and extremely pale, though not inhumanly so. Something like a pneumonia victim's. He found it attractive on her, and he liked her voice, gravelly but faint. Still, it would be easier to believe that she had once been a corpse than Ashley. Maybe this little black-haired cutie had been dead longer, lost her lust for life.

Grinning, he leaned close to her, just to emphasize that her feminine charms and zombie blankness did not intimidate him. "You bet I am, sweet-cakes. So tell me. Are you on a search-and-destroy mission, or are you just doing a bit of reconnaissance for God?"

Admitting that he was the intruder they were after maybe wasn't the smartest thing to do, but he refused to be afraid of these fanatics. Without a word from her frosty lips or so much as a wrinkle in her pallid features, she turned away to the street outside. Conspicuously unmoved, Vern would have called it.

"Okay. Just explain one thing to me. What the fuck is a paraclete?"

The woman got up and strode gracelessly out of the bar as if he'd just reminded her that she was late for an appointment. Vern regarded the bartender, a big brute of a man. "If you're not careful, man, this place could become known as a spook bar."

The big man blinked at him. "I almost never get niggers in here. Spics, yeah. This is the edge of the barrio, after all. But not coons."

He shook his head at such numbskullery.

"What can I get you?" asked the bartender.

A gun that shoots ghosts, he felt like saying. "Nothing. Thanks." After a discreet interval of waiting, approximately thirty seconds in length, he stood and followed after the woman, the mouse once more becoming the cat.

Maybe a cat who has just taken the bait in a trap, he warned himself.

It was dusk when Julian awoke, and the red light streaming into the loft reminded him of coagulating blood. He was famished but still mildly nauseated, so eating didn't seem to be an option yet. His clothes were sour with sweat and his body was positively ripe, but he didn't care. An oozing mire of self-pity beckoned to him to come and wallow and he almost did. Then his painting called to him. Not *his* painting; *the* painting. Something so alien and incongruous could not be his. But it was all he had. The shredded remnants of a dream—a wet dream, judging by the stickiness in his pants—combined with the ruddy rays of the sunset flashed the image back into his mind with neon brightness. Weak muscles raised him to his feet, moved him to the canvas, and reluctantly complied as he resumed his work.

This time it wasn't a totally enthralling effort, just an anxiousness to finish and be done with it. This will-sapping thing was in his head and he had to let it out before he could have any peace. But he knew that even then there would be no peace for him. He reinforced a serpentine line of purple. Loneliness would flood back in on him, even worse than before since he now knew just how happy he could feel. For so long he'd been sleep-walking through life. Now a chasm had opened up inside him, into which Ashley had poured her rousing, sense-devouring presence, filling it to the brim. Without her it would become a bleak desolation within him. Completing the painting would remove an annoyance. Losing Ashley would maim him with a merciless ache.

As he shifted his stance the drying semen in the crotch of his jeans pulled on some hairs, causing him minor pain. *Christ,* he thought. He hadn't had a nocturnal emission in over ten years. He'd probably had an erotic nightmare starring Ashley. Even in his sleep she came to him. Long-distance orgasm. Radar rape. What bound them together remained unaffected by time or space, was thicker than blood and immune to death. Maybe. Look at him. His life was deteriorating, but his heart had been transmuted from lead into gold, was driving him in unthought-of directions. He wasn't just painting the strange, dark, wild side. Now he was living it.

When he'd exhausted this fit of inspiration, two hours had gone by. It still wasn't quite finished, he saw as he threw down his dirty brush and stood back to see what he'd created. Everything but the center was done. In the peripheral areas of the canvas the cloudy disaster area of his original vision glowed redly among its broken columns and fallen arches, a totally discarded area of the composition. The imposing vision blazed within it and overlapped like a growing cancer. A white Maltese cross capped with four mushroom shapes projecting black spines spread over a diamond-shaped structure filled with wavy purple lines. Like snakes or lightning. Four bizarre gray forms bloomed diagonally from the diamond, something like mushroom clouds sprouting mushroom clouds. But he couldn't divine what lay at its core, a blank area roughly square in outline. Where this configuration had come from he still didn't know, for it seemed to relate to nothing he'd ever known and reflected almost none of his style. Ashley had bred this creation in him, sown the image in the field of his mind. It was not beautiful, but it *was* powerful and troubling.

Adrift in thought, he lumbered into the kitchen to see if there was any coffee left. There was, but it had corrupted into undrinkable sludge. The photographs still lay scattered on the table. He stared at them. Alive or dead, she had drawn something completely new and inexplicable out of him, at the same time saving him from his own living death. Whatever she was, wherever she was from, he had to find her again. An abysmal existence threatened him if he didn't.

Grabbing his jacket, he went down to the cold, dark streets and headed for the industrial wasteland to the west, driven by ancient hungers both ordinary and rare.

Vern shadowed the slight form of the woman for nearly two hours, until well after the sun went down. She didn't seem to have any particular destination, so he figured he'd unnerved her by turning the tables on her. When darkness fell, however, her aimless wandering slowed into a more purposeful pattern leading him onto her turf. The night gave her confidence, unsurprisingly. On the edge of her desolate, decaying neighborhood she walked into a dead-end alley and didn't come out. When he entered and explored it he found neither hide nor hair of her.

But that didn't mean she wasn't there, of course.

He wasn't shaken up, but this development did put him on his guard. If he *was* dealing with ghouls and goblins it would probably be a good idea to arm himself beforehand. Whether or not a roving cadaver could be killed, damaged, or at the very least remember what it was like to feel pain and have pieces of its body blasted away, he had no way of knowing. However, it seemed that now that night had come, the woman had decided to lure him back to the cathedral, no doubt with the idea of perpetrating extreme nastiness upon his person, aided by the rest of the gang. Maybe their power was greatest when darkness had fallen, for in their mutant eyes even he must be a creature of the light. Well, if they wanted to play rough, that was fine by him.

But he wasn't going to bite just yet.

He backtracked out of the area to a pay phone he'd passed, called for a taxi, and waited. She didn't reappear in the twenty minutes it took for a cab to pull up with its fat, bald, unhappy-looking driver.

"Where ya going, buddy?" snapped the man when Vern slithered into the backseat.

"301 Fremont. What took you so long?"

"Hey, you're way out here in no-man's-land. A few cabbies have gotten their lights shot out down here over the years. You're lucky anybody showed up at all."

Vern wondered if the guy meant their headlights or their life-light, and decided it wasn't worth asking about. They didn't speak further on the way to his offices. When they arrived he added a two-dollar tip to the fare and handed the bills over the front seat.

"Tell me something, man. Do you believe in life after death?"

The hack driver glanced at him with the slightest sneer as he took the money. "Yeah, sure. Ghosts and angels, maybe."

He found this answer sublime, for he might be playing with ghosts who looked like angels. Fallen ones, anyway.

"Thanks for the input, pal. Later."

The single-story office building housing Doyle and Hunt Security Systems was modern and polished on the outside, austere and immaculate within. Lots of glass, chrome, and dark marble. He'd bought out Simon Hunt's half of the business five years previously, but like Scrooge had left his partner's name on the sign and the stationery. The sound of it pleased him and he believed it helped bring in clients. Vern thought of himself as a hunter: of weak points where a residence or place of commerce could be unlawfully entered, of women lovely, soft, and yielding—and maybe, just maybe, on this night, of dead creatures creeping around among the living.

In the storeroom at the back of the building he opened a carton full of mothballs, dug through the small aromatic disks to the bottom, and pulled out a box of green metal. Inside was a nine-millimeter semiautomatic pistol with five clips of hollow-point bullets and a leather shoulder-holster. He promptly armed himself with the weapon and ammunition, then proceeded out of the building. The gun was unregistered, reserved for special purposes, which was why he kept it at work and not at home. If it should ever be discovered by the authorities, he could claim it belonged to one of his employees, let them take the fall. Lord knew many of them had police records, while his history with the law was pristine. Aside from a few juvenile offenses, that was. Vern had used the gun only once before, to settle a score with a romantic rival who'd hired four thugs to beat the shit out of him in the parking lot of a bar one night. Needless to say, the bastard now competed with no one for nothing anymore and Vern had gotten the woman all to himself. It was a pity their relationship had lasted only five months after that.

She was standing across the street just inside an alleyway when he came out the front door. Her hat, hair, coat, and glasses blended in with the black city night so that her ashen face seemed eyeless and the white skin of her lower legs disembodied in the light of a streetlamp. *Now, that is really fucking weird,* he said to himself. There was no way she could have pursued him on foot, but what had she used for wheels? Well, it was said that spirits could walk through walls and fly through the air, so there was no point in worrying about it. The game was on again.

His petite quarry walked and he followed, back toward the deserted boulevards. Her slow, clumsy gait had a bit more bounce to it, as if she were counting on him to stalk her now, even enjoying it. Vern's nerves were not quite as steady as when this thing had begun, for he had just been given pretty clear evidence that this woman was not completely normal. She'd performed a feat that some would have called impossible. Unnatural. Though he wasn't real learned on the subject, he knew that his distant ancestors had been tiny, furry animals who foraged for food during the day and got preyed upon by terrors in the night. Vern was experiencing some of that basic ancestral fear now, of the hell that night became when your devourers crawled from their nests, burrows, and caves. Feeling scared pissed him off, made him hate the source of his fright. He was amply armed and still highly motivated, however. There was no way he was going to blink first.

It was quite a distance back to her cathedral lair, and he had no intention of letting her lead him all the way there anyway, so he started thinking about making the first move. His edginess added to his sense of urgency about having it out with the bitch one on one before they got too close. Her fellow cultists might be lying in wait in the streets somewhere, and he didn't want to have to deal with that just yet. There would be plenty of time to go in and clean the place out later. Do it right. He wasn't quite clear on what he was going to do to this frail-looking wench with her bag of tricks when he got hold of her, but surely the laws of civilized humanity didn't apply to what she was. She was his for the taking.

She seemed oblivious to the people they passed on the sidewalk, though a few of them gave her curious glances. Vern slowed his pace so as not to make his pursuit of her too obvious. Traffic on the street was light. The faces he saw in the cars going by seemed remarkably complacent to him, unsuspecting of the kind of dark things he now knew dwelled in the world. In this city. All such complacency had been shaken out of *him*. He'd never look at anything the same way again.

All this walking was beginning to tire him some. Not so with her, of course. No. She moved as if she could keep going until doomsday and beyond. This was another reason to hasten his moment of attack. His mortal strength was waning while hers perhaps increased as midnight approached. Good fortune smiled on him as they progressed into a region of the city he knew particularly well, having lived in this vicinity for two years a decade ago. When she turned up a main avenue he ducked down a back street at a run. If he calculated his speed properly he would come out of an alley right on top of her.

Due to further good luck, and the dark lady's sluggish stride, he got it almost exactly right. Vern lunged out of the alley just slightly ahead of her, managing to startle her before she could react. He grabbed her arm with his left hand and with his right unholstered the gun to press it against her temple. A quick scan of the street revealed no potential witnesses. Then he dragged her deep into the shadows of the alley.

She stumbled in his clutches and dropped on one knee, her sunglasses flying. He roughly yanked her to her feet.

"Okay, bitch. Let's get down to it. Those of us with

body heat don't take kindly to getting stalked by cold fuckers like you." At precisely what point had he decided she really was a refugee from the grave? He couldn't say. "I'd be very interested to see if you blow apart like real flesh and blood. Should I pull the trigger and find out?"

Her expression remained dull, but he saw her eyes start to change and slammed her hard against the brick wall. "You stop that now or I *will* fire! I've killed people who were alive, so I have no qualms at all about shooting something like you to pieces."

Though they retained smoky purplish cataracts, her eyes darkened no further.

"That's good," he said, heaving his breath into her nostrils and slack mouth. "That's very good. You've shown me you can cooperate. All right. Now what's your name?" His adrenaline was really flowing now and the wildness was starting to come over him, telling him he could do almost anything in the next few minutes.

"Bethany Mulhare," she said in a whisper he could barely hear. Her body was not rigid with fear the way a regular female's would be. It just hung half limp in his grip like a rag doll. This only inflamed his ecstatic rage.

"Bethany, huh? Well, Bethany, I'll bet you died young, probably violently. That's part of the pattern, isn't it?"

She squirmed then, still without much effort. It was enough to trigger his fury and lust. He threw his weight against her, crushing her against the wall, then ripped open her raincoat. Buttons clattered to the pavement. Looking down, he was pleased to see that she was wearing a faded blue denim skirt. That made matters much easier for him.

"Ever been fucked by a live man?" he taunted her.

"Huh, cunt? Well, you're gonna get it now. I'm gonna drill ya and thrill ya."

Bethany didn't resist as he pulled up her skirt and tore away her panties, which were plain white cotton. Not much fashion sense there, he mused. He made sure everything looked normal down there and it did, very pale but beautiful in fact. His erection was long and hard as bone when he exposed it and rammed it into her as cruelly as he could, not waiting for her to lubricate or dilate. She didn't make a sound as he shoved himself far inside of her and began pounding away at her delicate tissues with a harsh rhythm.

Vern soon noticed things getting a little bizarre in his immediate surroundings. Her smell had been faint, like ashes and chalk, but he now caught a whiff of raw meat from her, like gutted innards starting to decay. Perhaps this animal act was awakening some memory in her cells of a time when they were bursting with life. He kissed her clammy, flaccid lips and tasted rotting flowers. His wrath, feeding on her subhumanly total submission, swelled further and he thrust into her even more savagely, wanting to impale her and split her open from vagina to sternum, batter her to pulp. One moment she felt like a complete body of warm blood-fed flesh; in the next she seemed to be only a shroud of parchment and bones crumpling and rattling in his arms. And for just an instant he thought she was something else, a creature with a wasp-waisted body and a batlike head, covered with silky black fur. Then the ground dropped out from beneath them.

They did not fall, just remained suspended in space above the hole. Vern believed he understood much then. This was the same pit he'd seen open up within the circle of worshipers in the cathedral, only smaller. Doorway to the hereafter, portal to hell, whatever it was it explained how this dead bitch he was fucking got from one place to another so quickly. It was also very likely how Ashley's corpse had absconded from the scene of her murder to be reborn elsewhere. He had doubted the evidence of his senses before this, but no longer. Everything he'd seen was real.

There was no point in scolding her for this horrifying manifestation; he had a feeling she couldn't help it. He was stressing her out pretty good, so she was bound to disturb reality somewhat around herself. In spite of the way his brain insisted on interpreting the infernal miracle, he could feel that it wasn't just below him but really gaped in every direction. He could see it out of the corner of his eye. If he stared down at the void too long, however, he knew he'd tumble into it, first his mind, then his soul, then his corporeal mass. It was not a sight meant for living eyes. So he concentrated on boring into Bethany with punishing force, finally working up enough friction against her intermittently substantial form to climax. His seed jetted into her barren interior, then he withdrew from her and jumped back, zipping himself up as he watched her collapse to the ground. The black pit faded before his eyes, like a puddle rapidly evaporating.

"Are we clear on things now, bitch?" he spat at her, heaving with exertion. "You stop following me or I'll hurt you even worse next time. Got it?"

She lay slumped against the wall, as motionless as a scarecrow.

"Answer me!"

"Yes." She gasped. "I won't follow."

"And the same goes for the rest of your clan. Keep away from me."

Bethany gave a convulsive nod in response.

"Good. Then we have an understanding. Thanks for the thrills, doll. You're the living end." He left her there, emerged from the alley, and started walking toward Julian's place. The need to share this experience with someone was like a full bladder inside of him, and Julian was the only one who could even begin to understand.

His head ached as he loped along, and he felt as if his vision was obscured, though the night was clear around him. Something *behind* his eyes was blocking his sight. An image, something like mushrooms encrusting a diamond with a cross on top of it. He recognized it as soon as it came into focus in his thoughts. It was the shrine in the chapel at the cathedral, the big stone sculpture. Now it had popped into his head shortly after he'd fucked one of the lady cultists. Vern was more than a little suspicious of this coincidence, but he forgot about it when the image faded a few seconds later.

On the way to Julian's, he had a twinge of regret. He wished he'd made Bethany go down on him, because then he could say that he'd been given death's head.

11

Ashley in Weirderland

What had he become and what was he doing? Julian asked himself this question as he walked.

In essence, when he looked back on the past three days or so he'd been fasting, starving himself in some kind of unconscious purification ritual. Preparing for he knew not what. Maybe this, whatever this was. The stale crackers, beer, and brandy didn't count. He also hadn't bathed. What did that mean? Clean out the inner man, but leave a layer of impurities on the outside. Like a mud-daubed savage. Or maybe he'd just suffered a lapse in personal habits caused by recent heavy distractions.

As for what he was doing, he was wandering aimlessly through a labyrinth of derelict factories and related disintegrating structures. If he thought about it for long, he'd probably admit that he was lost. He knew it was insanity to venture alone and unarmed into this urban wilderness, for there was no telling what sort of ruthless lowlifes lurked here. It was a favorite haunt of the Crucifixers, he was aware. As additional proof of his recklessness, he had no guarantee that he'd recognize the building Vern had described to him if he saw it, or even that it existed. His so-called friend might have dreamed the whole story up as a grandiose prank after learning of the curious circumstances surrounding Ashley's personal history. Certain details refuted this theory, but Julian was trying very hard to stick to the most rational interpretation of the facts.

Except when it came to what he felt. Facts be damned then. A woman wasn't just a fact. She wasn't a single one thing, but a myriad of memories, moods, moments, sensations, sounds, sights. Smells. Every time she moved she became someone else, a different face, another body. All this was even more true with Ashley. If she did know what it was like to die, then the thing she'd been uniquely unchained from was the burden of life. That was the supreme elegance he saw in her, perhaps. The living cling to life so hard that they forget to live it. She'd said something to that effect, hadn't she? Being alive was what she did, even if she failed to do it functionally all the time. Even that unnerving unpredictability of hers he found endearing. The outraged look on Anna's face after Ashley kissed her was a treasured memory to him now. Time had a way of turning shock and distaste into humor.

He rested in front of a big square structure that looked as if it was constructed entirely of intertwining pipes of various sizes, leaning on a guardrail. The sky above was black and full of diamonds. The skull of the moon was behind a cloud. Why hadn't he made this quest in the daylight? It reminded him of the joke about the Polish astronauts who planned to land on the sun at night so they wouldn't burn up. Yes, it was true: Ashley was a flame and he was a moth to that flame. It was more than sexual desire, however. She ignited an inferno of creativity in him, not just in his work but in the way he spent his days as well. In some sense she was the cure to his near-debilitating dread of perishing, his fear and hatred of death. He used his art to cope with it, as an attempt to transcend its terminating scythe and achieve a kind of immortality. In the ruins of long-dead civilizations survived the works of the hands of sculptors and painters, their talent and imagination still shining out from thousands of years in the past. He received a small measure of serenity in the knowledge that such personal longevity was possible.

As he looked around, he could just about believe that he was standing in the remains of an extinct culture. Not a sign of life or spirit could be discerned in the grim ugly shells of masonry and metal surrounding him. He was here in their midst now because he was impatient to join with the woman he believed he loved, to tell her that all the pleasure she'd given him eclipsed all the pain. She was in his blood and under his skin, he wanted to tell her. Her touch was the purest and most natural drug he'd ever known and the sight of her lithe, compact body in all its naked whiteness was the Holy Grail to him, filled with nectar for his own flesh. The little laugh she let out when she felt him coming inside of her was a siren song that overrode all his reason.

So he stood and began shambling through the maze of dark hulks once more, seeking out the beautiful, womanly artwork of flesh, charm, and fury hiding somewhere in its depths.

The pursuit and the rape had aroused his appetite considerably, so Vern stopped off at a taco stand that kept late hours to buy three burritos and a Coke. He munched these on his way to Julian's and felt very good about himself. How many people could say they'd stared a night-born beastie right in the eyes and beat it? Not many. Maybe no one.

The lights in the loft were dark when he checked them from the street, which told him nothing. He'd known Julian to sleep all day and paint from dusk to dawn, but the boy was quirky and sometimes obeyed normal rules of behavior. When he went up the stairs and pounded on the door there was no answer, however. For some reason little Julian was out on the town.

Vern set his food down on the hallway floor, fished out a tool from a coat pocket, and picked the lock in no time at all. Julian would be pissed, but he was too exhausted and overflowing with news to go home to his own place. He would just wait around here, finish his breakfast, and maybe catch a few z's until his friend returned. Then they'd talk.

He entered, nibbling away at his third burrito. The loft was badly in need of dusting and vacuuming, he saw when he flicked on the lights. When Julian's muse possessed him, he became oblivious to all else. Vern wondered if that muse was now exclusively Ashley. No, the man did seem to have an iron in the furnace, for there was a big canvas behind the wooden screen Julian used to cover his unfinished paintings. He wiped some sauce from his chin and peeked around the barrier.

What met his eyes almost knocked him off his feet and he dropped his burrito—*splat!*—on the floor. Julian was doing a portrait of the weird symbol from the cathedral, an object he couldn't ever have seen! He'd forgotten to mention that part of the adventure to the loverboy, the details about the god that the paracletes worshiped. Ah, but pretty Ashley could have told him about it, described it or drawn it for him. But why? What purpose did this image in oils serve?

It was incomplete, Vern noticed. The very center had not been filled in yet. Had Ashley intentionally omitted telling Julian what that part looked like? Was she setting some kind of trap for his creative soul? Dead things were no doubt prone to play strange games. If the cultists worshiped this image, and the cultists had the ability to come back to life after dying and take shortcuts through solid matter, then it must have power. Maybe Ashley had started to share that power with Julian, then suddenly changed her mind. Well, he could fix that. He knew what lay at the heart of the painting.

Vern sat down at the kitchen table and contemplated doing his friend a big favor.

He was just about dead on his feet by the time it happened, but Julian still couldn't believe he'd finally found the place. It looked exactly the way Vern had said it did, a hulking mound of Gothic masonry like the thick hub and short spokes of a giant rimless wheel. And there was the tree Vern had climbed! His goal beckoned, so with a fresh burst of vigor, he ran the remaining yards to the building.

The elation he felt was soon somewhat dashed, however, for though he stood knocking at the door for fifteen minutes, stretching into twenty, then thirty, going from one entrance to another, increasing the intensity of his pounding and calling out Ashley's name in a near shriek, he got no answer. If there was anyone inside they were studiously ignoring him.

Taking a break from his assault on the keep, fighting off a tide of frustration and despair, he saw someone walking down the street toward him. It was a woman in a hat and raincoat, dark, so she wasn't Ashley, moving stiffly and slowly. He stood his ground as she approached, and watched her go right by him without acknowledging his presence. She was attractive but unhealthily pale, and she looked like just about the most defeated, demoralized person he'd ever laid eyes on. So transfixed was he by the sight of this wraithlike waif as she drew forth a key and opened one of the doors, that he almost forgot to rush in and hold it open before she sealed him out again. As he grabbed the door, she glanced at him, weary pain filling her eyes, but offered no resistance at all.

She vanished into the interior of the building and he closed the door behind him. The front hall he was standing in consisted of bare gray stone walls and nothing else. He would be in total darkness if not for a faint light source somewhere down the narrow corridor in front of him. This place smelled like an old cellar, though dry, and it seemed to be unheated. Now suddenly he was afraid to shout Ashley's name, for he was in the domain of strangers, invading their turf. They could kill him and maybe get away with it, catching him in the act of unlawful entry. His fears were unfounded, however, for Ashley soon appeared in the passage bearing a kerosene lamp. Her face looked puzzled and annoyed as she came toward him.

"You must be a madman," she said without humor or warmth.

Her rejecting tone disheartened him a bit, but he gambled that she was just still upset. He didn't try to touch her, though. That much rejection might have made him turn back. Just to see her again was enough for now. She had nothing on her feet, her hair bordered on disarray, and she wore only a long brown skirt with a white blouse. The blouse was spotted with a few small, faint stains. No makeup. Though she wasn't looking her best, he still found her to be a most welcome vision.

"If I am, then you made me that way, Bittersweet." This he said with a smile.

"You're an idiot, Julian. Get out of here, now. You're not allowed to be here."

He took a cautious step toward her. "Why? Because it's hallowed ground or something? Am I too unclean to stand on it? Come on, Ashley. Are you really that much of a brainwashed believer?"

She turned away, annoyed, and bit on a knuckle. "I don't know what I believe anymore. There's no way I can know. I thought I could get away from this place, but I can't. And now I'm afraid I've done something terrible, worse than any of the other things I've done. I stupidly revealed too much of myself to an outsider. Now I'm in trouble, and you probably are too."

Unable to help himself, he tried to put his hands on her shoulders, but she pulled away. "What could possibly be so terrible, babe? Nobody can control you unless you let them. Why don't you tell me what the fuck is going on? What is this place?"

With a nervous shrug she looked back at him. "It's worth a try, I guess. I can't think of what else to do. We can try and sort this out with the masters, but I don't see how we can. Follow me."

His face had grown hot when she said the word *masters*. Who were these tyrannical bastards with such an overblown sense of themselves that they felt they could lord it over others, set themselves up as petty gods? And how could she submit herself to such maniacs? He held his tongue as he followed her down the shadowy passage to a dismal, claustrophobic sitting room, lit by a single oil lamp on a small table. The source of light he'd seen earlier, obviously. The gaudy red chairs there looked plush but proved uncomfortable. She set her lamp down on another table and sat in the torture device across from the one he had chosen, well out of reach of his touch.

"Who furnished this place?" he said, wanting to break the thick tension. "The Marquis de Sade?"

Rotting tapestries hung on the stone walls, depicting medieval scenes of dragonslaying and pitched battles. A threadbare Persian rug of red and gold covered the floor. Nobody seemed to have dusted the room in decades.

"Please try to be serious, Julian." Ashley was frowning with worry.

"I'll try, but it's not easy. I mean, here we are sitting in Castle Dracula with huge monuments to capitalist excess all around outside, while just miles away it's all bright lights and big city. The whole thing's just a bit too Halloween to take seriously."

She stared at him severely for a few seconds. "You're a lot farther away from civilization than you think. Just let me try to explain it to you." Her eyes focused inward. "I hardly know how to begin this. I guess I should just tell you the whole story. Or the *hole* story is maybe more like it." She leaned back and exhaled a harsh laugh. "My hole and the hole of my fucking masters.

"Uh, I blossomed sexually at a very young age, you won't be surprised to hear, and I quickly grew devious about it." Her voice was uncertain as she began, laced with unease at letting out so much intimate detail. "I guess I was a little mentally precocious as well. I realized that when you've got something that others need and you're willing to give it, anxious in fact, but only on your own terms—well, you've got real power then. I started out just doing hand-jobs, anytime and anywhere, had all those dicks tied around my little finger. I liked that. Guys are willing to give a lot for that oh-so-fleeting rush of come shooting onto or into a woman. It's always kind of amazed me."

Julian fidgeted, not at all liking the sound of this, what it seemed to be leading up to. The way she so casually spoke of her early, and many, sexual experiences left him jealous, hurt, and shaken, though he knew he had no right to be. Her story was as bleak as this improbable edifice they were sitting in, and he wasn't sure he wanted to hear any more of it. Coming here might not have been such a good idea after all, he thought. Vern was right: he was in over his head. Way over.

"So I misspent my youth getting what I wanted that way," she said, her eyes distant, her tone nostalgic and slightly proud. "Using my one talent. Fuck school, fuck career, fuck society, I said to myself. And the more I was willing to give, the more I was able to get. I was nineteen when I went professional."

Her gaze fixed on him to gauge his reaction. She still cared what he thought of her, he realized. Or was she just daring him to condemn her, as most people no doubt did automatically?

"Uh, I was pretty naive at first," she continued, looking away and tugging at her hair. "Everyone is. But I learned fast. I soon found that if I specialized in the rare stuff, what few other women were willing to do, well, then I could corner a very lucrative market."

She paused. "You got a smoke on you?"

He tugged out a Camel, handed it to her, and lit it for her as she leaned forward. Couldn't he ask her to skip this part? No, he had to trust her. If they were ever going to have anything together he had to have faith in her. And maybe she knew what she was doing, for while hearing about her past was hard, it was also purifying. No secrets between them. And wasn't that what he'd wanted most, for her to open up to him? Yes, but her secrets were a lot bigger and blacker than his.

"I had a bent for the more colorful and creative preferences of tricks. Don't quite know where that came from. There was an uncle who liked to pull down my panties and pat my bottom when I was a little girl, but that was relatively harmless. I wasn't an abused child, at least not physically. My father was a bastard who thought children should be like slaves, though. That's no doubt part of it. Maybe I was making up for a sense of powerlessness in my childhood. Because pain is power, you know. Not just the giving of it either. When you can take more pain than others, then that's a kind of power, too, isn't it?"

Her mood sounded lighter now, as if the telling of all this to someone was relieving her mind of a load. Bitterness still tainted her speech, however, and her flippant self-analysis couldn't entirely cover it up.

She curled her legs under her in the chair, still twisting a strand of her hair in her right hand. It was an unintentionally alluring gesture, thought Julian. "I was doing really great. The cops caught me in sting operations now and then, but I had girlfriends to post my bail. I was making a lot of money, but I was also spending a lot. Clothes, jewelry, posh restaurants, that sort of thing. Then one night a john got carried away and put me in the hospital. Goddamned motherfucker. Broke my arm and some ribs. This pimp named Cadge, who'd made polite overtures to me before this, sent me cards, candy, flowers, and came to see me. How touching. Told me that he and some of his boys fucked up that john real good for me. Promised to protect me if I became one of his ladies. Well, I was about to call it quits after that traumatic scene, but like he reminded me: What else did I know? What else could I do? I knew the streets, the more extreme techniques of Eros, but I was a moron otherwise. So I went back on the Sade-Masoch Circuit, at the end of Cadge's leash."

She sneered. "Huh. They call it being 'in the life.' Ain't that a laugh?"

That made him more restless than ever. The walls of the cramped room threatened to close in on him, and for a moment he had a hard time believing he was really there, in an ancient chamber of stone listening to a modern-day ex-hooker relate her sordid woes to him. It was just too crazy. What was even crazier was that he knew this woman, had made love to her, and might soon hear her claim to be a survivor of her own murder.

"Anyway, Cadge turned out to be a greedy, woman-hating psycho." She picked at her skirt, sounding disappointed now, somewhat regretful. "They all are, you know. Some of my clients were big-time dealers who made big-time bucks, and that looked really good to me. So the day came when I bugged out of Cadge's stable to strike out on my own in the drug trade. Naturally that pissed him off, and it was only a matter of time before he got his revenge. The details aren't important. It was just a fouled deal with a supplier named Ernesto Frost in the basement of the Grotto."

A bell went off in Julian's head. This was obviously why she hadn't wanted to go there on their second date. Too many bad memories. This just got crazier and crazier as it went on.

"I don't think they intended to kill me, just rip me off and rough me up some. Put a scare in me." Ashley grinned viciously. "Well, I would not be pushed around by anybody. I fought like a banshee. I did. I stabbed Frost in the groin, but he cut my throat. As I lay there gargling my own blood Cadge showed up, in a hurry so as not to get connected up with the body of an old acquaintance. But he did have time to spit on my face and say to me, 'Now you can turn tricks in the shit pit, spoiled cooze, with El Diablo as your pimp.'"

Lines and tics of agitation distorted her fine features as she hesitated again, breathing hard from the assault of the memory. She knocked ashes onto the carpet with a shaking hand, tremblingly touching her other hand to her forehead. "Uh, so there I was in a heap on the floor, growing cold as my blood ran out of me." Her eyes lowered; she strained to form a smile, but it kept fading. "All I could think was how I had wasted myself, squandered all that unused potential. I knew nothing, had experienced even less. I guess it took death to smarten me up."

Julian very much admired the way she'd so skillfully led up to this point, but his heart was thudding in his chest and he didn't know if he could bear to hear what was coming next. He pitied her, felt disgust toward her, even hated her a little bit now, and none of that wiped out his need to be with her. So he stayed put, for the torment he faced here was nothing compared to the devastating numbness that awaited him if he left.

"Um, now comes the really far-out part, Julian." She turned her eyes to the right, unable to face him and barely able to face what she was telling him. "I'll just tell it to you as I experienced it, and let you judge for yourself. I had a—a visitor before the cops and the medics showed up. This visitor floated above me in a hazy golden light, making me think of a burning bush. I guess I thought it was God come to give me hell for the sinful life I'd lived. I was surprised because I'd never believed in such a thing. *Well, do your worst*, I thought at the thing. I wasn't about to start feeling ashamed for just being myself, no matter what. And my visitor told me he wouldn't think of asking such a thing of me. He'd read my mind, which blew me away. And he hadn't come to inflict an eternity of damnation on me. Not exactly."

She shifted her weight abruptly, placing her feet on the floor and leaning forward. "His voice echoed in my head, telling me a bunch of really crazy things. I was needed as a guardian at some kind of gate. This gate kept the world from being destroyed. If I agreed to be one of these guardians I would be saved from death. Simple as that. I wasn't particularly terrified of dying, but living still seemed preferable. I'd have a chance to make up for all the things I'd missed. It still seemed like a really weird thing to be offered, a way out when your body's assuming room temperature. Might be the devil, I thought, trying to make a deal. But what did I have to lose? So I agreed. And what happened then made me want to take it back."

Taking a deep breath, she looked right at him. "Are you sure you want to hear this? It's pretty awful."

What could he say to that? He was trying to reserve judgment on her tale at this point, but if this was all a charade, it was already more elaborate than seemed possible. Best to hear it out to the end, see if it started to make sense and became subject to explanation. "Go ahead, Ashley."

A nod and a tilt of her head, as if to say, *Okay, you asked for it.* "The only way I can describe it is to say that all the shadows in the room swelled and swallowed me up. It was like getting digested by darkness. Cold blackness surrounded me, and I was being sucked through a dark, slimy tunnel. The room was gone, along with everything normal and real. All the light. Then the tunnel opened up wide and I was flying through an infinite void, just total emptiness. It was emptier than space because there weren't even any stars. For the first time ever I tried to scream, but no sound came out. Now that I needed to, my torn throat couldn't do it. So I was soaring through endless abyss, silent screaming, unable to move because my body was still essentially lifeless. And then *they* came."

A faraway look was hollowing out her gaze again, not because she was peering into the past but because she was visually recalling something unendurable. So it seemed to Julian.

"I thought I had to be in hell and these were demons. I had to give them a name, classify them, anything but face them for what they were. What they were couldn't exist. They were like tadpoles with clawed arms and gaping toothed mouths that never closed, swimming freely through the void like it was their natural habitat. No eyes, no faces, no jaws, just this yawning opening in the front of each of them. Somehow they sensed me, though, because a whole swarm clustered around me, studying me, hating me I think. They wanted to eat me, but they couldn't. They couldn't even touch me. I was immune to them physically, but the sight of them was raping my mind. I came out of that place finally, like a drowning swimmer getting hauled up from deep water, thinking that I should have chosen to die instead."

Ashley stood and walked to the back wall where a tapestry hung, staring at it without really seeing it. On the tapestry some monks were pointing frantically at a passing comet, probably fearing the day of wrath had come. The figures were so crude, they looked as if a child had made them. So Ashley had nearly died and suffered an intricate and nightmarish hallucination. It didn't really explain anything yet.

"I found myself lying in a big circular room with ten pillars in it," she said with nervous insistence. "It's located beneath this cathedral. We call it the Sanctum, and it's where the masters dwell. They shone above me, ten bogeymen just like the one who'd visited me at my death. They introduced themselves, but they all have strange names, probably not their real ones anyway. I had just passed through the Abyss, they told me. By its light I would be healed. Again, I'm just telling you how it happened. Rays of blackness seemed to shoot into the masters from below and their glowing bodies turned it into purple light, with which they bathed my body. It burned into my flesh, flooded me from head to toe, and I could feel it knitting together the torn tissues in my throat. My heart started beating and I felt warm again. I could move my muscles. Aside from the fact that I was probably losing my mind, I felt just fine. I was dead, but I was alive."

She turned around, leaned against the tapestry, and looked at him shyly. "Are you believing any of this?"

It wasn't what he'd expected, that was for sure. He scooted to the edge of his seat, as if to be just a few inches closer to her. "I'm trying, Ashley. It's a lot to accept. You must know that. You've got to give me a chance."

This seemed to satisfy her, so she crossed her arms and continued, examining her bare feet. "Then began my instruction by the masters. Now, I took it all with a grain of salt, and I believe it even less now, but they did pull off a neat trick with me at the end there. I can't deny that. But when it comes to religious stuff, I just never believed it. I sometimes thought that the devil existed and you could find him living in the hearts of some people, but all that spooky heaven and hell talk was just bullshit as far as I was concerned. So I don't know what's really going on in this nuthouse. All I can tell you is what the masters have told me. They say there's no God and no devil, but there is a hell. Hell is the Abyss I was brought here through on the night of my murder."

That would explain her body disappearing from the scene of the crime, he thought. Every time something she said made sense, it suggested an absurd conclusion. "Okay. So there's a hell. Who goes there?"

Pacing now, she pulled on the fingers of her right hand. "Well, no one exactly. This is kind of hard to explain, and like I say, I'm not sure I believe it myself. There are those tadpole creatures down there in the Abyss, but I can't say what they are. But according to the masters we all have this thing inside of us called a cumula."

"A what?"

"A cumula. As far as I can tell it's just a fancy word for soul. Anyway, if you live a really evil life, you poison and rot this part of yourself. All your murders, cruelties, and abuses accumulate in your soul, blackening it, deforming it. It becomes the essence of all the vileness inside of you, and when your body dies, it lives on as one of those things I saw in the Abyss. So you won't find Hitler or Jack the Ripper there, but they contributed their misshapen cumulas to the hordes of hell. See? We call them Coprolites."

At this point he wasn't afraid to say that he was believing none of it. In fact, he was afraid to say otherwise. "Coprolites."

Ashley nodded distractedly as she walked the short length of the room first one way, then the other. "Yeah. You know, because they're like the fossilized waste products of the dead."

"Uh-huh. Well, if the extremely evil become these things after death, what happens to the rest of us?"

"I don't know." She tilted her head as if wrestling with a difficult concept. "The masters claim that our spirits just disperse, go back to some kind of universal mass of spiritual energy from which they came. The masters are pretty vague on that point. I think they might not know the answer, but they do know how to keep someone from undergoing that fate if they choose to."

He didn't think there was any such thing as spirit, but it was an interesting cosmology she was drawing. It even had a certain justice to it. All the major belief systems were wrong, but a few religions had some of the details correct. "Someone like you?"

"Me and the other guardians. There's ten of us. Five women, five men, all at one time dead."

"And what is it that you guard?" Julian felt foolish asking the question.

"Harrowgate." She sat back down, rocked back and forth. "You see, the Abyss has always been there, but the Coprolites used to be able to emerge from it and roam the earth, terrorizing people and committing atrocities. They were the imps and ghouls of legend. They'd come out, haunt the land of the living for a time, then get drawn back into the Abyss like it's a black hole or something. And now they're kept in by Harrowgate. It shuts them out of our world. The masters claim to be ancient mystics who created the Gate, then sacrificed their humanity to stand watch over it. They have no control over it anymore, but through the guardians they make sure it is protected and maintained. That's what I do."

Now she was coming around to a subject that very much interested him. This complex fantasy hung together pretty well, but whether it was real or not, he had to know how to get her away from it. "And precisely what do your duties involve?"

Ashley slumped back with her legs thrust out, hands on her stomach. It looked like the telling of all this was taking a lot out of her, as her weakened voice indicated. "We are their arms and legs. And their senses, I suspect. I think they're pretty blind down there hanging above the pit. They can detect when someone within a certain geographical radius is on the edge of death and project themselves to him, but that's about all they can do. The other guardians and I figured out we all share that in common. We all died within ten miles of where the masters were dwelling. Not all in this city; the masters haven't always been here."

She issued a painful sigh. "We also must obey the dictates of the pact, to use the words of the masters. We perform the ritual of transfiguration in which we open up the pit to reaffirm our supremacy over the Coprolites." This sounded like a recitation, spoken with impatience. "It is also our duty to hunt down any Coprolites that by chance breach the Gate and invade this world, dispatching them back to hell when we catch them. No guardian has ever had to do this as far as I know. Other than that, our time is our own to do with as we please, though we aren't allowed to leave the cathedral without specific permission."

That was the opening he'd been waiting for. "What would happen to you if you left this place and never came back?"

Her face hardened into a mask. "The masters say we would die, but I've never felt any ill effects from being away from here. That's why I decided to escape for good last night. I was running away, but you acted like such a jerk that I realized how impossible things between us were. I can't live among the living anymore. I'm too different now."

Another mystery solved, but he cursed himself. If he'd been more understanding toward her, she would not have returned to this place. They would still be together, more than likely. "I don't think that's true, Ashley. I mean, are you so much stranger now than you were in your, uh, former life?"

"I don't know!" she snapped at him, glaring. "But it's hopeless. I've blown it for good. You see, I was never a happy guardian. I argued, rebelled, threw tantrums, refused to do as I was told. And the masters have ways of punishing us that you'd rather not hear about. The others get to go out a lot, on shopping sprees and stuff. Sylvio, the oldest guardian in both senses, comes and goes as he pleases. The masters trust him that much. Kristen could do the same, but she doesn't want anything to do with normal people. Iris refuses to learn contemporary speech and behavior, would attract too much attention if she went out, so she stays in all the time. Me, I wanted out. Bad. So I cleaned up my act for a while and I was finally allowed out for short periods of time. I made the most of it. I got that apartment, made some friends as Lamia, and dealt a bit of coke for mad money."

"Is that all you did?" he said, harsher and louder than he'd intended.

This caught her off guard. "What?"

Tears of rage stung his eyes as he pointed an accusing finger at her. "I mean did you go back to hooking? Turning tricks? Did you risk catching diseases that they hadn't even heard of ten years ago and maybe give them to me?"

Her mouth had gone slack. "How can you say that? Hurting you would be the last thing I'd ever do. Don't you see what you did for me? You made sense of what's been happening to me for the past ten years. You showed me there was beauty in it, meaning. From you I learned that I'm not the freak I thought I was. You are gentle, but your visions are savage. I wanted to be the same. I realized I could. Even though I dwelt with horrors I didn't have to be one. Not anymore. Because of you."

This surprise confession from her knocked his rage down from a force-ten gale to a mere squall. "But how do you know you didn't infect me with something?"

"Think about it," she said sarcastically. "Bacteria and viruses only attack the living."

The crux of all this remained whether he could totally abandon his reason and accept her assertion that she really was dead. He needed proof. Solid evidence. "Okay. So you died and came back. What are you now? Do you heal when you get injured?"

The question made her squirm a little. "Yes, but not in an ordinary way. My body is now sustained by the void-light with which the masters resurrected me. When I get a cut, the wound fills with a glow that turns to fluid and then it's gone. Or at least it looks something like that. And I might as well tell you now that I don't have this appearance all the time. In the ritual I change into something else."

He snickered grimly. "I know. A white rabbit. Without the ears, of course."

Her mouth did a slow gape. "How could you possibly know that? No outsider has ever seen the ritual."

"I have a very resourceful friend who broke in here and saw it. I told him about you and he was afraid I was getting myself into some bad shit, so he followed you last night."

She collapsed against the back of the chair, pounding her knee with a fist. "Oh, God. This is just great. How much did your friend see?"

The terror on her face tore at his insides. What was she so damned afraid of? "He saw the floor cave into a bottomless pit, some lit-up shapes floating in the air, and the supposed metamorphosis of you and your fellow guardians."

"Fuck. He should have stuck around longer. He could have seen me receive my punishment for sneaking out and almost running away. That would have been a sight he'd never forget. But it's nothing compared to what the masters will do to me when they find out he was here." She scowled at the floor for a moment. "Oh, but they know already, don't they? That's why they sent Bethany out tonight, to keep an eye on him. She doesn't like shopping and she has no interest in what this world has become. And she's pretty enough to bedazzle him. So at the next ritual I'll be scourged into a raw red horror by the masters, or worse. What the fuck have I done?"

He desperately wanted to put an end to her fear. But how? Whether what she'd told him was true or not, she certainly believed it. That was what he should deal with. "Ashley, I'm confused. If your masters are such benevolent beings, sworn to protect humanity from the monstrous things in this Abyss, why do they torture their servants? It seems contradictory to me."

"Argue about it with them!" she cried out, withdrawing into herself. She chewed on her knuckle, drawing blood.

Actually, her suggestion wasn't a bad idea. If it was proof he wanted, then a face-to-face meeting with the masters should provide it. And if he could demonstrate to her that they weren't what she thought they were, just maybe she would forget all this mystical nonsense and leave the cathedral with him. He slipped onto the floor and knelt at her feet. "All right. Take me to them. I'll tell them this mess is all my fault. If they have made such a monumental sacrifice for the sake of the human race, then they must have a profound sense of justice. It would be unfair of them to punish you further. I'll get them to see that."

Her expression was doubtful. "You're a fool. They're thousands of years old, Stormy. The youngest of them, Apassionata, was a Roman witch when a despot named Tarquin was deposed in a sex scandal. Or so she claims. They've had a lot of time to get to know human nature inside and out. Sylvio reads to them, fills them in on anything they want to learn about. You won't be able to put anything over on them."

Julian touched the hand she'd bitten into, caressing the wound, and she didn't move it. "Then I won't try. I'll just be my own painfully honest self." When he looked down again the blood was still there, but the teeth marks were gone.

With a weak nod she rose. "Okay. Come with me."

At the doorway she stopped him with a hand on his chest. "There's just one thing. Whatever you do, don't mention anything about the Shadow Prism. You were right about that. I stole it. It's forbidden to remove any of the cabalistic objects from the cathedral. Things'll be worse if the masters find out that I took it."

Her dread of the masters was really getting on his nerves. "If they're so powerful, why don't they already know about it? About my presence? Why haven't they sent anyone to do something about my being here?"

She stared at him for a few moments. "Oh, they know about you, I'm sure. Bethany or someone else has probably told them. But there's never been one of the living in here before, as far as I know. Maybe I surprised them, caught them off guard by accidentally drawing you here."

Putting her right fist to her mouth, Ashley turned away and leaned against the side of the doorway. "There's going to be hell to pay, you know," she said. "Things could get really bad for me. And you."

The words that came to his mind offered more encouragement than he felt. "But not for us. I think we should go through with this."

For a few seconds she stood motionless, appearing very uncertain. Then she nodded and led the way to the Sanctum.

12

Don't Reap the Fearer

The more he thought about it, the more it consumed him.

Vern sat staring at the painting, and he began to feel like the painting was somehow staring out through him. It was in his mind as well as on the canvas. If he could only focus his eyes in a certain way, the mental image would precisely superimpose itself over the painted image. Cover it and finish it where it was not yet done. But it was like trying to get one of those floating specks in your eye to stay in one spot. It kept drifting.

This was more than an intriguing riddle, however. His thoughts were being absorbed by this image, driving him to compulsion. Finish the painting. Make the shape in his head real. He'd seen it in the cathedral and stared at it too long. Was that why it preyed upon him? No, he'd seen it another time as well. After he'd fucked Bethany, this absurd conglomeration of shapes had formed in his brain like a psychic ejaculation from her. That was it! He'd stolen this secret from her in the act of intimacy. Not only had he beaten her at her own game, but he'd obtained the key to the downfall of her kind as well. This strange sign was surely the source of their power, and he could take it from them. If he finished the painting. Perhaps he'd jumped to conclusions concerning Ashley. Maybe she was a traitor to the dead, trying to hand over the vital element of their forces to the living enemy. And Julian had refused to accept it, most likely. They had fought about it, she'd run out, and now it was up to Vern to get the job done. As usual.

He stood and took long strides to the painting. Defeating demons and saving the world; these would be his latest accomplishments. Why, he was a goddamned bona fide hero. Did even he believe that a few well-placed brushstrokes with oils could strip a tribe of walking deaders of their mystical strength? After all he'd seen in the past few days, of course he could. Did he have the skill to finish the image? Don't think about it. Just act. He who hesitates is lost. So he squeezed some black paint out of a tube onto a palette, picked up a clean brush, dabbed the bristles, and extended it toward the bare region of the canvas.

And realized he could do nothing. His hand refused the signals from his brain.

Now, what the devil *was* this? The center of the image was perfectly clear in his mind, that of a square frame with eyes in the corners, almond-shaped eyes with vertical pupils. But he couldn't get his hand to paint it. All he could figure was that the shape was memorized in the hemisphere of his brain that he neglected, the one that artists and women were said to favor. Something about concentric thought versus linear thought. Once he'd read a boring article on the subject. He was beginning to get the unpleasant feeling that he was caught up in events that exceeded the capacity of his rather specialized intellect.

A bit daunted, he started knocking around the loft, smoking a cigarette and handling the various objects he came across. Julian sure collected a lot of weird shit, he mused. Kind of like the Addams Family's house. He saw a piece of junk made of purple glass sitting on a shelf, reached for it, and felt a jolt go through him when his fingers touched it. Suddenly, somehow he felt sure he could convey the image in his mind to the canvas. Now he could finish the painting. But why? What was this crescent-moon-shaped thing? Had it come from the cathedral, brought here by Ashley? If so, that only verified his theory. Another of their own weapons to use against them. He turned to the painting. It appeared almost luminous to him now.

Stomping out his cigarette on the floor and clutching the purple crystal tightly in his left hand, he stalked to the canvas, picked up the brush, and got to work.

"I think you know, it's not really a rabbit," said Ashley as they entered the central chamber, which Vern had described so accurately.

"What?"

"The form I take on in the ritual. It's not a white rabbit, or any other animal. It's an aspect totally unique to me. The masters say it conforms to my innermost nature, reflects what I have made of my cumula. Not as ghastly as the shapes of the Coprolites, it's also not as pleasant as that of someone who lived a less tarnished existence. Still, I'm not the ugliest of the guardians."

Julian tried to evaluate her words clinically. "No, I didn't think it really was a rabbit. That's just what Vern said, trying to be cute. So according to your masters there is some kind of moral imperative to the universe. But if there's no God to do the judging, how is the deciding done?"

"I don't know," she said faintly, as if she wasn't anxious to discuss it. "We all judge ourselves on some level, I guess. The harm we do others just ricochets back at us. I wonder what your soul looks like."

"Good question." And one that made him feel strange, like a woman wondering if the discomfort in her womb is a normal embryo or a malignant tumor. "I once did a portrait of myself as a satyr, all golden boy above and randy beast below. I hope it's something like that."

Then his gaze fell on the symbol in brownish stone standing against the wall, and his knees almost buckled. In three dimensions it didn't look quite the same and it was primitively carved, but there was no mistaking it. At least now he knew what went at the center of the blasted thing; seeing it made him tremble as he absorbed its details. Somehow this image had passed subliminally through Ashley into his nether mind, in the emotional maelstrom of sexual climax, and then forced its way out through his trained eyes and deft hands onto oilskin. He thought she'd inspired him, yes, but he'd believed the rest to be his own creative outpouring. For a magical configuration to transfer itself wholesale from one consciousness to another was a staggering occurrence, to say the least. He'd asked for proof of the truth of her words, and now here it was, plain as day.

Yet now he was more uncertain of things than ever. His instincts told him to trust no one. For instance, had Ashley been aware of what she was doing to him? Had it been her intention to get him to paint the image? And if so, to what end? He turned to ask her, but checked himself. No point in tipping his hand just yet. Find out what was going on first. But it sure was a shock. If this sort of impossible event had taken place, then maybe everything she'd said was also . . .

"Are you okay?" Concerned, she also sounded irritated by her own concern. "You look like you're about to puke."

"I'm okay, I'm okay. I haven't been eating right lately, that's all." Change the subject, quick, before he lost his nerve and got out of there. Back to the sweat-soured sheets of his bed where the nightmares couldn't chase him past the boundary of sleep. "Uh, this is quite a room here. Must be a fortune in polished marble."

She studied him curiously. "What did your friend think of our mass?"

"Uh, he thought it was a very nice light-show, excellent special effects. Vern's a very practical sort of guy. So where are the other guardians?"

Ashley stepped to the edge of the black spiral, careful not to tread on any of the eyes. "Oh, they're around. Meditating in their rooms probably. The Sanctum is directly beneath this chapel. I can't go with you down there. Like death, everyone must face it alone."

He wished she hadn't put it like that. Now that he knew there really was more to this unsettling situation than met the eye, he was afraid to see the masters. They might turn out to be more than he'd bargained for.

"Are you sure you're ready for this?" She seemed to be losing patience with him.

"Don't ask." Spreading his palms, he feigned a helplessness he was really beginning to feel. "How can I be sure? I should just go before it hits me what I'm really doing. Which way do I go?"

She pointed at the altar. "Behind the shrine is an opening. It leads to a spiral stairway. Go down it, follow the main hallway when you come to it, and you'll meet with the masters. Don't take any of the side passages or you'll end up in the catacombs. Iris and Nestor like to skulk around down there sometimes and they can be unfriendly."

Her warning made this idea even less pleasant now. "Can I kiss you before I go?"

With a tired sigh she said, "If you must."

Crossing to her, he gently clasped her arms and pressed his lips to hers. They still tasted of jasmine and patchouli, and the warm musky smell of her fortified his nerves. She gave him something to fight for. "Everything's going to be fine, Ashley. Don't be worried."

The look on her face was dubious, a bit pitying of him. "Just do what you can, Stormy. And try not to show them any undue weakness."

"Sound advice." He dragged himself over to the massive sculpture, studied it with mixed contempt and wonder for a moment, then slipped behind it and through the narrow archway in the wall.

Torches set in the sides of the stone passage lit the way, as if he'd just walked in on the Middle Ages. Or one of his own creations. He found the steps and took them as they wound downward. Into dungeons, he half anticipated. *Never should have gotten up this morning,* he told himself. *Never should have taken art classes.*

Most of all, he never should have gone to the Quarry that night.

He was fearful, but he was also curious. For so long

he'd been fashioning denizens of the strange in crayon, pencil, ink, and pigment. Was he about to confront some for real? In flesh that was not flesh? If so he would finally know if his search through the dark inner mindscape was for something tangible or if he'd just been chasing shadows all these years. Did the shadows of his childhood trauma have substance or not? He might soon find out. This plunge into the unknown was for himself as much as for Ashley, he realized.

At the bottom of the stairs another passage beckoned, with small arched doorways leading off from it at this end. He made a point of ignoring these, though the hairs at the base of his scalp prickled as he walked by them. The walls of the main passage were decorated with large primitive frescoes. It was difficult to make them out clearly in the dim torchlight, but he didn't much like the look of them. They seemed to show robed figures, maybe sorcerers or saints, driving hordes of grotesque creatures into the maws of vast pits. This was perhaps a depiction of the early careers of the masters.

Julian came to a columned archway, on the other side of which only darkness could be seen. It reminded him of what the ancients had inscribed on maps where they believed the earth's edge lay: *Non Plus Ultra*—nothing lies beyond. Well, it could be the end of his world as he knew it if he stepped beyond that point. When he came out, would he be the same person who had gone in? Would his sanity be ravaged or would his psyche be ablaze with wisdom? He wanted a guarantee that his eyes could still look upon beauty and appreciate it, needed to know that he would not see only horror after this. There were no guarantees, however. He stood alone.

Plucking a torch from its sconce in the wall, he went in.

Ten thick pillars rose up to the high ceiling of the circular room, mildly ornate and made of the whitest marble. Other than that, the room's only feature was a gracefully arching bridge leading to a round platform in the center. No masters, no monsters, no phantoms lurking behind the pillars. No one else was there. Was that it? Was that the joke? This was where you came if you wanted to imagine a conversation with invisible beings?

He'd been holding his breath and his heartbeat was racing, which made him mad. All that buildup from Ashley had had him spooked. She'd almost had him believing it. Almost. Turning, he started to leave, then thought twice about it. Was he really giving this a chance, or was he backing out at the first excuse he could grab on to? Okay, he would stay until he was certain nothing was going to happen. It seemed likely that someone was supposed to stand on the raised platform during an audience with the masters, so he obliged and waited.

Julian hated resorting to clichés, but he couldn't help feeling that he was being watched. The more time crept by, the more certain he became that he was not alone in the chamber, but he couldn't see anyone else anywhere. Then with a shock that nearly flung his spine out his back he saw them, ten faintly glowing shapes hovering above him in front of the pillars. They made him think of mummies, for they seemed to have heads and long torsos but no distinct limbs. When he lowered the torch, he could make them out more sharply against the dark, but it was a good guess that they were still in the process of materializing and would soon become more solid. It took everything he had to resist the creepy feeling churning his insides and not flee screaming from that place. He had to keep reminding himself that he was in no physical danger, though he wasn't really sure of that. And the mental danger was undeniable.

Finally the masters, if that's what they were, assumed considerable definition, and he could form some opinion about what he was seeing. Long-buried sensations threatened to erupt from his subconscious, for there was something familiar about the apparitions. They did indeed look waxy or glassy, like human bodies encased in exotically molded amber. Two sets of bulges protruded from the shapes, as of the elbows and knees of bent arms and legs. Some had a third set of swellings, which could perhaps be the breasts of females. These figures reminded him of what he'd seen one summer day as a boy when he'd found a butterfly cocoon hanging from a tree branch, torn it open, and exposed the pupa within. Its alien beauty had startled him. The masters looked much like it, though they shone with their own golden light, a steady aura that obscured almost all of their internal structure. They serenely radiated before Julian on all sides, several yards away from and above him. As he agonized over a memory deeper and more devastating than that summer day, one of the masters spoke:

"State your name for us." The tone was male and recognizably human, though very haughty and slightly echoed.

It took him a moment to remember he had a voice. "I'm—I am Julian Stormer." He had absolutely no idea what he was going to say to such presences, what he'd come down here to accomplish.

"I am Firdausi. I speak for the ten of us. Widdershins from me you behold Euterpe, Gemeliel, Porphyria,

Thelonius, Apassionata, Tervagans, Vulpeculine, Algolagnion, and Meraviglia. What is your purpose here?"

Right to the point, and not particularly friendly. *Widdershins:* he believed that meant leftward. Not that these introductions did him any good, for aside from the slight gender differences they all looked too much alike for him to distinguish them as individual entities. In time he might be able to discern their personal characteristics, but no time soon. Besides, he was only guessing at who was doing the talking, judging by the direction the sound was coming from and what he thought was motion around the facial area of the speaker as he heard the words.

"I'm not sure," he replied, feeling awkward. "To find out what's going on, I guess. What are you?"

"What have you been told of us?" Firdausi's tone was abrupt, a bit impatient with him, it seemed.

"Um, that long ago you created a barrier around hell to keep the demons from getting out. Now you watch over it to make sure nothing goes wrong with it." Standing in this grim, ancient-looking chamber, confronting such eerie hosts, the idea didn't seem as absurd as when Ashley had presented it to him.

"Do you have reason to doubt that this is so?"

"Well, it's not easy to believe. I mean, you speak pretty good English for someone who's been dead for over three thousand years. And it seems unlikely that a secret this big could be kept hidden from the world all this time."

"We learn the language of the land where we dwell." The master's voice sounded louder and even less friendly now. "We take pains to keep ourselves and our great work hidden, lest mankind face a truth it would find unbearable, that they are guarded by higher powers from a hell that many of their own kind infest after death. Look down at your feet, mortal."

Julian didn't want to comply, fearing he'd see something unpleasant there, but he had to look in case it was something he needed to defend himself against. He looked and instantly knew there was no defense against what he saw. The floor of the chamber was gone, utterly vanished! Only the bridge on which he was standing remained, spanning the blackest nothingness he'd ever seen or imagined. Julian grabbed the railings on either side of him, his body shaking madly between them. He was standing over the Abyss. It was the black of absence, a void, yet with a depth, a substance, to the blackness that somehow seemed alive.

"We are lords of that," said the master. "Yet you dare to question and defy us. Your ignorance and impudence are monstrous."

He wanted to ask Firdausi to make the pit go away, but he remembered Ashley's warning about not showing weakness. The vertigo he was suffering was tremendous, as if the void beneath him was sucking at his mind and flesh. He held tighter to the rails, unable to imagine staying, unable to move. The closeness of the Abyss tingled over his body.

He forced out shaking words, raising his gaze to them.

"I, uh, didn't mean to offend you. I'm sorry. I'm just trying to comprehend this."

"Your comprehension is not necessary. You were not to know of our existence at all. You should not have come here, to the cathedral or the Sanctum. No mortal is intended to behold such wonder."

It came as no surprise to find that these beings had

such a high opinion of themselves. Still, Firdausi had just reminded him of what he'd come here for. "That's what I wanted to talk to you about. My coming here is all my fault, not Ashley's. I don't want you blaming her for it."

"What is she to you?"

That wasn't easy to answer. Except that she was everything. "I love her. I came here because I want to be with her."

"Mere primitive emotion. What is that in the face of death and hell? You have nothing to say to us."

This was beginning to feel hopeless. His thoughts were distracted by the vast blackness below. While he kept his eyes focused on the masters, he couldn't settle on an interpretation of what they were. Now they looked like luminous sacs of flesh attached to the pillars by stems at their tops. How could he appeal to the emotions of such beings or outsmart the ancient intelligences within? He'd promised Ashley he would be honest with them. Well, he had to be honest with himself as well. A smothering sense of déjà vu was ripping at his brain, for he'd met the masters before. He was sure of it now. They were the Slug People his dying, terrified, five-year-old mind had encountered in his delirium. He must have been drawn here in spirit, had an out-of-body experience. Or had he passed through the Abyss and lost the memory of it? But how had it happened at all?

"Do you know me?" he asked meekly.

Firdausi took a moment to respond. "We do."

Julian gasped. "Then you *did* contact me when I momentarily died in that car crash?"

"We scan the souls of all who die within our sphere of influence. It was a matter of course, for two guardians had yet to be reaped at that time. We have them now."

Jesus! His whole fucking life had been leading up to this moment, this meeting, spurred on by that first incidental encounter. They had made him what he was. What gave them the right to mess up people's minds that way? His muscles spasmed with the impact of the revelation and he would have vomited if his stomach hadn't been empty.

"Why—why didn't you, uh, reap me?"

"You were a child." Firdausi spoke as if it was a matter of little consequence. "You were not truly dying. You feared death. A guardian must be one who fears death not."

The master's form seemed distinctly sluglike now. "You mean they have to want to die?"

"Suicides are also unsuitable. Those we select as guardians are humans who have bred monsters in themselves by the kinds of lives they have lived. They are not truly evil, but are originally sinful, conspirers with tragic twists of fate, hosts to imps of the perverse. They have lived in the shadow of death all their lives and this imbues them with a dark fearless strength that allows them to endure the Abyss and its inhabitants. You are an innocent, Julian Stormer, a fearer of life as well as death. We saw it in you even then."

The master seemed to be trying to goad him. Julian strained to gather his thoughts. Okay, so he was a believer now. Ashley's bogeymen were his personal demons and they were real. He'd sort out where that left his reason later. Right now he had to deal with what they were going to do to Ashley. God, poor Ashley! She'd been telling the truth all along, had really gone through all that torment. It was a wonder to him now that she'd held together so well. Would he?

"I c-came to talk to you about Ashley. I don't think she should be punished any more than she already has been."

"She has breached the pact and shall be scourged for it!" Firdausi's voice boomed in the chamber, making Julian wince. "To reveal our presence to outsiders is a transgression that cannot go unpunished."

Julian was beginning to notice something odd going on around him, something rising from the pit up to the masters. He decided it might have been there before and escaped his attention. "How can you be so unfair about this? She made an honest mistake. She has feelings and needs and they made her get careless. Besides, I haven't told anyone and I won't. And I'll see that my friend Vern doesn't either. We're the only ones who know about this place and we'll keep your secret to ourselves."

"We know that you will." That sounded like a threat. It certainly wasn't trust in his discretion. The stuff shooting upward from below seemed to be thickening, turning from smoke into fluid light, dark purple in color. It was beginning to give him the creeps, worse than he already had them.

"Your offer is insufficient," Firdausi continued. "Ashley knows the rules. Noblesse oblige, mortal. To whom much is given much is demanded. The guardians have been granted second lives and so must adhere to a strict code of conduct. They are unnatural beings who are untrained in their abnormal state when they enter it. Through harrowing we see that they are reminded of what they are, what they owe, where their duties lie."

Julian was starting to feel very strange. Unpleasant sensations were washing over his body, like a deadening of his nervous system. A sense of profound loss and utter aloneness shook him, as if he were adrift in an entire universe of which he was the sole inhabitant. He felt as if he barely existed, as if he was dying.

"We can offer similar lessons to the living," Firdausi told him. Was there a touch of sadistic glee in his voice? "We know your deepest secret fear and we can make you face it. It is better to face your fears and conquer them than to run from them, do you not agree?"

They were doing this to him, he was certain. Somehow they were projecting the Abyss into him, or some part of it, filling him with its horrible emptiness. Making him experience what death was like. Why? Were they trying to kill him? Drive him mad? He could see shadowy tendrils streaming from their eyes toward him, not unlike an emanation of the Shadow Prism.

"Why are you doing this to me?" There was hurt and confusion in his tone, more than he'd expected to hear.

"To show you this is no place for you. You do not belong here. You do not belong with the woman Ashley. She is not your kind anymore."

Grotesque and gruesome images swam fleetingly through his head: bodies splitting apart in oceans of brown sludge, lovers without skin dissolving into skeletons as they copulated, men transforming into giant gray scorpions, women getting penetrated by phallic worms that proceeded to devour their insides. His mind was sinking into its own depths, slipping away from consciousness toward its dark core. Someone less acclimated to such visions would probably have already lost his sanity, he felt sure. If he let it go on long enough, though, it seemed to him that his flesh would follow this descent, into the pit under his feet.

"Please stop this," he pleaded. "Don't hurt me. Don't hurt Ashley anymore. I'm begging you."

"Our decision stands," bellowed Firdausi, without a shred of mercy. "This audience is at an end. Return to the upper level and inform Ashley that we wish to see her. Fear not for her immediate safety. She shall not be harrowed until the next ritual. After you have told her, you must leave the cathedral.

No. Now he was getting cut out of her life completely. These *things,* whatever they were, had caused him nothing but pain from the very beginning. They'd scarred his personality and now they were trying to separate him from the one he loved. He felt nothing but hate for them, even if they were the architects of a hellbinding gate. They could go to hell themselves for all he cared.

"Fuck you all!" he spat at them. Their forms were fading, so he didn't know if they could hear him. The grim effect they were having on his nervous system was also receding, though the memory of it was hard enough to deal with in itself.

"Do you hear me?" he persisted. "I think you're shit-eating bastards. I think you're the lowest things in existence."

But he was alone; they were gone, and the Abyss along with them.

Julian took a few minutes to compose himself and recover from their assault. Then he crossed the bridge to the exit. He made his way to the end of the passage and climbed the stairs, casting away his torch on the stone floor at the top.

When he reached the altar room, blindingly bright in contrast to the ultimate gloom of the lower chamber, he saw that Ashley was not alone. A short, swarthy man in stained and faded khaki fatigues was with her. In spite of himself Julian suffered a spasm of jealousy. Still, as a living man he was confident that he had more to offer her than one of her fellow deaders. It was an unkind thought and he regretted having had it.

"Julian, this is Jorge Rios," said Ashley, sounding as if her mind was somewhere else. "He's a fairly recent arrival, like me."

Jorge didn't look too anxious to shake hands, so Julian didn't try. "Yeah, well, hello, Jorge."

The severe-looking man just stared at him.

Ashley rubbed her arms nervously. "So what did they say?"

He glumly faced her, his mood grayer than at any other time in recent memory. "They're as intractable as you said. They've thrown me out of the cathedral and you're still going to be disciplined. I didn't get anywhere with them at all."

She didn't seem surprised and there was bitterness in her voice. "Do you at least believe me now? I didn't make any of it up and this isn't a carnival funhouse. This is all really happening."

All he could manage was a weak nod. "They want to see you right away."

"Okay. Okay. Let me think for a minute." One hand on her hip, the other poking at her forehead, she briefly paced in a circle. "Don't leave yet, Julian. Wait here for me. I'll be right back."

Before he could even object, she disappeared the way he'd just come.

He looked uncertainly at Jorge, who broke into a scornful smile. "Hey, don't worry about me, man. I don't do the masters' dirty work. If they want to kick you out they'll have to do it themselves."

"I appreciate that." So Jorge didn't seem to like the masters any more than Ashley did. From what she'd said, some of the guardians seemed to be positively fanatical about their roles. Was there a schism brewing in the sect?

"Tell me something, aliver. What do you think you saw down there?"

Julian didn't really want to go into his childhood association with the masters, especially with a complete stranger. The torment was just too intimate. "I don't know. I guess they're just what they say they are. What else could they be?"

Jorge sneered. "What else could they be? Hey, haven't you got a brain, man? Think! They could be lots of things. Aliens, maybe, or invaders from another dimension. Who knows? Something we haven't even imagined yet. Jeez. You're not going to do us any good at all, are you? Well, I'll tell you something about them, something Bonita told me. She's been with them for a long time and she says that they don't look quite the same now as they used to. What do you think of that?"

He had no patience for this game. Too many mysteries and too few clues. "Whatever they are it's got nothing to do with me. I just want to get Ashley free of this place."

"Oh, but it's not that simple." The man was coming on in a condescending manner, moving his hands as if he were trying to get a simple point across to a moron. "No one gets away from the masters. No one here gets out, alive or dead."

"I will. When Ashley comes back I'm walking right out of here. I have to."

Shaking his head vaguely, he aimed a forefinger in Julian's general direction. "Yeah, and you know, that's the really curious part. No one on the outside can know about this big black secret in here, but there you go dancing out into nosy modern society knowing all about it. Now, how can that be?"

Good question. He was being sent out for a reason. So he would finish doing the painting? What would that do? Pointing at the intricate sculpture of the shrine, which he'd unconsciously duplicated on canvas, he said to Jorge, "Well, maybe you can tell me something, then. What exactly is that?"

The man looked surprised. "That? You mean you don't even know what that is? That's *it*, man. That's what the Gate looks like. It's what the masters put in each of us guardians so we could be their slaves. It's what rules our dead lives."

A deep chill slowed Julian's blood and spread rapidly throughout his inner regions of organ, bone, and flesh, frosting every nerve ending. All thought froze in his brain.

Except one: For some reason he had been chosen to be the opener of Harrowgate.

PART THREE

The Abyss Abides

13

Weekend Warriors

When it was finished, Vern was genuinely surprised at how well it had turned out. The part he'd done seemed to flawlessly mesh with the rest of the picture, even though his nonexistent style was very different from Julian's. His only artistic credentials consisted mainly of some brutal and lewd graffiti he'd adorned the city with in his youth. Yet this was masterful work and it had come very easily, as if he'd been tracing something that was already there instead of reproducing the image from memory. Now the painting blazed on the canvas as an organic whole, almost more than two dimensional in its vividness. He actually believed his friend would be pleased.

Exhausted from the day's exertions, he lugged himself over to the sleeping area, set the crescent of purple crystal on the orange-crate nightstand, and flattened himself out on the bed. He switched off the lamp and let his mind wind down to sweet oblivion.

All in all, he had to say it had been the strangest day of his life. He now knew there was a lot more to the world than he'd thought there was, but he didn't want to ponder the matter too deeply. In time he'd have to revise his view of things, but he was confident that he would eventually adapt to this new unknown. He always did. The first time he'd killed, he'd had to do some hard adjusting. It had torn some part of himself away, blackened a small portion of the area within him where his feelings came from. But he'd learned to live with that, even to savor the memory. No, in spite of the strange changes he was grappling with, he would be just fine. A bit of shut-eye would help considerably, and it soon came.

A change in the air made him jerk back from the edge of sleep, like a sudden static charge shooting throughout the room. Vern opened one eye to the shadows of the loft, still in a twilight state of awareness, and thought he saw something bulging out of the painting, a bloated black hump inflating itself from the center of the image. It silently floated free like a blown bubble, settling on the floor nearby like a fat toad in low gravity. It was about the size of a small man. There seemed to be a tail and two skeletal arms to the thing, but it was legless, and for a head it had only an empty cowl like an ever-gaping maw.

You're having the worst nightmare of your life, thought Vern.

He tried to wake up and found himself trapped solidly in consciousness. This was not a dream, nor was he out of it. The misshapen apparition was still there, and though it had no eyes, he was certain it was staring right at him. Through some sense it had fixed on his vulnerable flesh, perhaps the way a coldhearted snake detected the field of heat generated by its warm-blooded prey. Escape became Vern's highest priority just then.

With a leap that brought him down painfully hard on his left ankle, he hurled himself out of bed and scrambled for the door. In a sudden burst of speed the invader scuttled over to block the way to the exit, stopping him dead in his tracks. There was some kind of mind in the blighted mass, which only made it all the more horrid.

Vern couldn't decide which would be worse, dueling with this devil in the dark or turning on the lights and risking his sanity by seeing what it really looked like. At the very distant end of a long tunnel in the bulwark of his mental self, he felt the merest threat of that self coming unglued, unraveling into drooling, convulsing terror for the first time in his life. It wouldn't take all that long for that threat to come rumbling down the tunnel like a locomotive, derailing his reason when it arrived. He knew he lost something in that moment. Never again would he walk so casually bold through the ranks of his fellow men.

Hitting on a compromise, he retreated to the bed and clumsily switched on the lamp by its side. Further unwanted details were thus revealed about his opponent. Its skin was a brown-black crust, like dry, hardened shit, its back was humped and ridged, its bony limbs ended in vicious hooks, and what he'd thought was a tail was a smoky tendril bleeding off vapor into the air. Worst of all, its yawning, jagged-toothed mouth seemed to open on a vaster space than just its own hollow interior. It looked as if it could devour an entire world in there, swallow it whole.

One small victory was bestowed upon Vern, however. The monstrosity lurched away from the boundary of the light, so he resolved to barrage it with all the illumination he could. Rushing to the wall switch, he passed within ten feet of the creature, threw on the switch, and ran back to his supposed place of safety. His haunter lunged at him, but the bombardment of brightness from the overhead lights knocked it down and drove it back. Cornered against the door, the thing seemed to pass through its substance and disappear.

Vern let out a laugh that was not without a hint of mania. He was shuddering and he could smell the urine and feces in his pants, felt a soiled wetness he'd not known since the crib. Yet it wasn't quite over, for he had to find out if it had gone off in search of some other victim. On rubbery legs he staggered to the door and opened it.

There in the shadows of the hallway the ghastly aberration was waiting, daring him to emerge. And the switch to the hall lights was at the end near the stairs. It might as well have been a light-year away.

Closing the door and stumbling back to the bed, Vern took little solace in his reprieve from doom.

Jorge left, so Julian sat down on the cold stone floor and waited for Ashley to return. As a persistent delver into the sensory realms, he knew that his thought processes were often visceral and intuitive, lacking the rigorous appraisal of pure rationality, so he wondered if he might not be jumping to conclusions. A reality check, if such a thing was possible in this asylum, seemed to be in order.

If the diagram of the Gate had somehow been stamped on the very fabric of Ashley's being, then he could have perceived it by accident during their lovemaking. Or she could have known it would happen and had been using him, hoping he would paint the Gate and sow confusion among the masters and guardians while she made her escape. It would explain why she'd been so thrilled to find out he was an artist, especially one with macabre tendencies, for a talented hand combined with a morbid soul were probably the perfect ingredients for creating an outlet to the Abyss. He didn't want to suspect her, but he had to consider all the possibilities.

If he *was* some sort of pawn, who was behind it all? The masters themselves? The first time he'd been in their presence years ago they'd felt foul to him, vile even. Perhaps that initial impression was accurate. Ashley didn't trust them, and Jorge thought they were something other than what they claimed to be. Were those two just the disgruntled rebels of the team, the born malcontents? And aside from that, how could a rectangle of cloth with colored oils splashed across it form a sluice between this world and the repository of the malignant dead?

He was afraid he knew the answer to that. It was his suspicion that art was power, that in the act of creation he was tapping into levels of perception far beyond the normal senses. If so, then this precise configuration of line and shape might affect reality, form an attenuation in the veil of the real through which things might pass from one side to the other. The mute, icy lump of rock across the room couldn't generate the portal because it wasn't sculpted by talented hands, or maybe because it wasn't stained with pigments mixed with tears and sweat, the acids of human labor. Not like a painting. Lifetimes spent in study of the esoteric arts could conceivably yield the knowledge of just what that fearful symmetry looked like, but it took a heart burning with passion to bring it to life. Or so he speculated.

Ashley emerged from behind the object of his contemplations, looking grim and shaken. He stood, and she walked right to him, falling into his arms.

"My scourging will be administered in the next ritual," she said in a desolate voice. "I don't know if I can take another one."

He caressed her hair. "When will that be?"

"Tomorrow at midnight." She pulled back to look at him. "One good thing. You don't have to go after all."

"You convinced them to let me stay?" Full of caution now, he tried not to let himself feel too relieved.

"Huh-uh. It was kind of strange, even for them. Firdausi was carrying on in his long-winded manner about what a glorious thing it is to be a guardian, and then he just went silent in midsentence. He stayed that way for fifteen seconds or more. I think he and the other masters were communing. They don't have to talk out loud to one another, you know. Then he finished his spiel and ended by telling me you could stay if you wanted. So I don't know what's going on. They never reverse themselves once they've given an order."

This information made him even less inclined to rejoice. "We've got to talk. Is there someplace we can be alone?"

She tried to smile and failed. "Yeah. We can go to my room, though I can't guarantee you I'll be much of a conversationalist."

She took him by the hand and led him out of the sanctuary, through a maze of dingy, narrow corridors. Along the way she paused to peek into a room and inform someone named Iris that the masters wanted to speak to her. Ashley's room turned out to be the size of a monk's quarters in a monastery. There was a small black cat curled up on the bed and a variety of artwork reproductions taped to the wall. They were mostly erotica involving dominatrices, vampiras, and sensual witches, interspersed with Mapplethorpe reprints. Reminders of her heady, decadent past or aids to coping with her identity as a hybrid of soma and shade. Some ragged paperbacks leaned on a shelf set in the stone wall, next to a portable radio–tape-player, and a propane stove rested on a small wooden table in a corner. Ashley lit the stove and placed a kettle on one of the burners.

"Most of the others have pretty much forgone hot meals, but I can't live like that. You want some tea?"

"Sure." He sat down on the bed and petted the cat, who barely stirred. "There's no gas or electricity in this place?"

A curt shake of her head. "We have water because there's a well, but I can't vouch for its purity. The crumbling plants in the area are probably trickling rust and chemicals and petroleum into it, which can't hurt *us* any. This is made with store-bought water, though, so don't worry."

The discussion of such mundane matters after the tumultuous revelations of the day made his head spin a little. Few experiences in his life had equipped him to deal with these mind-blowing events, and changing gears so fast was a shock to his system.

"I like your decor."

"Do you?" She dipped tea bags into two blue china cups. "The kingdom of kink is my favorite domain. Always has been, always will be, it seems. I'm a demimondaine to the core."

She carried the teas to the bed, and he took his from

her as she sat down next to him. "What do you guys do for money? Property taxes and all that?"

Ashley sipped from her cup, even though its contents were still near boiling. "Well, they're real cheap around here, and it helps to be a tax-exempt institution, but the masters have accumulated a massive fortune over the centuries. This place is full of priceless antiques, for instance, brought over from the old country when the cult moved to America. The masters sometimes used to share their wisdom with ambitious men in business and politics, you see, and were given much in return. They don't do that anymore, I don't think."

Julian was having a hard time fixing on a point of reference here. Too much incongruous data in out-of-place surroundings he couldn't adjust to. "Where was the old country, Ashley?"

Her brow furrowed, suggesting to him that she wasn't used to doing so much thinking and talking. "The masters started out somewhere in the Middle East, but then they somehow ended up in Italy, in Florence. The palazzo they occupied was called the Black Vatican by some. It is said that the Borgias were among the masters' beneficiaries, and that Dante got his vision of hell from an audience with them. Then they moved to Baltimore for a century or so. That's where Nestor, Bonita, and Arlo were reaped. And then here. They seem to be moving ever west."

He had no trouble at all believing the bit about Dante. "Why did they come to America?"

"To stay in one place too long is to risk getting discovered, and people definitely aren't ready to learn about what's going on in this place. The bloody, fiery purge would begin and end in a single night. The very idea of what we are would have a harder time gaining acceptance here. This society is less steeped in a tradition of superstition."

"Can you be harmed, Ashley? Can they?"

She set her cup down on the shelf. "I don't know and I have no desire to find out. It's wiser just to keep a low profile. I think the masters can make one of us as good as dead if they choose to, but it's mighty hard to overcome something infused with light from the void. As for the masters themselves, well, I suspect they are among the things we are meant to guard. But I'd kill them if it would get me free."

This statement alarmed him a little. "What about the, uh, Coprolites? Who would keep them out then?"

Mocking eyes and a sarcastic smile turned to him. The disdain was not directed at him, he was certain. "Let me tell you something, Stormy. When I ended up here I was as dumb as a stump. I think I'd only read two books in my entire life. *Alice in Wonderland* and *The Razor's Edge*. But I told you what went through my head as I lay dying. I'd squandered my life and I wanted to make up for that. So when I came here I wanted to feed my mind. Not much else to do here anyway. Sylvio helped me. He was reaped at an old age, centuries ago. Firstborn of the dead, he calls himself. Sylvius Desiderius was his name, an alchemist, the greatest of all time to hear him tell it. He was the first guardian and he was the leader, until he got tired of 'minding the children.' Then he handed over the reins of power to sicko Kristen. Biggest mistake he ever made."

She seemed to be talking up a storm, in spite of her warning to the contrary. As he lit himself a cigarette, she reached out, so he handed her one. They lit both off the same match. "Sylvio and I have had a strange relationship over the years. He's taught me a lot, even how to read Italian, though I mutilate it when I try to speak it. There's an extensive library in the cathedral that he put together, something the masters tolerate but aren't all that pleased about. I've read just about every book in it. Can you believe that? It's like that old joke: You can lead a horticulture, but you can't make her think. Well, I've learned how to think. Sylvio had no idea what kind of monster he was creating. He's been mostly fatherly and like an uncle to me, but he did make a pass at me once. I can handle him. I know how to treat a john, and he's caught on to what I'm doing, but it amuses him.

"The thing is, I can't think of what he was planning on doing to me. See, he cut off his dick when he was alive to show the masters how devoted he was to them."

Julian's blood ran a little colder at hearing that.

"Anyway, I said I went through the whole library," she continued with some fervor, warming to her subject. "I found out that it contains not one hint about the masters, nothing concerning their origin or nature or anything. Made me think they might be hiding something, you know? So I got determined to learn about them. It was one of the reasons I started behaving myself to get permission to do some of the shopping. I decided to do some research, which was what I was doing on the phone the night we met. But I'm not very good at it."

This very much interested him. "But you found out something?"

She suddenly looked sheepish. "Um, not much. Research is a lot harder than I thought it would be. Some guys who work in the library at Nastrond University were charmed enough by me to help show me how to do it.

And to do a lot of it for me. One of them considered himself an amateur occultist. I did learn that there was this ancient Babylonian prayer that was supposed to expel a harassing devil. It goes, 'May it depart to the West; may he be committed to the care of Ne-Gaib, the great gatekeeper of hell; may Ne-Gaib keep them in strict custody. May his key lock fast the lock.' Makes me wonder if maybe Firdausi or one of the other masters isn't this Ne-Gaib character."

Smoke streamed from her lips as she recollected further. "Then there's the legends about King Solomon being a master magician with authority over all the fiends of hell, which he could catch in a net like a fish. The Ethiopian Christians had a picture of this net, called the Marbabeta Salomon, and it looks an awful lot like Harrowgate itself."

A long silence followed in which he couldn't tell if she was finished or gathering more wool. "Anything else?"

"Well, there's one more small bit of myth. It's Persian. What it says is that a group of magicians and witches got together and forged this thing called the sanction of hell. What struck me about it is that it says they glowed like embers heated in the winds of hell when they became lodged at its entrance after death. Sound familiar?"

"Yeah, but it's still not very useful." She sounded very sincere, but he still had to rid himself of some lingering doubts about her. "You were a big problem for the masters, and yet they let you run around outside the cathedral for this much time? I mean, three days in a row?"

Her hand waved in front of his face, dispersing the confusion. "No, no, not at all. I mean, I was always late coming home from the shopping trips. I was out with permission that day we met in the Quarry, but the other two nights I snuck out through a breach in the catacomb walls I found down there. And I planned on never coming back. See, I think the masters lie to us. I don't think the Coprolites are any danger to anybody. I don't believe they can survive outside of the Abyss or even come out of it. So I don't care about that shit anymore."

It sounded like her. Now he had to drop two bombs on the poor girl. He leaned over and put his hand on her leg. "Ashley, I think matters are worse than either of us knows. I realized today that I've met the masters before."

"Yeah, yeah, I know!" she blurted out, proud of herself. "That time you thought you died in the car crash, right? You were considered for reaping. I knew it as soon as you told me. God, I can only imagine how that would blow a little kid's mind. But there's nothing strange about that. I mean, you were croaking in the masters' sphere of influence. They must have examined every poor dying soul in the area and only accepted the really tough ones, like the others and me. The ones who agreed, that is. Oh, and according to the masters we all have one other thing in common, besides youth, a death wish, and a don't-give-a-shit attitude. They say we're all psychically sensitive, or else we wouldn't be able to see the Coprolites. More rubbish."

He noted all this for future reference. "Right. But there's more. I've done a painting of the Gate. I think the image passed from you to me while we were having sex. Then I painted it."

Ashley lost her smile. "That's crazy. How could that happen?"

She was asking him? "I was hoping you'd be able to tell me."

"Wait a minute. Shut up and let me think." This complication upset her a great deal. She stood and, frowning, began to pace again. "Shit. What the fuck is going on around here?"

Julian lay back on the bed, rubbing at his temples. All his strength was just about gone. "Well, what can a painting of the Gate do?"

One of her arms shot out, palm up, fingers spread. "Who knows? Almost anything. It's a piece of instruction the masters omitted to give us. An image of the Gate could *be* a Gate, I guess."

"You had no idea you were putting it into my head?"

"Of course not!" There was some hurt in the glare she aimed at him. "God, what do you think I am?"

He raised himself up on his elbows. "Okay. Then maybe it just happened. Being an artist I was just susceptible to it. I naturally made a picture of it. End of story."

A nod, biting her lip. "Yeah, maybe. And just maybe it's something else. See, I don't dislike the masters just because I hate authority and I don't like their faces, which they don't have. There's something very wrong about them. I think they . . . I don't think they like the world very much."

"In what way?"

"You know. Pleasures of the flesh. It bothers them."

This wasn't making sense to him. "Aren't some of them women, though? Don't they have mates?"

She sat down, leaning over him. "Not really. It's purely uti—utilitarian, Sylvio says. An alchemical union of opposites. I think the masters are puritanical. The flesh infuriates them. As an ex-whore I rile them the most. But imagine what the idea of the mass of humanity heatedly coupling every night does to them, all those sweaty bodies in frantic motion. It must drive them totally up the wall."

Was this the foulness he'd sensed about them—a rage against physical sensation? Or was Ashley off on a flight of fantasy? "Are you sure about this?"

"Yep. We have to undergo a purification before the ritual. Nothing painful, but it makes douches and enemas pale in comparison. Guardians aren't supposed to fuck each other, but they do. And Firdausi says things like 'Indulgence in bodily gratification retrogresses us back to the animal,' and 'Only meditation and restraint from stimulation can fulfill the being.' Bullshit like that."

Yeah, that sounded pretty bad, all right. "Christ, Ashley. I don't get it, then. If the human race disgusts them, why spare it from the wrath of the pit? If they have a loathing of, uh, experienced women, why bring one into their midst?"

She tapped his chest as she spoke, deadly serious. "My thoughts exactly. Maybe they don't have people's best interests at heart. And maybe they picked me to use me. To get to you."

Julian sullenly mulled this over, fatigue dissolving his concentration. "I can't think about this shit any more now. My energy is shot. I've got to sleep."

"Sure." Ashley rose, picked up the cat, and put him on the floor. "This is Necrophilus, by the way. I think the reason he's named that is obvious."

It was. Cats apparently offered their affections as freely to the dead as they did to the quick. Julian stretched out lengthwise on the bed and she lay down next to him, gazing into his face.

"What are we going to do, Stormy?"

There was worry tensing her voice, but it didn't sound

like it was anywhere near the amount he was feeling. "I don't know. Destroy the painting. Get you out of this madhouse. Fuck."

They kissed. He felt almost too weak to respond to her, but she seemed to understand this and invited him to rely on her strength; he did so without reservation. They barely had to touch each other before he was fiercely erect and she was moistly open. Then he was on her and in her, riding the crest of her rhythmic waves of motion. Intense sensation built up in them both, accumulating into an explosive mass of energy, threatening to become a beast with one mind and two hearts. The beast soon arrived, in a simultaneous orgasm, and he looked down at her in that moment. For a fleeting instant her human veneer melted away, revealing a somewhat animal shape beneath, covered with a white pelt. Now that he knew what she really was, he didn't recoil from it. It excited him, made him want to be flayed open by her, stripped of skin and muscle, down to the bone and beyond, so that his naked core mirrored her own bare essence. When they'd given and taken all the pleasure they could, they stretched out silently side by side.

Sex is ambiguous, he thought: a striving to transcend the flesh and the ultimate surrender to it. Something like Ashley herself.

Then he slept.

He was at a carnival at night. Ferris wheel, merry-go-round, roller coaster, tacky calliope music. The smell of popcorn and cotton candy cloying the air. Giant spotlights slashed their beams high across the sky. Julian knew it was a dream, or a vision, or some kind of intense extended revelation, in the tradition of John on the island of Patmos. It didn't surprise him to be having such an episode, considering that the whole internal structure of his head had suffered upheaval. A rocket-ship ride whirled around in front of him like his spinning wits. Screaming youngsters going round and round, up and down, in fat little silver spacecraft. The symbolism of this pointless machine didn't seem significant, so he started walking around, hoping to get to the bottom of this night fantasy as soon as possible.

Coming to a garish red tent, small, with a placard displaying an eye and a hand, he looked in. Madame Margie sat dressed like a gypsy at a table with a crystal ball. "Would you like your fortune told?" she asked, smiling vacantly. "It's a real wild one. 'And the fifth angel sounded, and I saw a star fall from heaven unto the earth: and to him was given the key of the bottomless pit. And he opened the bottomless pit, and there arose a smoke out of the pit, as the smoke of a great furnace; and the sun and the air were darkened by reason of the smoke of the pit. And there came out of the smoke locusts upon the earth: and unto them was given power, as the scorpions of the earth have power.'"

That was all he needed to hear of that. Moving on, he passed by the freak tent. Nolan Voight was there, as the fat man, looking even more colossal than usual, standing on an outside platform with the other oddities.

"Step right up," said Vern, the hawker. Dressed in black, wearing a top hat, wielding a cane. "Step right up and see these freaks of nature. All real, all living and breathing human monstrosities. Come and see this shocking menagerie."

A redheaded woman wearing only a snake and eating fire turned out to be Monique. "I'm the dragon lady," she said. "Dragons were alien serpents who fell to the earth from outer space. Their fire is the spiritual evil they breathe out, which we breathe in." She blew out a stream of flame to emphasize her point.

There was a juggling clown, who appeared to be Fred. His makeup and costume were in the "sad tramp" mode. He said to Julian, "Life is a carnival, but when you die you can't take it with you. All you get to keep is litter and trash left behind afterward."

Anna Kurtz, the amorous museum owner, as the tattooed woman, was the next exhibit. She was wearing a black bikini and looked okay in it. Snakes, spiders, vines, flowers, butterflies, eyes, ravens, satyrs, moons, stars, and ringed planets adorned her lean body, in mostly dark colors with startling bursts of blood-red in places. "What is written in skin is the only art that lasts." She winked at him after offering this bit of wisdom.

These were all just ghosts of his own angst, as far as he could see, so he headed for the exit. He'd never liked carnivals, even as a child. Having his organs jostled around on the rides wasn't his idea of fun, and crowds had always frightened him. On his way out he went by an arcade of game booths. One of the barkers called to him, in a very familiar female voice.

"Try your luck, mister?"

He stopped, turned, and saw Mercy leaning back in a chair with one foot propped up on the front of a booth. She tossed a ball into the air with her right hand and caught it again. She wore blue jeans with the legs rolled up, sneakers, a plaid flannel shirt, and a baseball cap backwards on her head. In real life she wouldn't have been caught dead in such an outfit. Her brown hair was cut short and curled forward, her green eyes gleamed at him, and her moderately full lips smiled with a touch of melancholy.

"Care to play, dude?"

It was a stunning experience to see her again, both painful and pleasurable. All sorts of memories and feelings stirred in him. He remembered kissing those lips, burying his face between those legs, squeezing those breasts. Going over to her, he started to ask her how she was, but realized the absurdity of it. This wasn't Mercy, just a faint trace of her floating around in his mental depths.

"Sure, I'll play."

She stood up and handed him three white baseball-sized balls of solid wood. "Just hit the target in the center and you win."

Then he looked at the target and felt his stomach lurch. It was his painting of the Gate, only it was completed. A black frame with four reptilian eyes in the corners enclosed the center, which was filled with darkness. What would happen if he did strike the bull's-eye with a ball? He decided to find out.

The first ball flew foul to the left. Second one hit below the middle. It was so big, how could he have missed it? He was unnerved, waiting for this whimsical dream to transform itself into a ghastly nightmare at any moment. The third ball hit the image dead center—and went in. Into the hole there, lost in blackness.

"You win," said Mercy cheerfully. "Here's part of your prize." She handed him a rough circle of rock about six inches across with a spiraled fossil embedded in it. The adder stone.

Of course. "You said this was part of my prize. What's the rest of it?"

Her smile turned menacing. "You'll see."

Julian walked on toward the exit, over which a sign said FAREWELL TO THE FLESH. Two huge spotlights raked the heavens just outside the entrance to draw attention to the spectacle. He looked up to see them brush the clouds, and something caught in the brilliance of a beam for just a second, some big hideous winged thing with a white tail. It was so brief a glimpse that he couldn't be sure he'd seen anything at all.

The streets were nearly deserted as he wandered along them, in the downtown section of the city. Something was odd about the streetlights, a violet tint to their glow. And there was a buzzing in the air. Some bees seemed to have found their way into the metropolitan areas. Big ones, he saw as some flew by him, strange looking and green. Like locusts with the tails of scorpions. Killer bees, maybe.

An old woman was walking down the other side of the street in the opposite direction. One of the mutant insects zeroed in on her, landed on her chest, and stung her. She instantly turned into a white statue. The grotesque bug then flew away.

Transfixed where he stood by the sight, Julian stared at the woman. Her life had been taken away in an instant. When he could finally move, he went over to her and touched her shoulder. Some of her came away on his fingers. Crystals. He smelled them, tasted them, found they were salt. She'd been changed into a pillar of salt, like Lot's wife.

As if on cue, the city exploded like Sodom. Out of the gutters, up from the sewers, millions of fat, ugly insects erupted upon Groveland, stinging every living thing in their path. He ran through the hurricane of hard, fluttering bodies and witnessed one massive atrocity after another. At the church wedding of a wealthy man's daughter he saw everyone present suffer the fate of Midas, dying as golden idols. All the children frolicking at a playground were injected with venom that hardened their small bodies into stone. And at a public auditorium filled to capacity, he saw the audience at a rock concert spontaneously combust into a holocaust when the lethal swarm descended on them.

He seemed to be protected from this onslaught, but he wanted to see no more of it. When he came to the tallest building he could find, he went inside and rode the elevator to the top. Heights were something else he liked to avoid, but a few mysteries were troubling him. Ashley had not yet appeared in this dream vision, which was a glaring omission, and he had to know if the flying creature he'd seen circling in the sky like a vulture was real. So he climbed the last few flights of stairs to the roof.

It was real, he saw, and it wasn't alone. There were ten of them, bloated bodies with batlike wings. They had riders, human. One of them was Ashley, waving.

"Never look a gift whore in the mouth," she called to him.

Julian snapped into consciousness. The revelation was over, but it had left him shivering. Or maybe it was just the coldness of the cathedral. Still as a tomb and almost as dark, lit only by the dwindling flame of the nearly empty lamp. He looked at Ashley, whose sleep seemed uneasy. Her brow was wrinkled and her eyes were restless under their lids. She seemed barely to be breathing at times, but then she didn't really have to, did she? In the dim light it looked as if her naked skin was threatening to dissolve away, suggesting the ghostly white form beneath. Her dream self trying to come through. Reminding him that she wasn't quite human.

Did he know her? Did he trust her? Was her heart, at least, human?

The worst part was not knowing.

He was awakened by a scream from somewhere below. In the echoing silence that followed, Vern struggled to get his bearings, recall the particulars of his heinous predicament. Some sort of animate blemish on reality had entered the apartment, somehow coming through the damned painting, and it was now somewhere else in the building. There was another tenant downstairs, a reclusive old eccentric named Bonewitz, and maybe he'd just met their vile visitor. Out of pity Vern hoped the man's death had been quick and not too unnatural.

Then he realized he might be able to get away while it was working its grotesquerie on the poor guy, especially since the sky was brightening outside. His heart pounding with the promise of escape, he flung the door open, rushed into the hallway, and instantly saw that it was too late. The twisted husk was floating back up the stairs already. Despair closed around Vern's brain again and terror almost froze his muscles, but he managed to dash back into the room as the creature scudded down the hall toward him. He slammed the door shut, locked it, and shoved a small bookcase in front of it. Then he stood well away from it.

What had just happened? Was the thing toying with him? More likely it had sensed his falling asleep and taken advantage of the break to feed on Bonewitz. Now it was back, no doubt keeping its vigil in front of the door. There were no windows in the hallway, so it would be immune to the dawn. He was still trapped.

He started thinking then about a way to climb down the outside of the building. Naturally, the fire escape was at the end of the hall opposite the stairs. The skylights were a good twenty feet above and the front windows faced on a sheer drop-off, too high to jump from. No joy there. Some old guy was standing in the street staring up at the loft, he saw. Looked familiar. It was that homeless bum Julian talked to sometimes. He couldn't be any help.

Pacing around the room like the caged animal he felt he was, Vern tried to grasp just how bad his situation was. Something horrible had come out of the painting and was now trying to get him. With that thought he ran over to the picture to take a good look at it, surmising that where one of the things had come through others could follow. Perhaps only the artificial light, now receiving reinforcement from the sun's rays, was keeping them from pouring into the room. And he knew it was probably true, for the design in the picture had dazzlingly changed, was alive with energy and motion. The purple serpents had become writhing bolts of lightning flaring inward toward the central square opening with its four eyes now glaring, and that opening was a fathomless, dizzying void. Black infinity bored through the heart of the image, like the bottomless pit in the floor show at the cathedral, like the hellhole Bethany had generated when he was fucking her.

He tore his gaze away, seething with panic and rage, and took a few steps back from the unbearable sight. She had gotten him into this situation, she and the other bitch, Ashley. If he survived this, he vowed to track them both down and rip them apart limb from limb, just for having put him through such torture.

At least he could slash the painting to ribbons and close the hole before anything else emerged from it. He slipped the jackknife out of his right boot, opened it, and pounced on the painting. The world seemed to make a slow roll and he slammed back against the floor, pain shooting up his arm. The knife flew from his fingers and skidded across the floor, smoking.

It took a few seconds for him to regain his senses. When he did, he looked at his throbbing hand, found most of the skin on it blackened as if burned. He searched for the knife, saw it smoldering near the wall, and crawled over to it. The blade was half melted away. A field surrounded the painting, it seemed, one that living flesh could not endure. It was probably beside the point anyway, he thought with creeping fatalism. If he should manage to cut away the canvas, the configuration would most likely still remain, hanging in the air and puncturing an obscene rent in the fabric of existence.

Julian had unconsciously worked his magic all too well.

Since her death Iris's sensibilities had narrowed to a very few hungers and obsessions, with very little in the way of rational thought. She had been morbid and melancholy in life, cruel to any animal or person that dared to get close to her. These traits had only amplified in her over the decades. They thrived in the absence of any stimulation from the outside world. Her fondest pleasure was preying on the occasional living victim who wandered into the area around the cathedral. Her second fondest pleasure was meeting with the masters.

It wasn't quite as exciting as it once had been, she mused as she descended the steps to the Sanctum. Gone were the days when their sublime unearthly appearance filled her with awe and rapture. Familiarity with their form had made them seem more commonplace, less divine. Still, they remained the shining suns in her dark universe. In their presence Iris felt real, important, integrated into the scheme of things. They were above humanity, undying, and they conferred this immortality upon a few special people, of whom she was one.

She entered the Sanctum, crossed the bridge to the central platform, and waited for them to appear. This was the holiest place in the world, she knew. Here she had received forgiveness, for the terrible things she had done, for the unwholesome thoughts she sometimes had. The same obsession that had plagued her when she was alive plagued her still, an unnatural affection for members of her own gender, but the masters told her that having such urges was not in itself evil. Only acting on them was. Under the guidance of the masters, in the austerity of the cathedral, it was easier to control her sinful desires.

Like beautiful ornaments hanging in the dark, the masters made themselves visible to her. It was seldom that she was summoned to stand alone before them, so she felt honored and blessed.

"Iris MacVay," said Firdausi, in a voice that she thought commanded respect but was full of love, "we are aware that on occasion you have ventured forth into the local environs to stalk and dispatch intruders."

She felt a flush of panic; was she about to be punished?

"It is perhaps an ill use of the living," said the master.

"However, you are a good and faithful servant. And that you keep away the overly inquisitive is of benefit to us. With this in mind we have a task for you. There is no more important work than what we do here at the cathedral. Sometimes, when so much is at stake, sacrifices must be made. Do you agree with the wisdom of this?"

"Yes," she replied, nodding emphatically. "Oh, yes."

"Very well, then. This mortal whom Ashley has brought among us knows too much and has seen too much. For the greater good of mankind his life must be sacrificed. You must put him to the death, in any way that you see fit. Just see to it that you do not leave an abnormal corpse lying where it can be found. Will you carry out this duty for us?"

Iris was thrilled that the masters would entrust her with such vital and unusual business. She was being given permission to hunt down and slay an aliver, and she would be gaining the favor of the masters in the act. "I will, my masters. Without hesitation."

"You please us, Iris. Some of the other guardians might not understand the necessity of this action, so we advise that you dispatch Julian when they are not present. During the ritual purification tomorrow, perhaps. We thank you for your devotion. This audience is at an end."

Their forms began to obscure themselves in shadow again, so she left the chamber, feeling elated. There would be fun and games the next day, and she would dream about them tonight.

If she dreamed anything at all.

14

Stigma and Stigmata

He was awakened by music, loud heavy-metal rock 'n' roll. It was the song "Fade to Black" by Metallica, appropriately enough. Julian lifted his eyelids and rolled over to see Ashley sitting on the edge of the bed, putting on makeup with the aid of a small round mirror on the bookshelf. The base of the mirror had tiny gargoyles adorning the four corners. Next to it the boom box blasted out the dark, forceful tune.

"I'm sorry. Did I wake you?"

Before he suggested that she was probably waking the dead he caught himself. She looked exceptionally lovely to him today, scrubbed and meticulously groomed, wearing black dress jeans and a lacy black tank top with no bra underneath, mascara and lip gloss masterfully applied.

"It's all right. Maybe it'll give me a whole new perspective on the day. What are you all dolled up for this morning?"

The smile she gave him was wan but affectionate. "It's for you. You make me want to take care of my appearance. There have been times in this place when I've really let myself go to pot, let me tell you. No one here to know the difference."

This was the second time she had come close to declaring her love for him, which in its own way was no less amazing than anything else he'd witnessed in the past twenty-four hours. It made him certain that he'd done the right thing in coming here, though he might have endangered his life in doing so. Maybe with her, for her, he could face death without being shattered by terror. She had given him that much. "I love you, Ashley."

Her body jolted as she heard the words. With lowered head, she fluttered her lashes. "You shouldn't say that. It's too easy."

"Not when you mean it. I mean it." He reached for her, but she arched her back away from his touch and stood up.

"Come on. Get up and get dressed. It's almost time for breakfast. We all usually eat the first meal of the day together. You're about to meet the other members of the family, the company I keep." She said "family" with irony, a bit of derision.

"Do you really think of them as your family?"

"Hey, I know it's not much," she said as she hooked a silver crescent-moon earring through her right lobe. "I've spent an awful lot of time alone with these people. I think I'll actually miss some of them when I'm gone. And it's basically the only family most of us have ever had. Bethany was an orphan, Bonita was a freed slave who got separated from her folks, and Iris's parents were killed in a train wreck."

She dropped onto the bed and squeezed his leg through the blanket. "Wait till you meet her. Iris. What a piece of work she is. Her family was poor relations, you know, so when her mom and dad died she was sent to live with rich relatives. They hated her, treated her like dirt, but she talks about them like they were gods. She thinks of herself as one of them now, a real aristocrat. Guess how she died."

Nothing much came to his mind. "Consumption?"

"Nope. I'll use the word she does. Vivisepulture."

Somewhere he'd heard the term before. "She was buried alive?"

"Bingo. Kept having these spells that made her appear to be dead. One just lasted too long and they planted her in the ground. Then, as Bonita puts it, wild Iris rose."

He sat up abruptly. "When did this happen?"

She had to catch herself to avoid getting bounced off the bed. "Sometime around the turn of the century. Why?"

"Well, think about it. What does that say about the masters? They knew she was there in her coffin, screaming and clawing, so they could have sent one of the guardians to tell somebody, but instead they let her die so they could recruit her. It takes a long time to die that way."

She thought about it. "Well, yeah, but maybe they can't sense a potential candidate until they're right at the point of death. I mean, I hate to play the devil's advocate, but I've had firsthand experience with this."

"So have I," he said, gently shaking a finger at her. "They brought me to them when I wasn't physically dead yet. Not completely. So maybe they could have saved Iris if they'd wanted to, if they really care about life the way they say they do. I don't think they care about it at all."

"Well, I told you I didn't think they did."

"No, you're not getting it!" He grabbed her by the shoulder. "The Gate is real. It's part of you and it passed through you into me, into one of my paintings. So it must have a purpose. You've been in the Abyss and you've seen what's in there. Those things are real. Now, last night you mentioned something called the 'sanction of hell.' Well, *sanction* is a funny word. It can mean the forbidding of something, the blockading of it, or it can mean the approval of something. Do you understand now?"

She disengaged herself from him. "Okay. I see what you're getting at. In other words, if anything escapes from the pit, a guardian is supposed to recapture it, not so it won't hurt anybody, but because it might draw attention to the fact that there *is* an Abyss, and that the masters are there watching over it."

Julian nodded and she nodded with him, fast and nervously. "That's what I'm thinking. And there's those murals in the passageway downstairs, showing the masters back when they had more traditional bodies herding Coprolites like cattle. Judging by that, I assume that when one of the things escapes into the land of the living, it can be controlled. Right?"

Her breathing was becoming noticeably more rapid, her fear breeding fear in him. "So the masters tell us. That present I gave you, the Shadow Prism, is supposed to have power over the Coprolites. If it's in your possession, they can't harm you, and it can be used to weave a net of shadow to capture them. Fuck me if that's true. I just liked playing with it."

"There's something else," he said, fighting off dread and a persistent sense of unreality. If things were the way they seemed, then no matter how bizarre they got, he had to keep himself convinced of their concreteness. Disbelief was not conducive to survival now. "Jorge was trying to tell me something when we were alone in the altar room, but I wasn't paying close enough attention. Has he ever said anything to you about what he thinks the masters really are?"

"Just that he thinks they're changing." Her knuckle suffered more abuse from gnawing. "He got that idea from Bonita. I thought maybe they're just aging or something. Maybe altering themselves because they're bored of being the same thing for thousands of years. Jorge's still a little paranoid. He's only been here five years. Got himself gutted in a barroom brawl while he was on leave. Everyone's kind of crazy for a while at first, but you get used to all the everyday strangeness until it just seems normal. He hasn't made the adjustment yet."

The thread of his original thought was threatening to unravel. In fact, it was totally frayed. "Uh, has anything unusual been happening around here lately?"

"Well, Sylvio hasn't been around much for some odd reason. And Iris has started making noises about deposing Kristen and taking over as leader. Other than that, it's been the same old weirdness. Hurry up and get ready or we'll miss the others at breakfast. I'm dying to see their reaction to you."

His head felt light and dizzy as he stood up. Too little food and too much fright. The lack of windows was disorienting, as well as claustrophobic. He disliked not knowing the time of day except by looking at his watch.

"There's some water in the basin on the table if you want to wash your face or anything," she said. "You can use my toothbrush. The toilet's down the hall if you need to use it."

He splashed his face, which had sprouted quite a growth of beard, and bristled some of the grime from his teeth. Then he went in search of the bathroom. It turned out to be a small square room with no door on it. Everything in it was made of bluish stone, including the raised circular hole, which he assumed was the commode. He urinated into it, reached for the handle to flush it, and didn't find one. Maybe it opened on a big receptacle that was emptied when it got full. If so, he hoped the Abyss didn't operate on the same principle.

Returning to Ashley's room, he got dressed and presented himself to her. "Okay. I'm ready."

She picked up a burning oil lamp and led the way. As they walked, a new worry started plaguing him. "Ashley, do all the guardians look, uh, normal? I mean, you and Jorge appear, um, ordinary enough, but you two haven't been here all that long."

"Seems like an eternity to me," she said with world-weariness.

"Yeah. But I met Bethany very briefly. Now, she doesn't look so abnormal that she'd attract a crowd, but she's awfully white. And you've said that some of the guardians are real old, so I thought . . ."

The look she gave him was annoyed but understanding. "Yeah, Stormy, some of the guardians look farther gone than others. But none of them are like movie zombies. A lot of the pallor just comes from not getting any sun. Like I say, some of them don't like to go out at all anymore. To ease the burden of shopping for ten on those of us who do go out, we have most of our provisions delivered in bulk. We claim it's charity for distribution to the poor families in the barrio, and we do in fact hand out some care packages there. But it's all canned and freeze-dried shit, about as palatable as military rations."

They entered the dining room then, which was a cavernous vault containing a long solid-oak table that looked to weigh over a ton. The thousand crystals and many candles of a chandelier sparkled above it. Eight of the other guardians were already waiting for them.

"Is Sylvio going to show up this morning?" Ashley addressed them as a whole, setting her lamp down on a sideboard.

"Sylvio is detained with an errand." The speaker was seated at one end of the formidable slab of wood. She was a tall brunette woman in a black leather gown, not unpleasant looking but with facial features too heavy to call attractive. Her sleeveless garment revealed muscular arms.

The people sitting around the table were staring at him. They were a diverse group, youngish, four males and four females, some looking more vibrant than others.

"Oh," said Ashley. "Then you can take his chair, Julian." She guided him to the vacant chair at the other end of the table, near her own at the corner right of it, and they sat down.

"Everybody, this is Julian," she said, a bit self-consciously. Starting with the woman at the head and proceeding counterclockwise, she introduced the group. They were Kristen, Bethany, the cool beauty named Iris, Jorge, a small black woman named Bonita, a burly bearded man named Rubin, a black man named Nestor, and a lanky scarecrow of a man named Arlo. In college Julian had known quite a number of people deep in the thrall of one drug or many; these folks exhibited the same lack of personal presence they had. He politely acknowledged each one in turn, then looked down at his plate of powdered eggs and reconstituted bacon.

For a while the guardians talked away among themselves, some in languages he didn't recognize, seemingly codes and slangs of their own rather than foreign tongues. They finally took their eyes off him. Bethany was the first to do so, Kristen the last. The latter woman addressed him, regarding him with cold green eyes.

"So tell me, Julian. Have the masters won your heart and mind?"

He studied her a moment, wondering how she'd died. "They have all but overwhelmed my mind, but I don't give my heart easily."

Ashley briefly beamed at him.

"You have stood before them and failed to absorb their wonder?" said Kristen, faintly accusing. "You must be blinder even than most other alivers. Don't you understand the rare privilege you've been granted? You have gazed upon divinity in the darkness, the lords of this world, yet you reserve yourself in the face of their glory. If I had my way this would not be tolerated."

Fanatic, he thought with disgust. "I apologize if my attitude offends you. I'm still trying to convince myself that all this is really happening."

"Oh, it's not as bad as all that," said Bonita, seated at the corner to his left. She was fetching in her way, with thick wavy red hair, a slightly flattened button nose, very full lips, and brown eyes with reddish whites. "Just think of it as a party that never ends, with kind of unusual guests of honor."

"Do you know what your friend did to me?" Bethany suddenly shouted with strained rage, all of it aimed at

Julian, who froze in his chair. "He dragged me into a garbage-strewn alleyway, threw me against the wall, and shoved his thing into me like it was a weapon! He would have killed me with it if he could have. He acted like I was less than a dog to him. The big brute tried to rape my soul along with my body, like the goons who took turns sticking their things into me before they cut me open and left me to die. That's what your friend did to me, and you expect me to sit at the same table with you? Well, I can't. Your people think I'm a horror? You're the horrors. You're a horror to me!"

Her whole body shook with fury as she glowered at him, leaving him utterly mortified. Had Vern really done that to her? Why would he do such a monstrous thing?

"Julian had nothing to do with that, Bethany," Ashley said crossly. "You can't blame him for what some other outsider did."

Bethany's breath caught in her throat. "It was like— like I didn't even have a right to exist. He was torturing me for being what I am, something that's already torture to me."

Was that the explanation? Had her unnatural condition repulsed Vern, evoked a purely primal response of xenophobic loathing from him? He'd punished her for being alien, for daring to be something different that he couldn't understand. Julian constantly submerged himself in such strangeness for his art, so when he came face to face with it he could accept it, was in fact drawn to it. He supposed the irony of it was that Vern, a man who was contemptuous of death, would make an ideal guardian while he, a lover of a guardian, with his dread of the grave could not be one.

It made him feel that his friendship with Vern had

been a lie, more of a parasitic relationship than true camaraderie. He hadn't thought Vern capable of such barbarism.

"Ashley is to blame for this," said Kristen sternly. "Sneaking out and mingling with the motley rabble out there, stirring up trouble. And another of your infractions has come to my notice, Ashley. Something is missing from the Arcade upstairs: the Prism of Shadows. You wouldn't happen to know where it is, would you?"

Ashley concentrated on eating. "No, Kristen. I have no fucking idea."

Her face scrunched up as if she smelled a bad odor. "I told you to curb your foul mouth around me. And I think you took the Prism outside of these walls. You'll pay for it tonight at the ritual when I tell the masters."

Julian watched Ashley pantomime a yammering mouth with her hand, but he could tell it was more bravado than bravura. The fork in her other hand was shaking. He looked down the table at Bethany. "I'm very sorry about what Vern did to you. There's no excuse for it."

She glanced over at him, her face slack. "All I do is serve. I've languished in this dungeon for over seventy years, doing just what I was told, because it's important work. And who is it for? Not us. Those creatures in the pit can't hurt *us*. And how am I repaid for my devotion? I get attacked and violated. I get reminded of my humiliating death all over again. It's not fair."

"No, it's not," said Ashley, looking up. "And it would be even more unfair if the work we're doing isn't even what we think it is."

"Oh, don't start that nonsense again," said Iris. She had a remarkably resonant voice, Julian thought, rich and strong. Her hair was long and brown, her nose was narrow, and she had small doelike brown eyes, the overall effect marred only by the cruel twist to her thin but sensual lips. "We are what we are and the masters are what they are."

"Yeah? Well, I've never been able to buy it." She tapped her fork on her plate. "Why should we believe them? People lie all the time, to themselves, to others. I should know. I had a lot of husbands as customers. Wives too. Nobody tells the truth. And nobody puts themselves on the line for anyone else. I never got this impression of deep-down goodness from our mighty rulers. They never struck me as the self-sacrificing types. I've heard some of you say similar things at times."

"Keep it up," said Kristen, smiling vindictively. "I'll tell them everything you've said."

"Oh, go ahead. I don't care anymore." Throwing her fork down, she crooked her right leg up into her chair and draped her right arm over it. "If they gave a shit about the value of life they'd value freedom as well. And if they were honest they wouldn't be afraid of questions and doubt. They're going to punish me for speaking my mind? For trying to have a life of my own? Let them. Fuck them."

It now dawned on Julian what she was doing. She was feeling out their loyalties, gauging their willingness to rebel, and doing it brilliantly.

"Ashley, you're always going to be an ignorant harlot, aren't you?" Iris again. "We aren't ordinary mortals. We have been chosen to perform a special duty. It requires discipline. Our work must be a secret, so the masters must take pains to see that it remains so. A rigidly governed unit like an army can work for the cause of freedom for others. So it is with us. Although this army could use a wiser general."

He'd been waiting for that, the political infighting.

"Like you?" Kristen, to Iris. "Hah! You're too full of yourself to lead, too handicapped by vanity. You would use power for your own glorification and neglect the principles that guide us. I serve the masters so well because I love them. You love only yourself."

Iris started to reply, but Arlo interrupted. "My, my, don't we all have a real high and holy opinion of ourselves here?" Short, almost skeletally thin, possibly the youngest of the guardians, he spoke with an unmistakable southern drawl. "Ain't we all forgetting one very important fact? We're all dead, and most of us didn't die very good deaths. In spite of what Bethany said, to the world at large we *are* horrors. We're their worst nightmares. They tell stories about us to scare the kiddies at night. So before we go putting ourselves up on pedestals like statues of Greek gods let's try to keep that in mind. We were scoundrels and gutter dwellers in life. Maybe our messy ends have made us even worse dregs of humanity."

"Speak for yourself, Arlo," said Kristen. "Better yet, be silent."

"Let him talk," Iris countered, probably out of pure spite. She couldn't like what he was saying any more than the other woman.

He directed his commentary at Julian. "I'm just saying the whole queer arrangement is no more wholesome than it looks. And we've gotten just what we deserve. Of course, little Ashley there doesn't quite see things that way, but then she hasn't been crossed over all that long, has she? No, she still insists on seeing herself as a victim of circumstance. And then you've got Kristen here, who sees all this as her glorious appointment with destiny. I think it's neither. It's the purgatory that we asked for, nothing more."

Rubin groaned. "Oh, God, I'm really tired of hearing that manic depressive ranting day after day. It's always the same thing." He looked at Julian. "You must understand, Arlo is a born masochist and he wants us all to flagellate ourselves along with him. It's all that guilt he brought along. Me, I think that here in the cathedral you finally see the real way of things, how they have been all along. Humans are a dark breed, a race of monsters wearing pleasant masks of flesh, still red in tooth and claw. To suffer and cause others pain is simply our lot as upright beasts not long out of the jungle. Mercy, love, and morality are far too feeble medicines for that hereditary disease. It's not a matter of sin, has nothing to do with good and evil. The only sensible gods for creatures like us are the masters. Gods who are as much dead as they are living. People have only been kidding themselves with grand illusions of angels, heaven, messiahs, saints, gurus, higher reason, and utopia. Is it not reflected in outside society, aliver? Where religion isn't dying it's being preached by fools."

Their attitude toward Julian seemed condescending, but the attention the guardians were paying him betrayed their true intent. He believed they were trying to justify themselves to him, get his reaction to what they had become. If they could gain acceptance by a normal human being, perhaps they could convince themselves that they weren't such monsters after all.

Ashley touched Julian's arm, leaning close. "Do you have any idea how many times I've had to listen to that?"

She slammed her fist down on the table, rattling the glasses and silverware. "I've said it before and I'll say it again. We are not any worse than anyone else, and the human race isn't totally awful. Yeah, sure, we're all fuck-ups here in the cathedral, but only because that's the sort of people who get themselves killed at a young age, and who learn not to value their own lives. That's what the masters were looking for, what they needed. I spread a lot of bad vibes in my life, but what was done to me was grievously wrong. It wasn't fair and I didn't ask for it. I think the same can be said for everyone else here as well."

"Speak for yourself," said Arlo, smirking.

"Then why do you submit to stigmatization, Ashley?" Rubin spoke with patronizing curiosity. "Why are you going to march into the altar room tonight and just stand there while the masters tear away more of your etheric body? If you haven't earned all those bloody badges, why let them be gouged into you?"

Her eyes met Julian's and they shared dread, both of the dire fate she faced and what the knowledge of it would do to him. "How can I stand against them?" she said, looking down at her plate. "There's ten of them and all of you. I have nothing to give me an advantage."

Arlo pointed a bony finger at her. "But you never so much as protest such treatment. You take your beating like a dog who's soiled a carpet and say nothing."

"And what do you do, Arlo?" Ashley's voice was high pitched with aggravation. "You don't do anything to bring on punishment because you've been cowed into submission."

His brows twitched ever so slightly. "I've learned my place. I don't act up no more."

"Yeah, your place. In what? To what? What if inside their pretty shells the masters are really hideous evil bastards? Huh? Have you ever thought of that?"

"Stop it, you're scaring me," he mocked.

Kristen stood, sighing scornfully. "I've heard enough of this idiocy. It's all completely irrelevant. Matters will be put right at the ritual." Then she glided out of the room with a suppleness that seemed unlikely for her rather stocky physique.

"Good riddance." Ashley leaned over the table, taking them all in. "I'll tell you this. I *will* resist tonight, but I need you all to side with me. If you don't, I may be ripped apart by the masters. I don't know what that'll be like, but I suspect there are worse things than death."

"Count me out," said Iris, standing. "You got yourself into this, Ashley. It's your problem, not ours."

Nestor joined her, grinning coldly at Ashley. "My advice to you is to learn to love the whip."

Then the two of them left.

"You know what I think?" said Rubin to Ashley. "You're just throwing up a smoke screen so that your lover boy there won't see the real you. You don't want him to know what sort of denatured freak he's fallen for."

"That's enough!" snapped Julian, catching himself too late and fearing Rubin had struck a nerve.

Arlo smiled broadly at him, then turned to Ashley. "Besides, even if the masters are somewhat less pristine than they present themselves to be, so what? I think I can live with it. They are unique beings in creation, and as their servants that makes us unique too. What more can you ask for in life and death, or in love and war?"

"And what is this?" she swiftly retorted. "Who do you

love and who are we at war with? If this comes down to a fight, which side will you be on, Arlo? I know that in a worldly war you fought for the forces of preservation and liberation. You had no trouble taking a stand then."

His grin trembled only a little. "Yeah, well, that was an awful long time ago. And I was a deserter, don't forget."

"Yes, I remember. You said you fled the battle not because you were afraid to die for your cause, but because you couldn't stomach the killing. You told me that you weren't a killer. A man who cannot kill cannot serve killers."

He met her gaze silently for several seconds. "Look at this. I'm getting an ethics lesson from a sleazy whore."

Ashley's determined expression remained unchanged. "You know I haven't been that for many years. And it was a service, not a vice."

"Ethics mean nothing to the dead," said Rubin tauntingly.

Jorge, the dead soldier, spoke up then, infuriated. "How can you say that, man? Didn't you say you got your head split open in a labor uprising? Weren't you a union organizer at a time when people looked at your type and only saw red? Now, it seems to me that you gave your life improving the plight of workers. You must have cared about something then. Why should your death change that? It was your body that died, not your judgment. You're the one who's killing that now."

"I don't want to see Ashley get scourged any more," said Bonita, meekly but with a touch of petulance. "What the masters did to her at the last ritual was bad enough. They might destroy her this time. She's our friend and we can't let that happen to her."

Rubin's eyes shot back and forth. "What are you asking us to do? Bring the whole house down on our heads? What will happen? Where will it end? We can't just overthrow everything. It's been this way for centuries."

"It's different now," said Ashley, more softly but still insistent. "Something has happened. I think the masters were counting on me creeping out at night, meeting someone, maybe Julian specifically or just any artist. Maybe they expected me to revert to my hooking ways. They knew that when I made love with someone, a vision of the Gate would appear in his mind. Well, that's exactly what took place. He saw it and he painted it. I think I've been manipulated into manipulating him into opening up the Abyss."

"I don't think it can be opened yet," Julian interjected. "The painting's not finished. There's still a big blank spot in the center."

"I see now." Jorge nodded pensively. "That must be why the masters were so anxious to banish you from here yesterday, so you'd go home and complete it."

Ashley puzzled over this. "Then they suddenly changed their minds and let him stay. I wonder why."

"Maybe they decided they weren't quite ready yet. Maybe they aren't through changing their bodies, but perhaps they soon will be."

"How?" said Bethany in a faint voice. "How could they be changing down there, suspended over the pit? They can't even come up out of there if we don't summon them."

Jorge fiddled with his napkin. "I figure it like this. I took a little physics before I dropped out of college, so I've come up with an analogy. I've told you guys about black holes, the collapsed gravity wells in space that suck everything into themselves. Well, if you could somehow land on one and survive on its surface, you could maybe perform miracles. You could convert matter to energy, energy to matter. Pure magic. I think the Abyss is like that. It exerts a force over the Coprolites, pulls them back into it. Some of that power was used to raise us from the dead. The masters might also be using it to undergo a metamorphosis of some kind. That's my theory, anyway."

Julian was very impressed with this analysis. It didn't seem quite so convincing to Bethany, however. "But why? What are they trying to do?"

Before anyone could answer, a gong sounded in the depths of the cathedral. All the guardians save Ashley quickly stood.

"What's that?" he asked her as the others filed out.

She slumped mournfully for a few seconds. "It's the call to prepare the altar room for the ritual. The masters demand that the chamber be absolutely spotless before they project themselves into it, so we've got to go and scrub it down."

"Can I help?"

Ashley shook her head. "You would be considered unclean by the masters. Stay and finish your breakfast."

They kissed and clung together, for a moment feeling totally alone except for one another, surrounded by a hollow, hostile universe. Its devastating vastness swirled past them but not through them, blocked out as it was by the sense of substantiality they gave each other.

Then she slipped from his grasp and left him. Alone.

15

Hunted and Haunted

Without Ashley by his side to reassure him Julian's anxieties began to run wild again. He found little comfort in the words of the guardians, who seemed to be a selfish and confused bunch at best. And he was convinced that the masters were bad news. Really bad news. Which left him with the dilemma of what to do next. They had used him to create the painting of the Gate, but he had been diverted from finishing it by Vern's interference, his pursuit of Ashley to the cathedral. First the masters had commanded him to leave, presumably so he would go and complete the work, but then they'd let him stay. Why? Maybe the half-dreamed vision he'd had last night offered him an answer. Or a warning. After a certain point a painting of the Gate might finish itself, or maybe the center didn't need to be filled in like the rest of the design. He'd seen a hole there where his brush hadn't made a mark, after all. However it might happen, there was a very real danger that the painting was done, or soon would be. Maybe he should go back to his apartment and check it out.

And maybe he should do it right away.

Julian rose, grabbed the lamp Ashley had carried in, and headed toward the outer exits. If he hurried he could get there and back in time for the midnight ritual, perhaps find some way to prevent Ashley's torture or even execution, though he still didn't like the idea of leaving without her. Getting back in might also pose a problem. As he threaded his way through the cathedral's tight passageways, he decided that he had no choice. He'd seen too much weirdness to just sit idly by and let things happen. That was his usual way of dealing with demands that were made upon him. No more.

He passed by doorless rooms, either empty or full of clutter, on each side of the corridor. Boxes, furniture, statuary, probably the expensive antiques Ashley had spoken of. Some of the objects looked precious, judging by his limited expertise, but he resisted the impulse to stop and examine any of them. It made him think of the masters as dragons, hoarding treasures and lovely young maidens but unable to make use of either. Such a comparison was not quite accurate, for the masters apparently applied their wealth, and the guardians were hardly maidens.

When he finally came to a closed door, he had no doubt it led to the outside, though it was obviously not the same one he'd come in through. This exit was located in a foyer with a fresco of homely winged figures, angels or devils or perhaps neither, adorning the walls. He studied the door and was relieved to see that it could be unlocked from the inside without a key, by virtue of an oval knob above the handle. It was reasonable to assume that the door locked automatically when it closed, so he resolved not to shut it completely once he was through it. He released the lock, turned the knob, then opened the door and stepped out into the sunlight.

Blinking in the sudden brightness, Julian set the lamp down against the door frame to help keep the door ajar. The area looked a lot different in the daytime, less sinister if no less dreary. And as confining as the atmosphere of the cathedral was, he felt exposed out here in the open. There were perils within and perils without. As he walked away from the building, he also realized that he didn't know which direction to go in. One of the perils he faced out here was getting lost in the surrounding industrial wasteland.

The way that seemed the most familiar was between two structures with high corrugated metal walls, heavy on the rust. So he set out, unsure of his path or his mission. If he reached his loft and found the painting finished, what would he do then? Set fire to it? Splatter it with black pigment? And if he found it unfinished . . .

Wait a minute, he thought, stopping in front of a chain-link fence and leaning against it. Now he wasn't even sure of his motivation. What if he was actually acting on an unconscious compulsion to go back and complete the painting himself, all the while deluding himself that he was intent on preventing its completion? He'd made love with Ashley last night and seen the image of the Gate in the wild vision he'd had. It remained in his mind in its totality; he could see it there still. Perhaps the masters had planned this, detaining him so that he would have sex with Ashley and thus imprint the Gate on his brain one final time. If so, he was falling right into their trap.

Ambivalence paralyzed him for a moment. Still, there was no way he could return to the cathedral without ascertaining the status of the painting. And he believed that now that he knew he'd been influenced into creating it, he could resist the impulse to finish it. Or preserve it. He had to go on, even at the risk of complying with the will of the masters.

On this journey through the maze of factories Julian tried to keep track of street names, if only to catalogue dead ends and roads to nowhere. It was noon and the sun was directly overhead, so he couldn't tell east from west just yet. Down Prime Way, turning onto Bush Boulevard, following a long stretch of pavement called Selva Avenue, he grew less certain of his course as he traveled. When he came to an intersection offering him the option of taking Avebury Street, he paused and thought about it. As he turned his head to the right, he caught a glimpse of a dark, slender shape some distance behind him, moving in his direction.

There was nothing there when he looked back the way he'd come, but there were plenty of places to hide. If he was being followed, it was more than likely by one of the guardians. This development didn't shed any light on the wisdom of his mission, for his pursuer could have been assigned to stop him or see if he made it to his destination. Or maybe just to remove him totally from the equation. With rising paranoia he kept on going straight, watching and listening for signs of his stalker.

It didn't take him long to verify that he wasn't alone, for whoever was walking in his tracks made no secret of it. She was a tall brunette in a brown dress, a glance over his shoulder revealed. Iris. Ashley had told him something about the woman, that she liked to lurk in the labyrinth under the cathedral on the off chance that someone would wander in to become her victim. Like a black widow in her web. Did the masters approve of such an activity? Hell, they probably encouraged it. And they had more than likely sicced her on him. He'd stupidly made her task simpler by leaving the cathedral, so that she could dispose of him without inviting objections or questions from the other guardians. *Smart move, Stormer.*

He quickened his pace and she matched it. She was still a hundred yards or so behind him, but he swore he could see the grin on her cruel lips. Should he just stop and casually confront her? Something told him that would be the worst thing he could do. Iris didn't like to venture into the outside world, he'd been told, so if she was out here it had to be with a definite purpose in mind. Chase, capture, torture, and execution, he guessed. Not wanting to find out for sure, Julian broke into a run.

One look back assured him that flight was futile, for her stride was so swift that she seemed to be skimming across the pavement. She was gaining on him, and he was running full out now. If he wanted to prolong his life, he had to elude her another way, forestall his doom until he could think of some way to deal with her, though increasing panic was clouding his reason. When he came to a bent and broken metal door in the side of a brick building, he yanked it open and fled into the greasy shadows beyond, desperate for a place to hide.

Light from the dust-coated windows and holes in the roof showed him that this was a machine shop of some kind. Drills, lathes, and grinding machines loomed in the dark expanse of the room, all going to ruin. It had not been a good choice; there was not much in the way of hiding places here.

"Hi de hi, aliver," said a sonorous voice from behind him.

He turned and saw Iris framed by the doorway, her lean but shapely form looking black and detailless against the brightness of the daylight.

"What do you want?" he asked her, trying to keep the fear out of his voice. Remembering the trick Ashley had done with her eyes in the Quarry, he worried that he might witness worse from Iris's gaze.

She advanced into the factory, and he retreated behind a workbench. "I just came to see if you needed help finding your way. It wouldn't do to have you get lost out here in all this wrack and ruin."

There was no sign of transformation in her eyes or her flesh, though he didn't really know what to look for. He was confronting someone who was beyond nature, which in itself wasn't so horrible, but this one had no love for him or his kind.

"I wonder why I don't believe you," he said, deciding that a bit of audacity might daunt her.

"Because you are a creature of so little faith. As such you are an affront to all that is pure and true."

As she spoke she moved toward him, driving him to duck behind first one work station and then another. She was as relentless as a panther in her approach, looking like a phantom from the past as she strode between the pieces of machinery.

"And just what is true, Iris?" His first strategy didn't seem to be working, so he thought he'd try being clever with her. Not that he had much confidence in this course of action.

She laughed lightly. "Death is truth, aliver. And you are about to receive it, and the truth shall set you free."

His remaining composure collapsed and he ran again, into an office, where he slammed the door shut, locking it. He grabbed a metal chair and lodged it under the doorknob. Now he was trapped, behind a barrier that probably wouldn't hinder her for long. Ashley's physical strength bordered on the superhuman, and so no doubt did that of her undead sister. A weapon of some sort might come in handy, so he looked around the room. There was a desk, a cushioned chair, a filing cabinet, a clipboard and a faded cheesecake calendar hanging on the wall, and a wooden box full of tools on the floor. Julian found a length of steel pipe in the box, drew a mote of comfort from its weight and solidity, then waited to see if he would have to use it. And if it would make any difference.

Iris's fist punched through the wood of the door with an impact that would have fractured most of the bones in an ordinary hand. She reached in through the splinters, turned the lock, and forced open the door, sending the chair flying. Her eyes still looked normal, if extremely intense, as she stood studying him for a few moments. There was a totally unintentional sensuality to her, in the swells of her breasts, the slimness of her waist, the length of her concealed legs, in her flowing black hair and dark eyes. He was attracted to her in spite of himself, even through his fear.

"I don't see what Ashley finds so fascinating about you," she said. "You seem like a weakling to me, just common riffraff. Then again, she's naught but a whore herself. How can you claim to love such a one?"

Was there a touch of jealousy in her voice? It was very possible that she'd never known love in her life, either emotional or sexual, judging by what Ashley had told him about her. Maybe she envied those who could still feel it.

"Love is blind?" he offered her with a nervous shrug.

"Hah!" she sneered, right before she lunged at him, knocking him against the wall next to the filing cabinet. The pounce came so quickly, he almost didn't have time to employ his weapon, but he managed to bring the pipe down with some force on her neck where it met her left shoulder. Its only effect was to knock her slightly off balance as her right hand closed around his throat. With her left hand she grabbed the pipe from him and tossed it away.

"Do not flee," Iris said with grinning glee. "Do not resist me. It is an honor to meet your end at the hands of one of the chosen. I shall fill you with the beauty of the void, the cold and pure darkness of it. Let me merge you with the Abyss."

Her fingers weren't icy but they felt hard, like wood, though they weren't yet choking him. The cuff of her sleeve was fringed with ragged lace, and she smelled like a forest in autumn, like fallen and decomposing leaves. Each guardian seemed to have his or her own signature scent, he mused crazily, perhaps indicating to a greater or lesser degree how much life they retained within them. It was strange the things one noticed when facing death.

"Shall I give you a gift first?" she asked him. "Shall I drag you alive through the Abyss before I fill you with its frigid darkness? Would you like that? Would you like to see firsthand what lurks there?"

He struggled in her grip, but it was like fighting against a statue. All he could think to do now was appeal to her sense of mercy, if such a thing still resided inside of her. "Listen, Iris. I know how you died. Your family hated you. I know that. Maybe they buried you alive on purpose. I think you believe that. It's them you're angry at. Not me. Not the living, but the people who didn't want you. The ones who thought of you as a burden so they allowed you to die a horrid death. It's them you hate."

She didn't even flinch from his words. "Wrong, Julian. It *is* you I hate."

"Wait a minute," he pleaded, grasping at straws. "If you kill me, it'll be like killing one of your own kind. I mean, I was almost one of you. A guardian."

Iris rigidly shrugged her shoulders. "So what if you speak the truth? That simply means that you were rejected as unworthy."

Her face moved closer to his, her eyes starting to darken. He tried to look away but his gaze was fixed, getting pulled deeper and deeper into successive recesses of darkness within her stare, into a whole world of hollow hurt yawning there. A pulsing blackness began to grow in the center of his brain in response to this glaring void. It started spreading, and Julian thought in his terror, *This is worse than I ever imagined death would be.*

Then Iris caught sight of the wall calendar, on which a beautiful young blonde in a string bikini was tugging at the bottom part of her suit as if about to remove it completely. Her gaze shifted to look at the picture, freeing Julian's eyes from hers. The sight seemed to freeze Iris on the spot, giving him pause to wonder if it was the open sensuality of the photograph or the date—June of 1972—that had so unsettled the woman. Either way, a lot had changed since the time in which she had lived.

"What has the world become?" she asked with a touch of awe and disgust, her eyes reverting to normal.

He shook his head as the encroaching shadow dissipated from his mind. Iris's distraction didn't weaken her hold on him, he discovered as he fought to get loose. It was relief enough just to have felt the withdrawal of the invisible deadening tendril that she'd somehow projected into his head.

"It's a place where nothing succeeds like excess," he answered her, startled by his own wit under such grim circumstances.

"Let him go, you fucking bitch!" a familiar female voice shouted from the office doorway. He was able to lean his head to the side enough to see Ashley standing there, tensed and ready for battle. With her eyes and her mouth narrowed to mere slits, she was indeed a terror to behold in her rage.

"Go back to the cathedral, Ashley," Iris said to her without turning, appearing only mildly annoyed. "This does not concern you. I am about the masters' business and you are in enough trouble as it is."

Ashley stepped into the room and shoved the desk out of her way with one hand. "I don't know if the masters told you to do this or not. I don't give a fuck either way. Leave him alone or I'll rip your heart out."

Looking down with a smirk of amused pity on her face, Iris finally let go of Julian and turned around to confront Ashley. He stayed where he was, however, uncertain about what might happen next.

"Very well," Iris said to her. "I have released him. But I will tell you something. I do not like to be threatened. And I do not disobey the masters. They want him killed."

"Yeah, well, they want a lot of things." She glanced at Julian, then fixed her glare on Iris. "Most of all, they want us to be their unthinking slaves. Think for once, will you, Iris? They claim to love the living, but they've told you to kill one of them for no reason at all. Now, how does that make any sense?"

Iris stood silently for several seconds. "They said that sacrifices must be made. He possesses too much knowledge about them and us, which is your fault. It is because of you that he must die."

Ashley shook her head in disgust. "You believe everything they tell you, don't you? I'm telling you, they lie through their teeth. Like, has it ever occurred to you that the masters could have saved you from death? They knew you were alive in your coffin, sensed you freaking out in the grave, but they just let you go through all that horror."

She thought this over for some time. "What of that? They have made me superior to the living. They were right to do what they did."

"I'm real happy you feel that way, Iris," said Julian, "but I don't want to be anything other than alive. I just want to live. Is that too much to ask?"

"We're sisters under the skin," Ashley said to her. "Both battered around by the world, given a raw deal. Let's not take it out on anyone else anymore, huh? Besides, he's my lover. If you had one, I certainly wouldn't want any harm to come to him."

Iris snorted at this remark, then walked toward the exit. In the doorway she paused and pointed at Julian. "He must accompany us back to the cathedral and be put under guard. He cannot be allowed to wander free with what he knows. And you are not my sister, Ashley." Then she was gone.

Ashley let out a sigh of relief. "We'd better do as she says or she just might change her mind. What are you doing out here anyway? I noticed Iris wasn't around for the cleansing of the chapel and I got a bad feeling. Then I couldn't find either of you in the cathedral and got an even worse feeling."

"I'm really glad you did," he said, going to her and hugging her. She barely returned the gesture. "I got worried about the painting. What if it gets finished somehow? I have to go and check on it."

"We'll sort it out later. I've got enough on my mind as it is. Come on. Let's go back."

When they arrived at the cathedral, Bonita was standing at the open door, apparently waiting to take him into custody.

"Iris told me to keep an eye on him," she said, smiling serenely. "It sure has been a strange day."

Ashley looked unhappily at Julian. "Why don't you wait in my room? I'll come to you when I can. Try to stay out of trouble."

He just nodded and let Bonita lead him back into the cathedral's depths, lighting the way with her lamp. Naturally he was glad he'd survived the ordeal, but he felt deflated and helpless and totally out of ideas.

"So what sort of game were you and Ashley and Iris playing out there in the no-man's-land?"

Bonita spoke with an accent, sort of a cross between a southern drawl and a New England nasality. He hadn't really noticed it earlier, but now he took a vague interest in her. She wore a sleeveless pink blouse and a long black skirt, and she smelled faintly of orange blossoms. Her way of dealing with her living-dead state seemed to be that she didn't take it very seriously.

"None," he replied. "Except that maybe I was the game."

She puzzled over this. "That doesn't sound pleasant.

But then, Iris can get carried away sometimes. I'm sorry you ain't having a better time here. I myself very much enjoy going out to be among your people."

This last phrase struck Julian as odd. He'd always thought of himself as an outsider among the living. It was difficult to think of them as "his people," but the guardians were even more alienated from them than he was.

They came to Ashley's room and he sat on the bed, she in the chair. An awkward silence followed, making him feel uneasy toward her. Somehow, the cheerfulness of this survivor of the grave was even worse than the darker attitudes her fellow guardians exhibited. He decided that making conversation with her might take his mind off his troubles.

"Won't you be missed at the purification of the altar room?" he asked.

Bonita wrinkled her nose at him, squinting slightly. "Um, maybe a little. But somebody has to watch you. You've caused quite a stir around here. Then again, maybe that's what this place needed. It was becoming too much like a tomb."

She scooted closer to the bed, scraping the legs of her chair across the stone floor. "Truth be told, I'm glad we have this little time to chat. We have something in common. I once worked in the arts."

"In what sense?"

"In every sense." She giggled. "Actually, I was an artist's model. I was also a free woman and a libertine. I loved the company of gentlemen and they considered it a privilege to share my company. Their wives and mothers didn't take kindly to it after a time, however. A mob of them cornered me in an alley one night and stoned me to death. What do you think of that?"

The years seemed to have drained the trauma of the experience from her; she told the tale casually. He felt sorry for her nonetheless. "I think it's a shame."

Bonita nodded emphatically. "Damn right it is. But the masters, they brought me back, made up for the injustice of it somewhat. I admit, it hasn't been much of a life in this dismal place, but at least it's life. And I have my dreams to keep me happy. Dreaming keeps me from fading away, from forgetting. But it ain't as good as the genuine article. Nothin' can match that."

Julian didn't know a lot about women, but he believed he understood what she was getting at. When she exposed the full length of her left leg through the slit in her skirt, he was sure of it.

"You're a very handsome boy," she said, cocking her head at him and half closing her eyes. "We could make some dreams come true for each other, right here and now."

He stood up as she reached her hand out to touch his knee. This was just too crazy, having one guardian try to kill him and then another try to seduce him. Oddly, he'd been more aroused by the one with the murderous intentions, but he had no wish to succumb to the desires of either. "Uh, hey, couldn't you show me around the cathedral some? I mean, if you're with me I can't do any mischief. What do you say? I'd really like to see the place."

Her lower lip protruded in a pout of disappointment. "I think what I had in mind would be more pleasurable, but I'll give you a guided tour if you like. Then maybe you'll do me a favor later if I ask."

She led the way with her lamp again as he counted his blessings for this reprieve. It gave him time to formulate a second ruse in case she came on to him again, as he wanted to avoid refusing her outright. There was no telling what sort of reaction you could expect if you spurned a woman who'd been to hell and back.

"There ain't a whole lot to see," she said in a light tone of voice. "But one thing is for sure: this place is a lot better than where we dwelled in Baltimore. That was just a run-down old lighthouse."

She seemed to want to keep up the friendly conversation, and he saw no harm in obliging. "Poe died in Baltimore, didn't he? Ever visit his grave?"

Bonita laughed. "I believe I met the man once."

That was possible, he supposed, but he doubted it. Julian wondered why the masters hadn't reaped the troubled, alcoholic, drug-addicted writer upon his death. Perhaps they'd tried and he had been found wanting somehow, as had Julian himself. If so, he was extremely curious to know what Poe's reaction to meeting the masters had been.

They followed several narrow corridors, passing by more rooms filled with antiquities; then they entered a fairly large chamber with wall-to-wall shelves crammed with books. The musty smell of aged paper and old bindings saturated the air of the room, which also contained some cabinets and tables of polished wood and three plush chairs. This was clearly the library of the as-yet-unseen Sylvio. There were about two thousand hardcover titles here, he estimated, some of them very old and rare indeed. They dealt with just about every subject, with a heavy leaning toward philosophy, poetry, and magic black, white, and gray. Latin, Italian, English, and French were the only languages he recognized. The others he couldn't be sure of. Now that he saw all these books, he doubted Ashley had read every one in here. These volumes would not be easy reading for a scholar, so even if she did have a lot of time on her hands, she would surely have found the going too tough. It seemed a harmless enough boast, however, an attempt to impress him with her newly acquired erudition.

"This is where Sylvio wastes all his time, poring over dull words," said Bonita with mild contempt. "When he graces us with his presence at all, that is. I fail to see how he finds comfort and pleasure staring at lifeless pages."

Julian pulled one of the books off a shelf. It was entitled *Clavicules de Salomon* and seemed to be handwritten in archaic French. As far as he could tell, recalling what little French he'd learned in high school, it dealt with the evocation of demons. In fact, it appeared to be a classic text on the subject, full of diagrams of magic circles and precise descriptions of necessary preparations. He wondered, could Coprolites truly be drawn out of the Abyss by these means, or was his painting of the Gate the only way, and these other methods only distorted echoes of it? Instead of inscribing a pentagram with a consecrated knife, he had rendered a grotesque pattern with an inspired brush, which was evidently a more powerful sort of magic after all.

"Maybe Sylvio just takes an interest in his work," he said to Bonita distractedly.

"Him? Hah! He's the laziest man I ever met."

A rank smell touched Julian's nostrils, more pungent than his own fermenting body odor. He had time to find it familiar before he heard a male voice say, "Ah, I thought I heard voices in here. Greetings, Bonita. And a sincere welcome to you, Julian."

He turned to look in the doorway and saw Fred standing there. Fred the tramp, the beggar, the wino. Fred who lived on the street near Julian's place and wore filthy ragged clothing, which he still had on.

"Fred? What the fuck are you doing here?" What else could he say?

Fred smiled cryptically at him. "Do you like my collection?" His accent was more pronounced now and unmistakably Italian. "It took me many years to put together. I'm quite proud of it."

Julian caught on then and his anger quickly followed. Apparently he'd been manipulated even longer than he'd thought. "You're Sylvio."

He bowed like an aristocrat. "At your service. I have long waited to have this conversation with you, my boy. Open and honest. I dislike deceit. I find it most distasteful."

Waddling over to a cabinet, Sylvio lifted a crystal decanter and poured some amber liquid into a snifter. "Would you like some, Julian?"

Julian's accusing stare was his answer.

"Your loss." He swished the brandy around, then sipped it, quite differently from the way Julian had seen him gulp down cheap wine from paper bags. "Ah. Quite an improvement from the swill I have been imbibing lately. What your degraded culture does to the fermented grape is a sin."

"What the fuck is going on around here?" Julian snapped at him. The man's casual attitude in the midst of this absurd situation was even more infuriating.

Sylvio plopped his bulk down in one of the overstuffed

green velvet chairs, daintily holding his drink. Clad in his dirty garments, he looked like a clownish thief invading a rich man's house. Yet something in his face, a residual nobility, betrayed that he was used to being among luxury and finery. "Please do not be vulgar, dear boy. This is a room of culture, after all."

As if to totally undercut this last line, he promptly stuck his left pinky up his left nostril, dug deep for a moment, then studied what he had withdrawn on the end of it. Exactly as Fred was in the habit of doing. "Please have a seat and let me tell you my story. I have not had anyone new to tell it to in a long time and I assure you that you will find it quite fascinating."

So many questions were racing through Julian's head that he couldn't settle on a single one to ask, so he decided just to follow Sylvio's suggestion. He returned the book to the shelf and sat down in the chair next to the man.

"I was born in the town of Cefalú," Sylvio began cordially, a bit boastfully, "a small port in northern Sicily, in the year 1161 A.D. As a young man I apprenticed myself to the alchemist Leontius, who bestowed upon me the name Desiderius because of my eagerness to learn the craft. Once I had absorbed all he had to teach me, which wasn't much, as he was more mountebank than magician, I began to travel in search of further knowledge. First I scoured the length of Italy for every scrap of occult lore I could find. Then I made my way across the continent, through the regions that are now Germany, France, and England, finding I had a talent for quickly mastering foreign tongues. Satisfied that I had acquired a scholarship of magic unparalleled in Europe, I returned to Italy and settled in Florence, where I established my laboratory in a hall of the palazzo of Count Utrecchio. He was much interested in the workings of alchemy, you see, and became my benefactor."

Julian noticed that Bonita looked bored and had taken to perusing a copiously illustrated edition of *Paradise Lost*. No doubt she'd heard this tale more than once before.

"I labored hard and fervently at my art. In time I succeeded in creating a spark of life in my aludel and transmuting a small amount of lead into gold in my athanor, but it was not enough for me. I longed for a truly great work."

Sylvio took a sip of brandy, his eyes gazing off into space, into the distant past. "So I resumed my travels, this time to the East. Cathay, India, and the Levant. Still I did not find what I desired. Until I heard tales of an abandoned temple deep in the Persian desert where the secrets of heaven, hell, and earth could be discovered, at the risk of life and reason. It was my destiny calling to me, I was certain."

"Sylvio, now that you're here, will you watch him?" Bonita suddenly said, sounding petulant. "There seems to be no reason for me to remain here."

"Do not interrupt, child," growled Sylvio, irritated that his epic narration had been tripped up. "If you have been charged with his keeping, then do not seek to shirk your duty. When I am through I must change my attire and report to the masters. So stay put and be patient."

Bonita pretended to ignore him, but she didn't go anywhere. The man turned back to Julian and smiled apologetically. "Now then, to continue: In the fifty-first year of my life, I set out across that tract of desolation known as the Sahra al-Hijra, the Wasteland of Desperate Pilgrimage. A perfect name for it, I thought as I trod its sands on foot. I took little food and water with me, for I sought to fast in order to purify myself, make of myself an empty vessel for the wonders I expected to pour into me when I reached the temple. After a time I began to regret this plan, for starvation and dehydration are not pleasant experiences, I found. And possessing only the vaguest hints of where my goal might be located, I soon feared I was lost. Fortune smiled on me, however, for on the fourth day of my trek, with lips cracked open and eyes nearly swollen shut, I beheld the ruins of a most ancient edifice half buried in the dunes. Exhausted, I had to crawl the final yards to it, feeling that it was only fitting that I prostrate myself before whatever powers lay within."

There was nothing useful or particularly surprising in Sylvio's words, Julian thought, considering what he'd learned up to now. Still, he listened intently to the guardian's enthusiastically told recollection, hoping for some scrap of knowledge that he might use to help Ashley.

"Needless to say," Sylvio went on, "it was the masters I met there, in all their glory. They told me that long ago it had been decided what must be done, that a gate had to be forged around the void that was hell, to keep the earth free of infernal predation. They were all men and women of like mind, masters of the elemental crafts who saw the need for this and came together to bring it to pass. So Harrowgate was made, using the force of the void itself. Then, again using the abysmal powers, they transformed themselves into a state between life and death to keep vigil over their creation, that it might never be undone. Further, they said they required servants to help guard the barrier that protected the world from the damned. These servants would have to be resurrected from the dead."

The guardian grinned and looked wide-eyed at Julian. "I volunteered without hesitation. The masters said they were unsure of my worthiness, however. I had an aura of lust and ambition, they told me. To prove myself to them, I took out my knife and cut off my male member and its attendant organs, lest they continue to offend. I bled to death from that wound, not knowing if I would be returned to life or not. Imagine my joy and gratitude when my eyes again opened and my heart beat once more. I had risen from death, like the Nazarene in his tomb. And mind you, my death was not suicide. I would have perished from thirst anyway."

For the first time Julian felt a bit appalled at the man. Self-castration was a sick act in any cause.

"I stayed with them for a time, telling them of how the world had changed since they'd imprisoned themselves on the edge of death and hell. Then I was commanded to return to Utrecchio's castle and there summon the masters through the Abyss. They needed to be among men, you see, in order to select more guardians. They never found any adequate candidates in Florence, alas. When centuries later I journeyed to the New World and summoned them here, our little circle began to grow. And now here you are among us, Julian. I would be most interested to hear your opinion of it all."

The story had left a bad taste in Julian's mouth and his expression showed it, but he didn't want to admit to the fact. "Why do you care what I think?"

"Because you are an individual of character." Sylvio gestured at him with his glass. "You treated me with dignity even though you thought I was a wretched vagrant. I was touched. And you are a talented artist. I have always much admired the creative urge."

Julian looked away and shrugged. "I don't know what to say about it all. It's just too incredible."

Sylvio laughed gushingly. "Yes, it is, is it not? By the way, there is somebody in your apartment. I believe it is that Vern fellow you associate with. I went there to see if by some chance you had the Shadow Prism in your possession, but he was there so I could not. No matter. I shall retrieve it later. Ashley is a very naughty girl for removing it from the cathedral, but I have always enjoyed her spirit."

What was Vern doing in his loft? "Why have you been spying on me?"

Sylvio sipped his glass dry. "Why? Because the masters instructed me to do so. They wanted you and Ashley to meet. I just kept an eye on developments. Fate did the rest. I am surprised you found each other so quickly."

"Why me and for what purpose?"

"The ultimate answer to that I cannot say," he replied in a reasonable tone. "I just did what I was told. Any talented artist would have been suitable. That is all I know. The masters weave a grander design than you or I can comprehend. Who am I to question it?"

The idea that he was really talking to someone who was almost a thousand years old made Julian feel a bit dizzy. "Listen to me, Sylvio. Your masters intended for me to do a painting of the Gate. I almost finished one too. Now, what does that mean to you? Would a Gate have been created? Would the pit open onto the earth?"

Sylvio rolled his eyes and laughed lightly. "That is utter nonsense. You cannot cause a breach in the barrier. You are an impotent mortal. Only we guardians can perform such a feat. In that we are superior even to our creators. And they would never let such a catastrophe occur. They have eternally stationed themselves at the mouth of the Abyss for that very reason."

Tapping on the arms of his chair, Julian tried to think. "Then why? Why all this deception and game-playing?"

"Well, I can think of one possibility." Sylvio pursed his fat lips and his eyes bugged out at Julian. "Perhaps the masters are preparing the way to reveal themselves to the world. It makes sense that they would first lay the foundations for this through artists. This is not a matter easily apprehended by the intellect, after all. It is in the gut, in the senses. It lies in the primal part of our brains, which knows instinctively that nature has a surface like a calm sea, beneath which nightmares devour nightmares in the dark depths."

That was all he needed: more doubts about what course events were taking. "All right. Maybe. I'm not sure about any of that, but I do know that Ashley is in grave trouble. The masters intend to punish her severely tonight. She's afraid she might not survive it. Now, she's told me that you took her under your wing when she first came here. You said you liked her. Can't you help her now?"

Sylvio stared at Julian for a long moment, his expression suddenly very grim. Then he looked away and set his glass down on the small stand next to his chair. "There is nothing at all to fear, my dear boy. Punishment is never that extreme. Now you must excuse me. I have many matters to attend to."

All the humor had gone out of his voice, Julian realized as the guardian stood and headed for the library door. There was something he wasn't being honest about. When he was gone, Julian turned to Bonita.

"How do you feel about Sylvio?" he asked her.

"I have already told you." She looked up from her book and closed it. "He is boring and lazy. And occasionally overbearing. What would you like to see next?"

"But do you trust him?"

She gasped out a laugh at that. "I am in no position to trust or distrust anybody anymore. Come along now. I will show you the upper gallery, the most interesting thing to see in this place."

That was fine by him. "Anywhere but the lower passages." He stood and followed her out of the room.

Night was coming on, and with it the fear.

As the day wore on the strain had grown, gnawing away at Vern's reason. He'd been sitting in the middle of the floor for hours, staring at the door, alternately sweating massively and shivering like a man caught in an Arctic wind. His back was rigid and he remained as motionless as possible, afraid that any energy expended on movement would weaken his hold on his shaky identity. Cramps throbbed in his legs and his ass was sore from the hardness of the floor, but he continued to sit like a statue, squeezing his gun, which he knew was useless, and scanning the walls as if he expected them to crack open and let in a thousand unknown horrors.

The real one was still waiting outside the door. He didn't have to check to know it was there anymore; he could sense it in the very roots of his spine. As hard as he tried, he couldn't figure out what it was, and he felt if he didn't come up with a rational explanation, he'd simply lose his mind. For lack of a better description he decided to call it a demon, even though it had almost nothing in common with that variety of mythical creature. This was something much worse. It was like a diseased organ from the interior of existence, never meant to be viewed by ordinary people, an abnormal growth formed in the hidden anatomy of reality. He'd fucked around and exposed it to the sane surface world of coherent shapes and logical systems.

And he had no idea how to cure this earthly realm of the infestation.

Its aversion to light was the only thing that had spared him up to now, but the fact that it could be held in check at all suggested there were other rules it would obey as well. Very specific conditions had been required for it to invade normality, so other specific conditions would probably destroy it or at least send it back where it had come from. And Vern knew exactly who would know what had to be done: Ashley and her weird pals down at the cathedral. That was reason number two to seek them out if he ever escaped from this fix he was in.

He looked up at the skylights. The salmon hues of twilight had been eclipsed by the purple shades of evening, and the black of night was soon to follow. All day he'd been asking himself if this day would ever end, and answering that he didn't want it to. Now it was. He had every light in the loft burning brightly, the three table lamps, two floor lamps, and even the dim bulb over the kitchen sink. Still, it seemed like feeble defense against the dark nightmare on the other side of the door.

The waiting was sheer agony. Vern was a man of action, always taking the offensive instead of just reacting to situations. He couldn't formulate any kind of a plan, however. His adversary was too inexplicable, and this situation was too grimly absurd. It was all way out of his league, but he refused to admit defeat. There was always a weakness in an enemy that could be exploited, no matter how powerful and inhuman it was. Or so he'd thought until now.

Night was here, he saw through the skylight. It seemed darker than any night he'd ever faced before. He lowered his gaze and a violet brightness suddenly burst across the room, branching out and creating explosions of sparks where it struck. Everything went dark, but for a few moments the afterimage of the glare persisted. Then his vision cleared, and he found himself sitting in a totally unlit room. Cold shock washed over him from head to toe as he realized what must have happened. Some of those bolts of lightning in the "painting" had lashed out at all the lights and shattered them. His doom had arrived.

Fortunately or unfortunately, he could see that doom approaching, for the demon was coming through the door. Not only were Vern's eyes quickly adjusting to the mingled shadows, but the creature seemed to exude an aura blacker than the dark surrounding it. This time it emitted a noise, a kind of metallic whirring within a howling wind, the voice of the void from whence it came. He gave in to terror, leaping to his feet and firing his pistol at the thing. His ears rang from the thunder of the discharges, which he was not surprised to see had no effect. Retreating across the loft, he threw the weapon and anything else he could get his hands on at his pursuer. Various pieces of Julian's bric-a-brac hit the demon and fell through it, though some seemed to get sucked down its maw and immediately come spewing back out, horribly changed.

His haunter was taking its sweet time catching him, but then it had no reason to hurry. He was trapped in its lightless element, so now he was just easy meat to it. The air seemed unbreathable and as in a horrid dream his limbs were responding slowly to his panicked will. His arm collided with the back of a chair, knocking it over, so he flung it in the demon's path. The demon went through the chair as if it weren't even there. Vern continued this strategy anyway, throwing furniture at the creature, but only his flesh seemed real to it. Everything else it either ignored or casually disfigured.

It was forcing him back toward the sleeping alcove, a husk of solid shadow swimming through the gloom like a shark. Past the cable-spool table and between two beanbag chairs, on it came. Always right toward him, using some unknown sense. He barked his shin on the bedpost, then crawled onto the mattress. For a fleeting moment he thought of hiding under the covers, as when he was a child and wanted to escape the evil things he imagined lurking in his closet. He raked his nails across the skin of his chest, in a deep despair tinged with penitence in these his last moments, and heard himself softly whimpering. Any second now he would go insane and be devoured by something that was the very embodiment of madness.

But he would not give up yet! If he went down fighting, it would at least lessen the thing's triumph. Rising to his knees on the bed, he reached out toward the nightstand, scraping his knuckles on its rough wooden surface as he looked for one more object to throw at the creature in a final act of defiance. His fingers touched the digital clock, which told him his time of death would be approximately six-twenty, then brushed against the singed metal of the blasted lamp. There were some books on the stand, a brass ashtray, and something else. Something cold, hard, and heavy, with a smooth, curved surface. Vern grabbed this unknown piece of junk and raised it to hurl it down on his attacker's malformed hide.

As if God had shone grace into the room, the creature stopped its approach and even backed off a little. Astonished, Vern caught himself before he launched the projectile and examined what he held in his hand as best he could in the dark. It was the crescent-shaped crystal that had helped to guide him when he completed the painting. Whatever it was, the demon sure didn't seem to like it. He let out a heaving sigh of relief. His reason kicked in again and he remembered that he'd already suspected the crystal had come from the cathedral. It had power. He was saved!

The idea that he might actually survive only made his heart hammer faster. He certainly wouldn't want to blow his chances now. Very tentatively, he slid toward the edge of the bed and waved the crystal at the beastie like a shaman with his rattle. It kept its distance sure enough, as if Vern were a suicidal maniac clutching a live grenade. The noise it was making sounded annoyed and alarmed as well. Even with this evident success, however, he was reluctant to leave the bed now that it seemed to afford him a measure of safety. Nerve was something he'd always had in abundance, so it didn't take him too long to decide that it was worth the risk.

He slowly lowered his feet to the floor and stood on unsteady legs. The demon still made no move toward him. First one step, then another, and Vern was actually walking away from it, around it and toward the door. It stayed where it was as he sprinted across the loft, finally breaking into a mad dash to freedom.

"I beat you!" he roared at the creature behind him. "I beat you, fucker!"

When he reached the door, something made him turn and look at the painting, a glimpse of some new motion within it. Glowing with its own infernal light, its dismal depths yawning, it revealed a sight that made him go rigid once more. In the center he could see more of the creatures coming, flying toward him as if from miles away across a void, and he didn't wait around to see if his defenses would stand up against an army of the things. Vern flung the door open, rushed out, and senselessly slammed it behind him.

At the end of the hall he flicked on the lights. *Can't have too much of a good thing,* he raved to himself as he half stumbled down the stairs, switching on the lights in the lower hallway when he reached the bottom. He stopped short as he came to the door of Bonewitz's apartment. No sound came from within. After a moment of deliberation he decided he had to know what had happened to the man. He took a step back, then kicked in the door. It splintered free of the frame, shot against the interior wall, and bounced partway closed. Through the crack he could see the wall inside reflecting the hall light back at him, so he moved slightly to change his angle. The wall was splattered with dark, glistening blood. As he followed its dripping lines downward, he discovered blotches of gore on the wall and the carpet, and, just sticking out from the base of the door, a bit of white that might have been bone.

This was the fate he'd just narrowly avoided, he

thought as his stomach did a slow flip. And now that he'd come through it alive, it was payback time.

With savage determination Vern set out for the cathedral once more.

Guilly, leader of the Crucifixers, was on the warpath.

He led his war party through the unlit streets of the industrial zone, which they called the Wasteland and considered to be strictly their turf. Here the teenage gangsters could carry out their trysts and orgies, marathon drug sessions, and pseudo-occult rituals in complete secrecy. A few interrogations, tortures, and executions had even been performed in the safely empty quarter, where blood and bodies could vanish without a trace. Now Angelo and Jesus had failed to return from their mission into the area, and Guilly was puzzled, curious. He was concerned that they'd gotten themselves killed or taken prisoner. Not that he cared about them personally, but they were from the neighborhood and former gang members. The Crucifixers took care of their own no matter what, so he had organized this modest expeditionary force to see what was up.

The contingent consisted of three *guerreros* besides himself, Arturo, Miguel, and Esteban, and two *mamasitas,* Paloma and Elpidia, in case they got bored while waiting for some action. In a pinch the female Crucifixers were also fine fighters in their own right.

"I'll be fucked if those two feebs were actually onto something," said Arturo, unhappy to be out on a cold night like this. He would much rather be home getting quietly stoned in front of the TV.

Guilly shrugged his broad shoulders. "Even idiots

have eyes. Those two have probably just gotten themselves into a mess that we have to clean up."

Esteban shook the spray-paint can he was carrying, rattling the little ball inside. "So there really is a freak commune or something living in that fucking pagan temple on Avernus Avenue? Maybe we haven't marked our stomping grounds good enough. I can fix that, though."

He parted from the group and sauntered up to a suitably blank wall, upon which he wrote large in flat black enamel: WELCOME TO THE WASTELAND. The youth wasn't much of an artist, deriving satisfaction instead from the sheer act of defacement, but he got the message across.

The others laughed and applauded, all but Guilly.

"Good one, Lobo," said Elpidia, scurrying over to him. She was pretty, if a little tough looking, a noble urban savage in her mind. To conform with this image she was a spectacle of pierced flesh. Both ears in a dozen places, twice in her right nostril, the studs anchoring a chain between right ear and nose, and with gold rings through both nipples of her hefty breasts beneath her pink T-shirt. Possessing more talent than Esteban, she took the spray can from him and signed the ambiguous warning with an abstract wolf, signifying the affectionate nickname she'd given him the first time they'd made love.

"Quit screwing around, you two," said Guilly, not terribly irritated. "We've got business to attend to."

"Come on, babe." Esteban was always quick to obey his leader's commands.

She refused to comply so quickly, however, and took the time to adorn the wall with a small, lethal-looking wasp, her own personal symbol. Then she rejoined the gang.

"I'm cold," complained Paloma after they'd walked a few more blocks. Taller than Elpidia and not quite as attractive, she had milder features and long, straight hair. Her only physical disfigurement was the dove tattooed on her left shoulder.

Guilly glanced at her. "Soldiers don't bitch, baby. Bitches bitch. Are you my little soldier or what?"

This brought a smile to her lips.

"It's not much farther. Just rub yourself or something."

That made her laugh.

They came to the cathedral, and it looked as lifeless as ever. A dead hulk in the dead of night. Guilly walked over to an open manhole and peered into it.

"We go in that way as a last resort," he told his lieutenants. "I'd rather break down one of the doors, make a frontal assault. But first let's check the place out, wait and see who comes and goes, if anybody."

At his command they pulled back to a parking lot a block from the cathedral, hidden from its view by a tall, square building. "Miguel, go get one of those oil barrels and roll it over here. The rest of you gather up stuff to burn. It could be a long night."

As they carried out his orders, he sat down on a cinder block and lit a cigarette. Guilly viewed command more as a responsibility than a thrill these days, a means to a more important end. By the time he was twenty-one he intended to rule the barrio or be out of it. His father was a minimum-wage slave and his mother a drunken slob; there was no way he was going to end up like them. No, he was meant for better things. In the meantime, running a gang would have to do.

The Crucifixers built a fire in the barrel and warmed

their hands over it, joking around and nudging one another, having a great time. This was as far as they would go, mused Guilly, for their poverty was in their minds as well as their environment. Their imaginations could not rise beyond it, like his. Of course, if he felt like it, he could take one or two of the females out of the depths with him, maybe even these two. But he couldn't allow himself to be held back from his goal by the company of street trash. When he made his break it would be clean and total.

"Let's spread out around the *iglesia* and keep watch. Stay hidden," he said. "If you see anything, signal by whistling. We'll all come running."

Reluctant to leave the light and warmth of the barrel, they slowly moved away in different directions. Guilly experienced no sadistic glee in sending them out into the cold darkness, for he knew Miguel would keep himself toasty with the bottle of sloe gin in his back pocket, Arturo would smoke several joints and feel no discomfort, and the inseparable Elpidia and Esteban would create their own heat. As for Paloma, she'd walk around for a while, then return to him, knowing that he had a certain amount of tolerance for her malingering, due to her willingness and skill in pleasing him. Everyone would be happy.

"Now we wait for our prey," he said to the night.

16

Welcome to the Wasteland

"Some portraits of me must surely still survive," Bonita said to Julian as she led him through the cathedral again. "If not, you could do a new one of me."

He actually had some idea of what it would be if he did: a woman of clay with flames roaring inside of her, reflecting Bonita's earthy but passionate nature. But he doubted he'd ever be able to apply pigment to canvas again, dreading that the fearful shapes he portrayed might somehow come to life.

They passed through an archway into a curved hall, which he deduced was a circular corridor that wound around the altar room. Torches burned along the way, so Bonita set her lamp on a small table of dark polished wood standing against the wall. About halfway around the circle they came to a flight of marble stairs. It gracefully spiraled upward to the second level, which appeared to be brightly lit. As Julian climbed the steps behind Bonita, he thought it felt a little like ascending into the light of heaven.

"I will even pose for a nude portrait, if you wish," she said coquettishly as they reached the top.

His attention was instantly drawn to the exquisite statuary lining the gallery, representing figures from many different mythologies. Then he studied the carved faces glaring and leering from the gray stone walls, wicked and whimsical in their expressions. All of this was illuminated by glowing white globes resting in the outstretched hands of bronze imps. Julian was fascinated, would have been delighted by these extraordinary pieces under other circumstances.

"Maybe I should consider a career switch to sculpting," he said to Bonita.

She smiled pensively at him. "Never modeled for one of those before."

"Where did these works come from?"

"From that castle in Florence that was the first home of the masters." Her tone sounded bored, slightly irritated, possibly because he was more interested in the gallery than in her. "That old Italian aristocrat was quite a collector, I guess."

He nodded as he wandered toward the outer circle of the gallery and commenced a circuit of it, trying to take in every bizarre form and surprising shape. At one point she assumed the lead again.

"If you want to behold something truly marvelous, I will show you."

Grabbing him by the hand, she hurried him along to a place where the gallery opened into an oblong alcove with mesmerizing decor. The floor and ceiling were pitch-black, but the three walls were a timeless, luminous blue, making the chamber seem simultaneously ages ancient and centuries into futurity, a room floating in space. Eleven white marble pedestals lined the walls, five along each side and one at the end. All of them had an object resting on it save one. This was obviously the Arcade, from which Ashley had taken the Shadow Prism.

Julian went in and examined the other curios. There was a small cube of black stone, a milky sculpture resembling the Venus of Willendorf, a tetrahedron with mirrored sides, and a nacreous sphere the size of a softball. The brown, manlike lump about the size of a rat, looking as if it were part plant and part animal, he took to be a mummified homunculus. Other objects were a jade phallus, a ram's horn, a snake skeleton coiled like a whip, and a tube of some shiny lavalike material. The exhibit standing alone at the end was a desiccated Glory Hand, yellow and waxy.

"You like?" Bonita asked.

"It's incredible." His awe was sincere. "These belonged to the masters, didn't they? These are the instruments of their human youth."

She nodded. "They are objects of powerful magic, though most of them have lost their potency over the centuries. I think. We are forbidden to touch them in any case."

Something seemed amiss to him. He soon realized what it was. "But if there are only ten masters, why are there eleven objects?"

"Sylvio told us," she said with impatience, "that one of the members of their order was killed long ago, before the gates of hell were closed. That enchanted hand was hers."

"Oh." He strode over to look at the glazed, upright appendage more closely. The precise lore concerning Glory Hands eluded his memory for the moment, except that they were supposed to be amputated from condemned murderers still hanging from the gallows. And that they had the power to immobilize victims. Maybe this one had been used to paralyze Coprolites escaped from the pit.

He half turned to Bonita. "When you say this was her hand, do you mean it was really once part of her?"

Bonita looked down coyly, then she rushed up to him and slipped her arms around his chest from behind. "Why do you worry about that old dead hand when I have two that are warm and attached?"

Out of reflex he lurched forward to get away, but he had nowhere to go because the pedestal blocked his way. His thighs struck the edge of the platform, the Glory Hand wobbled crazily, then it seemed to lean forward and grab at his crotch. An electrical shock seemed to pass from the lifeless fingers where they touched him, making him jump back into Bonita's embrace.

"Oh, yes, lover," she exclaimed with delight. "I knew you desired me."

He fought to slip free of her grasp, but she was as strong as the other female guardians he'd wrestled with. His balls stung from the shock they'd received. "Wait a minute here. I—"

Hold me, a voice pleaded in his head, soft, remote, and feminine. Not at all like Bonita's, so he didn't for an instant suspect her of pulling some kind of telepathic trick. It was someone else. Nothing that happened in the cathedral should have startled him anymore, but he wasn't prepared for this.

"Who are you?" he said out loud.

"The one who is about to bring you great pleasure," said Bonita, laughing.

Who are you? echoed the voice in his mind. *Come to me. I am beneath you.*

She sounded very lost and lonely, torn by emotional pain. The depth of her anguish tugged immediately at his heartstrings.

"Damn it, let go of me!" he shouted at Bonita.

"Oh, you like to tease, do you? Come, now. I know you like it." She slid her hand down his stomach, pausing to caress him there. This weakened her hold on him just enough for him to lunge to the right, almost breaking out of her grip. As soon as he ducked out of the way, the Hand leapt from its pedestal and fixed itself tightly around her throat. It glowed now with a faint golden light.

Bonita released him and clawed at the appendage, not so happy now. He flattened himself against the wall as the struggle unfolded, watching her stagger backward with the disembodied member closing on her windpipe. It seemed intent on killing her, assuming that was possible. The woman's eyes bulged out, and Julian thought he heard things snapping and crushing in her neck. After a few more seconds of this, Bonita fell onto her back on the black tiles, struggling with less energy now. Her body seemed to become hazy and unstable, revealing a form beneath, something rodentlike and covered with tiny red scales.

"Stop it," he said to whoever was controlling the Hand. "Don't kill her. Please. She wasn't harming me."

This one is a whore of Demogorgons.

The bitterness infusing her voice shook him. "She doesn't know what she's doing. Let her live."

She has not lived for many years. But since you ask, I will spare her.

The Hand continued to throttle Bonita until she stopped moving, then it let go and tumbled to the floor, where it remained motionless. Bonita's flesh solidified and she lay still, gazing sightlessly at the ceiling. She didn't seem to be breathing, but Julian knew that didn't necessarily mean there was no life in her.

"Is she going to be all right?" he asked the air.

She will be fine. You must come to me. We need each other. I have knowledge to convey, but our link is weakening. I expended much strength subduing this cat's paw. Take my hand. It will strengthen our contact.

He stayed where he was, staring at the Glory Hand as if it were a gigantic spider. It looked like a woman's hand, with long, delicate fingers and sharp nails.

Do not waste time. I am below in the catacombs. My remains are sealed in a wall. My hand will guide you to me. Pick it up.

Her voice sounded fainter now, more distant. It wanted him to go down into the basement, where the masters dwelt. The owner was in parts, she said. Hidden in a wall. He would be guided to her by the Hand. There were things she had to tell him. Just how badly did he want to hear them? Descending into those dark passages would be bad enough, but conversing with a mutilated corpse or babbling bones was downright unthinkable. Still, he'd been moved by the cavernous solitude in her voice, her urgency to help in spite of her vast agony. Maybe he should try. Many answers still eluded him, and he badly wanted to know who she was.

Walking over, he reached down and picked up the Hand by its stump of wrist. It instantly grew brighter. He wasn't frightened by it.

Come to me, said the voice, louder now that he held the Hand. *Come to me.*

Staring at the Hand, marveling at its permeating light, he shuffled uncertainly forward, out of the Arcade, along the gallery, and down the steps. What if this was a trick? he thought. This whole thing had been nothing but lies, games, and deceptions from the very beginning. Now all of a sudden he felt like trusting someone he couldn't see or even really hear. A wisp of misery and need, from below. There was definitely room for doubt about the wisdom of this course of action.

He paced the winding length of the hallway, wondering what he would say if anyone stopped him. When he came to the entrance of the altar room he carefully peeked in. No one could be seen inside. Apparently the scouring of its nooks and crannies was over. Well, he was about to defile it again. Ashley's company would have helped control his terror of going below, but he had no idea where she was. If she'd been free to do so, she would already have sought him out, so she was most likely still occupied. And if he went in search of her, the guardians might deter him from his task. Still the woman in the cellar called to him, her voice amplified through the detached appendage. How it was happening seemed less important than what it could mean. Steeling himself, he crossed the expanse of the floor, to the shrine and behind it.

Coming this way was no easier the second time. It was different, considering that he had an invitation, one that was even friendly in its way, but nothing down there could be pleasant to face.

"Lady, you'd better appreciate this," he said to the Glory Hand as he started down the stairs.

Come to me and I will show you, she replied.

At the base of the steps, the doorways in the sides of the corridor opened to his left and right. When he pointed the Hand to the left it flared more brilliantly than to the right, so he knew which direction to take. A lightless maze sprawled before him in the catacombs, the merest fraction of it illuminated by the Hand. Just to be on the safe side he turned to go back and get a torch from the head of the stairs. And found that he couldn't move.

You need no torch, said the voice. *I will light your way.*

Clearly, she was not going to let him go back. Only forward. Glory Hands really did have the power to paralyze. He had matches, but if he got lost in this jumble of tunnels, he'd expend them all long before finding his way out. So now he really had to trust the forlorn phantom woman. But not completely. He removed the buckle from his belt and used it to make scratches in the stone wall as the Hand guided him through the labyrinth, growing brighter when he headed in the right direction and dimming when he went the wrong way.

It brought him to a broad curving corridor, which he guessed surrounded the Sanctum. Which meant that on the other side of this stone wall were the masters and their pit. Did they know he was here? Would he suffer their wrath for trespassing in this place? *Don't think about it. Just go on. Get to your desti—*

Two bodies lay on the floor up ahead. One fat, one thinner. They looked human. Up close they were indeed young men. Julian knelt over them, using the Hand as a light. Something had burned out their eyes, blackened the sockets. He couldn't see anything inside their heads. No optic nerves, no brain beneath. The skin of their faces and hands was striated with dark cracks, as if their veins had filled with ink. Their bodies were split open, but there was no blood. He staggered back against the wall.

"I can't deal with this," he said, feeling his mind start to go black. "Whoever you are, I'm sorry, but I can't go on."

Leave them, she coaxed him from within. *Their time is past. But you must come to me or there will be more of this. Much more. Come. It is not much farther. Just a few more steps.*

It seemed too much to ask. But somewhere in his core he found enough will to heave himself from the brink and continue on down the hall, knowing he was at the edge of sanity. He gave the bodies wide berth.

"What happened to them?"

It is the voidlight. It can heal and it can harm, in the worst way possible. It devours from the inside outward. You are almost here! I can hear your footfalls.

He became paralyzed again, as if every muscle in his body had been seized by an invisible force. Then the Hand pointed at a place in the inner wall of the passage. This had to be the tomb of its owner.

"What do you want from me?" he said to the wall.

"Break in to me!" shouted a real voice from within it.

Julian jumped back, startled. The six-inch blocks of masonry here did look loose and ill fitted, so it seemed possible to tear them down and create a hole. The problem was that they might avalanche on him, smashing his feet or breaking his legs. Never before had he put himself in so much danger for the sake of a complete stranger. Nonetheless, he set the Hand on the floor well out of the way and by its light started prying the stones apart with his fingers. They rolled free fairly easily, tumbling away to the floor, scattering across the passage. A few minutes' work opened up the cavity enough for him to enter it, though he didn't yet. When the dust had cleared, he picked up the Hand and in its light saw its owner.

She was a naked torso, a head, two legs, and two arms, one without its hand. They were grayish, but otherwise perfectly preserved. Though separated, these remains had been chained to the walls and the floor in various ways. Before this maiming she had been a shapely woman and her exotic face was as exquisite as that of a Siamese cat. Julian didn't know how to react to the staring brown eyes, the full smiling lips, the brows and nose wrinkling at him, all from an upright head collared to a shelf about a yard above the ground. Her scalp was hung with many short black braids of hair. The body bound by steel bands to a stone slab was less disturbing, for it didn't move. Same with the manacled arms and legs.

" 'Tis a good thing that Sylvio is a sluggard," said the woman calmly, her voice thick and melodic, filled with a rich foreign accent. "Else you'd never have gotten through to me. Please bring my hand closer."

He stepped into her crypt and held it out toward her face.

"You may keep possession of it. I like the feel of your touch."

Since she was chained, she couldn't be a threat, and the amputation she'd suffered had not been crude, so she wasn't excessively horrific. His trust in her was not diminished. "How come you speak my language so well?"

"I am a witch, young fool. I have been inside your

mind." Her almond-shaped eyes looked him up and down. "What a sight you are. How things must have changed out there. What is your name?"

"Julian."

"And were you named after the Roman emperor?" She briefly closed her eyes and shook her head as much as she could. "Never mind. It is not important. We have no time for idle chatter. My strength is limited and I have much to tell you. My name is Ninanna. I was a member of the same order as those you know as the masters. I would be as they are if not for Firdausi's treachery."

Her lips frowned and her eyes widened with despair; some of that great loneliness he'd sensed in her seemed to be coming to the surface. "His real name is Damuzi. He was my mate. There were twelve of us in the beginning, and we joined together at a time when cities were something new in the world. We started out as exorcists, casters of *gallas* into the pit of Irkalla. Then came the plan for the great work, conceived by Damuzi. Harrowgate. Chase all the fiends into the pit and lock them in. Do mankind this monumental favor. Then we would use hell's cold, dark fires to form sheaths of timeless matter around ourselves to stand watch over it. I was proud of my husband and honored to be a part of it."

Julian shifted his footing nervously, holding the Glory Hand like a votive candle, wondering if whatever had slain the two teenagers still lurked in the passages. So far, Ninanna's story was more or less as he'd imagined it must have happened, within the constraints of sanity.

"Then Latarrek was killed during a purge," she continued, looking away as if relating a painful personal memory. "Even his amulet, a scepter of bone, was lost.

He was the mate of Shara, whom you know as Euterpe. Without warning Damuzi took Shara as his mate." A bitter sneer burst from her snarling lips. "She was the one he wanted to go through eternity with. Not me. I guess he thought I was too wanton. So I was the odd one out, as the magnum opus required an equality of sexes. I left the order in despondency. Some years later I was stoned to death for the crime of witchcraft. I was most surprised again when the masters appeared to me in ascended form to offer me resurrection. I became the first guardian."

Someone had just been caught in a lie. "It wasn't Sylvio?"

She shook her head again, her mouth pulled back in a jack-o'-lantern leer. "He was the second. He became the sole guardian after the masters tore me apart in a ritual shortly after we came to this country. This was done to me in the other city and I was transported here as so much baggage by Sylvio. Put back in a wall. The skeleton in their closet."

Her skull shuddered and he believed he saw similar tremors ripple through her other body parts. "Their punishment upon me was something I had not expected. Firdausi impaled me with a hard, sharp projection of himself and drained the life out of me. I died again, only it was worse than the first death. It was like becoming less than nothing. The sustaining voidlight was removed from my flesh, so that my inner body could not heal. Then my human body was ripped limb from limb."

Ninanna seemed to be sliding into a fit of self-pity, her mouth gaping and her eyes glazing over. Her feeling of devastation was understandable, but he wished she would get to the point so he could get out of there. "Ninanna, why did the masters do this to you?"

"Because I realized what they are becoming, what they are trying to do, and I sought to stop them!" Now her eyes blazed and her teeth were bared, making her look very much like a hissing cat. "They are as evil as anything in the pit to which they are bound, but they are transmuting their flesh into shells which are impervious to death and damnation. Soon they shall be free and flying over the earth, winged lords of hell scourging the world with the unleashed hordes of the Abyss. The mere worldly lust they so despise shall by the vaster and purer lust of the damned be obliterated. The time has now come. They are ready to emerge, so they had you open a Gate to release their army for them. And what a massive army it has become over the centuries, swelling even the margins of the void."

It was what he'd seen in his revelatory dream, a grisly apocalypse helmed by the masters. But where did the guardians stand in all this? Where did Ashley?

Ninanna's rage dissipated to weak gasps of fury. Her eyelids dropped. "They . . . can . . . be destroyed. I . . . can tell . . . you how to . . . do it. But I am fading. So little . . . vitality left. You must . . . bring me back . . . to you. Make me . . . aware of myself . . . through sensation. Make love to my body, Julian. Engorge it with . . . feeling. Hurry."

Looking at the torso, he instantly balked. In many ways it was beautiful, but it was not human anymore. As obsessed as he was with physical perfection, and as squeamish as he was about deformities, he just might have been able to have sex with an attractive woman who'd lost all four limbs. But a dead headless trunk? No, it just wasn't in him.

"I can't do that, Ninanna. It's too much to ask."

"Then . . . bring your . . . manhood close to . . . to me . . . to my head . . . and I shall . . . shall love it with my mouth. Feed me your seed . . . and I'll impart my revelation through your orgasm. Then you will know."

This was the maddest turn yet. Was she playing some sick seduction game with him? She certainly sounded as if she was weakening. The light of the Glory Hand was flickering, and her skin was becoming even more colorless. If she really was withdrawing back into some dismal coma and this was the only way to snap her out of it, shouldn't he be willing to do anything to learn from her what she knew? Even if she didn't have an actual scheme to defeat the masters and was just extracting some very twisted pleasure from his compliance with her request, at least he would have tried. And time was running out, his watch told him. Midnight was fast approaching.

Her eyes closed and her features went slack. Her mouth fell open, a deep purplish gray, and out came a last exhalation of fetid breath.

No, he couldn't do this either. There was no way he could live the rest of his life with the memory of getting fellated by a decapitated head. His sleep and his sex habits would be irreversibly disrupted.

"These are impossible acts you're asking of me. I can't carry them out."

Her lips barely moved. "Then you have . . . doomed us all." She sighed these final words and was still.

The light from the Glory Hand went out.

* * *

Vern wasn't sure precisely how unhinged this traumatic episode had left him, and he was beyond worrying about it. He'd never be the same, he knew, but he was going to make damn sure that a lot of other people weren't either. No mercy held him in check now, as little ever had. He was totally unbound and there was no telling where it would end.

On his way toward his destination he passed a crude sign that matched his mood perfectly, welcoming him to the Wasteland. Desolation was about all he could handle right now. The graffiti billboard seemed to extend a special invitation to wolves and wasps, carnivorous predators and poisonous stingers. Well, that was him, a wolf on the hunt. He hoped the stingers didn't follow.

The hairs on the back of his neck were as stiff as bristles and the skin there quivered unbearably, but he didn't dare turn around to look behind him. If he saw an entire swarm of faceless demons coming after him, the last train of thought out of his mind would go roaring off to the infinite horizon. He kept looking ahead and stalking forward, holding on to the piece of purple crystal for dear life and dearer sanity.

As he neared the cathedral, a shrill whistle tore through the chilly air, echoing against the empty buildings. It sounded human in origin, maybe one of the cultists alerting the others to his presence, though one might expect the active dead to communicate in a somewhat flashier mode. Continuing on, he believed he detected footfalls in his wake, and was utterly unable to check this out. Then three figures emerged from the shadows ahead of him. Vern knew he was about to be involved in a confrontation of some sort.

Six individuals in all approached and surrounded him,

four male and two female. They *were* human, he was relieved to see, just a bunch of Crucifixer punks, but he soon had second thoughts. He was alone and unarmed, on their turf in the middle of the night. It was not a good situation to be in. He damned himself for not having kept his pistol with him, for as useless as it was against his otherworldly foes it would have taken care of these two-bit punks with no trouble at all. To be killed by them after surviving an interlude of hell on earth would be unacceptably ironic, as well as totally unfair.

"You're a long way from home," said the one he assumed was the leader, a handsome brute with considerable brawn and an incongruously childlike face. If Vern recalled correctly his name was Guilly. He had a rep for ruthlessness on the streets.

"I'm on an errand of retribution," he said, reflecting that he was indeed a long way from home. So far that he could never go back. "Maybe you'd care to join in on it. You've got some real vile nastiness festering deep in your territory that you don't seem to be aware of. I think it should be wiped out."

Guilly grinned in a way that reminded him of a crocodile. "You mean that weird church and the loco fanatics living there? We know about it. How do we know you're not one of them?"

He raised the crescent of crystal over his head. "Because I'm their worst enemy, and I'm going to make them wish they'd never been born."

"Yeah? Well, they're on our turf, so why should they interest you? What's your grudge against them?"

The female Crucifixer with all the metal piercing her face made a strangled, gagging sound and went white. She pointed a wildly shaking finger behind Vern, and he felt his own features go similarly bloodless. Her subsequent screams came out in incoherent Spanish, but her gist was clear to him. His personal demons had shown up.

Oddly, only she among the youths seemed able to see the things, for the others looked completely baffled by her behavior. Maybe it required some degree of psychic sensitivity, he hazarded. In any case she was so insistent and fervent in her alarm that when she ran everyone else followed, even Guilly and Vern, like a stampeding herd of cattle.

When the hysterical girl was finally tackled by one of the boys, they were near an oil barrel with a fire burning in it. Had she intuitively known that its light would offer some amount of safety? And would it be enough? He doubted it. Now he could see the crooked funnels of charred crust sailing through the shadows toward them, dozens of the blighters, all wailing with that hollow, pulsating clamor. His last bit of stability held fast as he clutched the crescent to his chest like a Catholic with his cross and horrors converged on the parking lot.

The fire *did* hold them at bay, he saw. That was okay with Vern. He'd be very content not to see at close range what they did to their victims. Then one leapt into the circle of firelight just long enough to grab the girl with second sight and drag her out into the dark. None of the Crucifixers moved; they didn't have a clue what the devil was happening to her. Vern could see the demon all too well, like a wart-covered horn of plenty with bony arms. He stood petrified as the creature shredded her denim jacket and the pink shirt beneath with its meathooks, slashing some skin to ribbons with its delicate strokes as well. She screamed with lung-bursting despair as blood seaped from the cuts, and her comrades now realized that she genuinely was seeing something, though they still could not.

Guilly thought she might be having a spontaneous attack of stigmata. His crazy aunt Inez was extremely devout and spoke of such things, nuns sprouting holes in their hands and feet like Christ. Whatever it was he couldn't get himself to go to her aid. Neither could the others, not even Esteban, who had known so many hours of delight with her. Elpidia's plight was just too unfaceable.

Standing on its tail, the thing dug its claws deep into her flesh, seemingly studying her. Vern watched as it began tearing away her golden rings one by one, hooking its talons through the metal coils and ripping them out. Ragged bloody strands of skin hung from her ears, nose, and breasts, her sensuous body piteously ruined. Then the monstrosity seemed to expand, widening its maw, until it looked like a jagged hole in the night surrounded by a ring of organic matter, opening onto infinite darkness beyond. It sucked her in with tremendous pressure, not like a creature devouring its prey but like the mouth of hell swallowing one of the damned. All of a sudden she just wasn't there anymore. A moment later something came vomiting out of the orifice, a crimson slush that splattered on the pavement. They could only conclude that this was what was left of her, somehow digested and transformed.

This was more than the others could take. They fled the feeble defense of the fire and were quickly captured, all but Guilly. Their leader was smart enough to see that Vern remained conspicuously unpanicked by the invisible slaughterers and guessed that it was because of the object he was clinging to himself. Guilly ran over to him and they proceeded to engage in a violent tug-of-war over the crescent as the others met their nightmarish deaths around them.

Miguel was ingested and regurgitated in a shriveled, blackened form, as if burned to a crisp in perdition's flames. When Paloma tripped over a curb in her aimless flight, she was enveloped by a cold, hard husk that her eyes could not perceive. In Guilly's sight she just seemed to momentarily vanish from foot to head, then when she reappeared she looked like a million-year-old mummy wrapped tightly in ancient cobwebs. What happened to the others took place out of their view, which they both counted as a blessing.

"You did this!" Guilly shrieked at him. "You brought this down on us! What the fuck are you, man?"

Vern was not at all into words just then, so intent was he on retaining possession of the only thing keeping him alive. He kicked, scratched, punched, and bit at the maniacal Crucifixer climbing all over him. This seemed to be no time for fighting fair, but unfortunately he was getting as good as he was giving. They were turning each other into bleeding masses and threatening to do to themselves what the devouring apparitions were prevented from doing. Vern finally landed a solid kick to Guilly's groin, however, and the teenager blacked out from the pain long enough for him to get away.

When he was some distance down the road, he looked back once to see Guilly still half collapsed on the blacktop. Then he broke into a run toward the cathedral.

He knew that the pandemoniac horde followed.

17

Stormy Monday

I have answers but no solutions, Julian thought as he lit a fresh match and used it as a searchlight to find his mark in the wall. He estimated he'd negotiated about half the path he'd taken into this maze, backtracking along the trail he'd left. It was a lucky and amazing thing that his mind was still functioning on some level. Any level. His awareness had been raised enormously in the past few days, but unless he formulated a course of action, it would end up meaning nothing more than that he saw utter disaster coming slightly sooner than the rest of his kind.

The burden wasn't entirely on him, he reminded himself. Ashley and Jorge were far more likely to come up with something than he was. They'd struggled with the enigma for years, after all. His faith was certainly more in them than it was in his own abilities. What was he but a dreamer who spent his days baring his dreams to the world in lurid tableaux? He was woefully ill equipped for this call to duty. Like all of humanity's enemies, however, his powerful adversaries were destroyers of beauty, while he was one of its creators. As such, his role as deliverer might not be entirely preposterous, though he didn't feel the part at all.

With one match yet unburned he emerged from the labyrinth of stone, though still lost in the maze of his mind. Who was lying and who was telling the truth were yet nagging uncertainties, he thought as he stared apprehensively at the doorway of the Sanctum. (Was it a bit less dim in there than it had been before?) Someone had murdered the two boys in the catacombs, and it was more likely a guardian than a master. And as benevolent as Ninanna seemed, he found it bewildering that she had never tried to convey what she knew to the other guardians. Some of them must have had physical contact with the amulet she'd fashioned from her own limb. It now rested with the rest of her. She might not have trusted them after her experiences with Sylvio, in which case she wouldn't have tried to contact them. This sounded plausible at least.

At the top of the stairs and out from behind the shrine, he once again found the altar room empty. He elected to loiter around the main entrance, smoking his last cigarette. It was another last cigarette that had brought him to this point, sending him out to the bar where he'd met Ashley. The damned things really were hazardous to one's health. Soon he might be called upon to do something, more than could be reasonably expected of him. What he most wanted to do was disbelieve and forget everything he'd seen here, leave and never think of it again. Never look back. It was impossible, though. The very thing that made his life worth living was here, a most extraordinary person. And it hadn't been totally horrible for him in this place, had it? There were some marvelous phenomena here, but he had to wonder if they were all mere by-products of the imperious malignancies below, or if they could exist on their own. It was a crucial question, for the woman he loved was one of them.

He heard a sound of stone grinding against stone and turned to see the section of wall opposite the doorway slide open. The guardians appeared in their gray robes, some striding forth with enthusiasm and others straggling. Kristen grimaced at him, Iris smiled humorlessly, Sylvio offered him a dignified shrug, and most of the others ignored him. Bonita, none the worse for wear, made a point of not looking his way. They had problems of their own, he reckoned. Ashley was the last to come out, her face a study in despondency.

Julian went to her, but she held up her hands to ward him off. "You mustn't touch me," she said, barely above a whisper. "I've just undergone purification in the vestry. Your touch is impure to the masters."

"I don't care anymore. Do you?"

She lowered her head and shook it. "I always thought these religious trappings were ridiculous. But there's no point in aggravating *them* even more, is there?"

She sounded as if there wasn't a lot of fight left in her. Evidently her attempt to rally allies to her side at breakfast had failed. This bit of news disheartened him, but did not defeat him. Not yet, anyway. "Ashley, there's a lot I have to tell you. I went down into the catacombs. There's two bodies there. They look like they died in a weird way."

"Probably the work of Iris and Nestor. I could easily picture them indulging in atrocity for sport. They've deteriorated that far." It did not seem to be a matter of much significance to her.

Kristen whirled over to them like a stout dervish. Up close he noticed how big her pores were. "Are you finished prattling, Ashley? The hour is about to strike."

After a long pause she eyed the woman stolidly. "Who gives a flying fuck about the hour? It's always midnight somewhere, you know."

This outburst elicited a fleeting sardonic grin from Kristen. "Just be ready. I'm forming up the procession now."

"Yeah, yeah." Ashley shyly faced him, trembling like a small cornered animal. "Look, uh, whatever happens in there, we had what we had, you know? I mean, it means a lot to me. You mean a lot to me. With you I felt alive, even more than when I was."

He felt as if her terror was tearing him apart, severing the threads binding him together in body and soul. "I don't understand why you're going through with this. Why not just make a run for it?"

A tremor rippled through her as she inhaled through gritted teeth. "Because walking away from this won't solve it. I've got to see it through to the end, sort it out here. I've got to confront the bastards head-on."

An inkling he much disliked came to him. He'd been told that she had pain-loving tendencies, as well as the sadistic leanings he'd experienced firsthand. Could it be that on some level she was looking forward to this clash of wills? Did she in truth enjoy the pain her masters gave her? "If you feel you have to do this, then I'm with you. Uh, where should I stand during the ritual?"

She stared at him in dull surprise. "Are you sure you want to watch this?"

Not at all was the answer he kept to himself. "It's a part of you, Ashley. I need to know about it. And I want to be there for you if you need me."

Ashley's consent was more like surrender. "Okay. Just keep out of the way, then. And make sure you don't stare too long into the Abyss. It'll stare back." Her right arm twitched as if she'd started to reach out to him and caught herself.

"Aw, fuck it." She reached out, grabbed him by the back of the neck, and kissed him hard. "I'll stay in one piece for you," she vowed in his ear before breaking away to fall into line at the very end. Kristen eyed her with contempt for a moment, then led them into the altar room.

He followed a few seconds later and found a place on the sidelines as the guardians took up their positions around the spiraled circle. Did each of them have their own designated eye on which they stood or didn't it matter? Their actions offered no clue. Could he ask them? No, better not. The lords of this manor might take offense if an outsider spoke during a ritual. How *did* the masters punish transgressors? Did they shoot lightning bolts out of their luminous bodies? The moments dragged on, scraping his nerves to the edge, as the guardians stood in their ceremonial formation. Then they commenced chanting in perfect unison, words that he recognized as the names of the masters. The invocation was repeated several times.

Then the area of the floor painted with the spiral promptly dropped away into fathomless blackness, gaping open on the Abyss. Julian quickly looked away, obeying instructions. Directly above the darker-than-dark hole toward the ceiling the ten radiant forms of the masters materialized, or at least he assumed that's what they were. They didn't look quite the same as when he'd had his audience with them in the lower chamber. A seam or fissure snaked its way up the front of their casings, splitting open a bit on six of them to expose nearly inchoate structures within. If he had to hazard a guess, he would have said he was looking at folded wings, like those of a sleeping bat or an emergent moth. Now, it was just possible that the beings looked different when they were outside the Sanctum, but he doubted it. It was as Ninanna had said: They were about to come out of their cocoons, having completed their transformations.

Before he had a chance to adjust to this shock, the ten eyes shot their pillars of purple light upward, melting and remaking the very flesh of the guardians as it bathed them in its rays. He kept his sight on Ashley, though all he could see was the back of her head. When the shining shaft withdrew, it left her a creature with a head of pure white covered with short, soft, white down. At the tips of her fingers curved sharp delicate claws, like tiny blades of glass. Avoiding looking at what the others had turned into, he edged along the wall until he could see her face, and was massively relieved when he saw that she still had her own basic features. Except her eyes, which were now an icy dark violet with no whites at all. Her gaze was fixed on the masters.

"Ashley Praetor," said Firdausi, his voice echoing throughout the chamber. "Through your latest acts of misconduct and your persistent disobedience you have rendered yourself subject to harrowing. Prepare yourself to be scourged."

As if by reflex Ashley let her robe drop to the floor and revealed the badges of past punishments. In several places on her body ragged patches of her skin had been torn away layers deep, leaving raw red stigmata in the midst of her white velvety fur. From where he stood, he could see large ones marring her right side, her left breast, the right side of her neck, and her right hip. Many smaller ones mottled her arms and legs. None of them bled. Julian seethed with anger at these multiple mutilations, raging at the masters for having inflicted them, and at Ashley for having allowed such ravages to be done to her. And it looked as if she was welcoming more.

"Nooooo!" he screamed. Was she submitting out of habit? Had she forgotten her intention to revolt? "Don't give in to them! Fight them, Ashley!"

She looked at him, and the force of her stare almost knocked him against the wall. Her dark eyes seemed filled with the sight of everything that ever was or ever would be, and emptied by the sight of the end of all things. But she had heard him. Glaring defiantly up at her tormentors, she picked up her robe and covered her scarred, silvery nakedness.

"I refuse!" Shouting, belligerent. "I won't let you harm me anymore."

Firdausi sounded patient and still in control. "You cannot refuse. You are bound to the oath you took upon your anastasis."

Ashley sneered. "As if someone in that condition could make a rational decision. I had no idea what sort of twisted, inhuman maniacs I was getting involved with. I spit in your faces now!" Turning aside to Julian, she said, "The Abyss has been opened somewhere! I can feel it."

He wasn't sure he'd heard her correctly. "What?"

"Then you call upon yourself the ultimate penalty." Firdausi's voice was harsh, outraged, more thick with emotion than Julian had yet heard it.

Something long and white shot out of the base of Firdausi's body, a limb of some sort, and struck Ashley on the right side of her chest. She grunted as it thudded into her and flecks of blood flew as it dug in. It resembled a length of vertebrae and before it hit her Julian saw what looked like a ring of hooked claws or teeth in the tip, like the teeth of a lamprey. Ashley clutched at the skeletal lash, pulled it free, and part of her came away with it. A hole in her robe and another red wound were left behind as the whip of spine retracted.

He was going to lose her if he didn't do something quick. It didn't look as if she knew what she was doing. She couldn't save herself, was too unbalanced by fear and fury to think straight. So he had to do the thinking, though his own thoughts were in chaos. At least he didn't have to cope with the pain.

Something Bethany had said came back to him. The masters were summoned into the altar room. They couldn't project themselves from the Sanctum without the aid of the guardians. Presumably, the guardians could send them back. "Ashley, close the mouth of the pit! Send them back to the Sanctum!"

The fanged tendril was launched at her again and she blocked it with her left arm, to which it attached itself. She nodded her comprehension. "Let's close the Gate, everybody," she said with all the authority she could muster.

"No!" protested the gray, tusked, toadlike beast that was Kristen. "I forbid it! I say when the Gate is to be closed, and it is never to be done before the masters have withdrawn."

Tugging her arm from the grip of Firdausi's lash, losing more of her flesh, Ashley cried out in agony, then turned to Kristen. "Fuck you, you bitch. They're out to tear me to pieces."

"Good. Let them!"

She appealed to the other guardians then. "Close it now! Don't you see what they are? Power-mad tyrants, sick sadistic butchers. They're using us."

Would talking to them do any good? Could they be persuaded, now, at the last minute? He had to try, but he couldn't think of the words. Despair spun his mind into a whirlwind of incoherence. If he didn't act soon, he would miss the moment. He took a step toward the circle, feeling the horrid gravity of the void tug at his brain and body. *Give me the words,* he pleaded with his own soul, *the strength, the will, to prevail.*

"Li—listen to me! Your masters are monsters, just as she says. They aren't protecting the earth from the Coprolites. They're amassing them as an army to use against the living. There's someone buried in the basement, dismembered, a woman named Ninanna. She was a guardian like you. She'll tell you."

Julian was out of breath already. Hyperventilating, heart pounding so fast he expected cardiac seizure any second now. The punishing limb snaked out again, biting into Ashley's left shoulder, driving her to her knees. *Keep speaking, don't let her pain distract you.* Some of the guardians were actually looking his way.

"They're—they are evil." He pointed at the glowing masses above. "They hate the human race. They despise the sensations of life. You were alive and you came back from the dead, but they're neither, not life or death. They're nothing! And you've been duped into helping them. You've sold the world to hell!"

A creature with red scales and a ratlike face turned to the brown, apelike, leathery-skinned brute next to her. Bonita and Sylvio, he believed. "Was there ever another guardian?" she asked him.

The simian beast glared at Julian, who looked away in self-defense. "Never. He's making all this up."

"I'm not." *Give them so much proof that they can't deny it.* "Her name is Ninanna. She was to be one of the masters. She told me of others, Shara and Latarrek. You must know of them. The Glory Hand in the Arcade is Ninanna's, made from her body. How could I know that unless she told me? Please, stop them from killing Ashley!"

"Something is amiss here," said the minotaurlike hulk crowned with a dozen orange horns, standing where Rubin had been. "Lies have been told. Before we let one of our own kind be torn asunder, let's have the truth. I join in closing the Gate."

The segmented tentacle seemed to be drilling into Ashley now, maybe tunneling toward vital organs, draining the life out of her. He couldn't just stand by any longer, had to go to her aid no matter what. Could the lance of bone injure living matter? No point in worrying about that now. Around the circle of alien forms he ran, to where she was bowed down in her struggle with Firdausi.

"Silence, all of you!" the master blasted in their ears. "Any further impudence and you will all be punished!"

Julian reached for the tentacle and closed his fingers around it. His skin touched cold, slimy hardness, vibrating with inflexible might. He and Ashley pulled on it together.

"It's working," she said through a groan of strain. "The fuckers are showing their true colors."

"They can afford to, now that they've won. Don't talk."

The two of them finally dislodged the limb with a tearing sound, ripping a deep crimson gash in her shoulder. For his labors the spinal column whipped against Julian's skull and knocked him to the floor. No doubt about it; it could hurt him.

A reptilian creature with golden skin and long quills arcing from its head spoke up then. In his daze he figured it was Jorge, for it stood where the dead soldier had been. "I, too, think we should close the Gate. This is not justice. Certainly it's a far cry from mercy."

"I agree." This was said by the blue-shelled being with a knobbed, overlong head, which was Arlo, he believed.

"Yes, we should do it," said Bonita.

One final voice, that of a small black-furred creature with a batlike face and pointed ears, said, "Let's close the Gate." He thought it was Bethany.

A majority seemed to be sufficient, for the Abyss abruptly closed up and the masters vanished where they hung in the air. Apparently the voidlight didn't immediately fade, for the celebrants retained their altered forms.

"What have you done?" snarled Iris. Her face reminded Julian of a carrion bird—naked, beaked, and wrinkled.

Nestor, now something with a bulbous green cranium, replied, "They have undone everything." He sounded terrified. "The masters will never forgive us."

Julian and Ashley helped one another to their feet. She felt alive to his touch, but her many wounds repulsed him. He looked around, suddenly becoming fully aware that he was in a room full of monsters. Some of them he wanted to examine up close, but others made him wish he were blind. All of them struck him with a sensation profounder than sexual arousal or physical revulsion, the wonder of confronting in flesh forms as bizarre as those of his painted fantasies.

One of them he singled out for attention, the hunched, heavy-browed creature that was Sylvio. "You went against us, didn't you? You said you wanted to help her, but you lied. You lied about a lot of things, didn't you?"

"You told us that Ninanna and her mate were killed before Harrowgate was even made," Bonita challenged Sylvio. "As mortals. Now somehow she lives on somewhere in the cathedral. How can that be? What is the truth, Sylvio? What are the masters turning into and why have they secretly opened a Gate?"

Then Kristen started railing against the dissidents, promising them they would pay for their rebellion and blasphemy. Her nearly amorphous bulk quivered and oozed as she vented her anger. It took a physical effort on Julian's part not to vomit at the sight of her.

"Cavorting with cadavers, Julian?" said someone behind him, robbing him of a few heartbeats. "Mingling with monsters? Rubbing elbows with ghoulish entities?"

He thought it was Vern's voice he'd heard, but when he turned around to see, he couldn't be sure. There was a man there, but his face was so swollen and bloody that certain identification was difficult. A human face, even a ruined one, was a welcome sight here.

"Vern? Is that you? What the hell have you been doing?"

"I'll tell you," said Ashley, stepping off her glowing painted eye and striding toward them, still outwardly nonhuman. "The Gate has been opened at another location. I felt it reverberating across the Abyss. He's finished your painting, Julian."

One more shock will surely do me in for good, he thought. At first he was pissed at Vern for having dared to touch his art, but he was also glad for the man's company in this mad funhouse. He felt as if he hadn't had contact with the outside world in a very long time.

"Are you all right, man? You look like shit."

Vern smiled hollowly, studying Ashley with frantic eyes. "I'm just fine, no thanks to this cunt of yours."

Aside from Vern's insulting words, Julian didn't like the expression on his face. It looked unhinged, almost like that of a crazed animal. He started to fear his friend as much as he did anyone else present in the room. "Hey, take it easy. Has anything, uh, emerged from the painting?"

Turning to him, Vern cackled at this. "Yeah, you could say that, I guess. Something really fucking weird."

There was a Coprolite loose in the world. Maybe many. This realization was too vast and ghastly for Julian's mind to deal with, so for the moment it refused to do so. "Then why aren't you dead, man?"

Vern held out the Shadow Prism, grinning like a skull. "Handy little device, this. A whole bunch of Crucifixers got messed up real bad while I just stood there and watched, and not one of the grisly buggers touched me. Ain't that somethin'?"

On pure impulse Julian grabbed the object away. Vern

lunged at him to get it back, but he was suddenly held fast in Ashley's grasp.

"Let me go, you goddamn bitch!" He thrashed and squirmed to get away, but she hung on to him, digging her nails deeper into his flesh.

"No way, motherfucker!" she shouted into his ear. "We've got a score to settle with you. You raped Bethany, and because of you I just went through a hell the living can never know. Not only that, but you let those vile bloody shits out of the Abyss. You've got a lot to answer for."

Kristen and another guardian, the small black one with a vampiric face, left their places in the circle and approached. Julian thought he saw recognition in Vern's eyes at the sight of the latter creature. The other guardians formed a loose ring around the confrontation.

"This one is also here because of you, Ashley," said Kristen, glaring at Vern, apparently trying to rescue her position of authority. "Yet he, unlike the other, seems to have earned your wrath."

Ashley took a moment to respond. "Julian can be trusted. This piece of trash can't."

A smile seemed to form in the blubbery folds of Kristen's face. She turned to the diminutive guardian next to her. "Very well. Then he shall be judged. What do you think, Bethany? What would be an appropriate punishment for him?"

Julian saw where this was going and he didn't like it one bit. "Wait a minute. You can't pass judgment on him. You've got no right." It was a lame argument, he knew, but he'd pretty much exhausted his powers of persuasion during the ritual. Besides that, all the dark purple eyes looking in his direction were unnerving him.

"The dead have their own law," said Kristen. "What is it to be, Bethany?"

Trembling with fury, Bethany took a step closer to Vern, who was still struggling in Ashley's arms. "He let the damned out of the pit. I say he belongs there with them."

"No!" said Julian. "He didn't know what he was doing, any more than I did. This whole thing was set into motion by your masters. It's their fault."

Ashley looked at Bethany. "That *does* seem extreme. I mean, nature makes that decision when someone dies, whether they end up there. I don't think it's up to us."

"We *have* been given that power," Kristen insisted. "There is no reason why we should not use it."

Julian recalled that Iris nearly had, on him. "Are you sure you have that kind of wisdom?"

Unconcerned with these subtleties, Bethany threw herself on Vern and clawed into him with her own talons, pulling him free of Ashley's hold, a bit too easily, Julian suspected. As soon as his hands were liberated, Vern closed them around Bethany's furry throat, yelling furiously as he tried to strangle her. The attempt was futile. With a swipe of her right hand she slashed open the left side of his neck, obliterating his tattoo and exposing the plumbing and cables beneath the skin, leaving much of it torn and broken. Then she hurled his blood-spouting body to the center of the black spiral, where it landed with a bone-shivering *crack*. Vern rose up on one arm, but he could manage no more than that.

Julian stared at his grievously wounded friend, shaken and confused. The man was a rapist, and he'd just attempted murder, right before his eyes. And Vern certainly couldn't be trusted not to reveal the existence of the guardians. He seemed to have nothing but hate for them. Even so, he did not deserve the gruesome fate he was about to receive.

"Don't do this!" Julian pleaded.

Bethany faced the other guardians as she pointed at Vern with an outstretched arm. "You know what he did to me. You see what he is. He deserves the unending anguish of the void. I say we give it to him!"

"He was probably headed there anyway," said Ashley, more to Julian than anyone else.

Looking very pleased with herself, Kristen said, "Then let the sentence be passed."

All the guardians returned to their places on the eyes surrounding the spiral. Vern had time to shout, "Fuck you all!" as the circle fell out from beneath him into bottomlessness. He tumbled into it depths, shrinking rapidly, his inhuman scream echoing loudly after him. The opening quickly resealed itself and the spiral was restored.

Julian fell to his knees on the cold stone floor. Could he have stopped it? Should he have even tried? And how was he to react to the fact that Ashley had participated in the execution? Never again would he look upon her in the same way. She reigned over his desire and now his terror as well.

A hand touched his shoulder. When he looked up he saw it was Ashley, human once more.

"Do you hate me?" she asked solemnly.

Even though her eyes were back to normal, he was unable to meet them with his own. He shook his head.

"Are you afraid of me?"

Not wanting to answer, he just stood. The other guardians had all lost their monstrous aspects. As far as he could tell, they were just shuffling about. With the ritual over and a crisis upon them, they seemed to have become aimless.

"What happens now?" he asked Ashley hoarsely.

She studied her fellow guardians, frowning a little. "I think the shit's about to come down."

Kristen started stammering about some plan of action, but Sylvio moved from his spot and waved at her to be silent. She reluctantly complied. The man's features appeared very pained and weary, and when he spoke his voice matched the misery of his expression.

"It would be foolish of us to just stand around here and do nothing. I do not pretend to understand the meaning of this schism which has taken place here tonight, or the fact that an outlet to the Abyss has been manifested elsewhere. These events have occurred and we must deal with them. If there are Coprolites abroad in the natural world it is our duty to send them back and close the Gate through which they came."

"That ain't necessarily true," said Nestor, looking perplexed but sounding angry. "What if the masters wanted this to happen? They gotta have a reason for doin' this."

Jorge walked over to him. "Yeah, they do. So they can wage the biggest holocaust ever. The genocide of humanity. That's why."

The tension in the room increased tangibly and Sylvio tried to quickly defuse it. "That assertion is subject to dispute. Our course of action is not. According to the pact, we must keep the damned from invading the land of the living. That is what we shall do."

He motioned toward Ashley without regarding her. "I believe that Ashley and I can attend to this matter, with the use of the Prism. Julian should also accompany us.

His hand created the Gate, so by his hand it can be more thoroughly destroyed."

The guardians seemed to be making up their minds about this scheme. Kristen was obviously very unhappy about Sylvio taking charge, but he didn't seem any more thrilled about having to do so. In the end Sylvio simply left the chamber, Ashley followed him, and Julian went after her. He loathed the idea of coming face to face with the Coprolites, but he couldn't bear to be apart from her right now.

"Are you ready for this?" she asked him when he caught up with her.

He wished she'd stop asking him that. "As much as I'll ever be." The crescent of dark crystal in his hand conveyed strength to him, but it didn't feel like near enough.

Still, it would have to do.

He had survived, hiding in a Dumpster. It was a humiliating position to be in, but Guilly had been surprised to find that when it came right down to it, he would rather live on his knees than die on his feet. Those feet had been running as fast as they could until he realized how stupid he was being. There was some bad shit loose in the world, and only one thing could save him: the piece of purple glass that the weird motherfucker had been carrying. Guilly was convinced that the only reason he was alive was that he'd touched it during his scrap with the guy and its power had somehow rubbed off on him. The fight had left him bleeding in over a dozen places—on his face, his hands, and from his half-bitten-off ear—but it had been worth it. The thing had to be some kind of a charm, and he was terrified that the magic spell might be wearing off. He didn't know what he'd do then, though he had a vague plan about breaking into the cathedral. It was a lot closer than home, a place he feared he'd never make it back to in one piece. If anybody lived there, they more than likely knew about this weird shit. Maybe they'd caused it. He'd go in a few more minutes. Just a few more.

Images of his gang being torn apart filled his mind. They made him feel like he might start screaming and never stop. The worst of it was that he had never even seen who or what had been doing it to them. Poor little Elpidia had seen something coming, that was for sure. Whatever it was, somebody was going to pay for what had gone down.

The time had come to take action. He started to raise the lid of the Dumpster, heard people coming down the street, and checked himself, leaving only a gap large enough to use as a peephole. There were three citizens approaching, he saw, and he felt some satisfaction at having guessed right. The freaks from the church *were* involved, for two of them were wearing robes and carrying torches, like devil worshipers out of some old movie. One was an old man and the other was a stunning blond fox. Oddly enough, Guilly recognized the third person, the guy in the leather jacket and blue jeans, as the faggot whose ass he'd almost kicked down at the Quarry. And the fox was the freaky bitch who'd saved his skin.

Then Guilly saw light glinting off the purple glass in the guy's hand, and the magic charm seemed to fill his vision. His desperation to have it almost made him stupid, but he stopped himself. Three against one was not a good idea. He would wait. When they had passed, he came out of his hiding place and silently stalked them, pulling out his switchblade knife and extending the blade.

He would soon have his revenge.

Fear pressed in on Julian from all sides, as if he were miles under the ocean where no sunlight ever reached, where the currents ran ever cold. He'd seen pictures of the kinds of creatures dredged up from those depths, anglers with glaring eyes and needle teeth in gaping mouths, monstrous shapes that didn't dare blight the bright surface world with their hideousness. Now he was surrounded by even more obscene forms, the denizens of a dark hell hovering in the shadows of refuse-strewn alleys, derelict automobiles, and crumbling factories. They seemed to have congregated most thickly in the area around the cathedral, perhaps with the idea of assaulting the source of their imprisonment, but they didn't seem to be doing much of anything. As the three of them walked the streets of the wasteland, Julian had to keep reminding himself that his companions had mastery over the creatures, and that the crystal clutched in his white-knuckled hand conferred upon him a similar immunity. Indeed, whenever he came close to one it shied away with a tiny shriek. But the sight of the Coprolites had caught him off guard, for he couldn't have envisioned a worse nightmare. They were almost all mouth, leading down into impossibly vast gullets. Like living hollownesses, pure gluttony incarnate. And that perhaps described them best.

Julian moved close to Ashley, holding her back and letting Sylvio pull ahead. "Why are we trusting him?" he said as they advanced farther into desolation. "We already know he's a liar. And he left you to the mercies of the masters."

"I apologize for that," said Sylvio, turning. He spoke quickly and obsequiously. "I lost my nerve in there. You do not know what it is like. You have only served them a short while, but they are all I have known for nearly a thousand years. I could not go against them."

Ashley was unimpressed by this, her eyes darting at the murky shapes in the dark. "Shove it up your ass, Sylvio. You'll never get back into my good graces no matter what. I'm only going along with you because I assume you know how to use the Prism."

He nodded anxiously. "I do, I do. I have been fully instructed in its use."

"Then you're of some use to me. Why did you lie about Ninanna when you told us about the Glory Hand?"

Sylvio held out a pleading hand toward her. "It would have been awkward to tell the truth. I never knew why the masters executed her. She'd had no chance to tell me before and I thought she was incapable of doing so afterward. Julian must have inadvertently awakened her from her sleep of death."

The section they were entering was less populated by Coprolites, but they seemed more active here. Their motion seemed to be in the general direction of the cathedral. Were they massing for a siege?

"As leader," Sylvio continued, "I thought the guardians would be harder to control if they knew one of their kind had been riven apart by the masters. So I kept the secret to myself."

"Aren't we going to do something about these

things?" Julian heard the frightened whine in his voice and hated it.

"There's no point in sending them back until the Gate is closed," answered Ashley. "They'd just come right out again. Don't worry. There's no one in the area for them to hurt. And they can't enter the cathedral. God, I really didn't think they could exist outside of the Abyss. Anyway, we'll come back for them."

This made sense to him, but he wished the task were over with already.

"Oh, God," he said when he saw what was up ahead. "What is that?"

In the flickering light of a guttering oil-barrel fire lay two shapes of an unknown and unpleasant nature. One looked like a dried-out corpse rolled in spiderwebs, and the other looked like a body charred inside and out. Not far from them a large slick of reddish sludge stained the concrete, dotted with what looked like tiny chips of bone. Ashley led the way over, seemingly undisturbed by these sights, and examined them by the light of her torch like a detective at the scene of a crime.

"These must be the Crucifixers that your friend mentioned," she said, way too calmly. "Nothing like being in the wrong place at the wrong time."

He would have been slack jawed with shock if he hadn't had to close his mouth to hold back a severe bout of nausea. "I don't understand," he said through clenched teeth. "Are you trying to tell me that these were once human beings?"

She nodded, frowning a little.

"This is what Coprolites do when they are at full strength," Sylvio explained. "Very nasty."

He looked into the darkness, trying to make the creatures out. Only the occasional one seemed to be passing by now. "But how? Why?"

"Why?" The old man took a moment to frame a reply. "Well, they have been shut up in the void for a very long time, starving for sensation in a place of total deprivation. They are angry and hungry. On the rampage. If allowed to remain out for a while they would settle down some, but only after they had had their fill of victims. Even then, it would be extremely dismal having them around."

Julian didn't doubt it.

Sylvio tapped Ashley on the shoulder and she stood up. "I suggest we split up at this point." He withdrew the pearly orb from the Arcade from the folds of his robe. "I will use this to gauge just how bad the infestation is. That is its function. You and Julian proceed to his apartment to close the breach. Just aim the crystal at the painting, and when the umbral emanation appears, sweep it across the doorway until all is destroyed. Then let us rendezvous back here to purge the area."

She nodded and he started walking away.

"Some wild trip, huh?" she said to Julian.

He was amazed at the steadiness of her tone. Perhaps she was just tremendously relieved at having survived the ritual intact. "A bad trip. As bad as it is, I'd still rather be here with you than anywhere else."

The corners of her mouth twitched, along with her brows. "What a glutton for punishment you are, then. It shouldn't get any worse than this."

Julian started to respond, but suddenly had his breath knocked out of him as something tackled him from the left, stinging him in the side as it pinned him to the ground. It couldn't be a Coprolite, he knew, but it couldn't be anything else. He almost panicked, expecting unspeakable things to start happening to his body at any moment. Then he realized it was a man on top of him, and it was a knife sticking into him. Whoever he was, his attacker was grabbing frantically for the Prism, but so far Julian was succeeding in keeping it out of reach. The guy was big and he looked young, was wearing a gold jacket spattered with blood. A Crucifixer?

"Give it to me, you pig-bastard!" said the young tough. "Give me the goddamned thing!"

How he knew the value of the Prism, Julian hadn't a clue, but the guy looked familiar. In fact, as they wrestled, Julian saw that he was the gang member who'd wanted to rearrange his skeletal structure with a pool stick in the Quarry. Ashley seized him from behind, hauled him off Julian, and hurled him to the pavement several feet away, where he landed on his stomach. Julian carefully pulled the blade out of his side, wondering if anything vital had been injured. The wound bled profusely and it hurt incredibly, but the knife had stuck more in his jacket than his flesh. He'd studied anatomy so he could accurately paint both the outsides and insides of human bodies; judging by what he knew, he didn't think any major organs had been punctured, no muscles or arteries cut, but he couldn't be sure. At the very least he should probably get some stitches.

"We know this cocksucker, don't we, Julian?" said Ashley as she lifted the dazed teenager by his collar. She dropped him abruptly when she saw Julian's stab wound, the blood blossoming around it into his shirt. "Jesus, how bad did he get you?"

He pocketed the retracted weapon and stood up, grimacing from the pain, wishing he could be tougher: He felt as if he might faint. "I don't know. It's not too deep, I don't think. Anyway, I just want to get on with this."

"Are you sure you don't need a doctor?"

"I think I could use one, cunt," said Guilly, rising to his knees. "You broke my fucking arm."

Julian was about to tell the punk to shut up when he saw a swarm of Coprolites coming at them from the east, the direction of his apartment. These were new arrivals, obviously, a second wave. One of them looked even stranger than the others, a cornucopia-shaped husk with some of its human form still fused and intertwined with it. The head was stretched and bloated, the mouth was grotesquely distended in the characteristic maw, but this Coprolite was clearly identifiable as Vern Doyle, not yet having fully shed his mortal coil.

This misshapen fiend was the only one that Guilly could see, and even then only part of it. It looked like pieces of deformed human body parts flying at him, not all of them connected to one another. He scrambled to his feet and started to run, but he didn't get far before he was engulfed. In the bowels of an organic inferno he experienced an eternity of burning and grinding, the liquefication of his tissues cell by cell, as he was digested into putrid offal by the hollow monster. After praying for it seemingly forever, the vital lights in his mind finally went out.

Julian and Ashley watched with jaded eyes as the Crucifixer was consumed with some difficulty by the larval Coprolite, gobbets of flesh and gore spitting out of the huge orifice. Then the victim's remains were excreted out the other end in stringy streams of loose, bloody sewage, which splashed across the sidewalk. The thing that had once been Vern glared in dumb despair at the two of them, sensed their untouchability, then hurried on its way with the rest of the noxious flock.

This time Julian did vomit, but what came out didn't look near as bad as the hellish messes surrounding it. When he was finished he faced Ashley with wide eyes and pale features. "Let's get that fucking hole closed before anything more comes out."

She nodded solemnly. "It'll be over soon. Just hang together for a little while longer."

"If I can."

They made their way out of the Wasteland toward civilization.

18

Memento Morituri

The bleak grays, dusty browns, faded blacks, and dull whites of his neighborhood seemed like the landscape of another planet to him now. Hues perfectly reflecting his mood. Except for the great gulf of dread that had yawned open inside of him. There was no color for that. It continued to widen, and soon it would stretch so vastly that he wouldn't ever be able to scream it out. He held it in, fought it down, kept his fragile reason hovering on the edge. Must not let it fall into that blank chaos.

They must look a sight, he was vaguely aware. Bleeding man and torch-bearing priestess. Fortunately the windows along these streets were dark, the people behind them asleep. Or had all those lightless rooms become slaughterhouses? The Coprolites had passed this way. *No, don't speculate about that. Divorce your mind from the theory and practice of hell.* Concentrate on the task at hand.

Silence filled the space between Ashley and himself like a viscous fluid, through which his feelings swam poorly. He couldn't look to her for comfort for his fears, as she was now a source of fear to him. She had joined in a killing right before his eyes—of his closest friend, no less. Not much of a friend toward the end, having proven himself to be a wretched bastard. But Ashley had taken the prerogative of summary judgment upon herself and acted as judge, jury, and executioner. As far as he could see she was governed by her own laws, working toward her own ends. Was that what she'd been doing all along? Seeking her own freedom, no matter what? His suspicions had been aroused before. Now he wasn't sure they'd been completely laid to rest.

His building was up ahead. House of horrors, housing a gateway for nightmares. It looked just the same. They mounted the front steps, mocked by the gargoyle, and went in. The lights were on in the downstairs hallway, showing the open doorway to Bonewitz's apartment, the bloodied carpet beyond.

"I wouldn't look in there if I were you," said Ashley, her voice sounding tight.

Julian had no intention of doing so. "Poor guy. He probably never knew what hit him."

"Then he was lucky."

They climbed the stairs and approached the closed door of his apartment. He hesitated before opening it, fearing a breakdown if what he saw inside was too unbearable. His hand closed about the knob, turned it. The loft was dark, save for the almost neonlike configuration of the Gate, and when he tried the lights they didn't work. What glowed on his canvas stunned him for a few seconds, that this dreadful wonder had been wrought by his hands—and Vern's. More than alive, more than dead, more than artifact, it was like a confluence of forces drawn from matter and mind. Like the eye of God.

"We don't need any more light than this," she said as they crossed to the center of the room. "Hand me the Prism, Julian."

He gazed at her through a fog of panic, about to succumb to complete terror. "Are you insane? Just what am I supposed to use for protection?"

An impatient frown furrowed her narrow brows. "Don't worry. I won't let anything happen to you."

Her hand reached out and waited. His gaze went from her hand to her eyes, frenzied. He was sick and weak from the agony in his side, near witless from enduring one scare after another, and in a growing state of confusion. Ashley was asking him to put his life in her hands. Part of him believed that she must have a perfectly good reason for doing so, one of absolute necessity, but another part warned him that he was placing his faith in a ruthless, capricious, unstable personality. Just how sure was he of his facts? There was no point of reference for him to latch on to. For all he knew, the masters weren't real, were just externalized alter egos of the guardians themselves. Their guilt and madness incarnate. Was that idea any crazier than what they claimed to be? He had been manipulated all along, a living man in the land of the dead, so it was possible that he was still a pawn. Tonight the two of them had witnessed atrocities worse than the human mind could absorb and he'd not seen her bat an eye once. Underneath her extremely pleasing veneer she was a beautiful beast, white and wounded, but beastly in spite of her beauty. Could something like that truly love him? *Should* he allow himself to love such a being? It was a stupid question, for he really had no choice in the matter.

"You won't let them get me, will you, Ashley?"

Her face looked agitated, heated. "There aren't any Coprolites nearby on either side of the Gate right now. I can sense them. We'll have plenty of warning if any approach."

"All right." He gave her the Shadow Prism.

Ashley's body became very taut as she held the crystal out at arm's length, the horns of the vertical crescent pointing at the Gate. After a few seconds darkness gathered within the purple translucency and rays of blackness shot toward the painting. Where they struck, sections of the glowing pattern were blasted away, erased, more and more as she raked the beams across the intricate structure. The hole in the center started to close, then filled with some solid substance—which Julian recognized as the craggy rind of a Coprolite. It squeezed through just as the aperture sealed itself like a constricting pupil and the design around it collapsed, leaving only the painting behind.

The Coprolite shot straight toward Julian. Truly terror struck now, he pounced on Ashley, knocking her to the floor as he grabbed madly for the Prism. The impact made her drop it, sent it skittering across the room. He lunged after it with the creature hot on his heels, its breath like the stench of a rotting world. He saw Ashley throw herself onto it and cling to it in a bear hug, but that didn't seem to slow it down much. It feebly clawed at her with its skeletal limbs. Scrambling on his hands and knees, Julian searched blindly in the shadows for the crystal, knowing at any moment that he was going to be swallowed and devoured. It was almost upon him, nearly enclosing him. Then his fingers closed around the crescent, he rolled onto his back with the object thrust outward, and the roving maw backed off. Sensing it had no prey here, it slipped out of Ashley's grasp and soared away through a wall into the dark city.

He leapt to his feet, crossed the short distance between them, and seethed in her face. "What the fuck are you trying to do? That thing almost got me!"

"I miscalculated," she snapped at him, looking slightly muddled. "I thought the door would close before it could get there."

He didn't know whether to believe that or not. What the fuck was the matter with her?

"Anyway, you should finish destroying the Gate. You made it, so you ought to do the rest."

Glaring at her, he took the Crucifixer's blade and opened it, then stomped over to the painting. With savage strokes he ripped the canvas to ribbons and shredded the ribbons. This done, he broke apart the supporting struts and cracked them in two again and again. It did not feel like a complete enough destruction of the Gate's components, but it wasn't within his power to dissolve the molecules and atoms of which they were made.

"That's more than sufficient, I think," she said as if reading his thoughts. "Now let's go back and meet Sylvio, see about ridding this city of some undesirable elements."

He resented her humor on the heels of his near death. He felt as if he didn't even know her, had suddenly found himself in a crisis relying on a volatile stranger. She seemed to be off on some kind of trip all her own. As he crossed the room toward her, his legs suddenly wobbled, collapsed. He half fell to the floor and sat there

HARROWGATE

with the Prism cradled in his lap. Sleep called to him. It would be so easy to nod off into slumber. He needed to rest. He couldn't keep his eyes open.

Ashley knelt down in front of him, shaking him roughly by the shoulder. "Julian, you can't rest yet. I need the Prism, and there's a Coprolite loose around here. You won't be safe without it."

"What do you care?" he muttered. "You let it in."

She shook him again.

"It'll probably go to the cathedral like the others. Evil seems pretty stupid, doesn't it? Their one night out of hell and the demons are wasting it attacking an impregnable keep."

Julian limply held out the Prism. "You take it. Go on without me. I'm all out of willpower."

"Are you all out of love for me?"

He raised his head sharply, tried to read her expression. It looked bold, nervous, ambivalent, with an air of superiority. Like she was daring him. To do what? Love her? "No. I've still got that."

"Then come with me." Her lips pulled back over her teeth in a smile that was part snarl, reminding him too much of Vern. Worse than dead now. "Listen, Julian. I don't know what's waiting for me back at the cathedral. You might never see me again. Please. I don't want to face it alone."

That got him. Such an admission must have cost her. "All right. Let's go."

She helped him to his feet and they were on the move again.

Back in the deserted streets, passing by darkened buildings. Unless the buildings did conceal ghastly human remains, there was reason to hope that Bonewitz and the Crucifixers were so far the only victims of the Coprolites. Some of the local street animals had not been so lucky, Julian soon saw. One of the Coprolites, probably the last one to come through, had stopped for a snack. It was in an alley swallowing a rat. When the rat came back into view it was a writhing red mass of quivering organs and splayed bones, evidently turned inside out. There seemed to be no end to the inventiveness of the monstrosities.

"Oh, fuck," he gasped, turning away and staggering on.

"Wait." Ashley detained him by the arm. "Let's try to catch it."

"What? Why? How?"

She tapped the Prism in his hand with a fingernail. "With this. It was explained to me once, but I barely listened. It's not complicated, though. Just hold it the way I did when I destroyed the Gate."

Julian balked at her.

"Go ahead. And hurry up. It looks like it's about to run away. The filaments of the net are supposed to spin by themselves."

He relented and obeyed with a weak, unsteady arm. Dark tendrils flowed out from the crystal toward the Coprolite and branched out around it, joining together in a hexagonal cage with triangular facets. The skeletal formation of vibrating black bars started to shrink, while within its enclosure the creature curled up and seemed to swallow its own tail. It was soon reduced to a mote of blackness upon which the net collapsed. Then the lines of shadow withdrew back into the Prism so fast that he almost dropped it in surprise.

"I'll be damned," she said, studying the crescent in his hand.

Working up the required amount of nerve he looked into the Prism, but there was no sign of its captive. "Is it back in the Abyss now?"

Ashley looked at him, her eyes a bit spaced out. "Uh, I don't think so. I think it has to be cast into the pit. Come on."

That was something else to look forward to, wasn't it?

Sylvio was waiting for them back at the parking lot of the massacre, looking glum and uneasy. "It does not seem to be a major incursion," he said. "There are not more than a thousand Coprolites out, and all are in this technological desolation. Did you get the Gate closed?"

"It's closed." She crossed her arms and looked around restlessly. "You suppose the masters planned it that way? Set up house in the middle of nowhere knowing that if the things got out they'd shoot right to here? Attract less notice that way?"

"Who can say?" He turned to Julian. "Now, if you will give me the Prism, I can proceed to banish the Coprolites."

Recoiling at the very suggestion, Julian clutched the crescent so hard that it dug into his skin. "No. No way. Whatever needs to be done I'll do it. I've already caught one of them myself. I can get the rest. Just tell me what to do. Do I have to track them down one by one or what?"

The old man looked unsure, but he seemed to accept this. "Very well. This will be a mass purging. Same basic principle, except that you shall compel the whole herd to come to you. If you diffract a nether spectrum into the air over the intersection, it should draw them like a magnet and absorb them. So just hold the crystal at an angle and aim in that direction."

At the thought of a thousand Coprolites converging on the spot where he was standing Julian almost backed down. But he couldn't let go of the crescent, not after what had almost happened to him in his loft. He faced the crossroads and held up the crystal as instructed. It shot out its dark energies and continued to fire, forming a miasmic cloud above the blind and rusting traffic light. This black nebula thickened and roiled, then began extending smoky tentacles into the distance in all directions, like some huge, bloated octopus suspended in the night air. One by one the tentacles retracted, each with a Coprolite speared on its tip. As the creatures were pulled into the cloud they devoured their tails and wilted into shadowy spores, almost as if they were being unborn. When the last tendril had withdrawn with its squirming prey, the gaseous coagulation folded in on itself and receded into the crystal. The purging was apparently completed.

He stood trembling with the now inactive Prism held aloft, feeling that the night had suddenly become very silent and empty. What it had been emptied of, it was far better without, but what had been drained out of it was now his unwanted burden. With the area now cleansed of unearthly predators, however, he could safely give the crescent up to someone else. He held it out to Sylvio.

"No." The old man held up his palms. "I cannot accept it. They must be returned to the pit, and I am not going back there. I choose to take my chances out here among mortals."

Dismayed, Julian tried to give it to Ashley. "Why don't you hang on to it, lover?" she said, a bit coyly. "If some of the guardians or the masters are in a fighting mood, I'm going to have my hands full already. You can make sure the Coprolites are dumped into the void."

"But I don't know how to do it." That irritating whine again, but there was nothing he could do about it.

"It is simple," said Sylvio. "Just aim the Prism down at the pit. It will do the rest itself." He faced Ashley. "I am sorry I haven't been a better mentor to you, but you were a fine student. I am just a very old, very flawed man. And I cannot deal with what I fear is going on back at the cathedral. My wits are too frail."

Ashley stood with her right leg extended at an angle, glaring at him in disappointment. "Yeah, well, if you can't handle it, then you can't. You can't think of any way we can battle the masters? Anything at all?"

He shook his sparsely-haired head. "I am tired of thinking. My brain has worn itself out. Use your youth. That is something they have lost and can never have again. They are older and uglier than sin. Use that against them. I must go now. Farewell."

With a wave he shambled away from them, toward the city. Maybe to become a street person for real this time.

"That's what it comes down to, I guess." Ashley scraped her foot on the pavement. "Everything he's learned over all the time he's been alive, and he'll end up on skid row. Not enough ambition to make it on his own. Figures, huh? We've got a choice to make, you know."

Lost in the turmoil of his own distress, he almost didn't hear her. "What's that?"

"Which way to enter the cathedral. Through a front door, in which case we can maybe recruit allies and engage enemies among the guardians, or down into the catacombs. I know them like the back of my hand, so that's no problem. We go in secretly, march straight to the Sanctum, and unload the hellions into the pit. Then we take on my shining saviors once and for all."

It was obvious by the emphasis in her voice which tactic she preferred. "Take them on with what, Ashley? We've got nothing."

She grabbed the lapels of his jacket and shook him. "We've got us. We'll just fight them with what we've got, with piss and spit and filthy curses. Bite them, claw them, fuck in front of them, anything we can think of. Whatever it takes."

As crazed as she sounded, he didn't have a better idea. Or any idea at all. Her enthusiasm disturbed him, however. "You were afraid before the ritual. Aren't you afraid now?"

"I wasn't afraid of anything when I was alive. Why should I be now that I'm dead?"

"Because this time you could die for good." She seemed to be reverting to her hard-ass routine for some reason.

"I'm too much of a bitch to die. And if I do, we'll die together, giving them holy fucking hell."

That wasn't enough for him. He didn't want to die. Still, anywhere he went he would be facing death, along with the rest of the world. So he might as well go to the heart of the threat. And he couldn't leave her.

There was something going on inside of her, some compulsion too deep and basic for him to grasp. Better just to go along with it. Even with a rested untraumatized mind he'd have a hard time figuring out the mental dynamics of someone who had known death and rebirth. *Under stress we all show our real natures.*

"Okay. Let's go in through the back door."

They headed for the manhole, Ashley striding like a prowling cat with Julian plodding along behind. She descended first, positively spoiling for the combat. He followed and by the firelight of her torch he saw her face, the raging expression there. Ashley seemed to be filled with all the wrath of hell, the fury of a woman not so much scorned as used. Someone had thought of her as property, and now all that pent-up revenge had been triggered by—by what? By her ordeal in the ritual? By her wrestling match with the Coprolite? No way of knowing, but she sure was on a tear.

At the end of the tunnel they came to a hole in the cathedral's foundation. They entered the labyrinth and the moment they did he knew something was different. Horribly wrong. It wasn't dark, for a dim yellowish light seemed to be streaming from the direction of the Sanctum, right through the stone walls of the catacombs. It was accompanied by a reeking wind blowing from the same place. There was a buzzing in the air, as of flies at a rancid feast. And an unpleasant sensation made his skin twitch. It felt as if the pit was everywhere now, just on the verge of opening up all around them. The masters had to be rising from their transitional tombs, and from the Abyss.

As she led him through the maze, he felt like a child being dragged by the hand of his enraged mother, weak and helpless on the stormy seas of her rampant temper. He could only hope that she hadn't lost her sanity. His child mind was very much with him, for he had entered the labyrinth of his dreams, would soon face the Slug people from his death journey. They had ruled and ruined him long enough. Now he would defeat them or they would destroy him, but one way or the other he would be free of them. Long had they possessed his inner mind, as they had possessed Ashley in body. Both of them must now gain their release.

He was leaving a trail of blood through the passages, not a lot, just a few drops every two feet or so. They looked black in the sulphurous glow permeating the atmosphere. If he needed to find his way out by himself, they would work as well as bread crumbs or thread. To find his way ahead, to know what to do, there was no clear path to help him. Once again he was flying blind, participating in an event that must be extraordinary even to Ashley. All he had was his own sense of dead reckoning. It was what he used when he did his best paintings, letting instinct and insight guide his hand and his eye, so he would have to make do with it now.

They came out into the main passage before he was even aware of it, for the yellowish light made all the masonry look the same. The first thing he noticed was that the archway leading to the Sanctum no longer opened on pitch blackness, but framed a shadow show of swaying shapes bright and dark. The phosphorescence within looked distinctly unwholesome, like swamp gas or luminous mold. And the smell was that of an ancient slaughterhouse that had lain buried for a thousand years and just been unsealed.

They came to the doorway, and only then did Julian truly consider turning and running. The Sanctum now looked like not just the edge of the world, but the end of the world as well. There were jagged holes in the walls, burned away as if by tremendous heat, and through these holes could be seen nothingness, less even than the darkness of the Abyss. It was true void, total emptiness which his mind tried to perceive as a grayish haze while his eyes saw it for what it was. The nullification of everything. Existence was being uncreated in there, and walking into it would be like dying in the middle of the darkest dream. His heart was slamming against his ribs, and he felt as if he were sweating blood. All the oxygen seemed to have gone out of the air. The environment of hell wasn't fire and brimstone, his mind raved, but a vacuum in which thought and feeling rotted along with the flesh.

"What do you see in there?" she asked him in a small voice.

"Nothing." He sounded muffled. Remote.

"Yeah. That's what I see. Let's go."

How could she still be in such a rush? Getting his feet to move into the room was the hardest thing he'd ever done. They seemed glued to the spot, but as she tugged him, his leg muscles finally loosened and let him take a few slow steps forward. Then he was standing in the Sanctum.

Inside the chamber, though it was as cold as ever within, the walls seemed to be melting, and sections of the ceiling hung down like stalactites. Even the stone of the floor appeared to be warping, though the bridge arching across the center of the room still looked solid enough. The pit was wide open, and above it the masters, hooked to their pillars, looked drastically different. Every one of them was at least halfway out of its chrysalis, most of them more so, and they were struggling to break completely free. Their heads were little more than skulls with glowing eyes of dark violet, embedded at the top of yellowish-green masses of glistening translucent flesh, like short, fat worms, from which waved tiny arms as atrophied as those of a tyrannosaurus. They possessed vestigial maws like those of the Coprolites, but gaping from their swollen stomachs rather than the front of their bodies. Worst of all, their rib cages had unfurled to form struts for their manta-ray wings, which spread into twelve-foot spans of golden gossamer skin. Inside their barrel-shaped bodies, all their clustered organs seemed to have hardened into dull-colored jewels, probably utterly useless now. *The Slug People have sloughed off their skins and made themselves wings,* Julian ranted in his mind. They were getting away, escaping from him forever.

"Why don't you empty the Prism now?" Ashley said, squinting up at her changed masters.

He barely understood her words. "Huh? Oh."

Listlessly he crept to the rim of the pit, passing between two of the columns, all too aware that he was flanked by two of the emergent masters. Their grisly toothed tails could come sliding out any moment, as Firdausi's had during the ritual, digging themselves into his flesh. For a minute or so he just stood there glaring up at the winged worms writhing from their amniotic sacs, his mouth agape. Waiting for death.

"You shall be the first to die, harlot," Firdausi said to Ashley. The head master squirmed in his shell directly across the pit from Julian. "One less insolent corrupting slut fouling the world."

Her reply was filled with sarcasm, though it sounded forced. "Me? *I* foul the world? You should see what you look like. That's the body you want to live in forever? Ever see a nightmare crawling?"

Julian felt himself fading in and out of reality. The volume of her words was erratic, her voice echoing, unclear. Below him, the edge of the pit seemed to ripple like the shore of an undiscovered sea. He dropped to his knees and pointed the crescent at the dark hole, expecting one of the masters to fall on him at any moment. Instantly dozens of twisting shapes came spilling out of the crystal, expanding and uncurling as they tumbled into infinity below. In a way they were beautiful—the poetry in their motion, the anger in their fierce, tight bodies as they were swallowed by nothingness. He wondered why he was bothering to do this, for they would probably come flying back out as soon as the masters summoned them. No, that wasn't true. They'd needed him to create a Gate for them. Now it was closed. What *did* they plan on doing now?

"We shall be as gods," Firdausi bellowed. "You could have been a queen under our dominion, ruling a tenth of the earth after we have cleansed it of perversion. You see now what a fool you are."

"It's better to serve in heaven than rule in hell," she said with a hysterical giggle. "Your hell, anyway. I don't think I'd like what you would make of the planet. But how are you going to release your army? Your Gate is destroyed and we certainly aren't going to open one for you."

Julian heard a commotion behind him. Forcing his reluctant body into motion, he stood and turned, keeping the crescent pointing down into the Abyss to continue the flow of creatures. In the voidlight of the pit Ashley had transformed into the downy white creature she became in the ritual, and the other guardians were shuffling into the room around her. They changed before his eyes as well.

"What's going on here?" Kristen breathlessly demanded, tusked and blubbery, gazing in awe at the new forms of the masters.

"A Gate shall be opened," boasted Firdausi. "The artist will do it, if we hold you hostage. Or it shall be done by a majority of guardians. Be assured of it."

As Julian turned back to Firdausi, he noticed with shock that one of the Coprolites had managed to cling to Firdausi's column by its tail. He simply resigned himself to capturing it again and hurling it a second time into the void, after he'd dumped this loathsome load.

"You know," drawled Ashley with disgust, "I'm really sick of this heavy power-trip you motherfuckers are on. Yeah, you gave me life a second time, but only for your own purposes. I'm not your slave. I don't owe you anything. And I won't let you bring the curtain down on everybody else either. I'm tired of getting pushed around and told what to do and abused by sons of bitches like you. So you can just go fuck yourselves."

From the folds of her robe she pulled out a pistol and fired it wildly at the shimmering carcasses of the masters. Julian wondered where the hell she might have picked it up. She emptied the magazine, the shots sounding strangely muted, then Iris and Nestor disarmed her. It didn't matter, however, for every bullet that struck one of the grotesque bodies went straight through, leaving a hole that was instantly healed.

Kristen stepped forward, rudely elbowing Ashley, who broke free from the grasp of her fellow guardians. "Don't pay any attention to her, lords. She does not speak or act for all of us. There are those among us who are still devoted to you. We believe in you."

God, this chick is really screwed up in the head, thought Julian. If she could still serve the masters after seeing what they really looked like and learning without a doubt what their intentions were, then she had a truly barren soul. She needed a leader, any leader, to fill that hole within her. The masters had selected some of their servants extremely well.

"You can rely on me as well," vowed Iris.

"I stick by my oath to you too," said Nestor, apparently still loving the whip. "Tell us what to do!"

This was shaping up into a rumble. Gang war. Or maybe just a mob attack on Ashley. Fortunately the outpouring from the Prism had reduced to a trickle. One final Coprolite fell from it into the eternal dark. That vast blackness sucked at him, hungered to swallow him, and he had no will to resist it. Weakness had carved him out inside, removed the tension from his muscles and smothered the fires of his fortitude. Starved of sustenance, racked by mental upheaval, grimy with grit from his body and filth from the world, he felt degraded and humiliated. Lowered to a near-animal state of cowering disgrace. Since his earliest years he had been *their* victim, at some point graduating to the role of incidental puppet. In his most brittle vulnerable moment *they* had toyed with him, held his life and sensibilities in their hands. Now he'd come full circle and the situation was the same. That was the essence of his relationship to the Slug People, as victim to his indifferent tormentors. They had injected poison into his young mind, and he'd been dying of it ever since, exhibiting the course of the infection in the frames of his morbid masterpieces. The masters were the death he lived in terror of, Death itself. The Abyss was their collective soul, the voidlight their creeping madness, the Coprolites their diseased spermatozoa ejaculated into the world to lay it waste.

One more Coprolite hung on near the edge of the pit, flapping like a bladder in the downward pull of its forces. At least he could take care of it, do that much. He focused the Prism on the fugitive monster and a beam of darkness streamed toward it. Like a black laser ray the emanation struck its target, but instead of caging the Coprolite, the bolt severed the tail adhering to the pillar. The fiend dropped into the pit like a shot, astonishing him.

A thought assembled in his clouded brain, one that shook him like a tree in a hurricane. Maybe, just maybe, the Shadow Prism had just exceeded design specifications. Surrounded by walls pocked with windows looking out on oblivion, in the company of walking death and living hell, Julian actually smiled. There *was* a weapon he could use against the Slug People, and it had fallen into his vindictive hands. He'd received it as a gift from a girl with perilous eyes and a spirit in which night and day warred. She had saved him from gang violence and a bleak, loveless life. Now he had a chance to save her.

Holding the Prism out over the Abyss, he tilted it upward, aiming at the bloated gargoyle he believed was Firdausi. Darkness lanced out, curved through the air, and struck the pillar just above the master's leering head. A scream might have reached Julian's ears from across the bottomless pool of blackness, but he would never be certain. The stem securing Firdausi to his post snapped and the winged bulk plunged into the vacuous mouth it had so long tempted.

"Not to be!" roared the master of the masters, almost pleading. Was it surprise at being bested or a plea for nonexistence instead of never-ending despair? Firdausi flapped his wings once, but they were not yet strong enough to bear him up in the downdraft from the Abyss. They crumpled and he dropped, to the ebon surface and beneath it, never to be seen again.

Nine segmented tails unsheathed at the same time and lashed out at him, sending him leaping backward so fast that he stumbled, landing on his back. There was a scream behind him that was unmistakable, a guardian freaking out at the loss of one of their idols. He turned his head and saw Kristen lunging at him. Ashley grabbed her and pulled her back, and they fought. The fight spread quickly through the guardians, with Iris and Nestor trying to stop Julian while Jorge and Bonita defended him. Teeth and claws flashed among them while Bethany, Rubin, and Arlo looked on.

"This is the way it should be!" yelled Bonita. "Let him dispose of them. They have no place in creation."

"No!" shrieked Iris. "We need them! Stop him!"

Julian scrambled back, trapped between the fighting guardians and the deadly tails of the masters. They couldn't quite reach him. Ashley slashed viciously into Kristen's gray corpulence, but the glistening folds of her skin didn't cut easily. With sluggish movements Kristen closed her massive hands around his lover's throat and started to squeeze, blind fury even further distorting her flabby face.

"Do it, Julian," gasped Ashley. "Kill the others. Kill them all."

All he wanted was to go to her, pull Kristen off of her, but he wouldn't have a chance. Not that his chances with the masters looked much better. Alerted to the danger now, they swung their lethal tails back and forth like a jungle of killer vines, daring him to venture into their grasp. Turning, visions of Ashley's delicate skull twisted off in Kristen's paws skewering him to the quick, he contemplated doing just that.

Nothing could make him do it. There was no way he could survive an attempt to slay the masters, and if he sacrificed his life what would he be doing it for? Even if he succeeded in freeing the earth from them, what would he gain? He wouldn't be alive to enjoy the victory. Might as well just let the motherfucking devils reign over the world. Death awaited him either way. Death and its monstrous terrors. But what were those terrors? Where had they come from in the first place? From his ordeal in the crash, when he'd first met the Slug People. The masters. They had bestowed upon him the curse of the terrors. No, they *were* the terrors. He didn't know what death was, but he knew *them*. They had appeared at his little death, confusing him, making him think that they and death were the same thing. But they weren't, were they? It wasn't death he was afraid of. It was *them*. But the masters weren't death or life. They were nothing. Nothing to be afraid of. All they could do was kill him; he controlled his own terrors. He was the master of *them*.

"You didn't wound my mind!" he shouted at the masters. "You gave me a gift! You made me aware of my own fears and in knowledge there is power. Because of you I learned to expose terrors to the daylight. I can see you, and I know you, and I can destroy you! You've made me the master now!"

In a frenzy of anguish and euphoria he charged past the waving tendrils and rushed onto the arched bridge, not stopping until he was standing on the circular platform at the center. The nine tails of bone, thick as firehoses, whipped inward all at once, cracking like a justed spines as they curled toward him. Julian flinched against their impact, but every one of them fell short by a few feet.

The good lord protects heroes and fools, his mind murmured in its relief. He was glad he was a fool.

The nothingness below threatened to cripple him with vertigo, but he was so intent on his mission that he didn't care. Raising the crystal, he aimed its dark beam at the master next to Firdausi's vacant pillar, either Euterpe or Meraviglia, watching with glee as its cocoon broke free, slid into the pit, and sank into the dense shadows. Then he realized his choice had been foolish, for it had been only half out of its shell, while others were much farther along. He resolved to concentrate on those about to separate completely. With another flash of darkness from the crystal he sent to its doom one that had been about to take flight. With a quick look around he realized that this strategy wasn't going to get rid of them all. Now that they saw what imminent jeopardy they were in, the masters fought to tear themselves out of their cocoons with frantic gyrations. It was time to finish them off and get this over with.

The fight near the entrance distracted him for a moment as he noticed that the guardians were grievously wounding each other. He could make out broken bones, torn flesh, bared internal organs, and flowing vital fluids. Ashley no longer struggled in Kristen's clutches, but circled her now and swiped at her with sharp crystalline claws. Her body looked more red than white now, much to his dread. The only way he could help her was by killing off her enslavers, so he aimed the Prism and made another one dive into black oblivion. When he glanced back at the fight he was horrified to see Nestor rip

Bonita's head from her shoulders and cast it to the ground. Unobstructed now, Nestor started coming toward him, huge head and pincered hands like something from a madman's hallucination. The murderous guardian was grabbed from behind by Rubin and the two of them went at each other's throats. Their furious grappling carried them close to the pit, closer still, until a careless thrust sent them both careening over the edge. They were lost in fathomless black distances.

Such valor on Rubin's part could not go unmatched, thought Julian. With a vengeance he sent another master thrashing into the pit, and still another that glared hate at him with voidlight eyes. He could only imagine their rage at being thwarted by an ordinary man after millennia of waiting, of changing, of preparing.

One of them launched itself from its shredded casing into the yellow limbo of the air. Now Julian knew he was in trouble. At first he wanted desperately to cling to the idea that because it belonged to the pit, it would be repelled by the Prism, like the Coprolites, but that hope was dashed when the newborn creature came at him. As it swooped down, he ducked, but it lurched to a stop in midflight before it even reached him. Some kind of umbilical cord still connected it to its chrysalis. Puffing with surprise and relief, he stood up and fired a tongue of black light at its pillar as it struggled to break the tether. The stem of the cocoon seared away, along with that end of the cord, and the cocoon slipped into the Abyss.

Beating its wings wildly the freed master soared toward the melting ceiling. It flew at him again, and Julian flattened himself facedown on the bridge. As it made its pass over him, Julian felt himself lifted up slightly and dropped, and at the same time was seared by ripping, blazing agony. Warm wetness flowed down his sides to his belly. Blood, and lots of it. The master had ripped his back open with the hooks of its tail. It felt bad, worse than he could handle knowing just yet. Looking up, he saw the creature hovering at the lip of the void, about to glide his way again. The tiny feet at the ends of its withered legs had fused toes, he noticed, not unlike cloven hooves. Appropriate. And you could call its tail barbed. All of a sudden the master jolted, its membranous wings ruffled, and it toppled over into the pit. A guardian had leapt onto its back, one with a knobby, elongated head, knocking them both into the Abyss. Arlo had just saved his life.

And had his life been saved? Maybe not. He felt faint, woozy, as if his back were on fire. When he reached around to explore the injury, his hand stroked raw, slick meat and some naked ribs, the hard ridge of his spine. God, his back had been stripped of skin! This was it. He was going to die. No more worrying about it. No more putting it out of his mind. This was death and he was going to meet it. It was in him, devouring him, erasing his sense of well-being, ill-being, all being. He looked for Ashley. Needed her beauty, her light, the memories she gave him. Never again would he make love with her, but he could die this death for her. If it was for her, he could do it.

His vision was blurry, but he thought he could make her out kneeling over the mound of Kristen's prostrate bulk, tearing something out of it. Nearby Iris was yanking snakes of intestine out of Jorge, the golden lizard-man. This was not the kind of memory he wanted to have in his mind's eye when he breathed his last breath, but you paid your money and you took your chances.

Straining his way onto his shaky legs he stood, deciding to take as many of the enemy with him as he could. *Remember us who are about to die,* he pleaded with the heavens, wherever they were. He quickly dispatched two more of the masters and discovered they had devised a new strategy to get at him. One of them deliberately struck the bridge with its body in its downward course, smashing out one end connecting it to the floor of the Sanctum. Incredibly, the bridge did not collapse. The other caught itself by grabbing hold of the broken edge on its way down. They were clearly out to avenge the deaths of their fellows, oblivious to every other purpose now. Except to get him. *They were pissed off.* The remaining master hung from a column very close to the other end of the bridge, so if it managed to take that out with its hideous weight, Julian would go with it into a nameless eternity. As it was very near to emerging and the other one had nearly heaved itself up onto the bridge, Julian didn't have time to cross to the safety of the floor. He wasn't sure he had the strength to make it that far anyway. Staggering over to the hanger-on, he crushed its gnarled claws under his heels until it let go with a squawk, at the same time firing at the last of the masters. Sure enough, as it fell away, it collided with the bridge in its fall, causing the length of stone to crumble beneath his feet.

Julian took two running steps and made a leap for the rim of the pit. He struck hard, dropping the Prism into the icy darkness below. His arms were stretched straight out and his fingers found a rift in the warping floor. He was dangling in the void, too exhausted to pull himself up. In front of him the vulturine figure of Iris pummeled and pecked mercilessly at Ashley's smaller blood-drenched form, her ferocity undiminished by the fact that she had no lords left to serve. Bethany had curled up against the wall, apparently unharmed, while the remains of the other guardians lay around her in pieces. Ashley went down under the force of Iris's blows, looked his way, and finally noticed his predicament. As for him, his grip and his consciousness were slipping.

His blood dripped into the depths of the Abyss, into the numbing darkness in which he was almost totally immersed. Something was happening to his flayed back, as if the fluid of the void was hardening over it. Surely he wasn't degenerating into one of the damned. He wasn't dead and he'd lived a good life. Or so he believed.

Julian looked down and saw a swarm of Coprolites rushing up at him like piranhas in dark water. Then he looked up and saw Ashley running toward him.

Then all was blackness.

19

Ashley Wednesday

She stood in the Sanctum, still wearing her filthy and stained ceremonial robe. The chamber now resembled a cavern more than a room. Like wax or molten rock the material of the walls had solidified, and most of the columns had toppled. Of the bridge and the pit there was no sign. It had vanished after she'd pulled Julian's body from it. And the Abyss seemed to be gone for good. As a guardian her most startling power had been the ability to generate an entry point to the void, even travel through it to another place, as unpleasant as that was to do. Without more guardians around she couldn't open one. Even at a distance from each other they had formed what she believed was called a gestalt. That, too, was gone for good.

What she had seen in the Abyss just before it closed for the final time had shaken her. She couldn't be positive she understood what it meant, but she was fairly sure. In their maniacal gambit for control of hell and earth, the masters seemed to have torn the fabric of the Gate in many places. The integrity of the barrier was now in question. The rents in the mesh of woven voidlight might not be large enough for the Coprolites to pass through; the remaining threads stretched across the strained sites might yet be thick enough to hold them in. She was no expert in these matters. All the experts were dead, slain by her lover. Using one of their own toys, no less.

As for the guardians, Sylvio was out in society somewhere, having left even before the fighting began. Rubin, Nestor, and Arlo had met their ends in the pit. She had personally ripped out Kristen's heart and actually fucking eaten it, so while pieces of it still beat within her own body, it no longer kept the bitch alive. Kristen's disgusting corpse now lay buried in the yard, somehow still living but totally unable to move. Since it hadn't changed back to human form, it would come as a real big surprise to anyone who ever dug it up.

Jorge, brave, smart, and defiant, gutted a second time by Iris, now lay under a fallen pillar. She couldn't get to his body. Enough rubble covered him to serve as a burial, however. He was a tough street kid who had never gotten far, but who had never sold out.

Then there was poor Bonita, also interred in the church grounds, her head wrenched from her shoulders. She also had failed to change back. Ashley clung to some hope that the two parts would someday merge together once more, but she didn't know if such a thing was possible.

As for Iris, she had run out of the cathedral after Ashley broke off their duel. Good thing, too, because the bitch was beating her to a pulp. She had become human again after the pit closed, as had Ashley herself. Now Iris was out there somewhere, crazed by the loss of the guiding lights of her masters.

Bethany had survived, looked normal now, but was just about catatonic. She just lay in her room and remained about as motionless as someone who was dead. In time she might snap out of it. Her nerves were just overloaded or something.

And what of Julian? *Her* Julian? He had been in a coma ever since she'd dragged him out of the pit, barely alive. There was no point in taking him to a hospital. His condition was far beyond the scope of medical science. The knife puncture in his side and the peeled area of his back had been covered with some kind of smooth black scar tissue, as if the Abyss had cauterized his wounds. She'd never seen anything like it before, except in the carcasses of the two teenage trespassers in the catacombs. Their insides seemed to have filled up with a similar substance, like coagulated oil. And they didn't seem to be rotting. Had they been mummified by the preserving properties of the voidlight, injected into them by Iris and Nestor? Ashley knew that she could kill that way, with her eyes, though she never had. In milder doses her stare was good for striking a bit of fear in people. That was enough for her.

More than his body had been devastated by the void, however. He had in essence drowned in the sea of deadness in which the damned swam, so it was no surprise that such a shock had all but destroyed him. As his flesh had been drained of life, his sense of self had been cut off from all light, all reality, all connection to things that could be touched and felt. She knew. She'd been there, in that horrible place. The difference was that she'd been dead at the time. Maybe he had been, too, for a moment.

There was still breath and a pulse in him, but she was afraid she hadn't rescued him in time. He'd already spent a whole day in a dangerously deep unconscious state and so far there was no sign of recovery.

When she thought about what she'd done to him, she wished there were still a pit into which she could throw herself. Her actions had brought this gentle, sensitive artist close to a terrible death, while she was just fine. In fact, she would probably live forever. She'd ended his short life while hers remained endless. This was what she'd done to the guy who loved her, whom she now knew she loved. If he didn't live, she vowed to find a way to kill herself. Eternal life without him would be eternal damnation for her.

Ashley started back upstairs to check on him again, talk to his pale, inert form, try to bring him back from the brink of oblivion. There would never be a way for her to express how grateful she was to him. He'd freed her from her enslavement to the masters and that was all she'd really needed. She had long ago come to grips with her abnormal condition, as even in her natural life she'd hardly been a normal sort of human being. That part of it she could handle. To have her emotions awakened for the first time ever and then dashed by the death of her deliverer, a death that she had caused, was something else altogether. Never before had she cared about someone besides herself, more than herself. It was something new for her to have her continued existence depend on another individual, a scary and disturbing thing.

"Hello, Julian. How are you today?" She entered her room, sat down next to him on the bed, and began stroking his hair. His eyes were closed and his mouth hung open. Shallow breath wheezed into his lungs too few times a minute. "You know, you and Bethany are real boring company. I've actually started talking to myself. It wouldn't be so bad, but I'm beginning to lose my arguments with me."

As hard as she tried to sound cheerful, her voice fell flat. The cathedral was now a very lonely and depressing place, though its ghastly residents had been evicted. She mused that the only thing worse than a tomb was an empty tomb. Many of the guardians had been wretched people, but some of them had been her friends, and she missed having them around. Misery loved company, after all, and haunting the earth was easier to bear when you had fellow haunters.

"I guess I was pretty hard on you toward the end there," she said apologetically. "I thought I was doing it because that was the only way we'd get through it in one piece, but now I'm not so sure that's why. I think I might have pushed you into it for other reasons. You once told me a very personal story about yourself, Julian. I'd like to return the favor, tell you a story I've never told anyone else. I know I'm cheating because you can't hear me, but maybe on some level you can. Here goes."

Ashley shifted her weight on the bed, folding one leg under herself. "When I was fifteen I met a guy in high school that I liked. His name was Ross. It wasn't love, just infatuation, obsession, lust, but it was more than I'd felt for anyone else. It scared me, especially when he made it clear that he liked me too. I guess we were both really messed-up people because it was a pretty sick relationship. We fucked a lot but we never showed affection to each other. We couldn't. I think we both found the intimacy just too threatening. So instead of giving comfort to each other we gave pain.

"Ross was three years older, a senior, but I was in control. I'm the one who escalated the heavy games we played together. It started out simple enough, just trading punches until someone hollered uncle. Then we had biting contests. I've still got scars from those. One day I showed up with a hammer and dared him to try to smash my hand against the outside wall of the auditorium. I got my hand out right before the impact, but he wasn't so lucky. I broke some major bones in his left hand, but he still stuck with me."

Ashley withdrew her touch from Julian's bare chest before she continued. "I finally came up with what I thought was the ultimate game. It was basically just playing chicken on some railroad tracks. We'd stand on the rails across from each other when a train was coming. First one to jump off was the chicken. It was quite a rush, a real thrill, holding out until the very last possible second before leaping out of the way. I usually won. Then one day I decided I wasn't going to move, even when the locomotive was right on top of me. I didn't know why. I just made up my mind that I was going to stand my ground to the very end. So the train came zooming at us and Ross got a strange look on his face, like he knew what I was going to do. When the engine was almost on us he moved first, but at me instead of off the track. He pushed me clear just in time to save my life. The train smashed into him, plowed him under itself, and dragged him until it left him dead and torn up by the side of the tracks a couple of thousand yards ahead. And then I realized that was what I'd wanted to happen.

"That way he proved his love for me, but I didn't have to love him back anymore. I didn't have to give anything of myself. My emotional defenses were left intact. And I'm afraid I've done the same exact thing with you."

She stood up and slumped against the wall, gripped by a despair so deep, it made her face look almost haggard. "I don't think it was necessary for you to come back here. I'm not sure why I made you. It's possible that I just didn't want to be apart from you. Or maybe I wanted to see if you were as strong and crazy as me. And maybe I wanted you to die facing horrors trying to save me. If I'd been the one to empty the Prism, I might have seen what you did, that it could be used against the masters. Or did it take an innocent like you to defeat the bastards? I don't know. All I know is that I've done you terrible harm, while you've only tried to care for me all along. I guess that's just the kind of person I am. I'm that bad."

Her eyes ached, and after a moment the pressure behind them produced tears. Grudgingly, she let them flow, kneeling by the bed with her head on his chest. "You can't die, Julian. It just can't happen. Please live, damn it. Please speak to me!" Frantic in her frustration she threw herself across him and kissed his lips, her tears dripping onto his face.

"Don't die! Julian! Wake up!"

Then she collapsed on top of him, spilling her tears onto his skin and into his thirsty soul.

A lone, formless thought floated through space, little more than an urge to be, and it flickered like a flame in a whirlwind. Several times it had nearly been extinguished, but it raged against nullification. Finally it started to gather other thoughts to itself, like raindrops of liquid fire creating a brightly burning pool, until they flooded together into a blazing sea of memory and sensation and identity. Julian knew who he was once more, and where his body had been numb and ice-cold before, the blood now ran hot in his veins. His face was warm and wet, with a wetness that seemed to be seeping into his brain like the balm of life itself. Where it touched his cells he remembered himself and how to be part of the sensory realm again. Soon he was fighting his way back to consciousness.

There could be no doubt that the woman lying on top of him was Ashley. Her fragrance alone told him that. Ancient oils and rare spices. He could feel her breathing, so she was alive. When he opened his eyes he found himself looking at the tear-streaked side of her face, half covered by her tangled hair. She abruptly turned her head and her eyes met his. He'd never seen such gladness, surprise, and relief on a human face before.

"Hello, Bittersweet." His voice was not much more than a croak, but his words were clear.

"Stormy!" She raised herself up for a moment, then came back down on top of him, slipping her arms around him and crushing her body against his. "My God, I thought I'd lost you! I thought you were a goner for sure. But you came back."

Her unbridled enthusiasm was threatening to send him away again. "Hey, I'm not completely back yet. Give me some room to breathe, will you?"

Ashley hastily got off of him. "Sorry. You've been out for a whole day."

He sat up with some difficulty. They were in her room, in the cathedral, and he was alive. With a violent jolt he recalled that he shouldn't be. Part of his back had been torn off. Very tentatively he touched his right hand to his shirtless back, noting the nervousness in Ashley's eyes as he did so. A huge patch of flesh there felt different, like smooth leather, but his ribs and spine were no longer exposed to the elements. His questioning look caused her further pain.

"I don't know what it means," she said softly. "The voidlight sometimes acts like a fluid, as when a guardian's ordinary injuries heal. What it does to living people is something I don't completely understand. You saw those two bodies in the lower passages."

Julian looked down at his knife wound, saw it was sealed with a plug of black matter. "Oh, God. What am I now? What's happened inside of me?"

She took his hand in hers. "Do you feel all right?"

It took a moment for him to decide. "Fine, I guess. Extremely hungry."

"Then you're probably all right. The Abyss just gave you a parting gift. Your life."

This idea sprouted barbs of fright in him. "My old one or a new one? Am I like you now or something else altogether? And if I can still die, what will death be for me now?"

Grinning at him she massaged his chest, trying to soothe him. "It's just like you to ask that question first. Why not think about what life will be for you? I don't know what I am anymore, either, now that the masters are gone. I feel the same. Almost. But it's hard to tell. Maybe we'll live out normal lifetimes or age even faster. Or maybe we can never die. Who knows? Whatever happens we'll have each other."

The wisdom of her words struck home with him. He'd have to learn to live from moment to moment. Seize the day. Maybe these dark markings signified nothing more than the loss of his innocence. Baptism in the pit of his innocent flesh, his pure tissues. Well, they weren't pure anymore. And what of the pit, the barrier enclosing it? "What about the Gate? Is it still there?"

She looked down and away for a few seconds, then faced him again. "Harrowgate is stable, but I think it's been weakened. There are now places in the world where the Coprolites might be able to come through, maybe even the masters as well, though I doubt it. Only one of them completed its transformation. They're probably getting ripped apart by the Coprolites in there, or at the very least have their hands full fending them off. I only hope Rubin and Arlo can find their way out. But a few of the damned might stray through the tears in the Gate."

This was even more disturbing news, the possibility of those things getting loose in the world for a time, but there was nothing he could do about it. It was just something he'd have to live with. "It's all right, babe. You and I are going to be fine from now on."

She smiled at him, assuring him that it was true. The earth would be a more haunted place, but at least she would be there to haunt it too.

DISCOVER THE TRUE MEANING OF HORROR...

ABYSS

- ☐ **THE CIPHER** by Kathe Koja — 20782-7 — $4.50
- ☐ **NIGHTLIFE** by Brian Hodge — 20754-1 — $4.50
- ☐ **SPECTERS** by J. M. Dillard — 20758-4 — $4.50
- ☐ **PRODIGAL** by Melanie Tem — 20815-7 — $4.50
- ☐ **TUNNELVISION** by R. Patrick Gates — 21090-9 — $4.50
- ☐ **SHADOW TWIN** by Dale Hoover — 21087-9 — $4.50
- ☐ **THE ORPHEUS PROCESS**
  by Daniel H. Gower — 21143-3 — $4.99
- ☐ **WHIPPING BOY** by John Byrne — 21171-9 — $4.99
- ☐ **BAD BRAINS** by Kathe Koja — 21114-X — $4.99
- ☐ **DEATHGRIP** by Brian Hodge — 21112-3 — $4.99
- ☐ **METAHORROR**
  Edited by Dennis Etchison — 20899-8 — $4.99
- ☐ **ANTHONY SHRIEK**
  by Jessica Salmonson — 21320-7 — $4.99
- ☐ **DEATH'S DOOR**
  by John Wooley & Ron Wolfe — 21196-4 — $4.99
- ☐ **WILDING** by Melanie Tem — 21285-5 — $4.99
- ☐ **DARK DANCE** by Tanith Lee — 21274-X — $4.99
- ☐ **PENANCE** by Rick R. Reed — 21237-5 — $4.99
- ☐ **SHADOWMAN** by Dennis Etchison — 21202-2 — $4.99
- ☐ **FACADE** by Kristine Kathryn Rusch — 21290-1 — $4.99
- ☐ **RAPID GROWTH** by Mary L. Hanner — 21337-1 — $4.99
- ☐ **ANGEL KISS** by Kelley Wilde — 20728-2 — $4.99
- ☐ **THE MAKING OF A MONSTER**
  by Gail Kane Peterson — 21389-4 — $4.99
- ☐ **THE DARKER SAINTS**
  by Brian Hodge — 21113-1 — $4.99
- ☐ **MAKING LOVE** by Melanie Tem
  and Nancy Holder — 21469-6 — $4.99
- ☐ **HEART-BEAST** by Tanith Lee — 21274-X — $4.99
- ☐ **LOST SOULS** by Poppy Z. Brite — 21281-2 — $4.99
- ☐ **X, Y** by Michael Blumlein — 21374-6 — $4.99

At your local bookstore or use this handy page for ordering:

DELL READERS SERVICE, DEPT. DAB
2451 South Wolf Road, Des Plaines, IL 60018

Dell

Please send me the above title(s). I am enclosing $ _____ .
(Please add $2.50 per order to cover shipping and handling). Send check or money order—no cash or C.O.D.s please.

Ms./Mrs./Mr. _____

Address _____

City/State _____ Zip _____

DAB-12/93

Prices and availability subject to change without notice. Please allow four to six weeks for delivery.

SCIENCE FICTION / FANTASY

- ☐ **CHUNG KUO: THE MIDDLE KINGDOM** (SF)   20761-4 $5.95/$6.95 Can.
  By David Wingrove.
- ☐ **CHUNG KUO II: THE BROKEN WHEEL** (SF)   20928-5 $5.99/$6.99 Can.
  By David Wingrove.
- ☐ **CHUNG KUO III: THE WHITE MOUNTAIN** (SF)   21356-8 $5.99/$6.99 Can.
  By David Wingrove.
- ☐ **PSION** (SF)   50340-X $8.95/$10.95 Can.
  By Joan D. Vinge. A LARGE FORMAT PAPERBACK.
- ☐ **MASKS OF THE ILLUMINATI**   50306-X $8.95/$11.95 Can.
  By Robert Anton Wilson. A LARGE FORMAT PAPERBACK.
- ☐ **THE ILLUMINATUS! TRILOGY**   53981-1 $14.95/$17.95 Can.
  By Robert J. Shea & Robert Anton Wilson. A LARGE FORMAT PAPERBACK.
- ☐ **SCHRODINGER'S CAT TRILOGY**   50070-2 $13.95/$16.95 Can.
  By Robert Anton Wilson. A LARGE FORMAT PAPERBACK.
- ☐ **ZIMIAMVIA: A TRILOGY** (F)   50300-0 $16.00/$20.00 Can.
  By E.R. Eddison. Foreword by Douglas E. Winter. Introduction and notes by Paul Edmund Thomas. A LARGE FORMAT PAPERBACK.
- ☐ **THE WORM OUROBOROS** (F)   50299-3 $9.99/$12.99 Can.
  By E.R. Eddison. A LARGE FORMAT PAPERBACK.
- ☐ **REALITY IS WHAT YOU CAN GET AWAY WITH**   50332-9 $13.00/$16.00 Can.
  By Robert Anton Wilson. A LARGE FORMAT PAPERBACK.
- ☐ **THE CHANGES: A TRILOGY** (SF)   50413-9 $12.00/NCR
  By Peter Dickinson. A LARGE FORMAT PAPERBACK.
- ☐ **LOGAN: A TRILOGY** (SF)   50404-X $12.00/$15.00 Can.
  By William F. Nolan. A LARGE FORMAT PAPERBACK.

At your local bookstore or use this handy page for ordering:

DELL READERS SERVICE, DEPT. DFS
2451 South Wolf Road, Des Plaines, IL 60018

Please send me the above title(s). I am enclosing $_____
(Please add $2.50 per order to cover shipping and handling). Send check or money order—no cash or C.O.D.s please.

Ms./Mrs./Mr. _____

Address _____

City/State _____ Zip _____

DFS–12/93

Prices and availability subject to change without notice. Please allow four to six weeks for delivery.

6 DECADES FREE

By subscribing to **Analog Science Fiction & Fact** you'll receive a **FREE** copy of **6 Decades–The Best of Analog** with your paid subscription. Analog readers have enjoyed over 60 years of penetrating, absorbing science fiction and science fact. From the earliest and continuing visions of cybernetics to our ultimate growth in space–Analog is the forum of the future. Let the pages of Analog expand the realm of your imagination...as today's fiction turns to tomorrow's fact.

☐ **Yes!** I want to subscribe to **Analog Science Fiction & Fact.** Please send me 18 issues for only $28.97.

☐ Send me 12 issues for only $20.97

☐ Payment enclosed

☐ Bill me

NAME _____
ADDRESS _____
CITY/ST/ZIP _____

MAIL TO
Analog
P.O. Box 7060
Red Oak, IA 51591

OR CALL
1-800-333-4561

Outside U.S. & Poss. 12 for $27.97, 18 for $39.97 (payment with order, U.S. funds). Includes GST. Please allow 6-8 weeks for delivery of your first issue. We publish two double issues, in January and July. These count as two each.

ROBOTS FREE

By subscribing to Isaac **Asimov's Science Fiction Magazine** you'll receive a FREE copy of **Robots From Asimov's** with your paid subscription. Asimov's contains Nebula-award-winning stories, editorials by Isaac Asimov himself, and much more. Each issue is filled with provocative stories on the cutting edge of today's science fiction and fantasy... from worlds of myth to futures of imagination.

❑ Yes! I want to subscribe to **Isaac Asimov's Science Fiction Magazine.** Please send me 18 issues for only $28.97.
❑ Send me 12 issues for only $20.97.
❑ Payment enclosed ❑ Bill me.

Name _____
Address _____
City/St/Zip _____

MAIL TO
Asimov's
P.O. Box 7057
Red Oak, IA 51591

OR CALL
1-800-333-4108

Outside US & Poss. 12 for $27.97, 18 for $39.97 (payment with order US funds). Include GST. Please allow 6-8 weeks for delivery of your first issue. We publish two double issues in April and November. These count as two each towards your subscription.

MPSS-5